FOR ALL TIME

FOR ALL TIME

SHANNA MILES

SIMON & SCHUSTER BFYR

NEW YORK LONDON TORONTO SYDNEY NEW DELHI

SIMON & SCHUSTER BFYR

An imprint of Simon & Schuster Children's Publishing Division

1230 Avenue of the Americas, New York, New York 10020

SIMON & SCHUSTER BOOKS FOR YOUNG READERS

and related marks are trademarks of Simon & Schuster, Inc.

For information about special discounts for bulk purchases, please contact Simon & Schuster Special Sales at 1-866-506-1949 or business@simonandschuster.com.

The Simon & Schuster Speakers Bureau can bring authors to your live event. For more information or to book an event, contact the Simon & Schuster Speakers Bureau at 1-866-248-3049 or visit our website at www.simonspeakers.com.

Interior design by Hilary Zarycky

The text for this book was set in Adobe Garamond Pro.

Manufactured in the United States of America

First Edition

2 4 6 8 10 9 7 5 3 1

Library of Congress Cataloging-in-Publication Data

Names: Miles, Shanna, author.

Title: For all time / Shanna Miles.

Description: First edition. | New York : Simon & Schuster Books for Young Readers, 2021. | Audience: Ages 14 up. | Audience: Grades 10-12. | Summary: Through countless lives, seventeen-year-olds Tamar and Fayard have fallen in love, fought to be together, and died but when they discover what it will take to break the cycle, will they be able to make the sacrifice?

Identifiers: LCCN 2020050913 | ISBN 9781534485976 (hardcover) | ISBN 9781534485990 (eBook)

Subjects: CYAC: Reincarnation-Fiction. | Love—Fiction. | African Americans—Fiction.

Classification: LCC PZ7.1.M55668 For 2021 | DDC [Fic]—dc23

LC record available at https://lccn.loc.gov/2020050913

For Rochelle, and all the girls who deserve a happily ever after

FOR ALL TIME

Columbia, South Carolina, Present Day

TAMAR

YOU KNOW WHY FAIRY TALES SUCK? NOT BECAUSE THEY create unrealistic relationship ideals for girls, even though they do; it's because Cinderella and those other hags just sat around and waited for something to happen. They waited and talked to birds and wished and hoped, and eventually some handsome kidnapper appeared out of the blue sky and set their life in motion. In real life you have to actually do something. You have to get off your butt and send Prince Charming a text if you want a chance at happily ever after.

"Mirror, mirror, on the wall. I wish I didn't look like shit before the ball."

Fay pulls my hand away from the passenger-ceiling mirror and kisses the back of it. My palm presses against his palm, and my fingers fold into the soft warmth of his grip. He doesn't disagree with me, and for that I'm grateful. That whole back-and-forth about how beautiful I am when I know I look like day-old gas-station chicken Alfredo is tiring.

I close the mirror, my fingers brushing against Fay's rosary beads, a gift from his dead father that he loves more than clear skin on picture day. He never goes anywhere without them, despite the fact that he doesn't like to talk about his dad, ever. I've always assumed it's just too painful. They're hanging from the rearview mirror and swish with every turn the car makes. I settle back into my seat and watch as the ribboned citrine sky filters through the windshield, glimmering and aggressive. It's the kind of light that outlines moments so they can't be lost to time. Six thirty p.m. As perfect a moment as it gets these days.

Fay makes a sharp turn, and a freshly graded report slides across the dash. I pick it up and read the cover: REINCARNATION ACROSS ANCIENT CULTURES BY FAYARD DANIELS, WORLD CIVILIZATION. I flip through, scanning the essay, and I have to give it to him—it's pretty good, and with more than double the pages he needed to turn in. He got an A. Mr. Sato even tucked in a brochure for the Museum of Natural History in DC, glossy and inviting with a little sankofa bird superimposed over the building for some new excavation exhibit. The seniors class is supposed to be taking a trip there during spring break. Just another thing I won't be attending.

I throw the report in the back seat and adjust the heat to ninety, then turn the vents so they blow in my direction. I can see the little beads of sweat building on Fay's temples, but I can't help it. I need the heat on blast, even though the temps are climbing to over sixty in February. My body is like a Volkswagen Beetle climbing Mount Everest with a faulty engine. It's trying hard, but it's just not happening. I'm still cold.

"I know you had to study, but Andrea's tíat threw the sickest Super Bowl party at their neighborhood clubhouse. You remember Rick from Mock Trial regionals, right? He's got that gray patch on the back of his head?" Fay says.

"From Richland Northeast?" I ask, trying my level best to sound upbeat and interested in whatever the hell Rick did at yet another party I missed.

". . . and then we sacrificed a cat. It was lit!"

"What about a cat?" I ask, and he just smiles at me. I'm caught. "Ha-ha," I say dryly. "I have perfect pitch, remember? I hear everything. I was listening." I don't sound very convincing.

"No, you weren't, but it's cool. I ignore you sometimes too," Fay says, and winks.

"You do not. You hang on every word I say."

"Psssh! You make me sound whipped. And your boy is never that," Fay chides.

"Take me to Krispy Kreme," I say, and he doesn't even respond. Fay just makes a U-turn like it was the direction we were supposed to be going this entire time.

The red neon sign in the window glows to let us know the doughnuts are hot and ready, but we turn down the drive-thru instead of going in. Fay turns to place our order. "Can I get two decaf coffees, one black, the other with four sugars and two creams; one blueberry doughnut and two plain."

I fake the sound of a whip cracking. "How 'bout that," I say, fighting back the grin spreading across my face.

"Now, now, that's just me being an accommodating date. Besides, when is a little doughnut break ever a bad idea?"

Fay hands me my coffee. I wrap my hands around the steaming cup and let the warmth rush into my skin as the track changes to "Smooth Operator" by Sade. Fay places the bag of doughnuts next to me and slides his coffee into the holder, then switches to the next song and gives me a pitying look. He knows it's my absolute favorite melody to play on the saxophone, but my lungs can't handle the exertion anymore. Now my instrument sits in its case in the corner of my room gathering dust.

Fay backs into a spot right by the front door so we can watch all the other couples on cheap dates. There are at least half a dozen cars in the parking lot, with more in the drive-thru, but the cutest pairs are the older folks sitting inside by the windows.

"Those two are on a date," I say, pointing my stirrer at two middle-aged guys in New Balance sneakers and fraternity sweatshirts standing in line. "The guy on the left is recently divorced, and the other just moved back to town to take care of his elderly parents."

"You take point if the Q orders and pays. If the Sigma pays, the story changes."

I draw in the rich scent of the coffee beans and blow out a breath. "Why?"

"'Cause the two organizations have fundamentally different personalities. Q's gotta be the alpha, no pun intended."

"My granddad would beg to differ, but you'll find out once Morehouse sends you that acceptance letter," I say, and stick out my tongue to one side, imitating the countless Omega Psi Phi members I've seen strolling at barbecues, weddings, and at least one funeral. He doesn't laugh like I expect him to.

Fay turns his head and looks out the other side of the window. He's been avoiding the college conversation but won't tell me why. I decide not to press him today.

"What do you think they're talking about after forty years of marriage?" I ask, turning my gaze, and attention, to a couple who look to be in their sixties. Dressed in matching red polo shirts.

"Well, he's just retired from the post office, and she's just sent the last of their six children off to college. He's talking about how he wants to relax, and she's dreaming about seeing the country. She'll let him talk a bit, because she's learned how to let the old man tire himself out after all these years, before she springs the RV plan on him. He won't say too much about it now, but he'll bring it back up in a few days like it was his plan all along, and she'll let him believe it was," Fay narrates, his voice full of warmth.

"Wow! That's very detailed."

"It's a love story. That's us in fifty years," he adds.

I snort. "Let me stop you at six kids."

"What I wouldn't have done for a little brother. I hated being an only child," he says before inhaling his second glazed doughnut in a single bite. The pastries are pillowy soft when they're warm, but the plain ones make my stomach hurt now. It's one of those things I've only had to tell Fay once.

"But you got all your mom's attention," I say, slightly jealous.

"I don't know about that," he says sadly.

"So, it's your only-child powers that allow you to see into the future of Krispy Kreme's patrons?"

"Nope. I'm psychic."

I open my mouth wide to sneeze— "Bullshit."

We both laugh. Fay switches the music to a playlist we made together sophomore year for a songwriting elective. He was the only non-band member taking the class. It was almost two years ago, and even then, people assumed we were together. "Boyfriend" has always seemed too light a word for him—thin and arbitrary, like wrapping paper. "Girlfriend" is even worse. It comes with expectations. I don't like labels. I just like him. The playlist is full of super old-school cuts our grandparents love, like Sade, Prince, Donny Hathaway, stuff like that. Love songs.

My gaze settles on the horizon. All that's left of dusk is a coin's sliver of gold in the distance. The lo-fi rhythms are like a sun-warmed lake lapping the shore, calming and perfect. And, just like that, I don't care that I've got a purse full of inhalers or that the dress I bought only a month ago is a little loose. I'm just happy to be alive and seventeen.

My eyes are closed and I'm grooving to "All this Love" by DeBarge when sugar-scented fingers tenderly glide against my chin, urging my lips toward a boy with soft eyes; he tastes like lemon glaze and sweet urgency. Someone honks next to us, and he pulls away with the biggest smile on his face. I smile back.

"You're not getting into my panties tonight," I tease.

"So you say. I'm the panty wizard," he jokes as he settles back into his seat and starts the car again. We slowly drive out of the parking lot. It's better to pop the sexual-tension bubble early. Otherwise we'll be playing the will-we/won't-we game all night. Not that I don't want to, it's just . . . complicated. Fay would never urge me to do something I wasn't wildly excited about doing. I guess I take sex off the table so bluntly more for my benefit than for his. "Isn't that what they called that guy who was sneaking into people's houses in Winslow and stealing dirty drawers?"

"I'm a hustler, baby. You know how much lightly used panties go for on the internet?" he says as he gives me a wink, his face fighting to stay serious, one hand perched at the bottom of the steering wheel and the other hand squeezing mine tight.

I laugh so hard a tear winks out of my eye and I have to clench so I don't wet myself. We finally pull up to the school, and I can hear the bass from the gym as soon as Fay parks and turns off the engine. Seniors usually sit out the Valentine's dance so they can save up for prom, but May is so far away, and given how I'm feeling, there's really no telling . . .

"Back up in the spot!" Fay yells as he opens the car door and a whoosh of February air sends goose bumps across my skin.

"Ayo!" DeAndre calls from across the parking lot, expensive camera in hand. Fay and DeAndre have got a YouTube channel that's really getting up there in followers. They'll be filming all night.

Fay closes the car door to dap up his friend, and Selena waves to me from the sidewalk. I wave back and pantomime a chef's kiss to let her know I like her dress. I should get out of the car now. That's what I want to do, but my body needs just a few more seconds of the vehicle's warmth. How am I going to get through this night?

"You all right, bae?" Fay asks, face right up against the window.

"Yeah!" I lie, and I bite my lip getting out of the car, covering up my wince as sharp pains shoot from my sternum and radiate to each and every one of my ribs. I blow out a grateful puff of air when I'm finally on my feet. I pat myself on the back for deciding to wear my church flats instead of my damn-she-look-good heels. Like Nana used to say, *A girl can be stupid but she can't afford to be simple.*

Fay's talking so fast and laughing so hard I don't have to join in. I'd think he was completely preoccupied if he didn't slip off his blazer and drape it over my shoulders. I nearly melt from the residual body heat. I love these moments when he can read my mind. Selena joins us on the way in, and we find a table with some of the other kids from Mock Trial and Model UN.

"We missed you at regionals. Pilar tanked as the star witness," Selena yells over the bass of some song I haven't heard yet. I nod my head to the beat, making a mental note of it so I can flip it on my beat machine when I get home. When Pilar snatches Selena from the table to join her on the dance floor, Selena reaches for my hand. I wave them on. "Nah, I'll sit out. That's that lame dance for underclassmen," I joke, and they both roll their eyes.

I pay close attention to the moves, trying to memorize them in my head. I've been so preoccupied with doctors' visits I'm not up on the latest dances. I'll look it up online later so I can perfect it at home in the privacy of my bedroom—with the door locked. Jokes go over my head too—I don't get the references—but I don't want to think about that now.

My phone buzzes in my purse.

A: Hope you're having fun.

Crap. If she knows I'm gone already she must have nosy-ass Ms. Valdez next door watching the house. My sister always works double shifts on Fridays. She can't be home yet.

T: I am u know.

A: . . .

I wait for some snarky remark that never materializes and slip the phone back in my purse.

"Bored already," Fay teases, and reaches for my purse. "Maybe you texting some other dude. Telling him how lame this all is."

I roll my eyes. "Yup. He's gonna bring me some special brownies and Chinese takeout once all this is done." I wave my hand in the air like this is just the raggediest little backyard kickback instead of the most fun I've had in a year.

"Cool, cool. Tell him I like chicken lo mein and veggie egg rolls. He can get that thick-ass fruit punch, too, 'cause I'm coming along. You promised me the night, and you owe me for flaking out the last ten times."

"It wasn't ten times. Maybe . . . five."

"Uh-huh. You know I'm cool just sitting on your couch. We don't have to go out. I know you ain't always up for this."

"I know."

His smile widens in that Cheshire cat kind of way and he kneels down in front of me so he can wrap his arms completely around my waist while I'm in the chair.

"Can I tell you a secret?" he asks, his breath hot against my ear.

"Do I have to keep it?" I say, my lips drawing up into a small smirk as he leans back to check my expression.

He looks shocked for a second, and I pinch his elbow.

"You know I'm good for it. What?" I coax.

"Valentine's Day is my favorite holiday."

"For real? What about Thanksgiving? I mean, 'cause you can put it away." I laugh.

"You know my family is super small. I'm the only child of an only child. My dad's people are in the islands and we don't talk. Our Thanksgiving isn't ever like it is on television. I only get that when I'm at DeAndre's or that one time you invited me over with your fifty-leven aunties."

"Okay, then, why not Halloween or Christmas?"

"Halloween only knocks when you can still trick-or-treat. Christmas is cool, but it's kinda the same deal as Thanksgiving." He stops and studies me. "What's that look?"

"I know why you like Valentine's Day," I sing, teasing him a bit. "You've been getting valentines since kindergarten, haven't you? Who sent you a card? I know you got some candy cups at school today."

Fay is a flirt. He can't help it. It's less about attraction, but more how he relates to people. He's genuinely interested in them, and girls eat that stuff up with a spoon. There is no way that he didn't get some candy today, maybe even a few cards, with girls taking their shot while I'm away. He winces like he's been caught with his hand in the cookie jar. "I got you one. I was hoping you'd be back by now," he says, sadness tinging his voice.

"Yeah, me too. Online school is—"

"She's baaack!" Joo croons as she walks up to the table with her shadow, Brianne.

"Hey, Joo," I say. She's in a cherry-red bodycon dress with clear heels that are an inch shy of being fit for the stripper pole. As always, she's nothing but smiles as she tucks one of her jet-black strands behind her ear with a pointy, acrylic-tipped finger. We're friendly, but not really friends. She's smart and nice enough, but we've never clicked. I'd have to really think about it to say exactly why. She looks good and she knows it. I glance down at my home manicure and slide my hands under the table.

"Sup?" Fay says as he unwraps himself and stands to his feet.

Joo paints on an exaggerated frown and bats her lashes at Fay. A performance more for me than for him.

"So you not gonna say thank you?" she asks.

"Thank you?" I say.

"Oh, not you, T. Fay." Her eyes never leave Fay's face.

Now it's my turn to paste on a fake smile. I shift my gaze up at Fay with my best *I told you so* face. Fay and I aren't *official* official (my call, not his), but anybody with eyes knows the deal. Most people have manners, home training, that sort of thing—they know enough to keep a distance and be respectful—and then there's Joo.

"You sent him a Cutie Cup, right? Let me thank you on his behalf," I say with as much sincerity as I can muster.

Joo's fake frown turns to a real one.

"He told you?" she asks.

"Oh, girl, I assumed. Everybody loves Fay. All kinds of . . . people send him valentines. Friends, thirsty girls desperate for a chance, you know how it is. Oh, I didn't mean you. I'm sure it was just friendly. I'm sure you got a few too, right?" I say matter-of-factly. The more I talk, the more irritated Joo looks.

Brianne, who is the yes-man of yes-men, presses her lips tight, and her eyes go wide. I can't tell if she's holding in a laugh or waiting for a cue from Joo to throw the first punch.

I hold my expression. I may be a lot of things, but a punk ain't one of them. The DJ switches the track from a slow bop to something more fun, and a ton of people rush the dance floor.

Fay, eager to break the tension, opens his mouth to say something, but I rise from my chair and immediately need to sit back down.

"Y-you know, Joo. Why don't you and Fay go dance?" I say.

I quickly glance away and close my eyes tight, trying to stop the room from spinning.

"What you trying to do, T?" Joo says as she sets her purse on the table. I've disrespected her and she knows it, but it can still go either way.

"Chill, Joo," Fay says.

"Yeah, everybody chill. Why is it so tense in here?" I joke and turn back to look at them. "Fay, go dance with Joo. Brianne and I are gonna go to the bathroom."

Brianne, eager for an out, nods enthusiastically and hops from Joo's side to mine.

Fay squints as his body involuntarily moves to the beat. "You sure?"

"Yeah, you gotta thank her for all that sugar, right? We're all friends—right, Joo?"

The ball is in her court, and she knows she'll look stupid if she turns this into anything more than words.

"Yeah. C'mon, Fay," she says with all her teeth, but I catch her eyes cutting to mine a few times when Fay isn't looking, searching for the real reason behind my acquiescence.

I watch as he spins her twice before they make it to the writhing crowd. She laughs at something Fay says, and I take heartbreaking notice of how good they look together.

"Bri, help me get to the other side of the building. I don't feel too good," I say, and lean hard on my friend since Girl Scouts, hoping against hope she knows how to keep her mouth shut.

2

TAMAR

I'M NEARLY INCONSOLABLE WHEN MY SISTER AABIDAH FINDS me in the teachers' lounge. The crying brought on a coughing fit, so she had to bring the oxygen tank through a side entrance so no one at the dance would see. Aabidah eventually had to half walk, half carry me out of the school building. I'm no longer crying, but I'm still sipping breaths from my oxygen mask as she draws me a bath with Epsom salts and eucalyptus oil to open my chest up.

"You want to tell me why I had to come and get you? Or why you went to a dance when you know you're not supposed to?"

"I'm n-not a-a child," I say, fully aware I'm acting like one.

"I *can* forbid you from doing things, but I haven't, because *usually* you don't need me to be the adult in the room. You handle it yourself. But this? You could barely get up and get dressed this morning. There is a reason we're doing virtual school online. Why, why—"

"Because I'm seventeen. Because I want my senior memories to be more than doctors' visits and binge-watching singing competitions," I say, holding back the frustration and sadness building inside me as I pull the mask away from my mouth so she can hear me clearly.

"Mama would be on your ass right now," she mumbles to the tub.

"But Mama isn't here anymore, so . . ."

"So . . ." She turns to face me, then shuts off the faucet and lets her hand drag in the water a bit to break up the salt crystals settling in like fog.

"I saw Coach Letterman outside," she reveals.

"He tried to push up on you, didn't he," I say as I let the mask snap back in place.

"Yup."

"Ewww." My face contorts.

"I don't know how he keeps his job," she wonders.

"He only pushes up on the recent graduates. Once you cross that high school stage, you're fair game. He needs to be reported."

Aabidah nods a little too fervently, and I can tell she's hiding a smirk.

"Did you give him your number?" I ask, drawing in a pained breath of shock. She breaks into a fit of laughter, and I can't help but follow her. "Owwww. Don't make me laugh."

"I didn't give him my real number. But Coach Letterman is fine!" she argues.

I grimace. "He's old as hell, too."

"Whatever, I'm grown."

"See, y'all be encouraging that nasty behavior. What did Mama used to say? A fast tail makes a soft behind," I chide.

She sucks her teeth. "That is not how the saying goes. It's a hard *head* makes a soft behind."

"Whatever. You know what I mean." I take a beat to let my breath slow, and slip off my robe to get into the tub. "I'm sorry for going out. It was selfish. Fay called, and I don't know. I just couldn't say no again," I say, guiltily.

Aabidah shakes her head. "Shut up. You're supposed to go out and have fun, and you're supposed to do it behind your parents' backs. You don't have any of those anymore, so my back will do just fine."

I slip lower into the water and let the warmth do its work. Eucalyptus pushes past the blocks in my nose and chest, allowing me to breathe just slightly better than a few minutes before, but the feeling is delicious all the same. Aabidah gets up to go, but I stop her. I don't want this tension between us. I never ever let us leave a room without smoothing things out. Not after how Mama died.

"Tell me what you remember most about senior year."

Her shoulders slump, hating the change in subject. "After you tell me what happened with Fay."

My chin drops to my wet chest and I draw circles in the water with my finger.

"I ran. Metaphorically speaking. Really, I just leaned on this girl until I partially collapsed in the teachers' lounge."

Her mouth drops open in genuine shock. "Why?"

"I couldn't stand looking into his eyes and seeing so much hope there. The wanting. How many times can I say no when he wants to come over? I know he just wants to see me, but I'll be damned if he sees me with my face half drowned by an oxygen mask. The house smells like old sick people, no matter how much Pine-Sol you use. And I'm not blaming you. It's me.

"And Fay's sitting there at the table and he wants to dance. He doesn't say it but I know he does, and I keep coming up with these excuses because the truth is too real and too pathetic. I saw the looks on all the other girls' faces. Pity. Not for me, but for him. Those bitches smell the blood in the water, and you know what? I agree with them. Why would he want to be with me when he could be with one of them? One of those smiling, happy girls with a scholarship on the way and finals the only fear in her heart. Somebody who can twerk and drink spiked punch and laugh at dumb shit 'cause laughing is easy. I thought I could handle it, but I couldn't." I pause to take a much-needed breath, small though it may be.

"So that's it, then?"

"What's it?" I say, the grief giving way to anger.

"You just giving up? Like you did with Spelman?"

"Spelman's just on hold."

"Scholarships don't hold. You're a legacy. You'll be the fifth generation of women in this family to go to Spelman College and pledge. Pretty girls do what?"

I roll my eyes. "Wear twenty pearls. I know." We don't talk about how Aabidah missed her opportunity to continue the legacy because she had to stay home and take care of Mama. Her sorors are great, but the University of South Carolina wasn't her dream. I think it's too much for her to imagine that Spelman might not be my dream too, or that fate has intervened yet again to set fire to our family legacy.

"I know their music program isn't what you originally had in mind but—"

"We had a deal!" I whisper-yell, rising just a bit in the water so she knows I'm serious. This part of the conversation is over. "No college dreams, no future plans. I want scandal and intrigue. Four years ago. Spill," I demand.

Aabidah chews her lip and fixes the decorative towels on the rack so they line up just so. Thinking. She wants to say more and I'm waiting for it, but she doesn't go there. Instead she launches into a story about how the French teacher got caught cheating and his speech-pathologist wife tossed all his clothes onto the tennis court right before a match. It's funny. It's also a smoke screen. She gave up too easily, and if I know anything about my sister, it's that she never ever gives up without a fight.

3
FAYARD

I MISS HER THE MOST WHEN IT'S QUIET. THE AIR CONDITIONER kicks in and a low rumble fills the media lab with background music that I hate, and there it is. Loneliness. Not that I'm alone. DeAndre is rendering some footage from the Winter recital right next to me, headphones blasting something I don't recognize. His right hand, still a little dirty from automotive class, moves the mouse smoothly while his left is buried elbow deep in a bag of Wise dill-pickle potato chips. He chews with his mouth open and then licks his fingers.

"Want some?"

I shake my head. *Nasty.*

I've been staring at the same footage for nearly an hour, turning my rosary beads over in my pocket like a worrying stone. Dre set up a few GoPros before the dance started, so we got some great stuff: the dance-off between the freshmen and the juniors, Cathy Tran's promposal. But what I'm obsessing over won't even make it into the final cut for our channel. It's about a half hour after I arrive with T. She gets up from her seat at the table and then falls back down. I've got my head turned, mouth wide open, mid-laugh over something stupid, I'm sure. I didn't see her. I wasn't paying atten-tion. I zoom in closer, looping the strained pull of muscle in her jaw when she rises, the look of panic in her eyes as she gets to her feet, and finally the plastered smile she gives me when I eventually turn back around.

It's the smile that's the problem, because I didn't see it for the paper-thin mask that it was. I remember wanting her to dance and even resenting her for being so bougie. I thought she was bored. I lean back in my chair and let the loop play over and over on the screen, as if on the next play it'll be different: I'll notice how much pain she's in and take her out of the auditorium and to Finlay Park instead, carry her down the steps and let her watch the waterfall at night, wrap her in my mom's old FAMU blanket I keep in the trunk. Or I'll realize how dumb the whole dance idea was from the beginning and take her to Cool Beans, that coffeehouse on USC's campus. We'll sit in front of their fireplace and sip hot cocoa from cups the size of cereal bowls until curfew. I imagine all the scenarios that don't end up with her staggering out of the gym on the arm of a girl whose name I can't remember.

"You can watch it loop like that forever. It won't change what happened," DeAndre says as tiny bits of chip fly out of his mouth. He pulls his headphones off and pauses the track. "Just go over there. It's obvious you want to apologize."

"I called. She won't answer. I texted. I get one-word replies. I'm iced out."

"You know my instinct is to say"—he pauses and flips me the middle finger—"but I know how you feel about T. I don't understand it, but I acknowledge it. If you want my advice—"

"I don't."

"Nevertheless, I'm gonna give it to you. Use your resources.

Plebeians use lame stuff like telecommunications networks and social media. You a king or you a buster?"

"Be plain. I'm not in the mood for your riddles, Dre."

"What I'm saying is that T is no ordinary girl, so you can't go about this in an ordinary way. In Little League, what did Coach Barclay teach us about defeating your opponent?"

"The three *D*s?" I ask, not following his metaphor at all.

"That's right. T's avoidance is your enemy, and you attack your enemy by distraction, deception, or destruction. Which is it gonna be?"

"You know we lost nearly every game."

"Nevertheless. Which is it gonna be?" he urges, fully invested in this piss-poor advice. I gotta give it to him, though. He is trying.

I shake my head. Dre's got a sports analogy for every situation, and I don't know why this would be any different, but he does give me an idea. It's wild, but it is something. I shut down my computer and throw all my other equipment and books in my bag. It's Wednesday. Bible study night. If I move fast, I just might make it.

"Thanks, Dre."

"No prob! Don't get arrested! Wear protection."

"I don't think that applies," I say carefully.

He stuffs another wad of chips into his mouth and chomps down loudly. "It always applies!"

Sarah-Ann's already got her seat belt on when I squeal into the parking space right next to her at Shining Point Church. I knew that as head of the Teen Ministry, she'd be the designated driver for the Bible-study carpool. She's the church's oldest Girl Scout and co–troop leader for the Daisies. The parking lot is full of the tiny girls in their uniforms. I jump out and give a silent thanks to God the meeting ended early enough to let Sarah-Ann drive. Her twin brother, Bo, is the backup driver for the Bible study pickup. My plan would be dead in the water before it even set sail if he'd gotten the job.

She's about to slam her car door shut when I stick my arm out to catch it.

"Hey!" I say too loudly and too brightly, but Sarah-Ann smiles back.

"Hey to you! I haven't seen you around in a while," she says.

"I—I know. I have, uh . . . been doing a lot of silent study in my, uh . . . prayer closet. You've got to have a personal relationship with Christ."

For a second I think she's going to sniff out my bullshit, but she nods enthusiastically.

"Oh yes, definitely. But you've also got to consult people who've spent their lives in prayer and study like Pastor Roberts. Sheep need a shepherd."

That is not the analogy I would use, but I don't have time to get into that with her.

"Well, I was in prayer, and God put it in my heart to volunteer more at the church."

"You should! And the Teen Ministry would love to have you. We're cleaning out Deacon Riley's gutters this weekend, and then we're going to delouse Mother Bolden's three cocker spaniels," she says excitedly.

"Oh, wow. That does sound, uh, enriching, but I was hoping I could start today. As a service to you personally, I could do today's carpool," I say as earnestly as I can muster.

"You don't have to do that!"

"I'd love to! I want to! You serve God by serving others, right? And that includes you." I plaster on another big smile.

"Well, I could use that time to put an extra coat of disinfectant on the toys in the playroom," she says, more to herself than to me, as she thinks it over.

"Great! When one door closes, God opens a window. Is that the list of pickups?" I slide the list out of her hands and make sure the Christian hug I give her once she steps out of the car is just a tad too long. A soupçon of guilt to keep her from telling anybody I stole her job for the day.

There are four people on the list. Just enough to fit in my car. They're all kids I know, and they all live so close to one another that I could get the lot and still be thirty minutes early for service. So when I idle the car in front of T's house and walk up to the door, I've got reinforcements.

The bell rings and I can hear her yell "got it" from inside. I thought I was prepared for when she opened the door, but I'm not. She's in a pink T-shirt that says HOPE DEALER on the front and jeans that hug every curve. It's just jeans and a T-shirt, but to me she couldn't look better if she was in diamonds and lace or some luxury-brand stuff from the mall. She's water in the desert.

"H-hey," I say, and watch her lips quiver as she smiles. I surprised her, but she doesn't look mad about it. She leans over to the side to look past me at the car full of kids from our Vacation Bible School days.

She rolls her eyes and laughs a bit. "Clever."

I shrug. "Still coming?"

"You know it. Can't let the devil keep me from church."

"I'm not the devil," I say, giving her my arm so she can lean on me as we walk down the steps to the car.

"So you say."

Dina Slater leans half her body out of the back window to whistle at us. "Don't y'all look cute." Her brother Philip pulls her back into the car.

"Shut up, Dina!" he mumbles as he opens the car door on his side for T to slide in.

"Nice to see you again, Tamar," Bernard says in his uniquely formal way from the front seat.

"Thank you, Bernard. It's nice to see you, too."

"Fayard, did you know Tamar's name is biblical? The biblical Tamar's two husbands were killed by God for their wickedness, so she disguised herself as a prostitute to deceive her father-in-law Judah so she could bear a child," Bernard recounts.

"Uh . . . wow . . . uh. I did not know that," I reply.

I catch T's face in the rearview mirror: Her hand is over her mouth, trying to stifle a laugh. Bernard's got an encyclopedic knowledge of the Bible and board games. I went over to his house one Memorial Day for a BBQ and promptly got my ass handed to me in chess, checkers, Monopoly, and Clue.

Everyone but T files out of the car when we make it to the church parking lot.

"Loop around a few times," she says as soon as we're alone.

She doesn't have to ask me twice.

"You got it."

"So?" she asks.

"So . . ," I say back, suddenly at a loss for words.

"You have my attention. This was cute. It's nice to see you, and not in the same way that it's nice to see Bernard." She smiles, and the world slows down and clicks back into place again. I don't feel right when she's not around. I can't even remember what it felt like not to know her, and if all I get is this bit of time in a church carpool, I'll take it. Even if she's still in the back seat and I'm chauffeuring her around the parking lot.

"It's good to see you, too. I promise not to compare you to a prostitute," I tease.

"Well, let me do a praise break for that."

I keep glancing at her in the rearview mirror, grateful for the distance. Otherwise I might just stare at her the entire time and let the minutes tick by as I memorize each divot in her collarbone or try to calculate the degree at which each of her eyelashes curls.

"Pay attention to the road," she says softly, chastising me.

"I want to apologize," we say in unison, and then laugh.

"You don't have anything to apologize for," I say, and she stops me.

"No, please let me say this," she says. "I left you stranded. I didn't say goodbye. It was rude. I'm sorry. And you didn't deserve to be ghosted."

"You've been avoiding me too," I add softly.

"I'm sorry for avoiding you."

"That's it?" I ask, and she rolls her neck a bit at my tone, a little nonverbal *WTF*. I quickly backtrack. "Nah, nah, it's not like that.

I'm just stopping you 'cause you know you don't have anything to apologize for. I should have never suggested the dance in the first place. I wasn't paying attention to what you wanted, and I'm sorry. Please forgive *me*. I need you to."

"Okay."

"Okay?"

"Yes. That's it."

"You're not gonna ice me out anymore?" I ask.

"I didn't say that. I'm just saying I accept your apology. How long did it take for Brianne to tell you where I went?"

"Brianne! That's that girl's name!" I shout as I slap the steering wheel. "I've been trying to remember her name for days. Uh, I don't know, two songs, maybe three. It was unseemly what I offered her to tell me where you went, but she didn't break."

"Brianne's cool, despite her choice of best buddy. You and Joo looked good together."

I pull the car back into the church parking lot and turn to face her.

"Joo could sprout wings and I wouldn't fly anywhere with her. You know that."

She chews her bottom lip, trying to keep the smile she's suppressing from cracking wide across her face. Her eyes meet mine for a second, and there's that thrum in my chest that starts to warm my entire body. It makes me want to touch her, sit next to her, and think unholy thoughts on holy ground.

"I've got a lot going on, Fay. It's not fair to you that—"

"You don't get to decide what's fair to me. I do. I'll make that decision. Flip the coin, roll the dice, I'll always choose you. Even if

I have to sit through Pastor Roberts's warbling through 'Amazing Grace.'"

"That sound ain't sweet at all," she laughs, but there's something sad in her eyes. I want to press, ask questions to make sure that I'm still on her good side, that everything is smooth now. But I'm afraid that this truth is as fragile as the soap skin on sink bubbles.

"C'mon, then," she says, and opens the car door. "I'll get a stack of envelopes and let you pass notes to me through the service."

"What if I want to listen?" I joke.

"I stopped listening a long time ago."

"Then why do you keep going?" I ask, knowing how hard it is to hold on to your faith once God takes away something you thought was a given.

"The motions, bae. Sometimes you just have to go through the motions."

4
TAMAR

THE PROBLEM IS THAT YOU THINK YOU HAVE TIME.
When you're in high school, every minute before graduation feels like hours as you wait for your real life to start.
But that's not the case for me. I look into my future and all I see is
a brick wall.

I haven't talked to Fay in weeks, hoping he'll move on, dreading
the day he will. We rode to Bible study together a few times before
he left for the spring break trip. And one time he came over to
binge-watch reruns of *House*, but I had a coughing fit and we had
to call the EMTs and it was too much. Not for him. For me.

He keeps calling but I don't pick up. He texts but I don't reply.
At first it was just questions asking how I'm doing or what I'm
doing. Now he just checks in with updates about what he's doing
and how much he misses me. He's written a few letters, too. I read
them under the covers with a flashlight, afraid that even the fluorescent beams of my bedroom lights might bear witness to my
cowardice.

Aabidah's sensible gray Camry rolls to a stop in front of a squat
cement building way past the county line. It's attached to what
looks like a dilapidated dollhouse. Gravel pops like 'hood Fourth
of July as Aabidah and I let our eyes settle onto the grim facade in

front of us. I scrunch my nose up so bad that I have to readjust my oxygen line. My sister notices immediately.

"Don't do that, T. I asked around. She's supposed to be the best."

"According to who? *Backwoods Weekly*? *Meth and Homemade Biscuits Times*?" I joke.

Aabidah rolls her eyes and opens the car door; the scent of diesel fuel and honeysuckle wafts in on a hot breeze. Dolly's Mirror is a dive bar—I can tell that much from the yellowed and cracking road sign out front. Couple that with the SUV-sized American flag whipping above our heads and Dolly Parton's "9 to 5" spilling out from the screen door and you've got my country nightmare come to life. Aabidah opens the door for me and pulls my oxygen tank out so I won't have to lift it. I hoist myself out of the car, though. I need that little bit of agency, the tiniest morsel of control over my body.

"Ten dollars for your future. That's a steal!" I wheeze, letting the sarcasm sweeten the sight of me straining for air and wincing with every step. My birthday's coming up. I'll be eighteen. It's supposed to be great. I'm supposed to be excited about going off to college, getting to vote, being an almost grown-up. I should be planning an all-out bash with my friends, but I haven't seen anyone outside church since the Valentine's dance two months ago. And they say Tauruses are supposed to be devoted and responsible. Hardly. Too many doctors' appointments, too many hospital visits. Pity overload for the one girl in a hundred thousand who came out on the other side of a pandemic with the lungs of an eighty-year-old. But hey, there's hope; there's . . . .

"What's her name?"

"Rose," Aabidah says as her eyes go wide at the Confederate-flag doormat.

"We're already here, Aabidah. We might as well go in," I mumble.

Her head moves from side to side, searching, like all Black people do in a new place, seeking out another Black face. We don't find one, but we do see something that simultaneously surprises and reassures me: a child. A little girl about ten years old is pouring a beer into a frosted glass for a man in a pristine Carolina Gamecocks hat and matching T-shirt.

"Readings in the back! Put your ten dollars in the jar at the end of the bar," she announces without looking up. So much for Southern hospitality.

The jukebox switches to "Jolene," and somebody in one of the corner booths starts singing along . . . badly. When we walk through the curtain that separates the front area from the back room, the crooner is cut off mid-verse. Silence swallows us so completely that the squeak in the wheels of my oxygen tank echoes through the hallway. I nudge my sister forward with my elbow. She stumbles a bit but puts one foot in front of the other. This was her idea, after all.

The smell of sage mixed with boiled peanuts, briny and sharp, hits me as Aabidah knocks tentatively on the doorframe of the only open room in the hall.

"Y'all come on in. Take a seat on those cushions. I'll be right with you," a woman's voice says through the beaded curtain. We make our way in and sit down, taking in everything around us: the candlelight and tapestry-covered walls. A literal shrine to Dolly

Parton is in one corner, complete with burning incense and a fish tank with two goldfish swimming lazily in and out of a tiny church.

"You don't have to do this, you know," Aabidah says, nearly chickening out.

"Suddenly scared she might be the real deal after all?" I ask.

"No. It's just . . . this place is . . . I don't know. I've got a bad feeling. Why are you so calm, church girl?"

I roll my eyes. "I'm out of options, I guess."

Aabidah stopped going to the church after Mama died. I worry about what she'll have left if . . . when something happens to me. Sour bile rises up in my throat. I swallow it back down and then it starts, the bone-rattling coughing fit I've been trying to avoid for the last hour.

The psychic, a thick white girl in a beautiful form-fitting white linen shorts set, rushes over and shoves a steaming cup of mystery into my hands as I try and fail to catch my breath. My sister nearly knocks the thing to the floor as she tries to pry it out of my grasp.

"That won't help!" Aabidah grunts through her teeth, and pulls a handkerchief from her purse—one of Nana's old ones—and pushes it into my palm to catch the bloody phlegm.

"It's not for drinking. Sweetheart, put this cup under your chin and see if you can calm yourself enough to let the fumes get in your nose." She taps the cup with a blood-red coffin-shaped acrylic nail. "You'll have to pull that tube out, though." She holds up her hand and gives us a small wave. "I'm Rose," she says, and smiles.

"Like hell," Aabidah says as she struggles to open the sterile plastic bag holding my oxygen mask so I can get more air.

It feels like my chest is packed with hot rocks, but you know what, why not? It is almost my birthday. Ripping off my oxygen tube is the closest thrill I'll get for the foreseeable future. I pull the tubing back, settle myself enough to attempt to breathe in, hold the cup under my chin, and inhale. I don't expect anything, really. I've given up on expectations. But when I draw in a deep breath, it's the first full unhindered breath I've taken in nearly a year. It's clean and minty, energizing and cooling, and a tear falls from my eye before I have a chance to catch myself.

"Feels nice, don't it?" Rose says as she turns the knob down on her boiling peanuts and settles on an embroidered cushion in front of us. She's covered in floral tattoos from neck to ankle, and her fifties-style red hair is tied up in one of those dollar-store handkerchiefs you see gang members wear in movies from the nineties. A *Boyz-n-the-Hood-but-make-it-fashion* sort of vibe.

I take another deep breath in. This time the cooling sensation flows from my lungs down to the pit of my stomach. Goose bumps erupt on my skin, and it starts to feel like I'm floating.

"Are you okay?" Aabidah asks, but she sounds far away. I turn to look at her and it's like she's at the far end of a tunnel, or I'm looking up at her from the bottom of a well. *Shit, it's happening again.*

"What's wrong with her?" Aabidah asks Rose, the urgency in her voice muffling it into a desperate whisper.

"She's fine. She'll be back soon," Rose says calmly, winking as she drops a pillow behind me just in case I teeter.

I try to grab on to something before I fall, but there's nothing to grab on to when you're falling into your own mind.

5

Gao, Mali, 1325

TAMAR

"HAL 'ANT BIKHAYR?"

I blink hard against the sun and turn to the auntie who just asked after my welfare. "I'm fine," I say quickly, not wanting to draw too much attention to myself. "I . . . I lost my train of thought. I must have been daydreaming."

Al-Kawkaw is my city. I know the market, its beating heart, like I know the lines etched into my palm. My claim to her as my own is as valid as any girl born here, even though I was not. As its adopted daughter I know when I am being fleeced. I shake my head at the woman in front of me.

"It's too high a price, even for cloth so fine," I say, and turn the corner of the linen over with my hand. Iyin's ring, a half-moon agate set in gold, catches the light.

"Fine ring," she says, testing the waters to see if I have stolen it. I meet her gaze head-on. Yes, a slave has no use for fine jewelry, but neither does a girl whose fingers have grown too thin to wear it. It was a gift, but I don't owe this woman that story.

"Your mistress, daughter of an old family, a respected family, can't be seen in rags," the old woman says as she smooths the fabric with her wrinkled hand. I can only see her eyes, but they hold mischief. She could do this all day. I don't have even five minutes to spare.

I give her a short, dry laugh. "Rags? Is that what your competitors peddle?" I wave my hand at the stall at the end of the lane, where a man is hanging out some of the finest linen I've seen brought in since the last rains. The quality is not as good as what she has to offer, but the possibility of losing a sale is enough to make her bend.

"One week. I will have it ready for you," she says begrudgingly.

"That long?" I reply, and feel a twinge of guilt as the old woman's movements grow stiff with disappointment at her haggling skills. Iyin would have been fine with paying twice the price we have settled upon, but with the better deal, I can purchase food for the week, and food is worth more than envy. While Iyin is well versed in the price fluctuations of silks and linens, she couldn't tell you how much you'd need to purchase six eggs.

"I know cowrie is the expected payment, but I have been to every corner of the market today, and I might have been a bit impulsive. Will you take a trade? I purchased this scroll of poetry for my mistress, but now I'm sure she already owns the piece. . . ."

She nearly snatches the scroll from my hand. "Tomorrow," she says again, this time with more enthusiasm. She knows she's gotten the better end of the deal.

"Poetry, Khala Farheen? Had I known I could get away with paying in pretty words, I would have sung you all the ballads of Gobir," a young man interjects in an odd accent, plucking the scroll from her fingers and raising his eyebrows in flirtation. The old woman laughs.

"What do you know of poetry? All you soldiers understand is blood and war," she replies.

The soldier straightens his back, clears his throat, and takes a step further into her tent, his arm raised toward her . . . in a flourish.

"'All through eternity / Beauty unveils His exquisite form / in the solitude of nothingness; / He holds a mirror to His Face / and beholds His own beauty. / He is the knower and the known, / the seer and the seen.'"

The candlemaker in the adjacent stall claps.

"You know Rumi," I say, astonished that a soldier would know anything besides the price of wine.

"All he knows is death and gambling, girl," the old woman says with a sigh. "Ignore him. This place will be free of his kind soon enough."

"Oh, but I will miss you the most, Auntie. And who would I give my winnings to? Will you tell this girl that cloth is not all that you sell?" he says, his eyes dancing.

The woman throws up her hands and lets loose a monsoon of Idoma that I can't quite follow. Other than market visits, I am not allowed to talk with anyone outside the household, let alone travel to Enugu to pick up enough Idoma for conversation. While they joke and argue, I step away. I've still got to renegotiate the price of our weekly millet order, visit the midwife for an adjustment to Iyin's prescription of herbs, and hopefully find someone who can sell me a bit of that lemon-scented honey she loves from Timbuktu. I know of one peddler, but being the zealot he is, he refuses to sell to a girl shopping on her own. I tried to explain there were no sons in our household, but he wouldn't budge. So why give our coins to such a rude man anyway?

I smell my way, as much as I walk from memory, toward the fishmongers closer to the River Niger's edge. The newer stalls are more likely to be set up here. With the arrival of Mansa Musa's retinue, there's always something new to see, even if it is a bit more crowded. A sharp voice spooks a horse tied to a stall on my left, and a cart of melons spills to the ground from its flailing front legs. In a blink I'm off-balance and heel over head with no control over my body, bound for certain disaster. But in the next heartbeat strong arms cradle me and set me on my feet again.

"You must have a lot on your mind if you did not see that coming," the arms say as they spin me around. The Rumi soldier.

My first thought is to check my hair. It's wedding season, and Iyin was so generous as to allow me to have my hair styled along with hers. Braids no wider than flower stems bloom from the crown of my head and loop again and again, finally gathering in a lush ball at the back of my neck. Glass beads that flash green and gold dangle from their strategic homes on each braid and could easily slip out of place, but I needn't have worried. He caught me like it was his job to catch—a fisher of silly girls. His hands squeeze the flesh of my arms in a way that sends a shiver across my skin, followed by an internal desire I've never felt before. I snatch my arms loose. If he's offended, his smile doesn't show it.

I clear my throat, afraid the pitch in my voice might give away the nervousness churning in my belly. I have never been this close to a man I do not know, and I most certainly have never been touched by one. "Thank you," I rush, almost forgetting my manners.

"My pleasure. I am here to serve," he says and bows his head low.

I look around me to see if anyone is watching, prying eyes that might send a word to Iyin or her father about my inappropriate behavior. They would be lies, but it wouldn't be the first time. Thankfully, everyone is preoccupied with calming down the horse and the river of melons rolling down the street.

"Tamar! Are you all right?" a woman's voice cries close to my ear.

"*Yaa*, Adaku," I reply, and, seeing that I'm telling the truth, the midwife's daughter takes the opportunity to share the life story of her cousin who was once kicked in the head by one of the sultan's horses and never recovered. I have to squeeze her arm to stop her.

"*Ndo*, sorry. Who was that man?" she asks.

I turn my head. I expect the young man to introduce himself, but he's gone. "Nobody, just a soldier," I say, and loop my arm in hers so she can lead me to the midwife. Hoping with each step that I can shake the feeling of being in the soldier's arms.

6

Sumter County, South Carolina, Present Day

TAMAR

T-TAMAR!" AABIDAH YELLS.

"Jesus, why are you so loud?" I complain, and move the still-steaming cup of tea to my left hand and push it as far away as I can.

"You zoned out and I'm not that loud. What's in that stuff?" Aabidah demands as she shifts her scrutiny from me to Rose.

"It's my own blend. As I mentioned, you can't drink it, but hell if it don't open you up. Mentally and physically. I'll admit it's got a bit of a psychedelic edge, if you know what I mean," Rose replies, and adds a little shoulder shimmy for emphasis.

"Did you just give her drugs? She's sick, you psychopath!" Aabidah's eyes are full of fire.

She laughs. "It's not drugs. And it's definitely a lot less damaging than whatever her doctors are giving her." She turns to me. "Did they give you something to suppress the dreams?"

I nod quickly, almost imperceptibly. Just because she's a psychic, it doesn't make it any easier to admit a mental illness.

Rose shakes her head. "Those doctors don't know their ass from a pothole in the street."

I don't have anything to say in that regard. The visions started coming almost to the day I had my first real brush with death in the hospital. The doctors knocked me out and I woke up in Paris. I spoke fluent French and worked as a lady's maid for a Southern belle on her European wedding tour. I slipped into that life like I'd never had any other. It felt so real. Fay was there too, one of the *gens de couleur libres* attending a local university. I woke up ranting to one of the nurses in fluent eighteenth-century French for about fifteen minutes, and that's when they started giving me antianxiety medication. The language hiccup was blamed on some brain inflammation and the excellent foreign-language department at my high school.

Sometimes the meds work and I sleep fine, and sometimes, like today, they fail miserably. One moment I'm in the back room of a bar in South Carolina and the next I'm in West Africa, God only knows when.

The visions don't always come at night. Since my incident at the hospital, there seem to be triggers before they sweep me away. A smell, or a song on the radio. Once, I had a vision set off by the particular gurgle of a mall fountain. I blinked and I was standing on the edge of the Jet d'Eau near Lake Geneva in Switzerland. I pick up the teacup and place it under my nose again. Immediately, the fog behind my eyes lifts and blood rushes to my head. I draw in another deep breath and then another. Damn, it feels good to really breathe.

"I'll give you a bit of the tea to take home. On the house. So what brings y'all here?"

Aabidah, more annoyed and suspicious than impressed, shoves the unused oxygen mask back in her purse and flicks her waist-length passion twists over her shoulder. "You're the psychic. Why don't you tell us?"

I want to pinch her. I'm supposed to be the skeptic, but this breathing tea was worth the trip, so I'm willing to give Rose a bit of begrudging respect.

"Am I dying?" I ask with more volume than I've had the breath to give my voice in months. Aabidah's hand clutches at her shirt involuntarily. If she had pearls on, she'd be crushing them. I don't know why she's so shocked. She practically asked the same thing when we went to see my team of doctors last week. Their answer was vague, with talk about intubation and respirators, clinical trials and survival rates, the comically long waiting list for a lung transplant, but nothing solid. Nothing that seemed real, and everything with a hefty price tag. My sister can't afford much more of this. She's only twenty-two.

"I like you. Straight to the point," Rose says.

"Well?" I ask.

"We all are, honey, in one way or the other, but yes, your particular expiration date is much closer than your sister's or mine," she says as she unscrews the top of a bottle of expensive-looking alkaline water.

"How long?" I ask.

She tilts her head from side to side and looks at me, peering right into my eyes. "When's your birthday?" she asks.

"May twenty-second."

"Ah, well, sorry, kiddo. I don't see you making it that far."

My sister erupts into a litany of curses I have never heard spoken in real life, let alone out of my sister's mouth.

"Aabidah! Calm down. It's not her fault!" I yell over her.

She immediately stops. "This was a bad idea," she murmurs to herself, and then turns to Rose. "You're supposed to make her feel better. Reassure her," she says sharply.

"Honey, if I lied to people, don't you think I'd be in better digs than at the back of a dirt-road bar? I tell customers the truth and no more. . . . *But* I will say this. Tamar has a short life, but one of the oldest souls I've ever had walk in here."

"What's that supposed to mean?" Aabidah spits.

Rose sets her gaze on me. "Pour that tea into that aloe plant over there. It looks thirsty. But don't dump the leaves." Reluctantly, I empty the cup and hand it to her.

She looks inside, the scrunch of her red lips the only betrayal of what she might be thinking. "You're meant to have a great love, but a short life. You see here, each of these stems is exactly the same length, lined up the exact same width apart from the others." She whistles high and long and shakes her head. "I'd need a PhD in astrophysics to calculate how long you've lived or will live." She stops, peering into the cup as if she just saw something new. "Hmm, there's this bit of—"

Aabidah waves her hand in the air. "This is bullshit." She turns to me. "We're going to see Pastor Roberts in the morning. Got me out here in Klan country for this . . . ," she grumbles as she gets to her feet.

Rose is so mesmerized by my tea leaves she barely notices us as we slip through the curtains. We're just outside the car when I feel her cool hand grip my arm. "You forgot your tea."

Aabidah's still complaining as she slams her car door.

"You could have lied," I tell Rose.

She shrugs. "You would have been able to tell. Old soul, remember."

"What does that even mean?" I ask. I don't have a clue what she's talking about.

"Just means you are part of an old story. You've got a decision to make, though, right? The cryogenics center overseas? Fay?"

I chew my lip. Rose is the real deal. I didn't want to think about Fay right now. His presence in the equation that is my life doesn't compute. It's like a problem where instead of solving for x it's a fruit snack. And the cryogenics center? That's the absolute last resort. If it begins to look like I won't make it at all, then there's a trial I can sign up for. I volunteer to put my body on ice for a chance at revival once medicine has advanced. It's far-fetched, and Fay would say it's straight up B-movie science fiction, but it's a chance.

Rose helps me load my tank into the car.

"It's up to you. Part of all this human experience is deciding what you believe."

I should be grateful for her honesty, the cloudless sky, and the uncommonly cool breeze whipping the overlarge American flag over our heads. Instead I'm all tapped into my feelings, so I take my sister's approach.

"Sounds like bullshit."

We see the pastor the next day. He prays with us and, worse, assures me everything will be fine, and that I'm special, one of God's own.

And then the doctors call.

Turns out the pastor does have some spiritual insight worth something; I am special. So special my super-rare blood type means I'm almost impossible to match for a new set of lungs, which means we're on to plan E, the cryogenics center. Our last resort to try to pause the clock running out on my life.

"Hypocrite," I whisper, and then spit pink phlegm into the airport bathroom sink.

"You still thinking about Pastor Roberts?" Aabidah, asks.

I don't reply. It's embarrassing how much I wanted his approval after the debacle at Dolly's Mirror last Saturday. It's not like he gets the deciding vote on who gets into heaven and who doesn't. I even asked him, if I wasn't a virgin, what that would do for my chances. He dodged the question. Typical.

"Forget about him. You know Mother Jackson said he didn't even go to seminary. He's nothing but a storefront preacher with a high school diploma. He doesn't know everything. Don't . . . just try not to upset yourself. If you have an episode, they won't let us on the plane, and we're all out of that tea Rose gave you. The center was adamant about the window of opportunity for a case like yours, and we waited until the absolute last minute to book this trip. It's now Monday. We really should have pulled the trigger last Wednesday."

There's a bit of censure in her voice, but I don't pick at it. If I pulled that thread, who knows what I'd find beneath the seams? Maybe there is no experimental trial and all of this is just an elaborate exercise to give me hope, or—worse—there's no scholarship for patients dealing with hardships and she's going to go broke trying to keep me on ice, never living the life she's still got left to live. My heart starts beating too fast, and the health meter on my smartwatch begins to beep loudly, ricocheting off the sickly green bathroom tile. I take in a deep breath, or what passes for one these days.

"I know," I say, trying to avoid her gaze. "I'm trying."

"Do you want me to adjust your oxygen levels?" she asks, waving her fingers delicately across my oxygen tank. A lady with her young daughter scoots to the sink on the opposite side of the public bathroom, obviously avoiding me and whatever contagious disease she thinks I might be carrying. The little girl, maybe seven years old, with wide eyes and an LOL-doll rolling suitcase, openly stares.

A disembodied voice crackles over the speakers piped into the airport. "Attention, travelers: Homeland Security has raised our threat level to orange. Keep all carry-on bags in your possession at all times. Additionally, some flights may be delayed."

We both look up as if the voice will materialize into a person we can focus our attention on. When nothing else follows, Aabidah goes back to adjusting the tubes on my tank.

A sense of panic washes over me and I can't take it anymore. The trip. The sickness. The complete reliance I have on Aabidah. "Stop fussing. I can do it myself. Can you— I need a minute!" I snap.

Aabidah slowly straightens back up. She gives me an empty smile and tucks a braid behind my ear. Her brow is furrowed. For a moment she looks just like our mother: the little smile lines around her mouth, the flat eyebrows and lone dimple. You'd think having to raise your baby sister after your mother dies would put the years on, but you'd be wrong. I think she really enjoys it—loving somebody fully and unabashedly and having them love you back. She looks more solid than other people her age. Wise and polished. But now that I'm dying, tragically from complications of the same disease that killed Mama, the idea of having to be all alone for the first time is getting to her, and I just can't take her face right now.

Flat-out angry tears well up in my eyes. I should have gone with Fay to Myrtle Beach on Senior Skip Day last month and finally, finally told him I was ready for more than a few roaming fingers under my uniform skirt. I should have sipped that champagne at my cousin Letitia's wedding last year and kissed that girl in the bathroom. I should have stuck my head out of the sunroof at junior prom even though it's what basic girls do. I should have told Fay I loved him, even if it gave him a big head and made everybody start calling me Fay's trophy. I should be happy Aabidah got into that graduate program in DC.

Should, should, should.

My phone buzzes inside my fanny pack. I unzip it and look at the screen.

Fay: I had a crazy dream about u. Pick up!

Not as crazy as my visions, I want to say, but I don't. I close the screen and feel the phone buzz; now it's a call. I know it's him. I let it go to voicemail. Then on impulse I toss the phone, case and all, into the trash.

Who do I need to call? I've got a one-way ticket.

7
FAYARD

THE PROBLEM IS THAT YOU THINK YOU HAVE TIME.
Every kid, every adult, every dope boy trying to slang just
enough to get by, every big guy praying he loses the fifty
pounds keeping him out of the military, and every sad scar of the
human experience in this airport.

"Jesus Christ on the cross in springtime. Get up, Fay. You're
embarrassing yourself. Is that an engagement ring? Are you
unhinged?" Aabidah growls.

The sister. Always available to ruin a perfectly romantic moment.
Fate must have it in for me.

"Aabidah, this isn't about you," I say, exasperated. "And it's a
promise ring," I add quickly.

She is not amused. When T stopped responding to my texts, I
had to start hitting Aabidah up for updates, but other than con-
firming whether or not T was okay, she wouldn't give me much.
But she underestimated me. I got no shame when it comes to T,
and people love the idea of love, even when they say they don't. All
I had to do was lose a few games of chess to Benard to find out they
were leaving today.

"Are we on *Christian Catastrophe*? Where's the creepy host
who pretends to be a preacher? Don't answer that. She can't see

you. You'll just upset her," she says, trying to contain her anger.

I'm down on one knee. Luck led me into the airport only moments after Aabidah and T arrived, and I caught them heading into the ladies' room. I've been here ever since. I want to be the first thing T sees when she steps out of the bathroom. A few people start clapping right there in the terminal, but I wave them off. The mariachi band—if you can call two trumpet players from the middle school JV strand of the band—are waiting for my signal, as is their cousin, Javier, who's filming the whole thing with a digital camera we checked out from the community college. DeAndre flaked out on me.

"It's not for her. It's for her sister," I say, waving away the people passing. The cashier at the chicken place gives me a thumbs-up, and a handful of folks in the waiting area pull out their phones. Not everyone is happy, though. A guy in a FLYHOME T-shirt gives me a dirty look. He has a table set up and is collecting money for plane tickets for first-generation college students who can't afford to go home on their school breaks. I volunteered with them for a few weekends last summer. T and I both did. It was office work for a good cause that didn't tire her out. I shrug his way in some kind of half apology for stealing the eyeballs he needs for donations.

"You think you're helping but you're not. You'll just make this harder, and she needs to get on that plane." Aabidah stops mid-breath and shoots a pointy nude-colored nail at Javier. "If you don't get that spotlight out of my face, I'll tell security you're smuggling oxy."

Javier shuts the lens and lowers the camera, but I can tell from the blinking red light he's still filming.

"Why?" I ask. "And don't sell me some lame-ass story about a music scholarship. I looked it up. It doesn't exist."

Tamar's running away. I don't know why. Maybe she's running from me, but she's gotta know how serious I am about us before she gets on that plane. The ring is a moonstone, surrounded by diamonds, because she's my universe. Shit! The explanation even sounds lame, but it's the truth. My Gran was a hippie and it used to belong to her. I can't ever think of giving it to anyone but T. I've loved her since the first time we hung out together—well, maybe not the first day, but definitely the first week. We fit, and if you fit, why waste time looking for something you already got?

"Leave."

"Not until I talk to Tamar," I say defiantly.

Aabidah gets up in my face, snatching the ring out of my hands, so I have to stand to get it back. Her face is all screwed up, so she looks like the old lady she pretends to be.

"Listen, I like you, Fay. I do. You always seemed to really care for T, but the only reason I'm not kicking your ass right now is because we have a flight that we cannot miss. This is too much. You are doing too much. If you really love her, you will let her go." Aabidah sighs, and it's clear how exhausted she is.

And she thinks *I'm* crazy. "You don't let go of the things you love. You hold 'em tighter."

"Did you read that in a fortune cookie?" she asks, her fire back.

Damn, she's making this hard, and now I feel stupid for even repeating what that tarot reader told me at the senior carnival. Of course, Tamar wasn't there. She missed it, just like she missed prom, EJ's spring-break house party, and Yamilyera's epic beatdown when Sly finally told Cleo he'd been cheating on her and with whom. There's a twist in my gut and a scratch behind my eyes every time I close them.

I see T's face, not like the last time I saw her, coughing so hard she couldn't catch her breath, but smiling like on the first day we met. Sometimes I drift off and an image appears—her hair is different and I'm different too—and then I open my eyes and this shitty reality is still here. But T and I are bigger than reality. She has to know that.

Aabidah narrows her eyes and looks me up and down like she really is about to fight me, Then she lets out a big puff of air and dips back into the ladies' bathroom. I turn to look at my band in their EAGLE PRIDE T-shirts, eager and excited to help me with my grand gesture, at Javier who can't stop winking at every girl who passes by. *Am I doing this for her?* I gently close the box and slide it back into my coat pocket.

I turn to Javier. "Proposal's canceled."

My gaze shifts to an old lady sitting in the closest waiting area, eyes glued to us and the scene we've created. "Give the old lady the roses and stuff the bear in my trunk. I'll meet you at the car." Javier just nods and rushes off.

I walk the rest of the crew to the Krispy Kreme to buy them a dozen doughnuts and send them out of the airport too. I check the leaderboard and see that her plane has been delayed. I've got an hour to kill and sit alone with my thoughts. The air smells like sugar, and suddenly I'm sleepy. I put my earbuds in to drown out the voice in my head telling me I'm making a mistake. Aabidah's probably right. If Tamar wanted to be with me, she would have said it out loud, right? I turn the volume up and let whatever comes on play, as long as the bass is heavy, as heavy as my heart. I close my eyes and see T's face, her eyes boring into mine, her eyes saying what her lips won't. And it's there that I see her heart.

8

Philadelphia, Pennsylvania, 1924

FAYARD

DAWN IS THE BEST TIME FOR ESCAPES. THE SMELL OF maple and pillow-soft dough tickles my nose and coaxes me from sleep. Someone is making pancakes. Through the open window the breeze brings mystery and the clang of the streetcar, the bubble of the working man's coffeepot. At dawn you can blend in with the folk on their way to work. The hustlers are done for the night and the drunks are sleeping the drink off. The sun isn't really up yet, and if it is, it looks like a woman laughing, her head turned up just enough that you can't see her face. Like she's got a secret that's about to bubble right out of her.

A cool breeze blows the lace curtains in from the open window along with the sound of the early morning autobuses rolling by. I wipe the crust out of my eyes with my left hand; my right one's pinned under a warm, sleeping angel breathing feathers across my neck. Her heavy thigh is hooked over my stomach, pinning me down. I don't want to move. It's not that I don't like to slip out on a girl unnoticed—better the memory of me than the real thing. It's just that I'm so comfortable. Even with a price on my head and knowing her daddy could come home at any minute, I slept like a baby.

I lean over and kiss her forehead. She stirs a bit with a weak smile and yawns, cupping her hand over her mouth to hold in the stink. Now ain't that cute?

I slip my arm out from under her and roll my shoulder. Pins and needles shoot up my bicep. I like a girl with some meat on her, but heavy is heavy no matter how pretty it is.

"Shh . . ," I say softly, and try to find my shoes in the near dark. I snatch my shirt off the chair and button it blind. Her dark eyes finally open when I pull my cap over my head. Her hair is wild and shook loose of all the pins and things she put in before she went to bed, before I snuck in her window and made her promises I've got no intention of keeping. The guilt of it is tugging at my suit jacket, but I beat it away. I did what anybody else would do on their last day of freedom. Everything I damn well wanted to—I hustled a ticket to see Ethel Waters at the Dunbar Theatre (front row of the balcony, but still good), ate a steak at Miss Bethel's on Broad Street, and spent all but my last dime on a brand-new pin-striped double-breasted summer suit from King Fats's own tailor in West Philly. The very last dime went to flowers for Sable, the prettiest girl on Thirteenth Street, and when she turned me down, I pulled out one rose and took my chances with Ruby.

"Do you have to go?" she asks.

I nod. "You know I do."

"You have to write. You promised, and you said you always keep your promises," she says, her voice sweet yet pleading.

My guilt's grown a foot taller, and it's tapping on my shoulder now.

"You know Fats, baby. I gotta get out of town and fast. My uncle got me a job on the railroad. I don't know where I'll end up."

Her eyes flash, and I can tell she's seeing dollar signs. A Pullman porter is the best thing a colored boy can aspire to be besides a postman. For the next week or two, she'll probably tell all her girlfriends how she lucked out, while she waits for a letter that'll never come. My guilt grows fists and knocks me out the window I used to climb in here last night. My bum knee groans at all this early morning activity.

"Hey!" a woman yells from across the street as she makes her way out of her apartment. "I know that ain't Mary's boy!"

I lean up a bit on the ledge and snatch a violet from the window box of the next apartment and tuck it behind Sable's, I mean Ruby's, ear. She leans down for another kiss just before her daddy kicks open her bedroom door.

I'm down the rain gutter and across the street on feet that fly before he can even think to get his gun.

I'm still catching my breath, my new custom suit in a suitcase, when I find myself staring at my uncle. I can't say he ain't imposing as he stands there bald and red-faced, brown-freckled and seething on the train platform.

"Now, it wasn't my fault, Uncle Max," I lie. I'm late, so by extension I've made him late, and that is a direct violation of Mr. Pullman's 241 rules of conduct for porters. Uncle Max is a stickler for the rules. Makes you wonder how his only son ended up in Eastern State Penitentiary.

"Don't even bother," he says. "I don't care and I don't have time to correct you. The conductor is already on site. Just be grateful he's hungover and not looking to do any real work. I'll be the porter in charge for this run."

"Hey! That's a promotion! More money, eh, Unc?" I say excitedly.

His mouth pinches even further into a flat line. "You best tone down all that eagerness, boy," he says, his voice low and stern. "No. It ain't more money, just more work and more of a chance to get docked and into trouble. I need you on your best behavior. No, let me rephrase. I need you on *my* best behavior. Whatever you think I would do, do that. Anything else is a violation."

"You got it," I say, eager to please him. "Hey, I read the book, Uncle Max. I—"

He cuts me off and snatches the rule book I've pulled out of my pocket and tucks it into his. "Good. Now that you've read it you can focus all your attention on me. That rule book don't know everything about everything. I am your Bible and your Jesus Christ, and if you disobey me, you'll wish it was as easy as laying down and dying," he preaches.

His words knock the wind out of me. I guess that's the point. He looks me up and down and dusts invisible dirt off my shoulder before pulling my cap farther down on my head. I'm the mirror image of him now, tall and broad-shouldered, slim and long-fingered, in a gleaming white shirt, black pants, and matching jacket with six silver buttons.

"Your mama would cry if she saw you like this," he says softly.

My heart constricts. She would. This was her dream, the opposite of the living nightmare I put her through before she died. A defiance against that premonition she had, something about an untimely end. It scared her to death to think she might outlive me. At least God saved her from that horror.

I back away to put some space between my uncle and me. I clench and unclench my fists and turn my back so he can't see the water building in my eyes. I raise my hand and nod my head like I see someone I know just so I can blink away the tears and swallow the lump in my throat. When I turn around, I know I shouldn't have even bothered pretending, 'cause that dimple of his is winking in and out of my uncle's cheek as he tries to get his own emotions in check.

The Thirtieth Street Station of the Pennsylvania Railroad sits right in downtown Philly on the west bank of the Schuylkill River. It's big, open, damp, and busy as hell. Everybody I see has got somewhere to be and something important to get to. They've got adventure in their eyes, and luck trailing behind them like a trained dog. As for me, I've got work and lots of it.

"So, where do I start?"

"Hey! Gimme a hand with that trunk," someone yells.

I jog over to the guy, sweat soaking me to my draws. "Can't we take off the jacket at least?" I complain.

He told me earlier his real name is William Longfort, but everybody calls him Pal. Light-skinned and lanky, Pal shakes his head. "Against the rules. They'll let you die of heatstroke 'fore they let you take off that uniform. That's why we workin' so hard to get us a union."

I laugh out loud at that one, the first real hard laugh I've had in weeks. "Ain't no railroad union letting Negroes in."

He scowls and I have to swallow my smile. I put my head back down and try harder to carry the weight of the last trunk we've got to haul.

"That's where you're wrong. You playboys don't pay attention to the real world, how it's changing and how you got to make it change. The Brotherhood of Sleeping Car Porters will be the first colored union recognized by real industry in the nation. Mr. A. Philip Randolph been working for years to get us there, and when we do, we'll get paid for loading and unloading. Get us a real pension worth something, and get conductor pay when we do conductor work."

I nod. "That sounds real fine." I try to put more enthusiasm in my voice than I feel. I can tell a true believer when I see one. I just got here. I can't be too choosy about friends.

"Our time is long overdue. The AFL is gonna listen this time."

"Don't go filling his head with that Brotherhood nonsense, Pal," my uncle growls as he surveys the quality of our work. His cap hides his eyes from view, but you can tell they're angry. "I don't want you talking up the Brotherhood with my nephew. This here is his future, and that union foolery will kill his prospects before they even get a chance to take root."

"I don't know why you won't join us, Max. You need this as much as we do."

"That's right, I do need this. I got a sister with no husband, two daughters in high school 'bout to graduate, and if I'm gon' make sure they don't have to rock white babies to sleep at night for the rest of their lives, I'm gon' need money for secretarial school. Mr. Pullman's company been good to me. I aim to be good back."

"Not as good as it's been to the white folks," Pal says.

A flash of something hot sparks in Uncle Max's eyes as a train whistle, high and long, blows close by. I put my fist on his chest, knuckles right against his heart.

"Hey, Unc," I say softly.

Uncle Max points his perfectly manicured but rough finger at Pal. "You heard what I said."

Uncle Max and Pal stay locked in a staring contest for what seems like an hour. Finally, Pal breaks and smiles.

"You keep your nose clean, kid. We'll talk later."

I nod in understanding, but I'm distracted. There's a girl standing on the platform. Navy dress, black heels, red lips. Blooming, like she sprang from the concrete. I know her. No. I used to know her. I'm sure of it. I know her like I know family, even if we're distant. I've seen her sitting across the table at Sunday dinner spreading butter over hot cornbread. No, that can't be. I've seen her on the street outside my building. No. A girl like her couldn't walk down our block without Peanut, Blind Man, or Dee Dee saying something slick as she passed by. Then they'd call up to my cousin Shelby and he'd lean out the window to whistle. I'd do it too to see what was going on and then . . . No. I'd remember a fight like that. I'd lose 'cause it would be four against one and I'd have to do it because she deserves better than to be whistled at like a dog that's gone off her leash. No. I didn't see her at our table or on the block. . . . I could never have forgotten a face like hers.

"Stop staring. You look like you havin' a fit or somethin'."

"Sorry."

Uncle Max claps me on the back. It's quick and hard, meant to snap me to attention.

"It's okay. She is a pretty one. But keep your distance. Fraternization ain't allowed, and her daddy don't look too nice either."

I blink and look again. I didn't even notice the man standing in front of her. He's short with a thick, graying mustache and eyes like sharp teeth.

"Matter of fact, why, don't you help Willie get ready for dinner service."

"But I was on luggage with Pal," I protest.

"That's right. You *were* on luggage. Luggage is all packed. Now you're on dining service. I promised your auntie I'd keep you out of trouble, and that girl looks like a whole heap of trouble."

"But—"

"Let it go, boy. You need this job?" He narrows his eyes at me.

It's a rhetorical question. He knows I do. My knee pops as I start to move; it still does this when I stand in one place for too long, and it's been almost six months since my run-in with Fats. I take one last look over the old man's shoulder to see if I can see her face again, but she's turned her head and all I have is a memory. For now, that's enough.

9

TAMAR

COVER MY NOSE WITH ONE OF GRANNY'S GOOD HANDKERCHIEFS, a blue one, embroidered with a tiny bird bending its neck back. It's the only thing I got to block out the train smoke wafting through the air. Tears cloud my vision, but I dab the corners of my eyes like a lady when what I really want to do is cover my whole face. *Beauty is pain.* My sister, Patience, used to say that as she plucked her eyebrows to slits or squeezed herself into a girdle. I didn't get what she meant because I downright refused all that high-fallutin' mess at finishing school, but now I understand. Lord help me, I do. My feet pinch in shoes too tight and too high. My slip is bunched and makes my thighs sweat, and that's not to mention the pin keeping my cloche hat in place, digging into my scalp. Daddy made me wear gloves, too, like it isn't one degree cooler than hell's waiting room today. I set my cello down on the platform and cross my arms over my chest before I catch Daddy's eye. He doesn't even have to say anything. I know already what I've done wrong. I open my eyes wide to release the furrow in my brow and drop my arms to knit my hands daintily at my waist just like Miss Edith taught us. I'd grumble if I weren't so happy to finally be rid of the place.

"This is unacceptable!" Daddy's voice booms across the platform. "I demand to see the conductor."

The porter smiles even though Daddy's been as rude as he can be.

"Sir, I'm afraid that is impossible. I am the porter in charge for the duration of your stay with us. I assure you that you will be more than comfortable in a sleeping car all to yourself." He waves his hand over in my direction. "Not to mention how much safer it will be for your daughter."

"My daughter is none of your concern," Daddy says icily. He puffs himself up to his full height, which isn't much, and closes the space between the two of them. "She is under my protection and has no need of being relegated to inadequate conditions in order to appease other patrons. Our seats weren't held because the money from your white patrons is obviously worth more than that of your Negro patrons."

The porter's face doesn't betray anything. I have to wonder: IfI Daddy punched him, would he even flinch? Would that smile stay right where it is? "No, Mr. Williams. Your case is special. Most colored passengers who can afford a sleeping-car ticket are usually relegated to the less-expensive seats in the colored car once we move below Washington, DC, but I thought that an esteemed man such as yourself would prefer a private car. We aren't fully booked, so I've worked to move other passengers to the car ahead of you."

We're being upgraded, but that doesn't matter to Daddy. It's the principal. Being moved at all for white folks is an insult.

"Doctor," my father says.

"Excuse me?" says the porter.

"*Doctor* Williams."

Daddy continues to be awful, and I pretend not to see him

embarrass himself once again. A white conductor from farther up the train is found and Daddy pleads his case, albeit with a much stiffer back and a forced smile instead of a grimace, as the porter in charge gives instructions to other workers. One of them smiles at me real sly. He raises his hand to indicate he might take my cello, but heat rises to my cheeks, and instead of telling him to back off, I turn away.

Why did I do that? Feeling stupid, I turn back and he's gone.

Finally, the older porter, whom Daddy first spoke with, Mr. Max, leads us into the Pullman Palace Car. Daddy hasn't gotten his way. It smells like freshly starched linens and lemon oil. A chandelier hangs above the middle row of seats, and a scarlet rug runs the length of the car. Matching wine-colored silk shades cover the windows, and intricately carved foliage and fruit are etched into every wooden beam.

"There are bench seats here with a table for correspondence," Mr. Max says as he gives us a tour. "With a few added pillows and cushions, the benches can be converted into beds, and these wooden cupboards above your heads fold down and convert into beds as well. At the end of the car we have compartments with doors. Your ticket indicates two berths for you and your daughter, but as fortune has smiled upon us, you'll both be able to enjoy your own sleeping compartments in the private car. Take your pick."

He's trying to make it sound grand, like the privacy we're receiving is because we're very important people, like Josephine Baker or Duke Ellington. But our privacy isn't a choice. I wouldn't mind a little company. At best it would keep Daddy on his best behavior and give me someone else to focus my attention on. I choose the first of four small closet-sized rooms and slide my cello gingerly through the slim doorway.

"I will be your personal porter for this evening. I want to make sure your needs are met completely."

"Will we at least have access to the dining car?" Daddy asks, the anger he exhibited earlier losing steam.

Mr. Max sighs and leans forward a bit, like he's about to tell a child that he's just failed all his exams. "We want to make sure you are as comfortable as possible, Dr. Williams."

The emphasis on *Doctor* isn't lost on me.

"You and Miss Tamar will have access to the dining car from ten to ten thirty in the evenings and from six thirty to seven in the mornings for breakfast."

"And what will we do for lunch?" I ask.

"You're welcome to lunch in the colored smoking car. There are a number of—"

"No, thank you," my father says quickly. "We won't suffer the indignity of it. We'll have our meals brought here. Provide us a menu and we'll make our selections well ahead of time."

"As you wish, sir. Is there anything else, sir?"

Daddy shakes his head.

I wait until the sliding car door opens and closes before I kick off my shoes and fall back onto the bench closest to my room. "Did you have to be so mean to the man, Daddy? He's only trying to help," I say as I unpin my hat and toss it onto the table.

"And do you have to be such an embarrassment?"

"Me?"

"Asking about lunch like some gluttonous cow. Scowling like

an alley cat at every man and child as they pass by on the platform. We would not even need this trip if you had tried harder to find a place for yourself before graduation. This whole business was your mother's foolish idea." He paces the train car. "Sit up straight and put your shoes back on."

Tears well up in my eyes but I refuse to blink. I should be used to him speaking to me like this, but as hard as I try to steel myself against it, it still stings. The car drowns before me.

"I thought I told you to have your traveling suit tailored for the trip."

"I did," I whisper.

He grunts. He's scrutinizing me. All of me. As always, I'm coming up short. We never converse about it. He never says it out loud, but I know what he's thinking. My weight, my color—the richness of it, the depth, like good sleep and dark liquor. I look too much like Granny, his mother. Too much like who he really is, the person he tried so hard to run away from when he got accepted to Lincoln University. It was Granny's moonshine and juke-joint money that put him through college, but he'd never admit that to anyone who didn't already know. It's Mama's family that had the status, if not the money. My mother's mother, Grandmother Dawson, can trace her family back four generations before the end of slavery, not that any of that matters to her brother's creditors. He invested most of the family money and lost it. They're old Philadelphia, high status and high yellow. It was Grandmother Dawson who got Daddy his first interview at Mercy Hospital, and she's never let him forget it. I can't play this game anymore. I don't want to.

Patience knows it too. She takes after Mama, thin-boned and

golden, and sweet as ripe strawberries. She was never as good at her studies as I was, but maybe she is smarter. She watched Daddy, learned how to play into his hands, and maybe he let her. I, on the other hand, am sour rather than sweet. I'm not going to change who I am so that he can feel more comfortable slicing off parts of me to fit some notion of the ideal daughter. I guess my sister reminds Daddy of where he's going; I look too much like where he's been.

Patience, and Mama, even, kept their gazes low, nodded meekly when he exploded. But Granny was a tobacco-chewing, loud-talking, wild-mouthed, wide-hipped woman who let no man keep her from doing exactly what she wanted to do, especially her self-hating son. Her approach is infinitely more appealing.

10

FAYARD

THE WHISTLE BLOWS AND EVERYTHING MOVES LIKE IT'S been electrified. The radio crackles over the dishwashing station, and Bessie Smith's "Downhearted Blues" winds its way through the chaos as I enter the kitchen. The cook waves over a guy named LJ, as per the name tag on his jacket, who can't be but a few years older than me. His hair is shaved almost to the scalp and he's got a gap in his teeth that makes it sound like he's whistling when he talks.

"You know how to serve?" he asks me.

I shake my head. I don't know anything but running numbers, which made me perfect for luggage service, straightforward labor, but I've never waited a table a day in my life.

"No worry, all you really need to know is to do what you're told. Think you can do that?"

I nod.

"Good, 'cause you just lucked into the best-paying job on the line. Now, hip this, I didn't say it was the best *job* on the line, just the one that pays the most. Most fellas wait years for their chance at service. If you're good, you can put that sweet thing you got at home in a nice apartment and them kids you don't like into fine shoes with steak dinners every night. Keep your mouth shut and it won't get you into trouble. That's the first thing that'll steal this job from under you. Sass. No matter what the passengers tell you to do or how they tell you to do it, you hop to and you do it with a smile. You got a name?"

"Yeah, Fayard, but everybody calls me Big Time."

"Not anymore. Now your name is George."

I like to say I've got a poker face, but sometimes I falter. My jaw ticks, but I don't move.

"Don't look so put out, kid. My name's George too, and so's his and his over there. When you're on the floor, that's who you are. When you get off the floor, you're Big Time again. Got it?"

I nod. I do get it. We're not paid to be people with hearts, feelings, and dreams of our own. We're paid—no, *tipped* is more accurate—we're tipped to be buckets, willing to take whatever the customer pours out. No matter how bad a white man's day goes, he can always rest easy if it was better than the day of the colored man next to him.

I shadow LJ as I try to get my bearings. He's quick but thorough and explains everything twice so he knows I got it.

Right before we're done for the night, a couple of drunk white boys, not much older than us, try to get LJ to cluck like a chicken for a dollar. I feel every bit of the train wobble and shake as goose bumps ripple across my skin, and I'm waiting to see how he'll react—will he need a brother to go to war with him? Will this end in a fight or worse? I swallow hard. When he does it—chooses shame instead of pride—I close the book on him. You can't trust a man who'll give up his dignity for spare change. A guy like that will trade your life for his, or worse.

I don't ask any questions, though. I catch his eye after his little performance, and I think he knows he's lost me. His lips turn down just a bit at the corners and he doesn't meet my gaze again. For four hours I keep my head down; I smile; I hustle. At the end of dinner I shake off the snide comments, the rudeness, the casual and common inhumanity of well-heeled white folks, and take my pocketful of tips back to the laundry car for the real work. I haven't been on the train a full day yet and I already know there's no fighting who you really are.

Now there's only two things on my mind—policy and that girl I saw on the platform. It takes nothing but a whisper to get a numbers game going. Policy is like the lottery—well, not like, is—and every colored man with some change in his pocket plays. In Harlem, the New York Clearing House sets the numbers for the winner of the day at ten a.m. on the dot. I hear in Detroit they pick balls from a machine. And right now, on Mr. Pullman's train, I'm the only man with a plan.

For the remainder of the night, I slide in and out of each car like a pocket of air. Coins jingle so bad in my pockets that I sound like Christmas in July. I inhale big gulps of smoke-laced air, let it settle in my lungs and mark my journey. Soon my only wish is that I had a bit of mistletoe to take with me. I've got a date with destiny.

11
FAYARD

UNCLE MAX'S FACE IS SET, HIS BODY A SOLID WALL AT the back of the smoking car.

"No."

"But Uncle Max," I whine.

"You're too green and you got your daddy's blood in you. Ain't nothing you love more than chasin' a skirt."

I place a hand on my chest with pretend shock. "I am offended, Uncle Max. I would never do anything to jeopardize my new job here or to embarrass you. Besides, like you said, I'm green. You can put me in one of the other cars where I'm liable to make a mistake, or you can put me in the private car and all I have to do is take care of two people. It's like baby steps, easing into the job."

"No dice. Sharp's already turned down the beds and delivered the good doctor his dinner."

"*Sharp?* Even I know Sharp ain't the best." I met him while working luggage earlier. You had to watch him or you'd find yourself hauling everything alone, with him hiding behind a trunk with a cigarette.

"I don't need him to be the best. I just need him to babysit till we let 'em off in Atlanta."

I've got more argument in me, but Uncle Max turns and leaves.

"Uncle Max!"

The whip of the wind snatches my voice and tosses it along the tracks, but Fats always said an obstacle ain't nothing but an opportunity in disguise.

"Sharp?" I whisper. "Sharp?"

He groans and turns over in bed. With a near-empty car available, there's no reason to try to make up a bed in the smoking car like the other porters; he just picked the farthest sleeping compartment from the guests and claimed it as his own.

"Sharp!" This time I wedge a knuckle into his spine.

"Ow!"

"Shhhh!" I hiss.

"Man, are you crazy? What are you doing in here?"

"I'll give you two dollars if you let me take this assignment."

Sharp's lips bunch and slide to the side in suspicion. "You ain't got it to give."

I dig into my vest pocket and pull out a double eagle worth twenty dollars. His eyes bulge and he shoots up so quick his head cracks against the ceiling. Sharp winces and rubs the spot while reaching out to inspect the coin. I snatch it back.

"You stole it."

"I've never stolen anything in my entire life outside of a kiss. I'm just letting you know I'm good for it."

He's silent for a minute and then nods. Attending porters are required to stay close to their guests, and I want to be as close to the girl as possible. It might be the only joy I get on this job.

"All right," he sighs as he flops back down on the bed. "Ain't no point in me working this one anyway. Big-time coloreds don't tip worth a damn."

He slides off the bunk and disappears down the hallway as quiet as death. I guess it's one of those skills you learn over time. I don't even bother to undress, just pull off my jacket and unbutton my shirt before I hop into bed.

After the hardest day of work in my life, I thought I'd go out like a light, but my mind turns to sweeter things, like the girl asleep in the next room, her smile, the longing in her eyes, like she's looking for something she just can't find.

12

Gao Empire, Mali, 1325

FAYARD

EVERY DUMB ANIMAL HAS EYES, EVEN ME, BUT HERS . . . there are no appropriate words to describe them. Subtle and searing? No, it was more than that. Wide-set and wistful? It was only a few moments, but I see the girl from the market everywhere and nowhere. Her eyes staring into mine from around corners, and in my sleep. I've never been smitten like this before.

I bow low to one of the sultan's senior wives at the gate of the compound, removing my shield and smiling broadly so that she can see me clearly as a royal guest despite her rheumy and clouded vision.

She nods, and one of the guards lets me inside the wooden gates. While the city isn't protected by much more than the river and a few military outposts, the sultan does keep his family well-guarded, and as members of Mansa Musa's noble retinue, we are his guests.

"And where have you been all day dressed like that?" my father asks as he waves disdainfully at my borrowed foot soldier's attire.

"Nowhere."

"Ah, and with no one, I'm sure."

I laugh. Father knows I pretend to be a warrior so I can move freely in the villages, and chooses to look away. A title can be a burden, a fact he's well aware of.

"You are too predictable, son," he says as he gathers his prayer mat from the corner and hands me mine. "I wanted to wait until we returned home from the hajj to find you a wife, but you have forced my hand with this carousing. You are getting too old for this. Did you at least win anything this time?"

I blink hard. I thought he'd given up on the marriage talk after what happened with my last betrothal, or at least put it on hold so that we could travel in peace.

"I am seeing the world. Is it not my privilege to do so as the son of one of the most respected Mandinka chieftains, living or dead?"

"You flatter too easily, and that is your main failing. Marriage will center you, or at the very least occupy your days so that you don't risk defiling my good name or Mansa Musa's. Maybe we can outrun your bad luck."

"That silly old witch is senile," I say with irritation. Father is overly superstitious. Only a fool leaves his fate in the hands of some blind old woman in our home village who spins tales to earn her bread each night. Yet, he clings to the old ways and seeks out the advice of soothsayers and such for every big decision.

His eyes soften. "Forget luck, then. We will outrun your poor decisions."

I realize too late that his mind is made up and this is not idle conversation. I grasp at straws.

"B-but it was you, Baba, who insisted that I marry a Senufo girl like Mother."

He draws in a deep breath, no doubt taking the moment to remember Mother, her smile and her quiet spirit.

I lean into my argument.

"How would it look for your only son to return home with a foreign bride?"

He blinks hard and shakes his head. "It would look like a brazen attempt to get into the good graces of Mansa Musa, who is desperate to solidify alliances inside and outside his empire and among all the tribes of this land," he says calmly.

"So, this is political, then?" I ask, letting the deference fall from my tone. Father's ambitions are far worse than anything I do when the moon rises.

He releases a huff of air and leads me out into the courtyard and toward the mosque with the other men, lowering his voice so that we cannot be overheard.

"I am not immortal, Fayard, and this journey wears me thin. You are my only son, and I must see some things settled before I die."

I nearly throw up my hands in frustration. Father is legendary for his theatrics. "You are not dying, Baaba."

"We are all dying, my son, some of us a bit faster than others. I will tell you what my father told me when his time had come. He said, 'Love gives a man purpose. When we are in love, we are most like Allah.' It is time for a wife, children, and responsibility," he says soberly.

One of the palace guards greets Father warmly as we walk, and they begin talking, effectively sealing Father's edict. The conversation is over. I will be married before the rains come, and I will have no say in the matter. He speaks of love as if he can gift it to me like a candle waiting to be lit on his command. I know better. He will choose someone meek, dull, not too pretty, and very well connected. I don't have a year. All I have is a few weeks. And if I can only live for that time, I intend to do so for myself and not for political gain.

The next day I make it my business to find the girl in the market, and I know just where to start.

"*As-salaam 'alaykum*, Khala Farheen," I say, smiling broadly. For good measure I wave my hand over the auntie's fabric and beckon a few passersby to take a look.

She crosses her arms across her large bosom and squints her eyes in disapproval. "*Wa'alaykum salaam*. My answer is the same as yesterday evening. She is not here."

"But you must know something."

She laughs. "And why would I tell you? There are plenty of little birds hidden in every dark corner of the market whose time you could waste for the right price. The girl is a good customer. A respectable girl, and you are a brute," she teases. She likes the banter, but I am running out of time.

Tired of the pretense, I drop a small bag heavy with gold dinars in front of her. She nearly faints when she pries it open with a henna-covered finger. The intricate floral design is no doubt in preparation for one of the many weddings taking place every day.

"I knew you were a scoundrel, but now I see you are a thief. I will not take it."

"I am no thief. I am no soldier, either. There is enough money there to secure the transport of your grandson to Niani and with a recommendation to set him up as an apprentice to one of the city's scribes," I say quietly.

She claps her hands, then covers her mouth and eyes as her head shakes from side to side in surprise. Or is it despair? I cannot tell. When she does open them, they dart from one side of the stall to the other, making sure no one overheard. She even goes so far as to look under the tables.

Satisfied we're the only two in earshot, she leans forward. "I do not know who you have been talking to, but they lie."

I lean farther still and lower my voice as far as will go without losing its power altogether. "Even if the little bird is your lost daughter? Now, before you get too upset, please hear me out. I know what you thought you had to do to protect your reputation. A fallen daughter is hard to stand by, but the boy has no future here. He has no father who will claim him, and a mother who struggles daily to feed him. Do him this kindness. Save him from a life of poverty."

She closes her eyes, considering. I've played her a dirty hand, but what I'm offering is worth far more than the few coins I've tossed her way. The lies I'll have to tell to get the boy instated in Niani may cost me quite a bit in favors, but I'm willing to pay it; besides, it is a kindness. The boy will be better off.

She nods, snatching the bag of coins and whispering a string of curses in her native tongue. I exhale in relief and smile. I've got the better end of the deal, in any case. I would have paid three times that to see the girl just one more time.

"Give me your hand," she says, and I slide it forward. She shakes her head and clicks her tongue. "If I had paid close enough attention, I would have known these hands had not seen a day's worth of good hard labor. I will not make that mistake again."

And then, without warning, she slices my palm with a small dagger. I bite my tongue and taste blood. She grips my hand too tight for me to pull away, but instead of hurting me further, she wraps my hand in a strip of linen.

"Go and see the midwife. Tell her that I sent you to get a dressing for your wound. She will tell you where to find your girl."

"You could have just given me directions," I say, biting back the pain.

"This way is much more convincing and, for me, much more fun."

13

FAYARD

THE MIDWIFE LIVES IN A ROUND MUD HUT WITH A thatched roof at the southernmost tip of the city. I draw more attention than I want to when I arrive. I can feel several pairs of eyes, like the brush of fingertips, as I get closer to the entrance. There's a chorus of dogs and chickens that seem eager to nip at my heels and perhaps should, as they loudly bark and cluck, "Impostor!"

Of course I'm not allowed into the compound because I am a man, but a young boy, probably the midwife's son or nephew, comes out with the midwife and sets a small bench down for her to sit upon so that she can see to my wound.

"It is a very small wound to warrant such a long journey. I cannot imagine this was outside the expertise of the royal healers," she says. Her voice is deep as a man's but with twice the music of any woman I've met. There's a shrewd twinkle in her eye, but the rest of her face remains neutral.

I have my reply ready when I see the girl step out of the compound, a deep indigo Adire cloth wrap covering her from chest to ankle, copper coins winking from the ends of her braids.

"I . . . uh . . ."

"*Motashakr awi*, Khala Monifa," the girl says to the midwife as her gaze darts my way, once, I think. I hope.

"*Afwan*, my girl. If the cough becomes worse, you come to me," the midwife replies, then adds, "Tayo will walk with you as you head home."

The girl shakes her head. "No, no. I have many stops to make. I am trying to find that honey to sweeten Iyin's tea."

"I insist," the midwife urges.

"But I cannot pay you what is owed for such a kindness," the girl whispers, trying desperately to keep her voice low enough that I cannot hear. I pretend to be preoccupied with the pain in my hand, which has almost completely disappeared.

The midwife shakes her head and grips both the girl's' hands in hers. The girl bends down. Now I cannot hear the rest of the exchange, and before I have a chance to react, she's walking down the street with the boy in tow. I follow them at a distance. I'm not even that discreet about it,

The midwife doesn't try to call me back.

When the girl stops to buy spices, I pause at the opposite stall and pretend to haggle over sandals. When she stops for incense, I fall back a bit and purchase some sweet and spicy kelewele and nearly burn the skin off the roof of my mouth in the process.

"Everyone can see you are following her," the man jokes as he peels more of the blackened fruit and drops it in the oil.

"Following who? I am on official business."

He wants to draw me into a conversation, but as I said, I am on business. She is my business. He's right, though: I am not good at blending in. When she turns a corner on a busy street, she and the boy weave so quickly in and around the stalls, I lose them. It's clear this is their market and I'm just a visitor.

The whole endeavor is silly. I know this. Father has already set up meetings with the noblemen of the local mosque to inquire about several girls who are eligible for marriage and willing to travel, or at least be sent home to await my return from the pilgrimage. There is no need for me to meet the girl until nearly all the details have been set.

This is my father's plan, so he can keep himself busy. I am acting like a spoiled child. But this is the last chance I will get to indulge myself in the beauty and poetry of life. I walk a bit farther into the crowd, unsure of exactly where I am, and am caught off guard by the slave auction clogging the path. The host has hired musicians and servers to hand out sweetmeats, as if the whole affair is a festival instead of a horror show.

I've finally caught up with her. She whips her head to the side and catches me off guard.

"Why are you following me?" she asks feverishly. "No, no. Don't look at me. I can't be seen talking to you," she adds in lilting Bambara. The boy serving as her escort places himself between us and hurls his gaze up at me with the ferocity of a true warrior. I respect it. He would defend her if need be.

"How did you know I spoke Bambara?" I ask, curious.

"Your accent. We had a slave girl in our compound who was from Bamako. It was not hard to figure it out. Again, why are you following me?"

"I never admitted to such a thing," I say.

"You don't have to admit your crimes to be guilty," she says, a bite remaining in her tone.

"I have never committed a crime in my life. I—"

My mind draws a blank. I never considered that she might confront me. My plan always had me on the side of pursuit. And then I laugh.

"What is so funny?" she asks.

"Your boldness. I had planned to follow you from the midwife, find out what you liked, where you lived, maybe even your name, and then I would surprise you with a gift of dates or that honey you've been looking for."

"H-how?" she stutters, and breaks her own rule to look over at me. She quickly directs her gaze toward the auction. "Does that usually work on the other little birds in the market?

"What is this business of birds? Is it an insult?" I ask.

"They feed on the scraps thrown to them. Birds are beautiful and useless until they are eaten by larger prey," she says with ease. As if she's used this line to describe other girls before.

"Well, that is an insult. And, no, in that case I do not consider you a little bird, nor do I spend time with useless people. I don't consider people useless. Every person has value."

"Of course they do—this auction proves it," she says, and juts her chin toward the boy being sold.

"Not like that. Isn't there somewhere else we could talk?" I ask without shame.

"No," she says quietly but firmly.

I look behind us, and the crowd has filled in in such a way that it's almost impossible to make a discreet retreat.

"I could invite your family to the sultan's feast as my guest," I say.

"A common soldier feasts with the sultan?" she laughs, and even though it is at my expense, I instantly love the sound, like wind chimes just before a storm.

"Would you believe that I am not really a soldier?" I say. "I might dress like this to make it easier to move about in a strange city."

"If you're not a soldier, I'm not a slave girl," she says sarcastically.

Now it's my turn to laugh. The ring on her finger, the expert twists in her hair smack of nobility. She cannot fool me; I know wealth when I see it. I've made myself an expert in concealing it every day. The slave boy, thin and obviously unused to a lot of attention, is nearly shivering as potential buyers take him in.

"He has a mother somewhere. A father. Were they unfortunate casualties of war, or did they sell him because they could not feed themselves? What life awaits him?" she asks, her voice much quieter than before and laced with concern.

I fight the urge to look at her. "No one knows."

"His new master knows, because he will be the one to choose it for him," she says tightly, and then draws in a long breath as if to say something else, but stops. It's several moments later that she speaks again. "The lane is opening. I will ask you once more: Why are you following me?" She sounds like an irritated mother chastising her child.

"I want . . . I want to get to know you."

"Do you wish to sell me something?"

"Does that happen often? No. I have nothing to sell," I reply.

"When will you be leaving, you and the other soldiers and noblemen? How long will we know each other?" she asks. I don't miss the disconnect in her voice. She's already written me off. This has to have happened to her before. She is too beautiful not to be approached by men who promise her the world and leave every wish completely unfulfilled. She's too smart to be tricked by witty banter and a sly smile.

I was willing to lie, cheat, and bribe my way to her door, but she has asked an honest question and I have to give her an honest answer. She knows that whatever my intentions are, they must be brief, and what kind of girl gets involved with a man, a foreign man for that matter, who she knows will be gone before the rains begin? Tayo, less inclined with each passing minute to forgive my intrusion on their walk, presses close to her side and glares at me.

"Unfortunately, our time will be short," I say with all the joy leached from my endeavor. I realize too late that this was a fool's errand. My father was right, as he most often is. She's quiet for so long I think she might not speak at all.

"Good. It's gotten late, and I have an inkling where to find my lemon-scented honey. I will go to buy some tomorrow as soon as the market opens. If you can find the merchant, you will see me again," she says matter-of-factly.

I'm too shocked to ask questions, and I don't have the opportunity. She and the boy slip through the crowd like river eels.

And now the game begins.

I turn to the nearest three people and ask them all. "*Law samaht*, where can I find lemon-scented honey?"

14

FAYARD

WOKE UP ENERGIZED. I DREAMED ABOUT THE GIRL. I dreamed of searching for her. And I have to admit Uncle Max was right—I have a habit of chasing a girl or two—but this is different, and the dream seals it. Now I'm on a mission. I thought I was doing better than expected when I went to the kitchen early to get the doctor and his fine daughter breakfast. I piled the delivery cart with fresh cantaloupe, orange juice, those powdered ginger cookies they only set out for important people, hot coffee, tea, bacon, eggs, and two toasted New York bagels that somebody had tucked away in the larder where they thought nobody would find them. I draped the cart in linen and had a hell of a time moving from one train car to the next. The walkways are slim and you have to push the cart through the dining car, which is jam-packed with two-seater tables, then between the cars, opening the door from the one you're leaving and into the one you're getting on so you can lift the cart into the new car without spilling anything or waking anyone up.

More than one early riser in the berths asked how much breakfast in bed cost, and even tried to bribe me. I told them to take it up with their conductor after I lied about special services reserved for VIP passengers only.

I barely got any sleep, and my muscles ached something terrible when I rolled out of bed, still in my uniform. Thank God I was thinking ahead and paid the telegrapher at the Philly station to get a wire to New York and ask for the Clearing House numbers before we even left the station. I know I promised Uncle Max I was done with all that, but only a fool leaves himself with just one pot of gold. I should be able to pick up the numbers right after ten in Arlington. As long as no more than two people hit, and most likely nobody will, I'm good.

The cart rattles as I wheel it into the doctor's private car. I'm afraid that I'll ruin the effect of it all if I wake them up before I get the table set, but I don't have to worry too long, 'cause I see them both, fully dressed at not even six fifteen in the morning like a couple of seabirds looking for an early catch. The girl's eyes are red and puffy, and I can see the tracks of salty tears down her dark cheeks as she gazes out the window. Bright green fields stretch out like an ocean on the other side of the glass, and the sun lights up her face like that's its only job. Her father sits opposite her, head pressed forward, hands busy writing letters. He's already got a few addressed and stacked on the end of the table. She blinks wet eyelashes up at me and my heart nearly stops.

"Don't just stand there—the food is getting cold," the doctor complains.

"Yes, sir," I reply.

I get to work and fumble with the items on the cart now that it's not an empty table, but rather one already set with people. The girl pulls the book into her lap, and I have to work hard to catch the title etched into the top margin of the pages. *Cane* by Jean Toomer.

I haven't read it, but the name sounds familiar—maybe W. E. B Du Bois mentioned him in *The Crisis*. I'll have to dig through the copies in my suitcase to find out. The only other option is to ask Uncle Max, who's read everything, but that might tip him off.

"I didn't order all of this. I won't be paying anything additional," he says gruffly.

"Yes, sir."

She doesn't look up once as I set the table; her eyes travel across the lines of the novel like nothing else is going on around her. It takes all I have not to pray that the soft lift and fall of her bosom in her yellow dress will falter just enough for her to glance up and say thank you. I'd even take a snide remark, but I may as well be a part of the furniture as far as she's concerned.

"Are you enjoying your trip so far?" I ask.

The doctor rustles his newspaper but doesn't answer.

"I see you're traveling to Atlanta. Visiting family? Vacation?"

This time the doctor folds his paper and places it in his lap. He gives me a pointed look. "No."

"No?" It sounds more like a reprimand than an answer to my question, and I stop myself from placing the tin of sugar cubes on the table.

"No, we are not visiting family. We are not on vacation to the Deep South. Are you quite done?"

"Uh, yes, sir."

"Are you new?" he adds.

"As a matter of fact, sir, this is my second day on the job," I say as brightly as possible. He slaps his hand on the table and points a stubby finger at the girl.

"I knew it! We've been pawned off to the least of them. They have no intention of making this right. As soon as we get to Atlanta, I'll wire Graham Perry. He's just received his juris doctorate from Northwestern. I intend to sue."

"Uh, well, please let me know if I can be of any assistance," I say.

A sound escapes his throat, as if he is trying to hold back a laugh. "With the suit?" he asks with a small smile.

"Uh, no, sir, with the rest of your stay."

The smile is replaced with a scowl as he clears his throat and begins buttering the top half of a bagel. The girl sits motionless, save her eyes, which continue to flit left to right as she reads.

"Would you like me to bring something more to your liking, miss?" I ask.

The girl looks up as if to reply, but before she can say a word the doctor says, "This will do us just fine. She'll have a bit of fruit."

Like a puppet, she closes her book and places the bowl of fruit in front of herself. She stabs a large cube of cantaloupe with a fork and stuffs it into her mouth, all the while staring at her father as she strains to chew it without spitting it all over the tablecloth. Despite her efforts, her cheeks bulge and juice drips down her chin. One delicious drop slips down her neck and into her cleavage. I have to turn my head to keep myself from doing something dangerous. I've never wanted to transform into fruit before.

The directive is so quiet and icy I barely register his voice. "Go to your room."

She picks up a cloth napkin and spits the fruit into her palm before dropping it onto the table.

"Gladly," she purrs, and squeezes by me to get to her door. She's a big girl, and we're nearly chest to chest as she makes her way past. I can smell the fruit on her breath as she breezes by.

It's not until I hear the click of her thin compartment door that I think to move again. At least I know this. She likes books. She doesn't like cantaloupe.

15

Columbia, South Carolina, Present Day

TAMAR

T HE AIR FRESHENER IN THE BATHROOM IS SET ON A timer, so I'm caught off guard when it practically squirts in my face. Cantaloupe. I nearly gag.

I don't know anything about auras, but I do believe in energy, and Aabidah's energy is off when I step out into the airport corridor.

"What happened?" I ask.

She shakes her head and swallows hard, getting ready to lie. "Nothing. Ready?"

"Mm-hmm," I say, and scrutinize her as she flags down an airline attendant so we can get a golf cart to take us through security. It takes longer than I thought to get someone to stop, so I use her suitcase as a chair. It's utilitarian, chrome, without any frills or distinctions other than the two combination locks on the top and bottom. You wouldn't be able to tell it from any other soulless businessman's case if it weren't for a huge Hello Kitty luggage tag. She's in a kimono riding in the cockpit of a cartoon airplane. It's super cute and completely different from my sister's style. Even now, knowing that we'll have to drag ourselves through more than one airport, she's in a silk blouse, heels, and her perfectly applied signature liquid matte lipstick—a flaming red called Bawse Lady, from the Lip Bar.

"Where'd you get this?" I ask, fingering the tag.

"This guy I used to know."

I blink hard. Guy? I've never once seen or heard of my sister going on a date. Of course, she'll tell me if someone is cute or not, but there's never been anyone around long enough to start giving gifts. I really look at my sister, from her flawless nails to her twinkling diamond stud earrings. All that perfection takes work. Taking care of me and Mama took work. And she did it all without missing a step at school and at her job. If it weren't for her, I'd be living with our Aunt Ophelia in West Columbia. Which wouldn't be the end of the world, but it isn't home. Despite a hurricane of bad fortune, I've never had to leave my home—until now. And it's not the surgery or the poking and the prodding that scares me. It's the uncertainty of living, dying, and that little gray space in between that Aabidah's staking her hopes on.

"Used to know?" I ask.

"We don't talk anymore."

"But he was special? I mean, he had to be for you to keep . . . this. Not really your style," I tease. She doesn't say anything, but there's a ghost of a smile on her lips and a faraway look in her eye for just a moment. "What was his name?"

"Kouki," she says quietly, and draws in her lip, dreaming for just a moment, and then shakes her head. "It was a long time ago."

"Must be. I don't remember you talking about any guys," I say, slightly mad at her for keeping this information from me. I tell her everything.

"There wasn't anything to talk about. Like I said, he was just a guy I knew."

"I'm sure you've known lots of guys, but you've never accepted any gifts from any of them. Not even those Beats headphones from—what was his name?"

"Barry."

"Barry the Barber. He took us to the fair and won those very expensive headphones that you, honestly, could have really used, and you gave them to the church for the Toys for Tots program. I thought you liked him. *He* thought you liked him."

"T! Not everyone is looking for some grand love affair," she says with slight exasperation.

"So you did have an affair with Kouki," I prod, not willing to give in to her irritation. I don't have much longer to be the annoying little sister.

She leans back and draws in a deep breath, exasperated, but when she straightens up, she's smiling.

"Remember that weekend I spent in Aspen at the National Med Science Convention?"

I nod.

"I had to spend an extra day because of a blizzard."

"And?"

"And I wasn't snowed in alone."

Now the smile on her face cuts from ear to ear, wrinkling her nose and flashing her gums. It's a smile I haven't seen in years, one I'd almost forgotten. I want to call this Kouki right now and demand he return so that I can see this smile on her face again and again. It's a moment, a shining one, and then just like a sun shower in the middle of a drought it fades. Her eyes fall on mine, and surprisingly there's no regret there, just an easy happiness.

"Sometimes great things end, but that doesn't mean they weren't great. I felt good with our goodbye. I still do."

Instinctively, I reach into my pocket, my fingers searching for the phone I just tossed in the trash minutes ago. My heart sinks with regret. I don't feel good about my goodbye, and I know if I don't get a chance to talk with Fay again, I won't ever be. Now would be a great time to play something angry, and I think wistfully of my beat machine and saxophone, both packed up and mailed away this morning. No. This anger I'll have to sit with for the rest of the day, possibly the rest of forever.

16

Outside of Baltimore, Maryland, 1924

TAMAR

ACH'S CELLO SUITE NO. 1 IS THE BEST FOR WHEN I'M feeling mournful, but I'm not mournful. I'm angry. For that I usually play Schumann's *Fantasiestücke*'s third movement, but I dig into my papers and pull out a cello sonata from Chevalier de Saint-Georges, the Negro man who influenced Mozart. The composition is most likely a fake. Most of his original works have been lost, but it still holds a tiny place in my heart. I settle my fingers against the strings and cradle the instrument's wide body between my thighs. Granny introduced me to the violin, though she called it a fiddle. I upgraded to the cello once I grew a bit older. The cello loves me. The cello never lets me down.

The notes are a bit shy at first. I neglected her yesterday, and now my friend is jealous. The melody is harsh and unyielding, and the push and pull create something fiery that heats my small compartment to boiling. I don't dare stop. I don't dare open the door. I let the strings cry in a way I won't ever let Daddy see me crumble. I let the strings scream, ripping the air into shreds, wild and untamed and oh so unladylike. My music is not staid or proper, pretty or respectable. It is not for the mother looking for a biddable bride for her son at church or for the son looking for a pretty housekeeper to call his wife. It is adventurous and weighty, loud and boisterous, fuming when it wants to be and despondent when it needs to be. It is unapologetically emotional in a way I am never allowed to be without consequence. My music is a girl who behaves like a boy: flat shoes and comfortable slacks, loudmouthed and ready to take on the world. My music is black in a place where black isn't an insult: it's shining, proud, and unworried. I let myself transform into wood and sound and vibration. I play for hours, settling into the rhythm and rock of the train tracks until my hollow stomach spurs me out of my room.

I walk into the hall and make my way down the empty car to where Daddy is sitting with one of the three newspapers he reads everyday. Our porter, whose name I can't remember or maybe he's never said it, is clearing the dishes from lunch. I can see from the leavings that nothing was laid out for me.

"Good afternoon, Miss Tamar," the porter says brightly. He's got straight white teeth and bright eyes framed by wispy lashes that curl up in the corners. He steps back so I can slide past him to sit. It isn't a tight squeeze. He's got that lanky frame all the porters have, tall and wiry, except he's got a little bow to his legs. If my sister was here, she'd have laid herself out on the table as an offering, and if he saw her, he would have definitely obliged. Honey-tongued with a complexion to match, she's hard to deny.

"Good afternoon, uh . . ."

"Fayard, Miss."

"Yes, I'm sorry. Please forgive me."

"No apologies needed. I'm just glad you didn't call me George," he says.

"Why would I do that?" I ask, genuinely confused.

"It happens more often than you think. I can't say why, though," he replies.

Daddy clears his throat. "It's an insult, a holdover from slavery, where the slaves were often called by the name of the slave owner. George Pullman started the railroad company, so many misguided people call his employees by his name, even long after his death."

"Do they call the conductors George too?" I ask.

Daddy barks out a laugh that lets me know what I said was definitely not funny. Fayard's smile dims a bit but doesn't fall as he shakes his head. It was a bit of sarcasm, a joke for Fayard's benefit, but I guess I'm not the comedian I thought I was.

I look over the plates to see if there's anything left I can filch for myself. There's no way I'll be able to make it to dinner without something to nibble on.

"The kitchen isn't closed yet. I can bring you a menu if you'd like to—"

Daddy intercedes. He's returned to his newspaper so he doesn't have to look at me. "That won't be necessary. We adhere to standard mealtimes in this family. Those who find themselves absent during those times don't eat."

"But, sir, it really is no—"

"That will be all, Fayard," Daddy replies, the finality in his voice clear.

I clench my jaw to keep myself from saying something that could find me back home and under his clutches again. With Mama gone and Patience married off, there's no one to keep his dislike from boiling over bad enough to burn. Daddy was always mean, even to Mama, but I can feel his grief over her death curdling into something else.

I glance up at Fayard. The disbelief on his face congeals into something less appropriate. It's kind that he cares, but this isn't any of his business.

"Daddy's right," I say. I'm about to go into an explanation with a lie about how I'm not even hungry when another porter bursts into our car.

"Doctor! We need a doctor! Big Ti—I mean Fayard, excuse me." He turns to Daddy. "Sir, are you a medical doctor?"

Daddy puffs out his chest. "Yes, I am."

"We've got a lady in the colored car. She's carrying and she just passed out."

Daddy hops to. In a blink he's got his medical bag in hand, and in a flash he's out the door. And then I'm alone and not alone. I'm alone with a boy.

17
FAYARD

I KNOW THERE'S A GOD. NOT 'CAUSE JESUS CAME INTO MY heart all of sudden or I had some revelation. No amount of soapbox preaching could ever get me in a church on a Sunday morning. No, I know there's a God because my prayers have come true. I'm alone with an angel.

I clear my throat.

"Well, Miss Tamar, as your father is not here, might I interest you in some lunch?"

"Do you often disobey the wishes of your passengers?" she asks.

"When those wishes are meant to be cruel and mean-spirited, absolutely."

"Daddy is not cruel," she says hesitantly.

I take a chance and slip into the seat her father has just vacated. I feel a new rhythm of the train beneath me as her eyes fall on me. They flash for just a second, and her pretty lips part as if she's going to give me the boot, but she doesn't.

"Things look different from my side of the table. Any man who denies his daughter a meal can be called strict, maybe even a disciplinarian. Some folks like that sort of thing. I used to go to a Catholic school where they liked to do things like that. But a man who denies his child two meals in a day when he can afford it is definitely cruel."

"You don't know anything about him," she says with just a hint of censure, maybe even embarrassment.

"No, I don't. I'd rather get to know more about you."

"You're bold," she says, and her eyebrows rise and fall in a way that suggests she just might like that in a guy.

"You have no idea."

"It's gonna get you in trouble," she says. I can't tell if she really cares or if her comment is just a reflex. She's wearing a small, sad smile and all I know is that I want to make that smile bigger and brighter.

I almost don't make it out of the seat in time when the door slides back open and Uncle Max glides in.

"Good, you're still here. Good afternoon, miss," Uncle Max says, and tips forward a bit in greeting. When he rises, his gaze pins me to the spot like a specimen he'd like to dissect.

Tamar dips her head to greet him. "Good afternoon."

"Did you find the lunch satisfactory?" he inquires politely.

"I was just about to return to the kitchen for a roast beef sandwich," I jump in. "Miss Tamar decided to take a later lunch this afternoon."

Uncle Max frowns and pulls out his pocket watch to check the time, even though he knows exactly what time it is. I bet his heart beats in rhythm to the thing. Our eyes lock for a second before the air in his chest deflates. I know then that he's going to let the matter drop, and the relief feels like a cool breeze.

"You'd better get a move on, then," he says, and starts to place the remaining dishes on the service cart. "Lunch service ends in fifteen minutes. I'll help you with the cart."

• • •

With the cart stowed away and Charles working on the sandwich, Uncle Max takes the opportunity to lay into me, but not because I stole Sharp's gig.

"So, I hear you're runnin' game on my train," he says, voice low, his eyes narrow and calculating.

I try my damnedest to look shocked.

"Uncle Max, you know me. I wouldn't—"

"You would. You most definitely would, and I'm telling you to shut it down and shut it down now!" he growls. His finger is digging into my breastbone, and it's taking everything for me not to punch a hole in his chest.

"They pulled Coleman off at the last stop. Said he was lifting from the kitchens. Now, we haven't even restocked. How'd they know he was lifting?" he asks.

It sounds like a question I'm not supposed to answer, but he waits, so I shake my head.

"There's a spy on this train," he whispers.

It goes quiet, and I realize the normal trash talk that goes on in the kitchen has disappeared.

"I need everything on this run to be perfect! And I mean spit-shined! I know I've made my promises, but if you cost me my job, boy . . . ," he growls.

His lip starts to quiver, and there's a tick in his jaw as he looks at me up and down as if I'm for sale. He balls his hand into a fist and puts some distance between us before taking a deep breath. He then straightens his jacket and begins to head out of the kitchen, fully composed, as if this conversation didn't even happen.

"And I best not hear a word of fault from that doctor about you pushin' up on his daughter!" he adds, his voice trailing off under the rumble of the train.

Old Uncle Max. I didn't think he had a good threat in him, but I've gotta say, I'm almost scared.

Almost.

"You best listen to your uncle," Tall Jack says as he slices two oranges into quarters for the tray.

"You best mind your business. I'm fine," I huff.

"Yeah, you say that," he adds. "You seen Spark yet?"

I shake my head.

"Man's been looking for you. Say you owe him for his hit on the bolita."

I cock my head to the side and bark out a laugh. The bolita is the last two digits of the lottery number. It doesn't get you the full pot, but it does earn you a little something. "Spark didn't put in on the bolita," I reply.

"So you say. He says different."

"There were at least ten other guys puttin' in when he did. He didn't hit. Nobody did," I add. I don't like liars, especially ones who waste my time.

"Again, so you say. Maybe they remember, maybe they don't," he says lightly.

I've had enough. "Just gimme my tray."

I wipe a finger smudge from the side and add an extra cloth napkin so that it drapes under the carafe of iced tea.

Tall Jack whistles. "She must be pretty," he says.

"She must be one of the Whitman sisters with the polish he puttin' on that tray," Benny T pipes in.

The guys bust out laughing as I slide out the door. If they'd seen her, they wouldn't be laughing.

I turn my back on them. The more time I stay in the kitchen, the less time I have to spend with Tamar.

18
FAYARD

TAMAR PUSHES THE SAUCER OF LEMON COOKIES I BROUGHT FOR her toward me. It's cut to resemble an upturned flower—a rose, maybe. It's so thin it rattles a little on the tray but falls silent after a moment. My pleased reflection beams back at me from the polished table. Everything gleams here. From the wine-colored velvet bench seats to the chandeliers that hang in the private cars. Even the towels are embroidered with silk thread. I hadn't spotted that before.

"What?" she asks.

"I was just noticing how this suits you. The train, I mean." I bite back the compliment, not wanting to offend her.

"You're new. How do you like being a porter?" she asks, changing the topic of conversation.

"I'm not sure yet. It's very different from my last job. But I hear the work is steady, and it beats the steel mill. Even if I decide to stick with it, it won't be permanent," I say.

"Why not? What did you do before?" she prods, genuinely interested.

"I ran numbers," I admit. There's no sense in lying to her about who I am. Besides, it's clean work, and the only people who don't think so are the folks who want you to wash their drawers for a nickel and be proud about it.

She chokes a bit on her sandwich at my admission and I pour her a bit more tea from the carafe.

"Oh my. Went down the wrong pipe," she says quickly. Her voice is laced with a laugh but still harsh and ragged. She's got a smile on her face. "Do you think that's something you should be telling people?"

"I'm not telling people. I'm telling you. You've got an honest face," I say. She doesn't seem like the type of girl who judges people, but I could be wrong.

She sits up a bit and straightens her back like the class pet on the first day of school. "Actually, I lie quite convincingly."

"Really?" I say, fighting the urge to smile.

"Yes. For example, I was only being polite when I asked you to sit for lunch. I didn't think you would accept the invitation, given our obvious difference in position," she says in a level tone, her face inscrutable. There is a slight smile, but it's the same smile the milkman gives you when he's making his rounds: impersonal.

I fidget a bit trying to find the hint of a joke on her face, but I can't find one. In a last-ditch effort, I start to laugh, waiting for her to join me, but she doesn't. Her smile remains polite and unreadable. My face heats up and my skin starts to feel too tight, like the hair on my arms can transmit the electricity in the air. How could I be this stupid?

"My apologies, Miss Williams. I've been, uh . . . My apologies," I say as I move to slide out of my place at the table. I keep my eyes down, trying to look anywhere but at her face. When she places her petal-soft hand on mine, I'm forced to look up. Tears are in her eyes, and a silent laugh is choking its way out of her throat.

"I got you so good."

I nearly fall backward into the seat with relief.

"Damn, you're good. Oh, I mean . . . darn. Forgive my language," I add with a slight sigh. I need to try harder not to slip up when I speak.

"No, no, curse all you want. I prefer it. People choose their words too carefully around me and I hate it."

"You really are a good liar," I say in disbelief.

"I know. I've had lots of practice. Are you the brutally honest type?" she asks.

"My job required it. On the street, you're nothing without your word. People play their last dime for a chance at a win. You can't play games with people's dreams. They got to know that if they tell you a number, you gonna be straight with them and bring them their payout. Any runner can lie and say they don't remember what you told them, keep the money themselves. But then you're taking food out of babies' mouths, rent from some poor mother whose old man left her. People are real funny about who they trust. They should be. There are a lot of sharks out there."

"So you'd rather be a dream maker than a shark?"

"I would. As long as the money is good," I reply.

"Money isn't everything," she says.

"Sounds like something somebody who's always had it would say," I add, trying to keep the judgment out of my voice.

She frowns and looks out the window at the cornfields whipping by. "I don't have money. My father has money," she says, like her father is a stranger she's spouting facts about.

"Don't daddies spend the bulk of their money on their daughters?

I've only met a few who didn't, and they were garbage in a hundred ways than that."

"Let's not talk about fathers," she says quietly.

Her mouth is set in a line, and I'm missing the smile on her face from a few minutes ago. "Sure. Tell me where you're headed. Got a fella in Atlanta?"

"Do you know what Morehouse is?" she asks.

"Tell me," I say, more for the need to hear her voice and watch her lips move than for the information.

"It is *the* premier men's college for Negro scholars. Founded in 1867, it is responsible for more Negro doctors, lawyers, and theologians than any other institution."

"La-di-da," I reply in an airy tone.

Her words stir something deep inside, and a memory floats to my consciousness. Mama's face appears before my eyes. She's weak, but she could still walk then. I'd just won the recitation contest for my class. I was thirteen and no one clapped harder than she did. Mr. Loudermilk had told her I was his brightest student. He suggested an alternate course of study to prepare me for college. He even offered to find me a sponsor because "a mind like his should not be wasted." A week later Mama collapsed on the way home from the market. Two weeks after that I went to work for Fats.

Tamar's voice slices through my memory as she peels the rind from an orange slice and pops the flesh into her mouth. "You don't seem impressed."

"I'm not. Is this where you're husband fishing? The smoking lobby of some sissy college where they recite Plutarch and Lord

Byron after tea," I say, trying hard to cover a kernel of jealousy with heaps of disdain.

She gives me a funny look. Surprise? Irritation?

"Plutarch, huh? And you said you didn't know what Morehouse was."

"Didn't say that. I just told you to tell me more. I like to hear you talk."

She draws a deep breath in and holds it, eyes pinning me to the spot, but then she blows it out slow and wiggles in her seat a bit, her private thoughts a mystery to me.

"Who said that I was going there to find a husband? I may not marry at all. No, I'm going to Atlanta to attend an all-girls' school, Spelman College."

"I've never heard of such a thing. Why would a woman need college?" I ask, amazed.

"To be a teacher. To be a doctor. To be whatever she chooses besides a wife and mother." Her nose wrinkles a bit as she stabs a strawberry with her fork.

I hold up both my hands in surrender. "I don't mean to offend. It's just most girls I know can't wait to get married. If I had my choice, I'd love to be a girl. I wouldn't have to worry about nothing but staying pretty and finding some sick dope to take care of me."

"You'd rather be told where to live, where to go, and what to do your entire life?" she asks, incredulously. "You would trade your freedom for a life of servitude and imprisonment, where your father and then your husband will be in charge of everything—from how much money you can spend on groceries for the week to what color dress you're allowed to wear to church on Sunday?" She tilts her head, waiting for me to respond.

"All a decent woman needs to worry about is how to make good cornbread and where to find decent cigars," I reply. "You'd rather wonder where your next meal was coming from? You'd rather break your back on the docks for bread or troll the streets doin' everything the devil likes doin' just so the lights stay on at home?" I add. "No, you want to get your head cracked open in a card game some night 'cause a fella don't like how you looked at him. A wife isn't a prisoner; she's a refuge. A mother ain't a slave; she's a saint. Men make it possible for girls like you to keep they souls clean," I say, memories of my past rising to the surface.

"Oh, sing me the song of the virtuous woman!" she cries with passion. "I'm not most girls. I won't have my life defined by a man. I'd rather be free," she says defiantly, and then finishes her sandwich in three quick bites. Gotta love a girl with a healthy appetite.

"To be a *doctor*?"

"Uh, no," she says. "There are very few Negro women doctors. Even Daddy has trouble retaining work . . . at times. There aren't that many colored hospitals, and if it weren't for Grandmother Dawson, he might never have gotten placed at Mercy. I don't want that kind of uncertainty. I could be anything."

At that I have to chuckle. "Anything? Girl, nobody gets to choose anything. Life doesn't work that way. I think your pretty surroundings and that full belly got you a little blind to the real world. In the real world, a colored boy has three choices. One: scrape for white folks for *big* money, like the post office or what I'm doin' now. I got a boss who might as well be my master, and if I don't smile, I don't have a job. Two: scrape for white folks for *little* money—that's all the folks in the mills or on the docks breaking they back every day. And there's three: do for yourself with a little hustle and probably get killed in the doing."

"That's just not true," she says, and starts in on the work of that Randolph guy trying to start a union with the porters, then something else I can't catch.

"Do you have to stare at me so?" she asks, a bit flustered. Tamar blinks hard and turns her head to the window again.

"I'm sorry. I didn't know I was staring. I'm just listening. Really." She turns back to face me.

I'm lying. I'm half listening. I'm so taken by the way this tiny hidden dimple appears and disappears when she smiles real wide, how her lashes curl back on themselves, fluttering like bird wings when she's excited. Even when she's irritated, she's beautiful, maybe more so. She's got some funny ideas about men and women, but I can't begrudge her a dream. Fats says all the women have been dreaming a bit high for themselves since the war.

"You're not listening at all," she says, calling my bluff.

"I am," I say, forcing myself to pay attention to her words and not her mouth.

"Then what did I just say?"

"Uh-uh . . . ," I stammer.

"Exactly, you're just like . . ." She's scrambling to find the right word.

"Your last boyfriend," I finish for her.

Her head snaps back in surprise. I'm finding I like to surprise her.

"I-I've never had a boyfriend, not that it's any of your business," she replies tersely.

"Daddy keeps tight control, then?" I ask.

"Daddy doesn't run my life. I already told you that. Have you considered that there is no one I've found to be worth my time?"

"I have. I just thought it would be hard to turn down proposals from every man you meet. A girl as beautiful as you? I'm surprised you make it home every day," I say, trying to sound sincere instead of unsavory.

She laughs. "I enjoy compliments just like anybody else, but you're being a bit ridiculous."

"No, I'm not. Skin smooth as velvet and dark as twilight. Smile as bright as fresh snow. Hair—I haven't gotten a chance to touch, but I assume it's soft, too. Not to mention . . ." I let my fingers follow the outline of her body from shoulder to hip to thigh.

"Now you're making fun of me?" she says, hurt.

"What? I'm not!" I backpedal, trying to figure out what I said wrong.

She slides her plate across the table and stands in a rush to get out of her seat. "Mr. Fayard, I think I am quite full," she says formally, and snatches a book she'd set to the side of her that I hadn't noticed: *There Is Confusion* by Jessie Redmon Fauset.

"I—I apologize, Tam—" She fixes me with an icy glare, her fingers nearly vibrating with rage. "Miss Tamar. I am sorry if I offended you."

"Thank you for lunch. I'm retiring for the day. Please allow my father to make my dinner request."

And with that she's gone.

Stupid. I pushed too hard, and now I don't know what I said.

I jump up and rush the few steps it takes to knock softly on her door.

"Miss Tamar?"

Nothing.

"Miss Tamar?"

"Go away. I am reading and wish not to be disturbed. Isn't it your *job* to follow orders?" she snaps.

The way she says "job" stings in a place I usually don't allow people to reach. Light spills from under the frame, and I can see she's standing on the other side, my mirror image.

"Please see that this is dropped in the post," she says, so quietly I'm not sure I hear her correctly, until she slides an envelope under the door frame. Her feet disappear.

I've been dismissed. Discounted. I want to knock again, plead my case, but I can't.

In the space of a breath, there is her father, returned from his work, dishes that must be removed, and a smile that I can't let fade.

19
TAMAR

DADDY SLICES INTO HIS STEAK; BLOOD AND BUTTERY FAT pool on the plate. It looks delicious. I play with my spoon, moving it around the broth he's ordered for me, as if I'm an octogenarian who can't chew her food any longer. He's trying to pick a fight. I'm ornery when I'm hungry and he knows it.

A picture of Patience flashes in my mind, cutting Daddy's steak before dinner, and a pang of regret hits me in my chest. He's smiling up at her, no doubt seeing Mama's face reflected back at him: heart-shaped, the color of coffee that's more cream than anything else, albeit a bit pimply. I should have paid more attention to how she played him. I should have checked her the times she called me tar baby when she was mad, and then forgiven her right after instead of letting that wall grow thick as blackberry vines between us. There were things she could have taught me, things I needed to learn about how to be a girl in this world full of men who want to control you.

There was one time—Mama was sick by then, getting sicker by the day—that Daddy had gotten so bad he'd started sniping at Patience, too.

"Do you like boys?" she asked me later that day.

We were doing the laundry, placing the sheets on the line the way Granny showed us so that we didn't waste any space: pin left, pin right, smooth and pull.

"Course I like boys. I guess. Just don't have much time for 'em," I said, keeping my real feelings close.

"I mean, you never had a sweetheart, and you're almost seventeen now."

"So? I've been busy. Why do you care anyway?" I asked, irritation lacing my words.

"I *don't* care. Just curious is all. Mama's gettin' sicker and Peter's gonna ask me to marry him. I won't be here anymore, and you'll be in the house all alone with Daddy," she said, like it was a to-do list instead of our future.

Until that moment I'd thought she might adore Daddy as much as he adored her, but she looked at me straight on, letting the truth fill the gaps in our voices.

"If you not thinking about marriage, it might be good for you to talk to Mama about college."

"What's Mama gonna do?"

"Mama can make things happen in her own way. It may not be your way, but it works just the same."

The conversation ended and we never talked about it again. A week later Peter proposed and Mama made Daddy promise to pay my way through Spelman. I didn't give Patience enough credit then. I do now.

"Nutrition! Medical intervention would hardly be necessary if these people would follow simple commonsense guidelines to eating and basic care. It all comes down to the correct amount of vitamins and minerals that are essential to a proper diet. Lean meats and good milk. Fresh vegetables, not all of that fatback and collard greens soaked in pig grease," Daddy rambles.

He's excited, vacillating between moods, irritated one moment, energized the next. He's been useful today. Anyone would think we were having the loveliest of dinners, but he's not really talking to me—he's talking to my sister's substitute.

"Daddy?" I lace my voice with honey like Patience would. "What was it like in the main car?"

His eyes flick up from his steak and then back to his plate.

He grunts as if he's just realized I'm his sole dinner companion. "Claustrophobic. Odious. Filled to every corner with people talking too loudly or playing cards or checkers. Hardly anyone could be found in serious study of a book of some kind."

"Was there any music?" I ask, trying my luck.

His jaw works harder to chew the bit of meat in his mouth, as if my question has somehow made the steak harder, less yielding to his machinations. He swallows and takes a sip of water. His eyes find me again, lingering longer than before, but still less than a few seconds. I have to wonder if he's afraid of seeing himself reflected back at him or his mother.

"Someone had a harmonica. Another a fiddle," he adds.

"Did they crack open a window to let the devil out?" I say, and laugh.

It's one of Granny Lou Ann's old sayings. Even in the dead of winter she'd leave the door open in her place. She said too much of a good time could seep into your bones and make you turn away from work if you didn't let a little out. The corner of his mouth twitches upward, but it doesn't last. In fact, it backfires.

"Why are you suddenly so talkative?" he asks.

"I was just interested in your day. I've been cooped up in this car with no one to talk to," I reply. Which is partly true.

"Cooped up. Hmm." He considers the phrase but doesn't say anything else.

"I was thinking that there might be people that I could talk to in the main car. There might be some other girls traveling as I am."

"No." He bites off the word.

"But—"

"I said no. You'll stay right here in this car until we arrive in Charlotte."

"Charlotte? But we're going to Atlanta," I say, confused. What would he want to do in Charlotte?

"I've had a change of heart. I've received a wire from an old classmate to look out for a gentleman on our trip, a graduate from Allen University who is pursuing the medical field after a study of theology. We had a chance to meet in the main car. He has invited us to stay as guests at his home for a day or two. He was a great help to me as I tended to the woman."

"But classes start in a week. Why would we take time out of our traveling schedule to have dinner with strangers?"

"No brother Alpha is a stranger. Besides, he says that he has a sister that you might get on with, not to mention his mother. She's ailing and is in need of care; I'm sure you could help in that regard," he replies.

My stomach is in knots. I can't believe what I'm hearing. I can't, but I can. I just never thought he'd stoop this low. I am so foolish. So completely naive. Any man who would disown his own mother would do anything to make his life easier.

"You're marrying me off," I say in disbelief.

"Now, now. Don't get yourself into a tizzy. No one said anything about marriage. This is just a meeting. If you find that you and this boy suit, that would be a happy coincidence," he says, like we're discussing the weather and not the fact that he's sealed my fate without even consulting me.

"Will I have any say in the matter? Would I be able to pursue my schooling? My music?" I ask, the fury and pain building inside me.

"No matter what you do, you can always pursue your music. There is a great need in the community for accomplished classical music instructors," he says.

My head swims, and every cell in my body is vibrating. I can feel the strands of hair on my head standing at attention. My heart burns with the effort of beating double time. This was a trap. He had no intention of keeping his promise to Mama.

"No." It comes out small at first, but the force of it grows within me and I have to say it again. "No!" I roar. I slam my fist on the table, rattling the plates and dishes so much that the carafe of water tips and spills onto the floor.

"I will not marry a man I've never seen. I will . . . I won't go! I'll stay on myself and continue to Atlanta on my own," I say, trying to control the tremble in my voice.

"How dare you speak to me in that manner," he growls. "You will do as I say and when I say it." His voice is low, the anger snipping at the ends of his consonants.

"I have my own mind. I will make my own decisions. I'm no

longer a child. You don't speak for me!" My voice is at shrieking level now. I've lost all control of it.

He coughs, his version of a laugh, and rises to meet me nose to nose. "I speak for you and every woman in this family," he says, his measured voice full of venom. "You have no status. You have no money. Your name is not even your own; it is mine. You should be grateful that any decent man would want you as his prize." He puffs out a breath. "Do you think your music will earn you a husband?" he asks, incredulously.

I don't feel myself doing it; it just happens. My hands, my arms, have minds of their own. In their rage, they pick up the glass on the table and douse Daddy in a shower of iced tea.

He's slapped me before, for back talk and sass, but never this hard. My teeth rattle and I can taste blood in my mouth, metallic and sharp. His fingers dig into my scalp as he grabs my hair.

My mouth is open in a small scream when the sliding car door opens. Every ugly thing about us, about me, is exposed.

My eyes lock on Fayard's for just a moment, a moment of relief that is crushed when Mr. Max quickly slides the door closed as if they've seen nothing at all.

20

Columbia, South Carolina, Present Day

FAYARD

WAKE WITH A JOLT AND GET THAT SINKING FEELING, LIKE
I've just stepped off a platform that was too high without realizing
it. I was dreaming again. It's happening more often now, but this
is the first time it's happened during the day. I yawn loudly and
check my watch to make sure I haven't lost too much time. A kid
in a stroller in the food court gives me the evil eye. I slide out of
the seat and stretch hard. It feels like I've been asleep for years, even
though it's been only a few minutes.

Plan A involved romance, the big show with the band and a
ring and an audience. But after running into Aabidah, I had to be
honest with myself. Does Tamar want to be the center of attention
right now? Did I ask? No. It's what I want. I want the whole world
to know how I feel, but really the only person who needs to know
is Tamar, so on to plan B: saying goodbye.

I buy the cheapest ticket out of the same terminal as T's flight so
so I can get through security and hope against hope that I beat her to
the gate to say goodbye. I'm relieved to find that there are a few seats
left open for waiting passengers, but she hasn't made it yet. I settle in
to wait. Keeping a watchful eye on everyone in the walkway.

"Poop head!"

I twist around in my seat and see the same kid from the food court pointing his pacifier at me. On closer inspection he looks too old to be in a stroller, but who am I to judge?

"Poopy poop head!" he says again, and the kid's dad gently puts the boy's pacifier back in his mouth.

"It's rude to point," he says to his son; then he turns toward me and smiles. "Sorry, he's a bit . . . precocious. His grandma says he's been here before. He'll just pick someone out of the crowd and start jabbering away at them."

"Oh, uh. It's cool," I say, and shake the guy's hand.

"Flying out with family?" he asks.

"No, uh my . . . um . . . I guess you could call her my girlfriend, but she, uh . . . broke up with me. It wasn't anything I did. It was all a misunderstanding." I blow out a long breath of air. "It's . . . uh, complicated."

"Always is, kid. Fruit snacks?"

The guy hands me a small bag of fruit snacks and I rip into it, because why not? No need to tell him I'm not actually flying any-where, I just need to talk to my girl. That kind of confession is text-book suspect. Instead, I enjoy my complimentary bag of gummies and keep my mouth shut. The entire time, the kid is staring at me like I ran over his dog. The dad pulls out the pacifier so the kid can eat, and the boy takes the opportunity to throw another "poopy head" in my direction. I like to think I'm a pretty level-headed per-son, but there's something in this kid's eyes I don't like.

"Hey, Max, that's not nice!" the dad scolds, and something like recognition scratches at the back of my mind.

"What's his name?"

"Max, short for Maximillian. That was a real battle with his mom, but . . . ," the dad begins, but I just stare at the kid, meeting his evil eye with a level stare as I try to remember something that keeps escaping me. I could spend hours letting my mind search for the connection, but a plane full of military personnel unloads in the terminal opposite ours and a bunch of people begin to clap, breaking my concentration.

Through the crowd, I spot Tamar, her back turned to me as she rides on one of those airline golf carts for the injured and elderly. Aabidah's in the passenger seat, and when our eyes meet, her mouth is twisted in that serious scowl she reserves just for me. The cart stops just ahead of the service desk and I go to meet them.

"Daaaaamn," I say, letting the word draw out with a smile.

"I look that bad, huh?" T asks, a tissue in one hand and her oxygen tank in the other.

"No, no. You look beautiful. I . . . uh . . . I came to . . ."

She looks at me, those eyes that seem to see straight through me, what I was and will be, and she waits. She's thinner than the last time I saw her, like she's lost not just weight, but hope.

I can see now: the fear I had, that the disease had come back and that she didn't want to tell me, is true. She kept it hidden to save me. Maybe.

"I came to say goodbye."

She rests a frail arm on her hip and throws her head to the side, dramatic, mocking me. "And how'd you get past security?"

Aabidah pretends this is the first time she's seeing me and gives me a stiff hug.

"Fay is always full of surprises," she says, doing a really good job of feigning she's happy I'm there.

I just smile and take a chance at a kiss on Tamar's cheek. She shivers a bit, and I know it isn't from the cold.

"Babe, you know I have my ways," I tease. "The laws of space, time, and the great state of South Carolina don't apply to me."

"Why's that baby staring at you?" T asks, changing the conversation.

"Man, I don't even know," I whisper, wanting to get as far away from the kid as I can.

I take their carry-on bags from Aabidah so she doesn't have to lift them and set them next to one of the empty rows of seats in the terminal.

"You pissing off babies now, Fay?" Aabidah jokes.

"If you ain't got haters, you not really living, right?"

She rolls her eyes at me and reaches out a hand to help T sit down, but Tamar slaps it away. I catch Aabidah's eye and nod. T can be hardheaded when she wants to be. She doesn't like to look like she needs help, even if she's dragging an oxygen tank behind her.

"I'm gonna check on our seats and make sure we've got priority," Aabidah says, and heads to the ticket desk.

"Hey, you," I say softly, and watch as T tries to settle herself. I don't know if she's uncomfortable or trying to make sure she doesn't look uncomfortable, but I steel my expression anyway. I won't let a minute of this be spent on mixed emotions or imperfect impressions.

"Hey, back at you. So, you just had to see me, huh?"

"Don't do that. I came to your house. I know you were home," I say, wanting her to admit that she shut me out but I never gave up.

"Some people would call that stalking, Fay. I said what I had to say when I texted you."

"A text? Really? If you're gonna break up with me, you should at least say it to my face. How do I know your phone didn't get hacked?"

She rolls her eyes. "That's an excuse for celebrities when they get caught with endangered-animal porn or old MAGA paraphenalia."

"So, you were just avoiding me, then?"

She bites her bottom lip and picks at the end of her Carolina sweatshirt. Her nails are painted black with rhinestones on the pinky. They look so small.

"I can't lie to you, Fay, but I want to."

"What's that supposed to mean?"

"It means, why couldn't you make this easy and just find some other girl to . . ."

"To love?"

She pokes me in my ribs, and I fake like it really hurts, rubbing away the phantom pains as she picks something out of my hair.

"Yeah, that."

"I'll make a deal with you, then. I won't tell you that I love you and you can keep silent about how much you love me back. Deal?"

"I don't know what you're talking about," she says quietly, trying to look anywhere but at me.

"Perfect," I say, wishing more than anything that we didn't have to put on this whole front. "Are you going to tell me where you're running to?"

"How about you tell me what happened at the dance after I left? I never asked, but I want to know. And don't leave out the details. I want to smell it, it's so real."

"The Valentine's dance? Okay. Uh, it smells like cherry lip balm, latex balloons, and cheap vodka mixed with fruit punch. Oh, and vomit, lots of vomit."

"Gross. Also, you never told me if you got into Morehouse."

"I only applied because you got into Spelman, but that's all done, isn't it?"

"Okay, fine. But I know Morehouse wasn't your number-one choice. Spill. What about the others. How many?"

"It's irrele—"

"Spill! It'll make me feel better."

"Fine. Eight. Morehouse, Fisk, NYU, University of Florida, Carolina, Clemson, Howard."

"That's seven."

"It doesn't matter. I think I'm going to focus on the YouTube channel. Stay close to Ma." T cuts her eyes at me like I've just sneezed out of my elbow. She knows Ma isn't really a consideration. She works three jobs. I barely see her, and outside of check-in texts, she's been more and more of a ghost since Pop-Pop died a year ago. I'm the only family she has left, but most days it feels like she left me already.

"Seven. What's eight?"

I mumble, hoping she drops the issue.

"What's that?"

"Columbia."

"I knew you'd go Ivy League! And with your mom's income, you go for free?"

"If I go."

"There is no *if*. That's the beginning of what you've always wanted. You'll be in Harlem, so, like, if you get culture shock, you can always go kick it with the people." Her eyes are full of excitement.

"I'd rather kick it with you."

"Mm-hmm. Now who's avoiding?" she says.

Aabidah comes back from the ticket booth with an even deeper scowl.

"I'm going to Starbucks before they start to board. Want anything?" she asks. "Fay?"

T and I both shake our heads.

"She got into that grad program she applied for in Seattle," T tells me as soon as Aabidah's out of earshot. "She doesn't know I know. You're both putting your lives on hold. Life's not something you can just stop and start back up when you want to. You don't always get all the chances you want when you want them."

"Thanks for the sage advice, Obi Wan. Did you just age a thousand years without telling me?"

"No, I'm dying. It makes me wise."

I flinch. It's the first time she's said the words out loud. My first instinct is to make a joke, because I can't allow myself to believe it's true. But it is. As real as the tube snaking along her cheeks to the oxygen tank, helping her to breathe, like the paper-thin skin of her fingers. I rub my thumb over her wrist and feel her pulse. I count the seconds in time to her beating heart. If this is reality, I don't want to live it. I want the dream life. The delusion that everything is the way it's supposed to be. Where we are both whole and happy and so full of possibility that we can fly. We sit there, our hands entwined, quiet for a moment.

Weak light spills onto the walkway from the windows while a busker sets up his station at the restaurant right next to us. I scan the other seats for someplace she and I can sit where we won't have to talk over the music, but as soon as his fingers glide across his guitar, I stop. His first song is an acoustic version of "He Loves Me (Lyzel in E Flat)" by Jill Scott. Tamar's eyes close and her hand grips mine tighter. I wrap my arm around her for what may be the last time and close my eyes, too, wanting to sink into this peace, this feeling of being right and whole. There's a pop in the speakers, some tinny break that doesn't sit well in my ears. I hold T tighter, trying to parse the good from the bad, and failing.

21

Just Outside Richmond, Virginia, 1924

FAYARD

THE SLIDING DOOR TO THE CAR SNAPS CLOSED WITH A pop. I bite my tongue and taste blood behind gritted teeth. Uncle Max's arms are locked around me tighter than a jailhouse straitjacket.

"Ain't none of our business!" Uncle Max hisses into my ear.

"Like hell!" I spit, and try harder to get loose, but he's older and he's got that strength and strategy. I'm not the first man he's had to restrain.

"He's beating on her. We can't let that stand," I roar back.

"That's family business. We'll check on her in a bit. Let them calm down."

"She could be dead by then. Beat to hell by then," I say, losing steam at the thought.

"He won't. He's got too much to lose. Man like that loves his reputation. He'll do right," Uncle Max says solemnly.

"You can't be sure, Uncle Max." His thumb slips, and I'm able to pull my hand free, then my arm.

"She ain't yours!" he shouts over the din of the train.

My chest is heaving from the tussle, but I still got fight in me. My blood rushes past my ears and my teeth set on edge like a dog ready to bite.

"She ain't yours and she never will be. You always want what you can't have. Been like that since you could crawl." He draws in a deep breath, gathering himself. "It's not your business," he says with finality.

I know that. I never wanted to keep any girl. They were just girls. Fun to talk to, fun to touch and sneak around with. I ain't never wanted to call any girl my own, never wanted to fight for any of them, except this one. I want to kill her father. I could pull his head from his body with my bare hands, and I can't say why. I'm not even sure if she likes me, given how she acted earlier. But she looked at me. She looked at me, not with hope in her eyes, but relief, like I'd already saved her, like she knew I was gonna be there.

"Think, boy!" He's pleading with me.

I turn my back on him. Uncle Max can pick his own battles. I've already picked mine. I pull open the door with a clash and rush in, expecting a fight, but the car is empty. I walk down the hall slowly, straining to hear any sound. Nothing. I press my ear against Tamar's closed door. I don't hear anything, but something tells me to check the room I slept in at the end of the car. That's where I catch the faintest sniffle. I'm about to knock when I let my hand fall.

I clean up the mess of overturned tea glasses and ruined stationery—newspapers, too. I get a bowl of ice and a clean cloth and take a seat outside. Maybe Uncle Max is right. This ain't my business. But I wait. I wait so long I fall asleep.

"Don't you have somewhere else to be?" she says quietly, softly waking me from a fitful sleep.

"You're in the room I sleep in," I joke.

She snorts. I can't tell if it's a laugh or a puff of irritation.

Light spills out into the hallway from the room. Her back is pressed against the wall and she's sitting on the floor just across from me on the other side of the door. She's holding a cube of ice wrapped in cloth up to her eye. Her voice is ragged and raw like she's been crying, but there's no anger. She sounds like a sad little girl.

"Do you want me to leave?" I ask. "I just wanted to make sure you were okay."

"No," she says softly.

The silence rocks between us, and the rhythm of the track starts to feel like music: somber, but welcoming.

"He do that a lot?" I ask. I don't know where her daddy is, if he walked over me in my sleep or if he's listening at the door. I don't much care for my sake, but if he shows his face to get to her, I may not be responsible for what I do.

She shakes her head.

"No, not often. But . . ."

She stops and turns her head like she's trying to catch a memory.

"For as long as I can remember, on Sundays when I was a little girl, I'd get up, brush my teeth, thank God for the morning, and make my way to Sunday school at Mother Bethel AME. There's a candy shop on Sixth Street. They make lollipops, taffy, and caramel chews, and sometimes on special days they'd have these sweet buns. They'd bake them right in the store, and the entire street would smell like sugar and fresh bread and . . . oh! There wasn't anything in this world that I wanted more than one of those sweet buns, but Mama wouldn't hear of it. One day one of the church mothers gave me a dime because I'd played so well at the church picnic the Saturday before. I . . . I had to be eight, no, no I was nine, and it was the first time I had my own money. We were walking back from church, and Mama stopped to talk to someone. I don't know where my sister was, but it was just me and her. I knew this was my chance, you know?"

I nod. I'm right there with her. I know that candy store. It was one of Fats's operations, a candy shop in front and, for the right price, a speakeasy and numbers spot in back. Everybody knew what went on there. I can see why her mama wouldn't set foot inside.

"I broke away from Mama and I ran as fast as my legs would take me. I got pretty far, too. But she caught me as soon as my hand met the door handle. She said, 'Tamar, it doesn't matter how bad you want it. Some things you are never gonna get.' What kinda thing is that to tell your baby girl? I could see the buns; I could smell them; I even had the money. All that separated me from my heart's desire was just a tiny pane of glass, and I couldn't get there." She sighs. "All my life, I've felt like the future I want is on the other side of that glass, and no matter how bad I want it, I'll never get it."

She looks at me, eyes shining, and my palms itch to touch her. "You're going to tell me to have faith, aren't you?" Her gaze shifts to the floor.

"No. I don't have much faith to speak of, so I'd be the last person to say that. After my mam died, I felt like I didn't have control of anything. I just moved day to day, drinkin', shootin' dice, kissin' girls."

She laughs. "Sounds fun."

"Not as much as you think. My mama used to say that whenever you make a choice, there's another you somewhere making the opposite decision."

"What's that supposed to mean?" she asks.

"I guess it means that someplace, somewhere, you are getting what you want, or maybe this life is the best scenario. I'm not really sure."

She hums deep in her throat and then bites her lip. A few tears slide down her cheek, and I can't help but inch closer. I hand her another cloth from my apron and fit myself into the doorframe, my good knee up and my bad one lying straight just outside the door. I wince a little at the effort. Sleeping crouched on the floor didn't do my knee any favors.

"What happened to you?" Her eyes travel to my leg and I shrug.

"You ain't the prizewinner of terrible fathers. It's a sad story. I don't want to make you any sadder than you already are," I say.

"Tell me, please. I need to not think about myself for a second." She places a warm hand on mine and I forget how to say no.

"I told you I ran numbers, but there's only one person still alive who knows why. King Fats is the biggest banker in Philadelphia. Sure, there are other big-time numbers suppliers in the city, but he's the biggest, and from the time I was six years old he was like a father to me. He took me to Hilldale Club ball games—you know, the ones with the Negro baseball league? He bought me clothes, introduced me to people, everything. He was sweet on my mother, so he did it to please her. He might have even done it because he liked me. I can't say either way now." I pause. "You sure you want to hear this?"

She nods, eyes wet and searching, an inscrutable expression on her face before she turns and leans her head against the wall, closing her eyes.

"He would take Mama out, buy her flowers, cover the rent, all of that, but he wouldn't marry her. I was twelve when she got sick, thirteen when she stopped walking. She couldn't get around on her own, so I took care of her. Fats stopped coming around. As a favor, or for nostalgia's sake, he brought me onto his team. I needed the money, and I was the best runner he had. One of his soldiers told me he really was my daddy, but he'd never admit it 'cause the competition might kill me. I don't know if I ever believed that, but I was still too stupid to see I was just an employee. Mama got real bad, and the money I'd been making helped make ends meet, but it wouldn't pay for all Mama's treatments, so I went to Fats. I told him that he owed her, that he owed me. You think I'm cocky now, you shoulda seen me before my leg got busted up."

A hint of a smile plucks at the corners of her lips.

"The man laughed in my face, laughed so hard I thought he might fall out of his chair. Told me that he didn't owe us anything and that he'd paid for what Mama was giving him fair and square, and now that she ain't have nothing he wanted, their business was over."

The memory of it makes my temples throb. My fists begin to clench, and I have to loosen my tie so I can get a bit more air.

"I did not take it well. I said some choice words, took a few swipes at him before his security pulled me off. It was a baseball bat that crushed my knee. He laid down the blows himself. I'll say this for him: Everybody else who's taken a hand to Fats has ended up dead. I just ended up in the hospital."

I could tell her about the side hustles I ran to keep food on the table while Mama melted away to nothing. How King Fats came lookin' for me after I started makin' money with one of his rivals, hell-bent on killing me for leaking trade secrets, but I don't. I've already shared too much. Too much of the pain I've sealed away.

"I'm sorry," she says.

"Me too. You're the only person I've ever told what really happened." I lift my head and we lock eyes.

I don't know what it is about this girl, but she makes me feel like I felt when I had a mother, when I had a family and a place that was mine. She feels like home.

"Thank you for telling me. What do you tell people when they ask about your leg?" she asks.

"That I broke it jumping out a preacher's daughter's window."

She rolls her eyes. "You're too much."

"I try to be just enough," I say, and wink.

"He's marrying me off," Tamar says. Her voice is even, but it knocks me back just the same.

"What?"

"Tomorrow. In the morning. We're not going to Atlanta. Maybe we never were. We're going to visit one of his fraternity brothers. I will meet a man who will decide if he can tolerate me, and I will be expected to marry him," she says solemnly.

"He can't force you to do that," I say, angry on her behalf.

"Can't he? I have no money. I have no means to take care of myself. If he wants to drop me off at the side of the road, he can." Tears slide down her cheeks.

This time I don't stop myself. I lean in and pull her toward me. I let her sob into my chest and soak my shirt and I squeeze harder. She smells like rosewater and Overton's face powder, clean and sweet like Easter flowers.

Tamar pulls away and I get a good look at her. Her lip is swollen, but, thankfully, he didn't split it.

I take the cloth with the ice from her hand and dip it into the bucket of cold water. I wipe the tracks of tears from her cheeks. She's so beautiful it hurts.

"You're staring again," she whispers.

"I just can't get over how lovely you are. I know you don't like me to say that, but it's true." She drops her gaze, bashful for just a moment. I'm a little embarrassed, too. I don't think I've ever called anyone lovely. "I could kill your daddy for what he's done, and since you're a modern woman, you can help me."

At that, she chuckles. "I don't want to kill Daddy."

"So, what would you like to do?" I ask.

"This."

As her soft lips meet mine, the first thing that crosses my mind is that up until this moment, I don't think I've ever been kissed before.

22
TAMAR

MY LIP BURNS FROM THE PRESSURE OF KISSING HIM. I've never kissed a boy. Ever. I've kissed girls, sure, little nips on the rooftop of the finishing school. Sleepovers. This is different. He's like steel that only heats more with each kiss, but all I want is more. I want to be burned, seared by him. By this moment. He tastes like coffee and traces of lemon. I hold his face to mine, but it's not close enough. I want him on me, around me, tracing every inch of my skin.

I kneel in front of him, and when that isn't enough, I move closer, hooking my leg over his hips. He moves his kisses to my jaw, my neck, and I forget how to breathe. He grips my ankle to pull me even closer. His fingertips are rough and sure, calloused like mine. Does he play music as well?

Thunder rolls under my skin and he strikes lightning down my collarbone to the top of my dress. He nudges the light cotton of my collar to the side with his nose. I kiss his face, his ear, his neck. I lick the skin there and he tastes just like unripe watermelon, just ready enough to shake a bit of salt on to bring out the sweet. And—

An image flashes across my mind, and my heart squeezes and flutters. I've been here before. Together, with him, like this. The rhythm of the train rocks us in its arms and—

I *know* him.

I see Fayard. I see us, just behind my eyes, in a memory I can't place. Our fingers are entwined under a tree at the edge of a farm. I feed him strawberries. The juice stains his lips, my fingers. He's laughing at something I've said. We're both dressed a bit funny. Him in a loose-fitting white shirt made out of coarse fabric and loose homespun pants. His hair is longer, but his smile is still the same. My hair is tied up in a scarf and tucked under a straw hat.

Flash.

He kisses me as tears slide down my face. Why am I crying? We're tumbling through tall grass at the edge of a lake. His face is scarred with ritual markings on each of his cheeks. He looks at me as if I'm food. He always looks at me like this, but it doesn't scare me. I'm the opposite of scared. He strokes my face and tackles me so that we're a ball of laughter tangled in soft, sandy ground. He traces kisses down my belly.

Flash.

I remember. And remember. And remember.

He's in short pants on a beach, wrapped in a white robe at the edge of a desert, bent over double planting rice.

My father is asleep nearby. I place my hand against his chest, and his eyes, they plead, full of hunger—they look just like they did at the edge of the lake, and now I am afraid.

Flash.

"I'm—I'm sorry," Fayard pants. His chest is heaving and sweat gathers on his brow. His whole face is glowing, just like it did when he had that fishing accident. His father, Ade? Adesola! Adesola had sent him out early and he'd caught his leg in a net and . . . that didn't happen.

I shake my head and close my eyes to shut out his too-familiar face as I come crashing back to the here and now.

"You don't have to be sorry. I'm the one who kissed you," I say.

"Oh, yes, you did. Uh . . . did you . . . while we were . . ."

I cover my hand with his. Whatever he's about to ask, I don't want to answer. I need to catch my breath. I need my mind to slow down. I hinge back a bit to rest my head on the frame behind me and I see his face twitch.

"I'm sorry, let me get off," I say.

His hands grip gently but firmly on my hips and hold me in place.

"Please. Stay. Having you sit here is the best my leg has felt in a year."

"How bad is it?" I ask, because I care, but also to get him to talk.

I need him to tell me about the *real* him, the train porter Fayard. He looks at me, a bit surprised, but with that same intensity, like he's peeling away the layers of my mind to get to what's underneath. He says it's worse in the morning and tells me about his stay in the hospital. I watch his mouth move and try to keep from looking him directly in the eye. It doesn't stop my brain from conjuring up images of him somewhere else, sometime else. He continues and I remember listening just like this, knotted in a pretzel of limbs on dirt, on sand, in a bed of hay, a bed of silk.

I tell him to stop and climb off. I push myself against the wall and I see a rope of hammered gold around his neck and a braided white cloth wrapped around his head.

"Are you okay?"

I don't hear him at first, but I can tell from the way his brow knits that he's concerned. He says it again and again until he pushes himself up from the floor on his one good leg and leaves, returning with a glass of water. I drink all of it.

"I must be tired," I say when I'm done, and I almost believe it. I could run a mile with as much nervous energy as I have built up in my body, but my mind—my mind must be weary. "It's the excitement of the day, I think."

"Or the worries of tomorrow," he replies.

The concern has deepened his voice. I can't look up at him.

"Do you really think he's gonna marry you off? You came all this way. It ain't that much farther to Atlanta."

"Daddy doesn't make threats, and he never changes his mind. He prides himself on that. Once he makes a decision, that's it."

"Wasn't it his idea to bring you to Atlanta?" he asks.

I reach back in my memory to pick apart all the words he used regarding the trip, me, Mama, and Spelman. Not once did he ever say the words "I'm taking you to college." It was me who reminded him of the start date. I sent off the letters of confirmation. I even arranged the travel. He just nodded his head whenever I told him what I'd done.

"I don't know. Mama said she told him what she wanted for me, but I wasn't there. I didn't see him promise her, and he never promised me, not to my face. I . . . I'm in real trouble," I say, fighting the urge to cry again.

The panic rises in my chest, and Fayard bridges the distance between us. He places his hand on my back, drawing small circles up and down my spine until my breathing evens out.

"I can help you," Fayard says.

"No one can help me."

"I can. I've got money."

I chance a glance up at him, grateful it's just him there and not some other version of him, slightly changed and bewildering.

"I hustle. I told you that. I just needed to get out of Philly, and this was the easiest way. I haven't really thought about what would come next, but maybe, maybe you're what's next," he says in earnest.

"But you don't know me." No one has ever been this generous to me before. We just met. And while my mind is telling me that I know him deeply and completely, it doesn't feel right.

"Don't tell me you didn't feel what I felt when you kissed me. Like we fit together somehow, like I've known you all my life. I felt it the moment I first saw you on the platform."

I tear my eyes away from his and drop my arms from around his waist. When did I put them there?

I shake my head and straighten my dress. Suddenly I'm desperate for a mirror. "You're mistaken. Maybe you're not as experienced as you think you are. Kisses are always like that." I'm rambling.

He hooks a finger under my chin and lifts my face so that I have to look at him again.

"No, Tamar, they are not."

I don't think either of us registered that anyone was approaching until they were there. Two warriors waging battles of their own—Daddy and Mr. Max, quiet and accusing in the doorway.

And whatever fairy tale I might have thought I'd fallen into is over.

23
TAMAR

FAYARD'S MONEY WEIGHS DOWN MY TRUNK LIKE A DEAD body. I imagine police at every turn just waiting to search my luggage and unveil my deception. Desperation, that's what I'm blaming this on. Daddy and his lies made me do it. I tell myself that, but is it true? Did Daddy turn me into this, or is this what I've always been?

"Smile, for God's sake. Nobody likes a sullen woman. Just a small detour and . . ." Daddy stops himself. The lie isn't worth the effort. We both know what this is. I've already created the most believable excuse for the eggplant-colored bruise along my jawline. An accident. I was playing stickball with a few kids at the orphanage where I volunteer on the days I'm not providing cello lessons to the children of the Philadelphia colored elite.

"It doesn't even hurt," I tell the driver as he loads our bags into the car. Mr. John squints hard, eyes flickering to Daddy, before he decides to go on with his polite introduction to his hometown.

The train station gets smaller in the rearview mirror, but I can still see Fayard's face when I close my eyes.

"James Shepard is a great man. After he and Mr. Fitzgerald started that Mechanics and Farmers Bank—we call it the M&F Bank—colored folks in town really had something to call they own. I was right grateful for them, too. My brother's got a farm 'bout twenty miles outside of Durham. If it hadn't been for Mr. Shepard's bank, we wouldn't have got the mule we needed to keep the family name right. My family ain't too big, you know. I can't work like my brother on account of my arm. . . ."

He yawns on, but it's all just a blur. A lot about the great Mr. Shepard and how smart his nephew is, as if I care. My mind is racing, trying to figure my way out of this. I thought we'd be close to the train station, or at the very least someplace close to the city, but the hours stretch on as we get closer and closer to Hayti, "the best colored town this side of creation," to hear Mr. John tell it. All I know is that it's near part of Durham, far away from the train I need to get back to, to escape, to start fresh, to apologize. Maybe not to apologize just yet. Apologies hit better when you can make up for what you've done. Replace what you've stolen. Mend what you broke, and I need this money for tuition, for my ticket to Atlanta, to get a small start. I'm in no position to say sorry, not yet.

"Well! Here we are. Durham, North Carolina, but some folks call it Bull City. Down that way is the Bottoms. I wouldn't recommend fine folks like yourself going down there. Folks with names stay up on Parrish Street near St. Joseph's AME Church. Over there is Bankers Fire Insurance Company, and in that building you got the National Negro Finance Corporation. We got our own banks and volunteer firemen, so we ain't got to worry about what happened in Tulsa in '21 happening to us."

I hold my breath and wait for Daddy to start in on what really caused those white folks in Tulsa to burn out and murder thirty-five full blocks of Negro businessmen, doctors, and schoolteachers a few years ago. Ten thousand people were left homeless, just like that. Everything they worked for, up in smoke, all 'cause some shoeshine boy had the audacity to trip and fall on a white girl in the elevator. Black folks say it was an accident. White folks say it was attempted rape. "What kind of girl works an elevator?" he'd start. It was all Daddy could talk about a few years ago, but he doesn't take the bait. He lets Mr. John just prattle on. Finally, the car stops.

The house is large, much larger than our brownstone, with a wraparound porch and rosebushes bursting with flowers lining the walkway. African violets spill out of flower boxes on the second-floor windows, flanked by bright white shutters covered in the kind of ivy that's left to wander as it destroys. A man—short, barrel-chested, and bespectacled—stands regally at the top step, clothed in the kind of righteousness that old families tailor for all their sons. It makes his creases sharper and the pigments in his ties brighter. It reminds everyone that humility is for the middle class.

Father bounds up the steps, nearly falling over himself to greet the patriarch of the Milton homestead, admiration smoothing the folds between his eyes. He can smell their money, and even I can't miss the perfume of their position in the community. It's the aroma you get after you've had generations removed from struggle, while Daddy's still got the stench of Tennessee moonshine on him.

I smile and nod like a good girl all day and well into dinner with the entire Milton family, where Mrs. Edith Barbara Milton—and one must use all her names when addressing her—is attended by the housemaid. The girl is nameless, with downcast eyes and a blinding white apron that I marvel at as I watch Mrs. Edith Barbara Milton's trembling hands and insistence on feeding herself. The cold soup is a disaster in slow motion. I'd no idea soup could be served cold until now.

Once she's had her fill, her voice rings out, high and sharp as she addresses me. "Spelman? Fine school for girls, but it really is unseemly for a young woman to be separated from her family by so many miles. My son-in-law founded the North Carolina College for Negroes. It's just become four-year. It's important that we develop Negro teachers to educate the race into the future," Mrs. Edith Barbara Milton says.

I want to reply that I've never seen myself as a teacher, but more as a performer. I want to ask if there is a music concentration, but I bite back the question because I don't want to know. I don't need to know how I can force-feed myself this half life. No, it's better to go on as if this is a hell of my father's design that I must escape. I need a good reason for what I've done, some excuse for what I've allowed myself to be. I let my selfishness turn to salt in my mouth, and I'm suddenly not hungry, my belly full of guilt and my own sharp-edged desires.

They've seated me across from Norman Shepard, the nephew, my father's future for me. He's got the flat forehead and light eyes of his uncle James, glasses, and an air of haughty satisfaction with the world and his place in it. Unfortunately, he's also got his grandmother's weaselly voice.

"We all agree. The question is to what extent. We should ask ourselves what we must sacrifice in our zeal to move forward at all costs. Our women are sent to work as teachers and secretaries and nurses while the work they are divinely ordained to do, as wives and mothers, is neglected. Can the race be uplifted if the family falls apart?" Norman says.

"You don't talk very much, do you?" Norman says when the meal is over and we all thankfully begin retiring to our separate rooms. He's been ignoring my usually very effective nonverbal cues. "You should speak up more around here. Your father led us to believe you were at least agreeable to conversation, if not a wit."

I turn slowly on my heels and look down at him from my higher position on the stairs.

"And what else did my father say about me?" I ask, curious to know whether he fell on his habit of backhanded compliments or decided to go for half lies to sweeten his deal.

Norman blinks, obviously pleased I've decided to engage him in some sort of wordplay.

"Ah, well. He said you were well raised . . ."

I take a step down, closer to him.

". . . considerably trained in the arts . . ."

I take another step, and he clears his throat.

"Did he say anything about my beauty?" I ask.

Norman chuckles under his breath as if I've made a joke. I stare at him, waiting for an answer to a question he was sure he didn't need to reply to.

"Did he?" I press, a little bolder now. I won't pass any paper-bag tests, my skin is far darker than your average lunch sack, and my hair isn't straight as a ruler. If Norman is as shallow as he seems to be, then I'm sure that's what he's looking for—light, bright, with no naps in sight.

"Well, uh, he didn't really say. Everyone applauds a girl's bright complexion, yes, but there are other laudable qualities. He let us know up front that you were dark-skinned so there would be no surprises."

"'Us'? Surprises? When exactly did *we* have this discussion about my future?" I take another step down, so I'm now on the first step with him, close enough to smell the cigar smoke still clinging to his sweater vest. I look up at him through his lashes. I can tell he's had little experience with girls, dark-skinned or otherwise. I'm much closer than good manners would allow, much closer than any good girl would dare, but I am not a good girl. I am an angry girl.

I hear the creak of the floorboards as Mr. Milton and my father approach from the den. Norman jumps down a step as if he's been stung, but I hold my ground and my stare as the two approach.

"When, Norman?" I snarl.

"Oh, you two are still getting acquainted. That's good to see," Mr. Milton announces cheerily as he waves his pipe in the air, missing my tone entirely. Father isn't nearly as excited to see Norman and me talking.

"Norman was just telling me about how long you and Daddy have been planning to get me down here," I say, fighting the fury rising in my throat.

"Really? I'd say it's been about six months since we first had a chat about it, eh, Joseph?"

My stomach drops, not just because it's the first time in a long time I've heard anyone use Daddy's first name, but because six months ago my mother was still alive, still making firm plans for my first year in college.

He always meant to defy her. He always meant to do this.

"Well, you really should have included me in the discussion," I say, exaggerating my shock. "I don't think your nephew and I suit at all. He seems to be able to overlook my dark skin, but I'm not able to overlook . . . him."

The words feel good out of my mouth, but it's Daddy whom I've misjudged. I thought there was no way he'd show who he really was in public. He'd never risk his reputation to drop the mask.

I was wrong.

24
TAMAR

CLENCH MY EYES AND STEEL MYSELF FOR THE BLOW, BUT IT doesn't come. All I can feel is Daddy's hot breath billowing out near my face. I take a step back and peel open one eye to look at him, surprised to see Mr. Milton holding tightly to each of his arms.

"In this house, even if the women speak out of turn, we don't hit them," he says angrily and with just a hint of surprise. Daddy grunts and snatches his hands away, only to trudge up the stairs. I don't look at him as he goes. I don't flinch when Mr. Milton lifts my chin up with his hands, peering down to get a better look at my thinly veiled bruise.

"He do that?" he asks.

I nod quickly, an infinitesimal move he can feel, even if he can't see it. A tear teases the corner of my eye and I squeeze my eyes shut before it can be fully born.

Mr. Milton sighs loudly. "I had my suspicions."

He turns to his son. "Norman, pick up that pipe."

"But . . . ," Norman protests, and immediately bends down to do as he's told.

"We'll get your arrangements settled for your trip to Atlanta the day after tomorrow. We observe the Sabbath quite strictly here."

"Of course," I croak, my voice choked with emotion and gratitude. "Thank you."

I tell myself that guilt will keep me from sleeping and that if I never sleep again that penance will be enough, but I do sleep, the evidence of which is clear when I'm jarred awake by clicks against my window. The taps come sporadically, too far apart to be the hands of a clock, sharp interruptions in the still darkness of my room.

Moonlight from the window pools in the middle of the floor, bright enough that I don't need a lantern to see the ground below.

I'm shocked, not by Fayard's presence, dark and unashamed in the bushes, but by my ability to keep breathing as I take him in. It feels like it only takes a breath for him to scale the magnolia just outside the window, and just one more before he's standing right in front of me, wincing as he sets both feet down. He bends his knee a few times. Instinctively, I reach out to him, to touch him and soothe that pain like it wasn't me who caused it. I stare at my rebellious arm and snatch it back.

"I want my money," he says plainly.

"I know." I don't ask how he got here or how he found me.

"I. Want. My. Money," he repeats.

"I—" I start in on my excuse and notice the black eye to mirror mine, the split lip, the blood on his shirt, the dirt at the hems of his pants. "What happened to you?" I reach out a hand again, this time to touch his face. He knocks it away.

"Don't pretend that you care," he spits. His voice is low, but these walls may be thin. I can't be too sure.

"I do care. I just . . . I *am* sorry."

"You're sorry? I beat Spark for a cool five minutes for stealing from me before I figured out he wasn't lying. Do you understand how long that is in a real fight?"

I shake my head.

"No, you don't, 'cause you're a high post girl and you're used to bloodless competition. You're the worst kind of people. High class folks who talk about 'us' but are really just out for themselves. I bet you weren't ever really going to Spelman, just sold me some story so you could make it to Slick downstairs with a little change for yourself. What you think you're gonna do with the money? Buy a new dress? Some sheet music for that sad instrument you play?"

"It isn't sad," I say weakly, glad for the barrage of insults. I deserve it.

"It is! Just as sad as you, so beat-down you can't tell when some-body sees you. You couldn't wait a day for me to figure something out? You couldn't leave me an address so I could write? Come and see you?" he finishes in a rush.

"I don't want your help!" I cry, trying hard to keep my voice down. "I didn't have time. I could wait all day, all year, all my life and look up and find it's passed me by from all the waiting." I spit, "I might as well be a slave." I'm rambling about possibilities like . I've got any idea what comes next. He's a stranger, but there's this familiarity that is so scary to me. "I'm not making any sense," I add, my tongue slow and stupid with guilt.

"So you steal instead?"

"I didn't mean to do that! I'd lost an earring and I thought that maybe I'd dropped it when I was in the room, your room, and the money was just there. You were gone and I knew there was no way

I could say goodbye or ask you and it just seemed like the universe was giving me a chance to get what I really wanted."

"And you never thought about me?" The pain in his voice is tangible; it rises at the end, accusing me. I know the question is deeper than a thought. He saw what I saw. I'm not just a girl who got greedy and he's not just a boy on a train. There is something else pulsating between us, real and elemental, like ocean currents.

A part of me wants to give in to it, align myself with him, become *we* instead of *I*, take a chance. The other part of me knows that this can't be right. This time, this place, this moment is off-balance, the wrong boat for us to climb aboard together. We haven't figured out who we are by ourselves, let alone together.

"I just met you," I say, and even as the words come out of my mouth, I know it is the biggest lie I've ever told. His shoulders fall inward, crumpling from the weight of my betrayal.

He closes the space between us and leans forward, his lips just a finger's width from mine. Our eyes meet, and my heart stops, waiting for the kiss that doesn't happen. He backs away, anticipation leaking out like steam from a kettle. Suddenly I ache like I've never ached for a kiss, for his arms to wrap around me. I'm desperate to feel the sense of rightness that was there when he kissed me, before the visions, something other than this painful loneliness digging into my body and scooping me out.

This will be the last time I see him. I know this like I know the sun will rise. This is the last time we will be together, and it will be my life's great tragedy. Not this house with Norman, not Daddy's superior love for Patience, but tonight in this little room in North Carolina with a porter boy.

I'm surprised at how quickly I give in. I'd hoped that maybe I was stronger than this. I didn't want to be the kind of girl who folds after a kiss. I was wrong. I find the money bag packed neatly next to my clothes in the chifforobe.

Fayard shakes his head, a slow, pitying movement, and allows himself to collapse onto the windowsill, his bad leg jutting out like a punctuation mark. He opens his mouth once and closes it again, thinking, and then says, "You don't have to hurt people just because somebody hurt you. You know that, don't you?"

I'm not sure how to answer him. Sometimes I act without thinking, and sometimes I overthink so much that the decision gets made for me, but I know I won't ever get over hurting him. I hand him the bag just as the first rays of dawn start to light up the sky, inky blue shot through with violet and lavender.

"So where are you headed?" I ask, wanting to tease out just a few more minutes with him.

"I'm a city kid. Chicago, maybe? Baltimore."

There's this rising halo of light around him as he's indulging me. I have no right to keep him here or to subject him to whatever punishment my father would inflict if he found him at my window, but I can't let him go. Not yet.

"I'm not going to Spelman."

He blinks hard.

"I don't have to marry Norman. I messed that up for Daddy. But he'll never pay for school now."

"What's your plan?" he asks.

"I don't know. Go back home. Maybe I can stay with my sister and teach music until her baby comes."

He frowns and leans against the windowsill, like he's tired of the conversation, and my stomach drops because I know this is it.

"I'm gonna keep this quick because there's no need to drag it out. I'm not saying I forgive you, but that doesn't mean I can't hold a grudge on the road. There's enough money here to get us set up for a little while with my mother's cousin in Harlem. We won't even have to share a room if you don't want to," he adds with a slight smile.

"You would do that for me?" I ask, my voice so small I can barely hear it over the subtle roll of thunder outside.

He opens his mouth but the thunder snatches it, and then I realize the sound is in the house. Someone is banging on the front door.

We both turn to the window and see a girl standing in front of the house, huge with child, her hand on her hip like the handle of an angry teapot.

"I guess Norman had his own plans too," I add.

There's rumbling inside, and I'm glad I locked my door. It only takes a few minutes for the scene to blow fully out of control as the girl's father, rifle in hand, gets into a screaming match with Mr. Milton right out there on the front lawn.

"So?" Fay asks, his eyes pinned on me rather than the ungodly scene below. "Will you come with me?"

The sun is up now, the halo on full blast, surrounding Fay with a spotlight that must be coming from God himself.

I don't need to think about my answer this time. I kiss him and my whole body is a live wire, a plucked string vibrating to the tune of possibility. I pull away and run to the dresser, ready to fill the world with music.

25

Columbia, South Carolina, Present Day

TAMAR

THE SOLOIST SWITCHES TO SOMETHING WITH A BIT more bop, a rendition of some K-pop song I can't remember the title of. I pull my head back from Fayard's shoulder and smooth my thumb across his eyebrows.

"Remember the first day we met?" I ask.

"Vacation Bible School. Y'all had just moved from across town and I was like, I don't know, *thunderstruck* might be the word. I was smacked by that thunder when you walked into the church basement with those little purple overalls you liked so much."

"Wow, I don't remember what I was wearing."

"I do. You wore them at least once a week, but that first day you had on this white crop top. You still got it somewhere?" he asks, lost in the memory.

"Uh, that was two cup sizes ago, and don't act like you weren't scoping out all the girls' "crop tops.""

"I love fashion," he jokes.

"I did not want to go, but Mama was determined to get us back to the church with everything that was going on after quarantine. What was that girl's name? The one who liked to break out into a praise dance every time Reverend Trish gave a sermon?"

"I don't know who you're talking about."

"You know! The one with the super-hairy legs."

He's thinking, the little lines etching into his forehead, and for a few moments I get to stare and soak in all the details. How he smells— soap and Murray's pomade, ironing starch and the tiniest hint of pine from the air freshener in his car. I need to memorize his face and hope I'll be able to see him just like this in my dreams when they put me under at the cryogenics center. There are these freckles under his eyes, pinpricks of cocoa against a pristine canvas. Boys always have better skin than girls, but his glows. It's not just good skin care or genetics; it's something from the inside that lights up every cell. He's good, a genu- inely pure soul, and I want to keep him preserved in my mind just like this. Solid, clean-smelling, kind, and unworried. Hopeful.

A shadow passes over us and breaks the moment.

"Awww, look at you two!"

"Barbie?"

Barbara Engelman is the best Mock Trial lawyer in the state and beat me several times in regionals. Then she beat our entire team junior year, the last year I was able to compete. Someone else got the title this year. Not because Barbie lost a step, but because she didn't compete at all.

"I thought you were in Israel," Fay says as he stands to give her a side hug.

"I was. Spent a year with my aunt and uncle to see if I liked it. Now I'm back. Are you guys running off to elope?" she asks, tossing her hair over her shoulder. Barbie has the best hair: super thick, super curly. It makes her look like she should be playing a harp in a castle somewhere. Of course, she hates it, but we always hate what makes us stand out.

"T's running away from me. She's going to some summer program in the Dominican Republic," Fay replies.

"The DR? Really? I spent two weeks there the summer of freshman year. It was this language-immersion camp thing. My Spanish is still shite but I did learn to French kiss," she says, and winks. "Did you decide what school you'll be at in the fall?" she asks as she takes a seat next to Fay and plops her bookbag between her legs. It's covered in buttons and patches from all over the world. Even though we're the same age, she's got this confidence that makes her sit up straighter, a shine to her eyes that lets me know she's seen things, talked to people twice her age about everything from politics to sex, and they listened. I've never been jealous of anyone, I've always felt it was a waste of time, but looking at that beat-up Jansport gives me a twinge of longing like nothing ever has. Barbie is what freedom looks like.

"I was looking hard at Clemson but finally went with Brandeis. My father's a rabbi. Why rock the boat? So, spill. Where are you landing?"

She's so expectant in her signature red half-moon glasses, waiting for my answer, for Fay's, like she doesn't even see my oxygen tank. I wonder if she knows about me, but she has to—everyone knows.

"I'm looking into a gap year," Fay mumbles, his long arm arcing over his head so he can scratch the back of his neck. It's one of his tics. He gets itchy when he lies or when he's nervous. The other arm slides into his pocket. I don't see, but I know he's rubbing his rosary beads raw with this thumb.

"T? What about you? When you come back from the DR?"

"Me too," I say quietly.

"Are you guys sure you're not eloping?" she says, not catching the slightest change in the mood. "The way you gunned for me at state the last two years I just knew you were gonna go for political science and go right to Princeton. I heard Randy Shivers from Spring Valley, got accepted there. He won Best Witness last year, remember?"

I shrug as if this is all a big joke, but I can't muster a smile.

"Don't answer. None of my business, but, Fay, if you don't have plans for the summer, there might be an opening for a four-week thing at NASA I heard about. It's a joint partnership between Brandeis and Howard University. They're, like, trying to get more religious people and more Black people to pursue space exploration as a goal. Totally free. I know it's late, but one of the guys got into this freak safari accident and there's a space open."

"What the hell kinda accident is that?" Fay asks.

Her eyes get wide and then she leans in close. "I dunno, but I heard it was some kind of sex thing. The US consulate got involved. Scandal. I don't know. I do *not* know! I can't say for sure, but he's gone," she rattles on. Barbie's a fast talker.

"I'll link up with you," Fay says breezily without any real hint of conviction, and it's then I make it my business to get him to email her in the next half hour to secure that spot. I know Fay—he can get obsessive. If he doesn't have something to do, he'll make grief his whole life. I don't want that for him. I want a bag full of buttons for him just like I would want it for me.

"Cool. I've got your email. I'll shoot you the details. My sister's dating a guy on the selection committee, so I can get you in no problem."

"This isn't like your cousin with the fifty-dollar iPads, is it?" I joke, trying to lighten the mood for myself.

She rolls her eyes. "That moron is dead to me. It's nothing like that. Promise. Hey, I gotta go before they lock this place down."

"What do you mean?" I ask, and she points to the marquees, which have all changed from a basic black background to orange.

"There's some demonstration outside. You guys don't travel as much as I do, so you don't know, but I can smell when something is about to go down. I'd rather be home when it does. I hope your flight doesn't get canceled. It was great seeing you two. Make sure you post pictures from your DR trip!"

As soon as Barbie leaves, Aabidah walks over with a bag full of French macarons. I do a little happy dance and immediately feed one to Fay. He takes a bite, exaggerating how good it is, and licks the tip of my finger.

"Stop!" I playfully push his face away.

Aabidah rolls her eyes. "Our flight's been delayed two hours. They're doing extra security checks."

"Are they going to can—"

She cuts me off mid-breath—"No!"—and then takes a deep breath of her own. "No. They won't. It's just a delay," she says firmly, but I can tell she's not sure. "I'm going to find one of those massage chairs. I'll meet you back here in ninety minutes." She doesn't even look back at me for a confirmation, just walks away, leaving a cloud of anxiety trailing behind her.

A cancellation would be a death sentence. I don't want to think about it, though. I look over at Fay, who's still pretending that salted caramel macarons are the best thing he's ever eaten.

"So. A delay means I get you for another hour and a half. Can you stand? Walk?" he asks, and I wonder where he's going with this. He gets up, brushes the crumbs from the side of his mouth, and holds out his hand like the chivalrous prince in a fairy tale.

"I can walk. Where are we going?" I ask again. I push myself to my feet and place my hand in his. He's got that Cheshire-cat grin on, and I'm wondering what he's got cooked up in his brain. An hour and a half isn't that much time for an adventure, but this is Fay. Anything is possible.

"We're running away," he says.

"Oh!" I reply, and place my hand on my cheek in mock surprise. "Can I ask where to, dark prince?"

"To the moon. To the stars."

26

Alpha 9, Lunar Base, 2260

FAYARD

THERE ARE GALAXIES BEHIND MY EYES AND THERE IS music in my ears, a slow melody that makes me sad and comforted at the same time. It doesn't want me to wake up, but I fight it. I'm trying to say my name, but it keeps coming out slurred. Spit dribbles down my chin, and after some more coughing fits and expelled phlegm I'm beginning to regain sensation in my lips. A few minutes after that, my tongue comes back on board, and I'm able to answer the baseline questions that'll get me out of processing, into a bio-controlled uniform, and to the cafeteria for a real meal.

"Name?"

The voice is disembodied, so I'm not sure if it's attached to a real person or a program. The intake room is featureless, just an aluminum box with a door where they shove all the newly arrived cryopods. In the more rural colonies they don't even shove you in a room; they just set the pods out in a field, crack the seals open, and wait.

"Private Fayard Leanthony Azikiwe."

"Leanthony, huh?"

Well, that proves it's a real person.

"Vital signs are in the normal range. Look directly ahead of you:

the eastern wall is a monitor and will display a series of images. Please tell me the name of each image you see displayed."

"*Oui.* Yes. I mean, okay."

"I see here that you're a polyglot. Which division have you been assigned to?"

"Counterintelligence," I reply, and feel a pang in my right temple. I reach up and feel an electrode attached to my head and then feel one on my chest; I didn't notice either in my post-cryo fog. They're collecting more than vital signs. I take a deep breath and focus.

"Your intake will take slightly longer, in that case. Your first image is ready . . . now."

"Earth, cloud, *cinq*—I mean . . . the number five. Bowl, spoon, hovercraft, filtration tank, mountain." The images speed up and slow down, changing in size to test my visual acuity and in complexity to assess my memory. I've gone through about ten slides when the voice pauses.

"Could you repeat what you just said?"

I kind of zoned out, so it takes me a second to remember. "Um, shoe. I think."

"No, you said cat."

"Okay, cat."

"Private Azikiwe, cat is the next image, not the last. Have you been given prior knowledge of the intake assessment?"

"No."

Silence. I have made a miscalculation, but I can't see how. I've never seen the test, and there's no way to know what is on the tests anyway. They're random. I would have to be able to see through walls to cheat. My temperature is rising. I know they can see this in the vital signs, but this isn't a normal tangent for intake. They don't need any reason to dig into my background. I take a few deep breaths—in for four counts, out for eight. My heartbeat slows. I'm turned inward when they finally come back.

"Private Azikiwe, did you dream while you were under?"

"Yes. My dreams are always quite vivid when I'm in cryo."

"Can you tell me what they were about?"

"They're nonsense. I'm always myself, but I'm on different colonies. A ship's docking station? A lake? Possibly Earth. I can never hold on to the particular details when I wake up. There is a girl."

"Her name?"

"I can't remember."

"What does she look like?"

"Beautiful, with, uh . . . I know that she's got, um . . . I can't really remember right now." It's always like this. I wake up with a warm feeling akin to being hugged by someone you love, and then nothing. Every detail evaporates as my awareness of myself settles into my current reality.

Silence again. They're watching my vitals, I'm sure of it, trying to see if there is a lie stripped bare in the binary, but there isn't. Not this time. Eventually, they come back on.

"All right, private. Let's do this again."

The first days out of cryo are the worst. Your muscles are stiff, your brain is mud, and the only thing you want to do is eat. Couple that with your body's need to acclimate to whatever new atmosphere you've just landed in and you've got a recipe for unchecked emotion. We're military, so planet-hopping is part of the deal. Some people laugh, like my bunkmate, Ralphie. He giggles, even in his sleep. Even when he's awake he's always smiling. Predawn five-mile run? Smiling. Midnight gray-water duty? Smiling. Rapid-fire jab to the solar plexus? Big grin.

"That's the aggression I want to see, 675! 459, stop smiling and recover," Captain Baqri bellows from the observation booth. 459 doesn't take the advice, and the other soldier gives him an impressive beating, despite their small size.

459, otherwise known as Ralphie, limps off the mat, helmet still secured but a slight bit foggy on the inside.

"A beast," he croaks.

I nod and help him get his gloves off so I can attach an anesthetic patch. No one's allowed to go to the infirmary before all the matches are done. Captain's rules. You have to be near death before you're allowed to be carried out. It's only happened once, and I think that was because the poor fool was moaning so loudly no one could concentrate. He was transferred. Of course, we didn't realize who it was until the next day and he was gone. The numbers aim to keep things anonymous; the gear is full-body, and helmets are tinted. But after a few matches you can figure it out, especially if you're on the same team.

The room we're practicing in is quite small, but the virtual-reality overlay makes it look like we're all in an arena. The observation booth is probably twenty meters away, but the illusion has it situated a few kilometers above us, with the captain and other members of the instructional staff looking down on us like gods. A single spotlight shines from the ceiling on the dueling pairs of students below. The rest of us wait patiently on the sidelines for our numbers to be called at random. You could fight twice in a row or not at all. It just depends on the luck of the draw. I assume it's to build stamina in the uncertainty of war, but in the moment it just feels cruel and unnecessary. I'm bored. I can fight, but I prefer more effective strategies for disarming my opponent. Besides, most of these other kids have been raised on military outposts with food rations and artificial sunlight. I was raised on an ally colony, separate and used to its own ideas, like freedom of religion and sustainable farming. As a result, I'm taller than nearly everyone else, and a few stone heavier.

"Aren't you gonna take one of those for yourself?" Ralphie asks as he leans back on the bench. His mouth has started to relax, and his vital stats, visible on the leaderboard hovering next to the observation window, are beginning to level out.

"Not yet. They slow you down."

"You've already fought twice today. They can't call you again." Ralphie coughs, still a bit out of breath.

Captain Baqri's voice booms out over the intercom. "Next up, 675 and . . ."

"What's with the repeats?" Ralphie asks.

"Azikiwe," I hear in my helmet. "You're up."

"Fucking hell," I hear one of the kids in our group say as they encouragingly slap me on the back. But I decide to be like Ralphie and smile even though I'm angry.

"Final match, 675 and 712. Four minutes. No breaks. Hand to hand. No gloves."

A collective groan erupts among the bystanders. Hand-to-hand matches are grueling. This is an endurance test as much as anything else. 675 is small, much smaller than me, but judging from the previous matches, and judging from their earlier match with Ralphie, they're fast and strategic, waiting for just the right opportunity to strike somewhere debilitating. I'm pulling off my gloves and reconfiguring my helmet to something lighter. It still covers my chin, but it's mostly flexfilm. Great for temperature control, not so great for protection from broken bones. After detaching key pieces of the helmet and stripping down to just shorts and my full-body flexfilm, I bound into the arena and stop cold.

675 is a girl.

27
TAMAR

CAN SEE HIS MUSCLES GO SLACK ONCE HE GETS A GOOD look at me. I'm guessing he's a guy. With the suits there's no real way to tell, but it doesn't matter anyway. We can politely hash out pronouns after I've won. This is going to be harder than I thought. I don't need any special considerations just because I'm a girl. Most of the guys don't care, but there are a few from the more isolated colonies who hold on to ancient beliefs about inferiority or some crazy idea that I need them to protect me. I can tell by 712's reaction that he's the kind of guy to throw this match, and if he does, we might be here all day. The captain adds overtime if it's a draw— he doesn't believe in ties, only winners and losers. He'll want to show that girls can take as much punishment as the guys. That's my worst-case scenario. Most likely I'll end up in the infirmary or in an artificial coma, neck deep in nanigel while my muscles are rebuilt. Who has that kind of time?

712 is frozen for a beat or two before he begins to bounce again. He's warming up those fatigued muscles after two previous fights, and I notice that he's favoring his left foot. There may be a weakness there I can exploit. I stand stock-still while I continue to look him over. He's tall. Thin, but covered in lean muscle. If he doesn't knock me out in the first minute, I may be

able to run him down, let his fatigue topple him without a hit.

"712, 675, this fight is judged on hits, deflections, and total knockout. You have four minutes on the clock in ten, nine . . ."

The adrenaline begins to build and I can't keep still. Suddenly I'm on beat with my opponent. He's hopping from foot to foot, totally in the zone. The mat changes from yellow to green and rises six feet in the air to keep interference to an absolute minimum. The buzzer sounds and I go for it. Two layouts, a tuck, and a half twist. It's showmanship and requires more grace than aggression. He's surprised—I know because I'm able to get in three quick jabs to the side of his right knee and a kick to his shin before he thinks to retaliate. He doesn't hold back, either. His hook rattles me, and I see double before my vision sensors recalibrate. It takes longer than it should, and he has time for another shot, but he doesn't take it. He should have. I would have.

"Visual acuity seventy-six percent," my helmet tells me.

I run at him and hit the mat on both knees, avoiding his swing. I'm small enough to bend back and suffer only the slightest hit from his fist. I'm in the perfect position for me to home in on his weak spot: his ribs. My hits aren't as powerful as his, but they are effective, and I can hear his anguish when my jab connects with his body. He tumbles back several feet and nearly falls off the edge of the mat before he catches himself. I hop up and back away quickly.

He twists and groans between short panting breaths. He tries to straighten and folds almost immediately. He looks like a wounded animal, and there's no way for him to make his pain end other than to go through me. I'm squat, moving, both hands in front of my face, ready, but I'm thinking more about him than myself and I don't move fast enough. In seconds he's got me off my feet and over his head and, *smack*, my back is on the mat.

"Visual acuity thirty-two percent."

I can't breathe. Every ounce of oxygen has been knocked out of my body. My mouth opens and closes like a fish, but no air is coming in. Fire builds in my chest, and I've lost control of my arms and legs. Two beats later I gasp, and sweet air fills me again as 712's helmet comes into focus right above me.

"Seven, six, five . . ."

They're counting my knockout. I can't be knocked out. I wriggle, I squirm, and somehow I make it onto my knees as I try to crawl.

"Three, two . . ."

At the last second, I stumble upward. My back is on fire and my legs are filled with stone. He's returned to his corner, but he doesn't look much better. 712 is no longer hiding the fact that he's got a broken rib—maybe ribs, plural. One hand is holding his side protectively as he keeps the other balled into a fist right in front of his jaw. There's still time on the clock. Hits don't matter now. It's about survival. If I attack him this time, he'll have to come at me hard. Maybe knock something loose that isn't so easily repaired, and I don't have much left in me for hits. I need to run the clock. I can't win, but I can move around the mat and hope for the captain's mercy. 712 is limping, but he's already shown that he's unwilling to decimate me in a head-to-head battle . . . which gives me an idea.

"Helmet, give me a capoeira rhythm. Berimbau. Mid-tempo," I mumble beneath the plastic lens in front of my face.

"Berimbau. Received."

I fall into the ginga, the sweeping left-to-right rhythmic dance of capoeira. My opponent stops moving. For a moment I think maybe I've misjudged him, but it only takes a second before he falls into the rhythm with me.

Two minutes on the clock.

We start easy with a meia lua de frente, a kind of half-moon frontal kick. I swing with my right leg, foot flexed, and he mirrors with the left. We try again, moving closer together so that the movements are a pantomime of a real fight, where we come within a hair's breadth of touching each other. He can't hear the same beat that I hear in my helmet, but it feels like he doesn't have to. He's in the moment with me. One breath, one heartbeat, one sliding parry after the other. Armada, a kind of spin kick. Esquiva lateral into esquiva baixa, he kicks out, his long legs nearly toppling me over as I bend and almost kiss my right knee, arms stretched out like bird wings.

"Increase tempo."

The berimbau speeds up and so do my movements. Without a word, 712 follows me, arms, legs slicing through the air with the kind of grace you can only be born with and matching me so smoothly it's like we've been doing this for years. It's fluid. We aren't an orchestra; we're the metronome. A feeling, deeper than déjà vu, sends a shiver across my skin, and a twist in my gut erupts like a bomb. I fumble. Just long enough for his foot, which was in an arc above my head, to come crashing into the side of my face. I fly before hitting the mat with a thud just as the buzzer sounds. Match over.

The mat decompresses, and I'm suddenly surrounded by people.

"Visual acuity ten percent."

I see a face, blurred but too familiar to be a stranger, fading into the crowd.

28
TAMAR

"HEY, SIL? HAVE YOU EVER BEEN ON A TRAIN?" I ASK.

"Huh?"

"A train. A transportation device. Old. Pre-wipeout technology," I reply.

"Do I look like a transpo scholar? Maybe that guy rattled you a little more than you want to admit," Sil says as she adjusts the fuel levels on her side of the cockpit.

I let out a nervous laugh, suddenly embarrassed about something as silly as a dream. Then for a split second I wonder if I should go for a mental review. My grandmother had visions she swore were premonitions. They committed her. Nope. Best to just shake it off. It's probably a symptom of the nanigel.

A day of rest in the infirmary and I'm back to training. Alpha 9's been ravaged by religious civil war for hundreds of years, and there's little more than rubble left. Military conscription is mandatory for all citizens of the Republic if you want to have some kind of life for yourself. Ten years of elementary indoctrination and then another five of secondary training, followed by your choice of a number of military posts for advanced training. If you're smart enough you can test out of those last two years of secondary, like Sil and I did, and skip right on up to advanced. Sure, you can decide to opt out, but if there's ever an evacuation for a plague—or, God forbid, another atmospheric collapse—you're on your own. Worse still, you could be sent back to Earth, and not even God can help you in that hellscape.

Our base is a temporary outpost, just thirty-five thousand people if you don't include the prisoners in the supermaximum-security jail, and the handful of corporate execs sent to oversee investments. It's one of those quick and dirty operations made for people with ambition and a strong stomach. Our units are here to either find something or destroy something.

Sil and I pull up slowly to our attack position on the dummy course. We're doing a reconnaissance drill. The instructors are somewhere close by, but we can't see them. The abandoned city we're using for the drill looks ancient and eerie at this time of night. Hologram citizens flicker in the broken windows.

"Cue horn grenades to clear out the citizens. We'll give it ten minutes and then drop us down a few meters. I'm gonna turn off the boosters. We should be able to reduce our noise output by thirty percent and stay hidden for a while."

"You sure, boss?" Sil asks.

"You've been second-guessing me since the match," I whine.

"Hey, now, don't get mad at me. I'm just wondering if you lost your edge. It was you who decided to turn a death match into a ballet," she says, and laughs loud and openmouthed. "If you weren't knocked out, you'd have seen him. Beautiful and damn near distraught over your unconscious corpse. Don't worry, your lover boy was pretty beat up, too. His team had to carry him off to the infirmary."

"They didn't send a hovercot?" I ask.

"They did. He refused it. Lover boy is all heart and honor."

"Ha-ha. Happy you got your laughs in? We gotta focus, and I need you to never say 'lover' again. It sounds gross when you say it."

Our ship has been kicking out too much heat during this conversation, making us visible to the enemies infrared devices.

I chew the side of my lip. I haven't lost a fight in a really long time. Maybe that's why I'm feeling off. This is going to drive me crazy. Trains. Weird.

"Stop daydreaming," Sil quips. "They're serving Andelurian food for lunch today and I don't want to miss it. I can almost smell the whipped pasha and rulin sauce. I read once that Andelurians have twice as many taste buds as most humans. A crazy surgeon in their primary colony used gene splicing to apply the mutation to all the following generations. You know how much infantry eats? There might not be anything left."

I cue up the sound cannons and check to make sure our shields are at full strength. Our reconnaissance ship was built for maneuverability and speed, so it's small, with little in terms of defense upgrades. This kind of mission is meant to be more of an education than anything else. It's supposed to teach us how to stalk, manage our emotions, work as a team, and follow orders. It's low risk, but that doesn't mean no risk, so you still have to be careful.

"You know," I say, "one of the first markers of civilization is the existence of art, very often music. Music is a marker of life. It's ironic that it can now be an instrument of death."

"Okay, Wise One, can we get this show on the road?" Sil groans. "Just pulse it and be done."

"Where's the fun in that?" I reply.

"Decimating a city isn't supposed to be fun," she says flatly. "Stop wasting time."

I cue the beat panel on the console and switch it to manual while I roll my shoulders. Adrenaline shoots through my veins as I test the levels, and the pod vibrates with pure unadulterated funk. I love that word, "funk." It's old, and dirty, and so right for what this is, for what I do. I look over at Sil, barely able to contain my smile. "For their sakes they'd better be ghosts. This is war. They know what to expect."

And I let the beat drop.

Sil lets out a battle cry as soon as we're released from review and I punch her arm.

"Superior! It's just a coincidence the head of the review team is from the same colony as I am," I say.

"There are no coincidences. If we keep this up, we'll be off this backwater in no time. Maybe we'll be transferred to Section Nine in the Risha Quadrant. I heard there's a law that restricts shifts based on daylight, and for nine months out of the year the days are only six hours long," Sil says.

"Sounds depressing," I add.

"That's 'cause you don't know how to club like I do."

"Whatever."

"Let's celebrate. I got a friend in the engineering department who found a thin pocket. We can go gliiiidiing!" she sings. "C'mon.

You know you want to. I'll even see if he'll let you do the first blast."

"Let's do it," I say with a nod.

Sil makes the call, and a few hours later we're dressed in our biosuits, helmets secured, with about six other trainees from engineering and linguistics. It isn't an official mission, so we have to walk, but two hours later Bilal, the engineering guy, raises his hand.

"This is it," he announces.

At first glance it doesn't look like anything, just a salt bed of cracking and baked gray clay. We're nowhere near the grasslands, but there are mountains rising in the distance. Cave systems snake beneath the surface of Alpha 9 no matter where you are, but you need someone who really knows the topography to find someplace thin enough to create a gulch.

"You the blaster?" Bilal asks, and I nod. "You're up. The edge is right here," he says, and drags his boot across the ground to make a rough line. "Walk about twenty paces and you should be dead center."

I drop my bag and pull out a bass grenade. It looks like a silver pancake with a spike in the center. Our ragtag group is full of nervous excitement, chatting across the same comm frequency. They're all ready to jump and so am I. I run out to the center, stomp the grenade in with my boot, and give the gang a thumbs-up before I pull the pin and run.

I'm booking full out because I've only got ten seconds before it erupts. I barely make it before the first boom rattles the ground, knocking everyone off-kilter. I fall flat on my face, and one of the linguistics guys pulls me up. I have only another second on my feet before the smaller tick-tick-ticks of the snare package programmed into the grenade kick out and he grabs me with both arms.

"This is pretty cool," he says as the first cracks in the ground erupt like trapped lighting, spidering out to the farthest edges of the hidden canyon.

"Thanks," I say, and straighten up as best I can.

"I know this song. It's a backbeat, isn't it?" he asks.

"Uh, yeah. Most people don't recognize my rhythms."

"My mama filled our home with all kinds of music, especially classical jazz. Let me guess. It's—"

The final drumbeat cracks through the ground, and the grenade disappears into the roof of the canyon along with an avalanche of rock and soil. Dust fills the air and everyone cheers.

"Max Roach," he yells over the din as he scoops me up in the excitement.

My body freezes and warms all at the same time, and he must realize his mistake because he puts me down as quickly as he picked me up.

"Sorry."

"It's fine," I say.

"No, really. I shouldn't have. I was just overexcited. I'm new here. Fayard." He juts out his hand for me to shake and I take it, making sure to squeeze hard.

"Tamar."

"It's a pleasure to meet such a lover of violent music," he says smoothly. Light glints off his helmet, and for a moment it's like the entire planet has decided he should be in the spotlight.

I want to hold on to my offense, but his smile is so warm I let it go.

"I wouldn't call it violent, just effective."

"Definitely," he says as he falls back into the canyon, nose-diving until his gravity sensors kick in and he shoots up like a champagne bubble, somersaulting in the air. I don't realize I've been holding my breath until I hear his breathless cackle in my ears.

One by one we take turns diving into the center of the canyon, waiting until the very last moment to turn on our boosters. Sil's paired off with some ballistics girl, her arms pinwheeling in the air like a puffer fish. After the initial rush of diving wears off, I find the perfect place to flip onto my back and float.

I've just gotten to that meditative spot where your mind and body melt together and vibrate with everything around you when I catch a flash of arm in my periphery.

"Peaceful, isn't it?" Fayard says.

"It was."

I try to get back to that thrum of oneness and fix my gaze on the rising twin moons, but there's too much movement. He's on his belly and then his back again, backstroking in the air.

"How are you doing that?" I ask. He should be bouncing wildly, but he's as steady as a duck treading water.

"Gravity stabilizer."

"They don't issue those to trainees."

"I won it in a card game off a captain in the geology unit. Alpha Two is a lot looser than Alpha Nine."

He flips in the air again, graceful, his long legs arcing lazily in the still-dusty haze. The tiniest sliver of the setting suns casts light on the crumbling canyon, making the dust look like glitter and him like a man-sized dragonfly.

"Thank you," he says.

"Why are you thanking me?"

"Because this is a perfect moment. Without you, this would not be possible. It's hard to block out all the noise at base, and I am very happy right now, so thank you."

I don't know why, but a deep sensation of bashfulness washes over me. I turn my head slightly to look at him smiling. I look away and swallow hard.

"You're welcome."

29
FAYARD

THERE'S THIS OLD SAYING: "RIGHT OUT OF THE FRYING pan and straight into the fire." It's a clunky cliché, but hell if I don't feel it the moment I make it back from my final check at the infirmary. Nanigel supercharges your white blood cells and accelerates muscle and bone repair. It can be painful if you don't take your recovery seriously, and since I spent all of yesterday afternoon gliding over a fresh canyon, my bones feel like they are on fire from the inside.

"Can you even see straight?" Ralphie asks as my eyes roll back into my head. The shocks on these field tanks are barely functional. We're bobbing and rattling like dice, and before I know it, I'm detaching my harness.

"Get back in your seat, newbie!" First Sergeant Clemmons barks from his position up front. I can't reply because my head is in the nearest bin, throwing up bile. I haven't eaten in forty-eight hours, and all that comes up is this acrid, noxious phlegm.

"Damn!" Salvador bellows.

"Why is he even here?" Pham asks.

"Phew!" Ralphie shouts.

A chorus of irritated and disgusted comments rings out, along with a few whistles and a handful of claps from some of the older recruits on the transport. Ralphie and I are the youngest, and by far the least prepared. When we get to the field site, an abandoned city with a blast crater in the middle of it, we all pile out. The city's filled with buildings of different sizes and heights, roads overgrown with carnivorous snake grass and piles of shattered triptofilm, this planet's version of glass. It's pretty obvious the site has been hit with multiple sound cannons by the way some of the buildings have collapsed and by the complete lack of a single intact window.

Ralphie is partnered with an excavation team and given a shovel when he jumps out of the transport, but First Sergeant surprises me when he pushes a neutron rifle into my hand not a second after I've secured my helmet and passed through the oxygen lock.

"Grab an extra weather-tent capsule off the ledge there and stuff it in your hip bag, just in case. You're coming with me," he says.

"I don't know how to shoot . . . yet," I tell him, not wanting to admit I have an aversion to guns of all kinds. Not that I'm scared of them or of violence—I'll fight anybody hand to hand—but there's something about guns that makes me uneasy. I can't say why.

"It's point and shoot, son. But don't worry about it. It's just a precaution."

A precaution, like the weather tent. WTs are two-meter-by-two-meter-by-one-meter ploy-aluminum flexi-fiber creations included in every soldier's go bag. They are crude, airless, and coffinlike, and they can save your life if you're caught in a storm on a planet with subzero temps or need to survive an avalanche. It is a lifesaver, like the gun. Neither of which I thought would be necessary on what should have been a glorified field trip.

"I thought we were on a collection expedition," I say.

"No one told you to think, private. Now tell me, 'cause I need to make sure. How many languages do you speak?" he asks.

"Seventeen, sir. Twenty if you count variations in dialect," I say with confidence.

"Good, good. And you're versed in ancient languages too?" he adds.

"Yes, sir. Old Mandarin, Tipu, Latin, and Hebrew."

"Just what I needed to hear."

We hop into another transport. This one is a hoverbed. They're mostly used for hauling debris and supplies short distances. If I didn't know better, I'd think this was a hit. But I do know better than to ask more questions, so I'm silent for the fifty minutes it takes us to get to a cave system I've never seen listed on the maps. I use the time to think about the girl I met yesterday, Tamar, her legs twisting in the air like soft ribbons, her laugh guarded but genuine.

"Switch your biosuit to stealth."

"Yes, sir," I say, and watch the LED lights in the seams of my suit go dark while the fabric adjusts to the color signature of the surroundings. As a team, we'll be nearly invisible unless you know what you're looking for.

The caves aren't accessible from the valley floor, so we have to climb up and over a few boulders to find an entrance. I remain silent, just like I'm trained to do, until we make our way into a man-sized hole and find two other officers staring intently at detailed cave paintings carved into the wall, as high as ten meters, and a Sueronese girl behind them poised to stab both of them in the back.

• • •

Despite my inexperience I am the first to shoot. Lucky for her, I'm the only one who had their gun set to disarm rather than kill.

"I want to be mad you didn't kill the girl, 'cause she's an attempted murderer, but if you did, we couldn't interrogate her. So . . . that's something, ain't it." First Sergeant claps me on the back, and it isn't a smile on his lips, but like he said, it's something.

"I'll be pissed for you, First Sergeant. In the field, newbie, you set your gun to kill. Always," one of the faceless soldiers says as he pushes the girl to her knees and ties a restraint around her wrists and ankles. She's spouting a number of curses and speaking so fast I can't really catch what she's saying. That is until one of the other soldiers tosses a translation disk at her feet. They're great for basic conversation, but in pitch languages they can get glitchy, and you never want to use them in a highly sensitive situation. Best to have someone to blame for a misunderstanding. Now I see where I come in.

"Death bringers, whether you carry a rifle or not. Every one of you is a murderer," she yells. The disk breaks up the words, but her point is made. She's bald and blue-skinned, young if her height is any indication. A full-grown Sueronese woman can be twice as tall as any human, and though the Sueronese have similar body types to humans, they differ in distinct ways. They have a respiratory system that's twice as efficient as ours, with two spines and two sets of lungs instead of one. Her nostrils are nearly flat, with two additional holes to help her breathe in the thin air. Their blue skin isn't really blue, but tinged by a special mud they use to protect them from the UV rays of their twin suns. There are other differences, but I can only speculate, because the Sueronese are notoriously private, and everything we know about them is secondhand and distorted, the musings of missionaries and military envoys. She's dressed in a gray-green jumpsuit with an elaborate bundle cinched near her shoulders in the same fabric.

"She's a spy," I say.

"Well, you are as smart as I've been told. I'm impressed. This girl was caught sneaking in and out of this little cave by one of our drones. Imagine our surprise when we stumbled upon one of the most important discoveries in Sueronese and Republic history."

I gaze up at the wall, now illuminated by field lights. Above the glyphs is a giant sankofa bird, its neck bending back to tend to a glittering, blood-colored, egg-shaped gem the size of a grapefruit.

"It's a translator," I say. "Alphabets in each language stacked at the top, one above the other. I don't understand most of the glyphs."

"We tried digging out the gem, but it retreats back into the wall the closer you get to it. Looks organic, but there's some machinery at work; has to be. You do understand some of them, yes? The glyphs?"

"Yes. The fifth from the top is Hebrew."

He claps his hands excitedly and grips my shoulder too tightly. "Godsend is what you are. Major Thorisdottir is our language expert on site, but she's down with trench flu and we can't risk this getting out digitally. She recommended you as a stand-in. What else can you tell me?" First Sergeant urges.

The message is growing out of the stone instead of etched into it. I've seen this method used on other colonies, sometimes for religious reasons to mark a holy spot, sometimes just to advertise coffee on the side of a building.

"Uh, you'll have to take video, because it will disappear once the weather changes. It's the same message repeated over and over—at least that's what I'm seeing from the lines I can translate—but it doesn't make any sense. Loosely, it says:

> A blessing to live but a curse to die if only love
> the heart does find
> On the wind of chance does the goddess climb
> To turn the many-faced head of time

"It could be 'crown' instead of 'time'; I'm not sure. The rest is a jumble of letters and numbers."

The girl's face, previously an angry grimace, softens into something shrewd. She's pretending not to understand English. My answer surprises her, so I focus on not making eye contact with her again.

"Letters and numbers, huh," First Sergeant says, a little skeptically.

A groan from deep in the cave erupts from the blackness and brings with it a stench so powerful it makes it through the filters in our suits. This isn't good. That smell could only mean one thing: volcanic activity, shifting fault lines, and a possible collapse of this very old cave.

First Sergeant raises his voice and the disc begins to translate. "Looks like we're running out of time, sweetheart. I have a cryptic little message and a teenage spy, just small enough to creep through that hole up there and read it. And if my years of experience don't fail me, I'd hazard to guess those letters and numbers are coordinates of some kind. Now, my higher-ups, and even the head of the Republic, seem to think the Sueronese are a bunch of primitives on a backwater planet that even they don't want to defend, but I know better. Even a cowardly dog will bite if you get close enough."

First Sergeant picks up the girl's discarded blade, curved in the middle but sharp at the end. He holds it up to her neck, and I look to see if anyone is going to stop him. Killing POWs is against the rules of occupation. Even witnessing a murder can put you up for a dishonorable discharge.

"First Sergeant," I say tentatively, my voice clear but not too aggressive. "What are you doing?"

"Hush, boy. Now, sweetheart, I'm gonna need you to tell me where those coordinates lead."

"Rubbish. It leads nowhere. It is a children's rhyme to teach the youth to listen to their parents," she says dismissively.

"Ah, ah, ah . . . don't you lie to me."

The girl's chin is pointed as high as it can go, and her nostrils are flaring with fear, or it could be rage; I can't tell. First Sergeant presses the blade in farther.

"This knife would be enough for me. A blade like this is unmatched, I'll give you that. Sharp enough to run through a man, but curved just right to cut a man's throat," he adds.

"It is used for fruit," the girl says, and begins to laugh. "All you see is killing and death. We are a people of light," she says proudly, unfazed by the blade. "It will take more than a blade and a polyglot lover boy to pull anything other than poetry from my throat," she says. Her eyes dart to mine, unsettling me with their focus, and then she laughs a bit more.

It unnerves the sergeant so much he pulls the dagger down a bit, but that doesn't make me feel any better. Men like him would rather be wounded than laughed at. I'm debating whether I'll have to tackle the sergeant to keep him from killing her when the ground starts to shake, sending us tumbling to the floor. A split second later all the lights wink out.

The girl continues laughing. "It is the goddess. The winds are changing."

One of the other soldiers gets a flare going, bathing the shrinking cave in orange light as he leads the way to the opening.

"The cave is collapsing!" he shouts. "Everybody out."

We all run, with me pulling up the rear, and I realize that the girl is down there, her hands and feet still tied.

"What about the girl?" I shout as we run.

"She's the enemy, newbie. Let her figure it out."

Maybe she knows some way out of here that we don't, but just in case she doesn't, I do the only right thing, hoping no one sees me, hoping it's enough. Then I full-out sprint to the exit, squeezing through the hole just as a boulder shifts and closes the opening completely.

We barely make it out before the entire cave system shudders and collapses, shaking the ground for miles.

We ride in silence, our mission failed, but I'm glad to have time to think about what the girl called me. *Lover boy.* Where have I heard that before?

30
TAMAR

THE ALARM RIPS THROUGH MY EARBUDS AND CUTS OFF the constant waves I need to sleep. I can't tell if it's a drill or the real thing, and I bump my head on the top of my bunk when I bolt upright. The knot is rising on my forehead; I'm sure it'll easily rival the size of a golf ball by the afternoon. I'm a little unsteady on my feet because of it, but this isn't my first drill. The lights have been dimmed to emergency levels so that all residual power can be diverted to life support and the exit ramps. I grab my go bag from the corner of the bunk, a uniform shirt from the shelf, and jump into my boots. I let them tighten on my way out the door. I run into Sil in the hallway.

"Drill?" she pants. She's hopping on one foot as she tries to get her boots on. She's still in her underwear, a uni shirt and what look like gym shorts slung over her shoulder.

"I don't know. It might be the real thing," I say as quietly as I can, hoping that I'm not right.

A twinge of panic rises in my chest as we both run, nearly tripping over each other to fully dress. It could be an attack or a full biodome collapse. I pull off my bonnet and stick it in my pocket, grateful that I decided to rebraid my hair last night.

"Look at you with the big reveal," Sil teases, a little out of breath.

"I knew that linguistics kid got to you. I saw you guys talking. Fate will turn you into a romantic yet."

"Whatever. One must be well turned out for the end of the world," I joke as we run. My head pounds, and the more I run the less convinced I am that this is just a drill. When we make it outside, it looks like an anthill has been kicked over. The world is scrambling.

"Evacuate, calmly. This is not a drill." A disembodied voice crackles through my comm. I slide my finger along the bone behind my ear to increase the volume, but it doesn't really help. I'm still healing, so it doesn't work as well as it should just yet. Brain procedures are delicate. You can't rush the recovery. "Move quickly and calmly to your designated evacuation site. I repeat, this is not a drill."

A great boom reverberates around us, and the ground shakes violently for almost five full seconds. We watch in horror as the general classroom building collapses.

"Jesus, this *is* real." Sil coughs. Dust and debris kick up into the air from the destruction.

"Shit! The doll. I gotta go back!"

Sil grabs my arm. "Are you crazy? We gotta get out of here."

I shake my head. "I can't be the one who lost it. I'll be out in a minute. Don't wait for me."

I pull my arm free and run back inside; the sound of Sil screaming my name pelts me as I run through the corridor. My room's on level one, so it's not far. I'm fast, and even in the dark I know exactly where it is: an arm's length above the sink, which is two steps from the door. Two turns and a thirty-second jog and I'm there. I grab the doll and an external account card just in case—if we get dropped on a colony with less than favorable refugee considerations, I'll have a few credits to live on. The sound of my boots echoes in the empty hallways as I make my way back out the same way I came, but another boom rocks the building and throws me to the floor.

This time the alarm kicks out for a minute, and an eerie silence fills the corridors. I'm plunged into darkness, but I jump up and keep moving. It'll take a minute or two for the generators to kick in, and I might not have that. I can't risk being caught in a building if the ground collapses. I won't know for sure if it's an aerial attack until I get outside. I take a deep breath in and get my bearings. I have to turn around to find another exit, but all the buildings are symmetrical, and an exit on one end has to have a twin exit on the opposite side. This time I move a bit slower because of unfamiliarity, but I'm still able to make it out. The trip, the fall, and the exit take all of two minutes, but those two minutes save my life.

It's gone. The building, the spot where I left Sil, my bunk, all of it. Wailing, sirens, the boom, crackle, and crash of metal on concrete, rock against soil, all crumbling, fill my ears.

I buckle myself into the right side of the escape pod, fingers trembling, tears streaming down my face. The escape drill is the first thing recruits are taught when they arrive at a new base. Tucked into the median of each road, the pods look like architectural flair with a curved awning here or an adjacent bench there to hide their functionality. Light panels cover most of the outside shell of every pod: bright yellow for singles, and vivid green for doubles. I'm so disoriented by the time I make it to the nearest pod station that only doubles are left.

There's a boy already inside. His hair is full of fine dust that covers him from head to foot. A trickle of blood and sweat easing from his forehead cuts through the dryness like a river. He's smiling, though his chest is still heaving as he gathers his breath.

Fayard.

"Tamar!" he gasps in surprise. He must have run here too. "Sinkhole?"

Of course it was a sinkhole. It left behind a crater so deep I knew it was futile to try to assist with any rescue efforts. I watched it swallow everything in the quadrant, just a couple of hundred feet to the left of me, including Sil and all my classmates as they were making their escape. My chest hurts. It's an old ache, not from the running or from the ash in the air, but from loss. Sil was my friend, one of my only friends. Space is vast—it swallows you up without regard for your dreams or hurts. Some people like that feeling of being part of such a large whole. Right now, it just makes me feel insignificant, and like Sil was insignificant too. My heartbeat won't slow down even though I've stopped running. I know that I'm safe now, but knowing and feeling are two different things.

"All that damn drilling!" he yells, and I nod. Thousands of drones are now hovering above the sinkhole, diving in and out of the dust gap. Some come up with an officer or recruit twisting like a caught fish, but too often the bodies aren't moving at all.

This is supposed to be a drilling accident? Engineers would have checked and rechecked for that kind of thing. Not to mention the alarm systems set up for evacuation. No, this feels more like an attack. I purse my lips.

"Why are you yelling?" I say as I look him over. "No . . . don't. It's y-your . . . ears. They're bleeding," I shout, realizing I'm doing the exact same thing.

He puts his hands to his ears as if this is the first time he's noticed the blood.

"Got a tissue?" he asks.

I pull my silk hair bonnet out of my cargo pocket and hand it to him.

"*Merci*," he says, loud and bright. "I got caught just outside the quadrant when the building came down. Good thing the linguistics department is on the outer edge. If I'd been in engineering, I wouldn't be here right now."

His accent is thick. It's got a rhythm to it like the Kreole spoken on the outer colonies. I didn't notice it out in the canyon.

"Can you please stop talking? My friend just died and . . ."

My voice snags in my throat.

"I'm sorry. I talk when I'm anxious. This is a lot for the first week of school. I've never been caught in a sink before," he says, trying to keep his voice steady; he taps the inside of his forearm a few times. I wonder if he's gotten an anxiety patch installed. I know a few kids who swear by them. I decide to soften a bit.

"It's fine. Sorry. Talk," I say, feeling bad for snapping at him.

The air is snatched from the pod as the countdown begins, and the pressure from the ascent makes my ears pop. My muscles are screaming and my eyes are watering from the pounding in my head, but I'm in one piece. All my senses can be accounted for. I don't know if he can say the same. A part of me wants to offer him my first-aid kit, and another part of me wonders if I should keep my multitool in hand, just in case he gets . . . however some people get during bad times.

"Are you okay?" I ask, softer this time.

Fayard smiles as he points to my uniform. "I can't hear you too well, but it's pretty easy to read your lips. You've got a pretty mouth, 675."

The pod rattles. Is he flirting with me?

I look down at my uniform and shrug. I don't get it.

"675," he says, and I look to see my serial number stitched right above my name. He points to his. "I'm 712."

He's the guy who knocked me out! The biosuits covered our ID numbers at the canyon. He continues to smile and puts up his fists in slow motion. Sil's voice echoes in my brain: *There are no coincidences.*

"My apologies," he says.

"No need," I reply, and take a good look at him without his helmet on. Sil said he was handsome, and as he takes a cloth from his go bag, I can see what she meant. Even covered in dust he's got a warmth to his smile, long wet lashes, and full lips that have a hard time frowning. His face seems more familiar than it should; maybe we met before on another colony? No. It doesn't matter, though. I don't want to talk about the fight. I don't want to talk at all.

"Can I see?" he asks, pointing at something on my right.

I look down at the doll. The sealed case is cracked and the panels are covered in dust, but I can tell that it's still fine inside. I saved it. And it saved me.

I shake my head. "No," I say softly. "It's very old."

"That's fine. Not yet, then," he says patiently.

For some reason this makes me smile, because now I know he's crazy. Crazy I can handle.

"Prepare for cryosleep in T minus thirty seconds," the pod announces. I settle back and take off my boots, nestling the doll in between. My stomach lurches as the pod rises. I hate cryosleep. I always have these vivid, nonsensical dreams. 712 stares at me, the same goofy look on his face.

"Oh, right," I murmur to myself. "Ears." I point to the ceiling and mouth slowly, and with real exaggeration, *CRYO SLEEP. THIRTY—WELL, TWENTY SECONDS.*

"Oh! Cryo is the worst. It gives me nightmares. Okay. Well, I'm glad you made it. I guess fate has brought you to me."

"What?"

"I said fate. She brought you here. Don't you believe in fate?"

My eyes fall to the sankofa medallion on his chain. He's a zealot. Great.

"I-I . . . my best friend does." *Did.* She *did* believe. I swallow hard.

He grabs both my hands in his.

"We're going to be okay," he says, a fervor in his grip and in his gaze.

I want to believe him. God, I really want to believe him.

31

Columbia, South Carolina, Present Day

TAMAR

DON'T HATE THIS. HAVING FAY HERE IS EXACTLY WHAT I
wanted, even though I wouldn't let him know that. He makes
everything seem like it will be okay. I don't think I've admitted that
to myself until just now. I kept that gospel tucked away, because it
would mean all those things I never said out loud were true: that I
love him, that I need him. That those fairy tales where the prince
sweeps the princess off into a happily ever after weren't bullshit.
Aabidah's right. He makes me want to stay—stay and fight.

"Give me your foot."

"Why?" I ask as I lean back on the cushioned bench in the sky
lounge. It's quiet with just a few businesspeople holed up in separate corners of the place, their heads glued to phones or pinned
to computers. Fay and I are the youngest people here by at least
twenty years, but Fay worked his magic. He's leaning back against
the wall opposite me in the one booth that isn't visible from the
attendant at the bar.

"I want to touch you."

I suck in a tiny breath of surprise and Fay laughs.

"Not like that—well, I do . . . but . . . not right *now*."

"Not like this, anyway," I say quietly, and adjust my oxygen line,
feeling too on display all of a sudden.

"Shut up. You being wild disrespectful to my generous offer," he jokes.

He slips off my sandal and cradles my heel in his lap and begins to rub all the kinks out of my arch.

"That feels good."

"I know. I am a champion foot massager. And before you get started, it's 'cause of my mom. She works long hours. I rub her feet for her."

"I wasn't going to start," I say, warring with myself to decide whether to apologize or confess. Is it pride I'm fighting? Embarrassment? What am I afraid of?

"What's wrong?" he asks.

"I wish we'd . . . you know," I say, and raise my eyebrows.

"I know what?" he asks.

"You know. That night at Renata Tripp's pool party last summer. Everybody was downstairs, and we went to the basement to dry off and talk, and we started kissing and . . . I should have. We could have—"

Fay holds up his hand to stop me.

"No, we shouldn't have."

I freeze as a bolt of embarrassment rises in my belly. I thought. . . I'm not sure what I thought, but . . .

"Relax, that's not what I mean. What I mean is yes, I wanted to do *that* with you that night too, but I'm glad we didn't because that's not how I wanted it to be with you—in Renata's unfinished basement on some moldy-ass towels while ESPN played old highlights in the background? Trying to do it quick so we wouldn't get caught? Nah. If you had told me you were ready, I would have tried a lot harder. We both deserve better than that."

I nod tightly, unable to meet his gaze while I sit with all my regrets. He slides my sandal back on and picks up the other foot. The warmth of his hands is a cross between a cozy blanket on a cold night and that feeling of complete peace when you float in a pool on the first day of summer. I let myself drink it in and consume me for just a minute. I'll give myself that little bit because I deserve it. Even death-row inmates get a final meal.

"I was going to propose," he says quietly.

"What? Why would you?" I sputter.

He shrugs. "You know I like to make things . . ."

"Big," I finish.

I don't know why it's those words that start the tears. I didn't even cry at Mama's homegoing. Maybe I was more prepared for that than this. Family love is different from romantic love. You expect it and demand it in some ways. It's supposed to be unconditional, and you don't have to do anything to get it.

The attendant walks by and smiles hard at Fay on her way to some back room. She's got lustrous hair that shines even under fluorescent lights. Her matching shorts set hugs every curve, and her makeup is perfect. She doesn't even try to act respectful with her reckless eyeballing and juicy-lipped smile. Fay doesn't even know she exists, but I can't keep my eyes off her. I must look like a charity case. I might as well be the poster child for the March of Dimes with Fay's beautiful ass as my last wish.

I pull away from him. His touch is too hot on my skin right now. I suddenly feel ridiculous sitting here together. "It's because I'm sick."

"You're out of your mind if you think that's true," he says.

"You have to see all this. I'm sitting here attached to an oxygen tank. I've lost fifty pounds and gone down two dress sizes. I've got tubes snaking out of my nose and—"

"And I don't care. You could lose another fifty pounds or gain a hundred. I don't give a—"

"How can I believe you're so sure about me, Fay, when you aren't sure about anything else? How can you be all in with me when I'm like this?" I hold up my hand. "Don't answer that. I know how. It's because this tank and this disease make it temporary. You can play pretend forever without it having to be real."

"You're scared."

"Of course I am."

"Not of the disease. You're scared of me and scared of yourself when you're with me. You did this at the dance. At your mama's funeral when you left in the middle of the service to make sure the house was clean and ready for the folks afterward. Even before you got sick and DeAndre had that kickback on that half day and you kissed me for the first time. You kissed me and, hand to Christ, I thought I was gonna pass out. You left right after. You don't like to feel anything."

"Are you a psychologist or something? Who are you to . . ."

But he's right. I don't like to feel, 'cause when I do it runs so deep that it feels like I'm drowning in emotion. I never even agreed to be his girlfriend. We never had the conversation, and I was glad because I didn't want to risk him saying it wasn't true. We just became us, a unit.

He looks at me with so much love, it makes me want to get

up and run so far my heart won't catch me, but there is nowhere to run. Wherever you go, your heart's still there, still beating and waiting to break.

His watch beeps and I know time's up. We sit there in the moment, until his hand slides from my foot to my calf and up to my thigh as he scoots closer.

I can taste his tears when his lips meet mine.

Ahem.

We break, avoiding the attendant's reproachful stare, and walk slowly back to my gate. I'm searching for something profound to say, any words that will make this feel less like a goodbye and more like an intermission, but then there's an outbreak of sound, like gunshots in the air, and everyone screams. My heart leaps into my throat and Fay grabs me around my waist just as an alarm starts to wail.

For a full minute there is absolute terror, until someone yells that it's fireworks going off outside and I can breathe again. At least, I try to breathe again, but I can't.

"Tamar?"

My hands claw at my throat. I twist my oxygen up to full blast, but I can't take in any air.

"Tamar!"

Fay lays me on my back. There's a crowd, but all I see is his face. All I feel are his hands cradling my head. Maybe I always knew I wasn't going to make that flight.

"Help is coming, Tamar. I'm going to fix it. Just stay here. Stay with me! Don't close your eyes. Stay with me. Stay with me," he pleads; his eyes bore into mine before he lifts his head to the sky, his lips moving in prayer.

32

TAMAR

T HE CALL TO PRAYER RINGS OUT ACROSS THE CITY. I open my eyes and I run. My robes threaten to trip me as I try to catch my breath; I stop just in time to gather them. It is a mistake. His legs are longer, and his stamina far outweighs mine, or a gift of his military training. I am no match for him, and I can do nothing when he wraps me in his arms.

He found the honey stall and gifted me with dates the likes of which I'd never tasted before. The next day it was an ivory comb from Timbuktu. I hid it inside my sleeping mat and dreamed of him. Each day he brings a new gift. Each day a new adventure, a sweet reprieve. We melt into the shadows and soften where life has made us hard. This is a respite made sweeter because I know it won't last, these stolen moments, an hour here, an unnecessarily long errand there. I've told him every secret except the ones that matter the most, and I don't let the knowledge that I can't have this forever cool the warmth of his embrace.

He tastes of salt and the spice of good meat and raisins. He tastes of wealth, much more than a simple soldier can acquire. He too has secrets. I break the kiss, stare into his eyes, and search for the truth. I decide that I do not want to know.

I turn and run, faster now. He will not chase me much longer.

. . .

Hours later my lips still burn with the memory of him as I pray with my mistress, Iyin.

"What is this smile, Tamar?" she asks. "Afternoon prayers rarely make you this happy."

I wipe the smile from my face as I roll up my mat in the common room. I gather her much more intricately woven mat as well and place both in a basket in the corner. Weak light spills in from the window, along with the smells from the cooking fires in this corner of the city, as we make our way to her room.

I can hear the calls for the last ferry of the day across the river and feel the tension that can only come from so many people pushed into one place. But there is joy in the frustration as well. There is so much life before the rains come, so many people bustling about, things I never get to taste for myself. I wonder where my soldier is now, what preparations he must make before he is gone again, what—

"Tamar?" Iyin chuckles.

She is thin, with skin the color of pale copper and soft eyes that weep too easily, but beautiful nonetheless. We are the same age. She should be married by now, but none of the acceptable men from good families will have her. Despite her beauty she is fragile, with a cough that shakes her entire body and leaves her covered in sweat. Her monthlies are but a trickle if they come at all, and some days it is all she can do to sip a bit of broth. She was born too early, and the midwife insists that each day is a gift her father should be grateful for, but he is too stubborn to accept the finality of good wisdom and instead prefers to pay money we don't have for doctors who give her a more favorable diagnosis. Childbirth will surely kill her. Still, her father exhausts himself as he looks for a suitor, even if he must go looking among the enemy.

"I am happy for you, *sayida*. Tonight you may meet your husband, *inshallah*," I reply, not answering her question.

She laughs, a weak and wispy sound that would be pretty if it weren't so faint.

"*Inshallah.*"

She's done this before. Yet another introduction. We are weary with it. The preparations, the costly feast. Music. An exchange of gifts. And, after a night of fearful anticipation, rejection.

Iyin looks at me with those fierce eyes, as if she's about to tell me something, and then she's overcome with a cough. The first one rattles like bones spinning at the bottom of a cauldron. More follow, and it is as horrible as it has ever been. I serve her the midwife's tea with the lemon honey she prefers. It helps, but not enough.

"I will not make it through dinner with the amir," she wheezes after a few tentative sips.

"Of course you will."

She shakes her head, a few tears leaking out of her eyes. "I grow tired of this. I detest the pageantry, as if I am a prized cow, up for the highest bidder. Except no one is willing to bid."

She laughs mirthlessly and takes another sip of tea. It helps the cough but also soothes her nerves. I find a small cushion and slip off her sandals so that I can massage her feet. Her eyes close in bliss as I rub shea-nut butter into her arches.

"Sometimes I envy you."

I blink in shock, unable to understand her meaning. When we

were much younger, she would sometimes play cruel tricks on me, compel me to answer riddles that would put my ignorance on display, but she hasn't done that in years. Still, the urge to distrust her is there.

"Why?" I ask tentatively. I am a slave, even though she no longer likes me to remind her of that.

She shakes her head and manages a real smile this time. "You think I don't know when you slip out of here on your little adventures? How you wear my wraps and pretend you are not who you are?"

My instinct is to deny it, but to add lying to my list of sins would be too much. I remain silent, head down, unable to lift my eyes to hers. Even if we are the same age, even if we have grown up together—closer than any pair of sisters—she is still the mistress of the house. It is a wall between us that keeps us apart, a wall that gets thicker with each year and more impossible to scale.

She waves a hand at me like she's shooing a fly before taking another sip of her tea. "Do not worry. Your secret is safe. Jealousy burned within me after I discovered your deception, but I had to be honest with myself. We must all take our joys where and when we can. I would do the same if I could."

"How did you find out?" I ask, hoping this question won't put her over the edge.

"One of Father's spies. A candlemaker in the market. You are kind to him, so he told me instead of Father. He is duty-bound to report, but he guessed I would be more lenient with you."

"I must thank him," I say quickly.

"No," she says sternly. "Do not remind him of his disobedience."

I nod, and my face heats with humiliation. I am not as clever as I thought myself to be.

"What is his name?" she asks.

"Who?" I say, trying to feign ignorance.

"The soldier. What is his name?"

And just like that, my humiliation is multiplied. How can I tell her that I do not know? How can I say that we speak of dreams instead of the cruelty of our reality, our attraction as natural and necessary as a thirsty man's pull toward water? I cannot admit that it was her name that crossed my lips when he asked.

She laughs that wheezing laugh again and my heart pains for her. "Tamar, do not worry yourself. I overstep. I wish so much to be free of these shackles and find my own adventure and joys. Does he know who you are?" she asks lightly.

I shake my head. I can't believe how well she is taking this. Perhaps her condition is wearing on her more than I've realized, leaving her little energy to care.

"We speak in his home tongue. To him I am a merchant's daughter playing a dangerous game, but nothing more," I say. He probably prides himself on his conquest. From his clothing, his status is no higher than mine, but his hands are smooth. Every truth he has told me could be a lie, not that it matters.

"I guess those shared lessons paid off. You have always had a regal bearing. It represents us well in the community. But these meetings will have to stop. If you dishonor this house, please know that Father will not hesitate to make an example of you. He will have no choice. Our family name must remain unstained," she says, her voice cold.

"Yes, *sayida*."

I am not new to my position so my face betrays none of the pain, but my heart beats wildly in my chest. She has saved my life. Did I know that I was risking it at all? Yes, and I did so with reckless abandon. I made the wrong choice, but that doesn't mean I did not enjoy it. I knew the day would come when I would give him up, when I would discard him like the few others and recommit myself to God's will, but something about him has made me want more. Too much more. I lock eyes with Iyin and see pity on the surface, but, like mold on once-fresh fruit, there's jealousy around the edges.

"I apologize for my shamelessness," I say softly.

She doesn't reply. She is lost in her own thoughts.

Light from the lanterns dances along the walls as I help Iyin dress in her rooms. Her grand boubou is made of the finest Yemeni silk, the color of fresh dates; a cinnamon-tinged purple is woven throughout, with gold thread and tiny gold rings. I nearly drool at its magnificence as I help her tie the matching wrapper that will flow out from underneath the garment. The wide sleeves make each flick of her wrist the answer to a question you didn't know you'd asked, and the billowy cut hides her skeletal frame.

A bell rings from the courtyard.

"They are here," she sighs.

"Do not be nervous, *sayida*. You have been here before," I say, trying my best to encourage her despite my own belief in the futility of the endeavor.

"That is what I am afraid of. The new taxes are cutting Father's profits to the bone. He has no sons, and he is not as respected as he tells himself he is. I do not know why this amir has accepted his invitation. I must wonder what he is really out to gain," she says skeptically.

"The legend of your beauty," I reply in my best imitation of her father.

"Father's words sound strange in your mouth. Do not taste them again," she snaps as her mood shifts from anxious to frustrated in the fraction of a second.

"Of course, *sayida*."

"Leave me," she says without looking in my direction.

I am in no place to argue with her when she is like this. Her father is a snake, and there isn't a man, woman, or child in the market who does not know it. I try to shake off the bad energy before I make it into the kitchen.

"*Mihofnima*, Binta," I say to the cook.

The Fulani woman grunts, sweat pouring down her face and arms. She has been cooking nonstop for days.

"They are here already. Did you know that? The griot has already begun *The Epic of Sunjata*. Do you know what that does to my timeline, oh?"

She isn't really talking to me, just venting. She's had to do most of the preparations herself, when two years ago she would have had a staff of five or more.

"If he is skilled it will be quite a long time before he is finished," I say.

"And then they will be ravenous, devouring every bite of my creations in seconds flat. What have I done to deserve this, eh? And why haven't the rains come and driven this heat away? Sira! Fan!"

Sira, the youngest of the house girls, jumps at the sound of her name and struggles to effectively handle the imported bamboo fan, Binta's pride and joy. The thing is nearly half the girl's size and only serves to move the hot air around. I shake my head and try to hide my smile.

"Don't delight in the misery of others, little girl," Binta admonishes, and then turns to look at me, mischief in her eyes. "Have you practiced at all while you were out with your soldier?"

"Does everyone know?" I say in shock.

She chuckles. "We were all young once, and there are no secrets in this house. Get your kora. You will play tonight."

Deep breaths. I draw the air into my lungs and marvel at the aromas wafting from the feast. Yusuf Ibn Mustafa, Iyin's father, has outdone himself. The house has been stretched thin in the last two years, so there have been no feasts or cause for celebration, but when Mansa Musa arrived with a caravan of twelve thousand slave women, three hundred camels, and enough gold to put the sparkle back in the eyes of every hustler in the market, it put a dance in everyone's step. My head swims with the scents of ginger, hot pepper soup, fufu, and fante kenkey. I send a silent prayer that I play so horribly the entire party will retire early and allow me to gorge myself on their leavings. I can almost taste Binta's jinjinbere washing down everything, the hints of lemon and sugar from the sweet drink lingering on my tongue for hours afterward as we wait, inevitably, for Iyin's formal rejection.

Voices drift into the hallway while I delay interrupting the conversation for as long as I can. I don't like to draw attention to myself, and in these lean times a pretty slave girl with a talent for playing the kora might be just the souvenir this amir has a taste for. I've always had a gift for music, and in more prosperous times it was quite fashionable to purchase lessons for the house staff.

I should be grateful. Sayid Mustafah is many things, but I can say he has never looked at me with lust in his eyes; in that I have been blessed. I was purchased when I was only four years old, to be a companion for Iyin. I don't even remember my parents, whether I was loved and then sold to save me from a harsher fate, or if I was a burden, the last in a long line of unwanted children. When I was younger, I dreamed that my fate was all a mistake. I prayed that my real mother would come to the door looking for me or, better yet, see me in the market and recognize me as her own so that I wouldn't have to deal with the awkward explanation that I was never really a slave at all, but a lost nobleman's daughter. The fantasies were fun for a while, but as I grew older, they brought me more sorrow than joy, so I gave them up. Now I don't live in daydreams. My joys come with each present moment, singular temporary delights.

Laughter rolls in waves on the back of perfumed smoke, and a twinge of familiarity unnerves me. I hover closer to the door but stay out of sight.

"You must excuse my nephew. He spends all his days at the local madrassa. Since we arrived, I have not laid eyes on him for more than a few minutes."

The man's rich tenor booms out over the few guests in attendance. It commands attention to his clipped Arabic, betraying that the language is his second or maybe even third. Although the accent is one I have heard before.

"Fayid, I admire your dedication to the faith. If Iyin had been born a boy, she would have surely followed the same path, maybe even to the famed Sankore Mosque to study. It is such a blessing to have a future mullah in our presence," Sayid Mustafah says, his voice effusive. He is used to giving praise in a way that seduces men from their money.

"*Inshallah! Inshallah!* Have you ever traveled to Timbuktu to visit the mosque? It is magnificent," the amir says.

"Sadly, no, but my daughter has had premonitions of marrying into a traveling family, so there is an incentive. Her grandmother was also gifted in this way, so we shall see," Sayid Mustafa says.

They all laugh.

"I guess that is my cue," Iyin whispers. I nearly jump out of my skin. I didn't hear her walk up behind me. "Play me to my cushion?" she says quickly, and busies herself with straightening nonexistent wrinkles and ridding herself of invisible dust.

I nod and walk stiffly to a stool that has been placed in the center of the room. My eyes stay downcast as I begin to pluck the strings of the kora. Its long wooden neck reaches far past my shoulders, but I have slender fingers, and the wide body of the gourd that makes up the instrument fits perfectly between my legs. The men fall silent as I play, and I close my eyes as I let the notes create a cloud for Iyin to float on. I float too, allowing myself to be buoyed up beyond this place to an oasis where I am bound by nothing. The music settles my nerves. My heart beats to its rhythm, letting the melody erupt from deep within me, root me to the spot where I can tell the world who I am without opening my mouth. I feel their eyes, but I don't care. I am my truest self right now, and for the fleetest of moments, I wish there were someone else here to witness it—someone I actually want to bare this side of myself to—but it is a silly desire.

When I am done, the small audience explodes in applause. I open my eyes and offer them a rare smile, a smile that I root firmly in place to hide my shock. I make certain to lock it there and back slowly out of the room.

He stands front and center, his confusion plain, in finery that eclipses anything Sayid Mustafah owns.

Fayid, the amir's nephew and honored guest, is my soldier.

33
TAMAR

THE NEXT MORNING HE IS THERE, MORE BEAUTIFUL IN the full light of day than he has ever been in the cover of the darkened market stalls. He is dressed in a jewel-toned djellaba; the loose-fitting robe flows down to his ankles like the river on a calm day and mimics the inky blue of a cloudless sky turning into night. When I knew him as a soldier, I believed that his confidence was born from practiced invincibility, or an assumption that he could defend me against any attacker. But there was always a kernel of doubt: his smooth, callus-free hands, his love for poetry. It hinted at something more. Now I see it for what it truly is: the sickly-sweet stench of extreme wealth and the power that comes with it.

Beauty is deceiving anyway. They say I am beautiful, and what has it gotten me?

Binta leads the betrothed into the main room and presses herself into the corner as chaperone and spy. She pretends to shell peanuts as she listens. I sit opposite Fayid, too outraged for pretense.

"As-salaam 'alaykum," he says as I enter the room.

"Wa'alaykum salaam," I say, chafing at the formality. Is this the same carefree boy who fed me dates in an abandoned river stall? Which one is real, this prince or the kind pauper I grew to care for?

"Sayid Mustafa sent word that he has discussed my proposal with you."

I nod. "I would like the opportunity to speak truthfully," I say, unable to hold my feelings in any longer.

"*Now* you would like to speak truthfully? It seems quite late in the day to start there," he replies. He looks a bit taken aback but then relaxes in his chair, letting his long legs fall out a bit wider. A small curve of his lip hints at an irritated smile. Here is my soldier, not the nobleman courting Iyin at the door. "You let me think you were a merchant's daughter," he says.

"I told you, plainly, I was a slave," I reply, knowing full well I wasn't believed.

"How could I have known? You—"

"You saw what you wanted to see, and then you lied in turn," I finish, tired of this game of deception.

His fist clenches but he doesn't deny it.

I swallow deep, trying my best to hold back my indignation and replace the tide with something that feels more like courage. "Sayid Mustafah has informed me that I am to be a concubine, serving my master as a servant as she serves you as your wife. Congratulations on finding such a wife. You have reached high. You are blessed indeed," I say, void of any emotion.

I stare defiantly at him, waiting for him to deny how advantageous his choice of wife is to a man of his standing. This is a strategic step for him, a noble name to add to his military connection. A lineage to attach himself to in this region. Maybe if we'd talked more than felt, I would have guessed at how adept he was at politics.

"Marriage is not so simple," he says, a hint of annoyance lacing his words.

I grip my arms tighter, willing myself to stay calm. Bile rises in my throat, and I swallow the acid back, grateful for the reminder that fate is not my friend.

"Tamar, you cannot be so stubborn. I have done what I can," he says, his voice breaking. "I asked for your hand. It will always be known that you were first in my heart." He leans closer, his voice dropping in pitch for my benefit. "You will always be first in my home."

"But not in name," I croak.

He leans even closer, but with less softness. His other side shines now, the man with a title, the kind of person who is used to getting what he wants without interference. But I will not make my own subjugation easy for him or anyone else.

"Do you remember the first time you touched my hand? I had been following you again, waiting for a moment where we could talk without being seen. You purchased a fish from a stall and plunged your hands into a pot of cool water to rinse them. I found some reason to rinse my hands as well, and your fingers slid across mine. I lost my ability to speak after you touched me."

He laughs at his own story, and I hate myself for thinking how beautiful he is when he is laughing. "You pluck a string in my chest that I can't stop from vibrating. Every night I dream of you. Nonsensical dreams that say that I am meant to be with you," he whispers. He settles back onto his stool and winces as he rubs the leg he favors when he walks. If I'd paid more attention, I would have known he wasn't a soldier by that fact alone.

"Dreams are not reality. You know nothing of what it is to be a woman or to serve." My voice strains under the weight of his betrayal.

"It is your service that makes you strong. Very few women enter the market alone, bold in their pursuit of the things they need. They allow expectations and fear to cow them, but not you. It is your strength that I admire most."

I don't always want to be strong. It is a mask I hide behind. But I put on the mask now, and for a moment I imagine again what this new life might be like. Fayid takes this opportunity to make his plea.

"Tamar, I may not be able to lay the moon at your feet, but please allow me to give you the stars."

34

TAMAR

S TARS. TWISTING, BURNING SWIRLS OF COMETS. GALAXIES, supernovas, moons behind my eyes. It's peaceful here. I want to stay here in the quiet. Floating.

Someone's shaking me, but I can't tell who; my eyes feel like they're sewn shut. Thick and impossibly strong fingers grip my jaw and shove something long and spindly down my throat. I thrash. I can't breathe. Oh God! I can't breathe. My arms are like lead, but I will them to move and try to pull the thing from my throat. The hands are too strong. I struggle to yell, but I don't have air. I'm using everything I have to shift the weight off, but I don't have enough to get going. Awareness gives way to blackness.

"Vital signs. Stable. Private Tamar Blanchard. Age eighteen. Weight: seventy-five kilograms. Height: one-point-seven meters. Blood type . . ."

I draw in a deep breath and jerk upright. The stars are laid out above me, and up ahead I see nothing but endless fields of dimly lit kinograss, cerulean and glowing, no higher than my elbow if I stick my arm straight up. It's been harvested recently. The same twin moons I've seen every night for the last twelve weeks greet me from the sky. We're still here. Fully exposed. Not on base, or in the rescue pod, but still on the class IV planet where a sinkhole just . . . A tiny jolt of panic squeezes my heart. How long have I been out?

"It's okay," a male voice says.

I run my fingers across my face, or at least I try to. I'm in a biosuit. When did I put on a biosuit? I take a deep breath, letting myself get used to the feeling of the oxygen tube down my throat.

"It's okay," the voice says again, but I don't hear it; it's in my head. I jump backward as if I've been stung.

A guy squats in front of me. 712. "Fayard."

Fay. Call me Fay. I'm sorry. I had to set up a telelink. You weren't breathing well, and I wouldn't be able to hear you, so I thought this would be better, he says without moving his lips, though I can hear him just fine.

"But my chip blocks teleware," I say.

I don't like people in my head. I've heard horror stories. Sometimes people forget who they are or start to believe that God is talking to them when it's just the enemy hacking into their feed. I slide my hands over my body, taking an irrational account to make sure everything is still there. I glide my hand across my hips and groan. He would have had to take off my pants to get me into the suit.

I was training in counterintelligence. There are few things I can't get around, he says.

"You're a spy," I say accusingly.

I didn't say that. I'm a linguist, but we are military. Every person has a gift that can be a curse to someone else, he adds.

We sit in silence as the wind moves the grass in that eerie way that it does on this rock.

"Our pod crashed?" I ask, surprised. It takes a strong force for these pods to falter.

He nods.

Must have happened right after the cryosleep kicked in. I woke up just in time to see a thousand escape pods fall to the ground like some kind of hellish hailstorm. Some burned up in the atmosphere; others cracked open like eggs as soon as they hit land. I was able to switch the autopilot to manual and get us down before we met the same fate.

My "thanks" die in my throat. "How long have I been out?"

A few hours. I tried to wake you, but the disorientation had you. You fought like a demon when I tried to get you in the biosuit. I thought you might not make it, he says, his eyes filled with worry.

I dip my head, a poor excuse for gratitude, but it will have to do. I swallow, and the tube grates against my esophagus. I slide my finger across my wrist to access my controls and disable the breathing mechanism. The ropelike straw retracts and forces me to hack spit and phlegm into my suit for a full minute before I feel normal again.

Sorry about that. I couldn't hear your vitals breakdown with the damage to your chip, and I didn't want to take any chances. It's hard to tell if someone is breathing through the suit.

"It's fine. I'll be fine. Where's the pod?" I ask, looking around.

The pod is gone, he says.

"What?" Instinctively, I duck lower and peer into the distance, wondering if we've been seen.

We're in rebel territory. I mixed up a dissolving agent as soon as we were both in the suits, he says, trying to reassure me.

I can see my eyes reflected in his, and I jump to my feet with awkward and frantic speed. It takes considerable effort to take even a few steps. The gravity on this planet is hard to acclimate to, now that we're no longer in a biodome, and we've both still got the effects of cryosleep to shake off.

Slow down. It's right here, he says, already knowing what I'm looking for.

Fay points to two small bags at his feet: one I've never seen before, and the other, mine. I rush over, as much as I can, and peer inside. The doll is intact. My body is whole. I realize that I owe Fayard everything, but there's something that keeps me from the shower of gratitude my mama's manners are begging me to give him.

"Can you hear my internal thoughts?" I ask, fully aware of his eyes on me.

Only if you would like me to. I didn't install that kind of programming.

"But you could if you wanted to," I reply, not sure if I entirely believe him.

I stand and throw one bag over my shoulder and hand him the other. *Where are you going?* he asks.

"To find somewhere to bed down. We can't stay out here. Storm's coming."

He looks up at the sky as if he's searching for something.

I've never seen a sky so clear, he observes.

"That's how you know it's about to hit," I say. "Haven't you ever been out in the field?"

Of course, he says, all defensive. *But intelligence training is not the same as what they teach in combat units. Our agents don't go out into the field unless they are fully prepared for all scenarios. It takes years.*

I roll my eyes. This guy saved my life, that's true, but damn it if I feel like babysitting a newb in enemy territory. Although he did dissolve the pod, so maybe he's not completely useless.

I turn to face him and walk backward. It's important to always keep your eyes on your team in the field, especially when your senses are muted in the suit.

"Beta-Sueron is notorious for its storms, so we're going to need to find some shelter. If that's the field bag from the pod, there should be a transmitter in there, but once the storm gets going, it won't matter if it works or not. Nothing will be able to get in or out, and that's if the rebels don't use it to track us and kill us before we can be rescued," I say, feeling like I'm back to my old self.

He smiles and my stomach flutters. I thought he was flirting before, but this smile is different. This one has intention in it or maybe even a promise. It makes me uneasy. I turn around and start to move a bit faster.

"How long have you been on base?" I ask.

I was late. My transfer didn't go through properly, so I got in a few days before our fight.

"That was a week ago. Field training takes a month. You don't . . . you don't know anything about Suerone do you?" I say.

I read the in-flight magazine, if that's what you're asking, he says smugly.

"Do people think you're funny?" I ask.

Some do, but I take it that this is not the time for funny, he says, and tries to put on a more serious face.

This guy annoys me. "If the storm doesn't kill us, or the rebels don't kill us, we still have to survive the night chill," I reply.

He doesn't say anything, but I can hear his next question in the silence.

"They wouldn't put that in the manual. When the Sueronese think that colonists—that's you and me—have touched down in their territory, they like to cue a weather bomb. It's small-scale environmental terrorism. Basically, it triggers a drop in temperature that can freeze anything with a pulse right where it stands," I add.

That's a myth. It's based on one of their old folktales about a woman with icy breath, who kills her lover after he leaves her for another, he says.

"I don't know anything about folktales. I know war, and we are trying to win it and so are they," I say. This life is as far from a folktale as any I've heard of.

There are no winners in war, just one side that suffers more than the other, Fay says.

"Or decides to end their suffering early. I guess it depends on who you're asking. It's not like any of us volunteered for this. We were born into it," I say bitterly. Whose side is this guy on?

I wasn't, he replies.

I'm surprised, but I don't show it. I let the sound of our boots crunching through the low grass fill my aching ears. Everything aches, but I pretend that I'm feeling okay, for his benefit and mine. I notice just how low the grass has been cut where we've crashed. It's not a good sign. There could be rebel camps where we can't see them. In fact, I'm almost certain there are.

"Hmm? What?" I ask.

I said, why do you call them rebels?

I shrug. "I don't know. It's what my commanding officer calls them. It's what the manuals call them. It's what we use in training."

Okay.

"Just okay? No, lecture on the state of the displaced Sueronese and their need for agency in the New Republic?" I reply, already anticipating his response.

He laughs. *I take it you've heard that already..*

"I have. It's an old song. People love it, especially officers in units that don't see combat," I say with irritation.

I wouldn't know. My service is mostly academic. My interaction with the enemy, as you call them, is in a hospital, in a prison, or through a monitor.

I think I see something out of the corner of my eye, but it's just the wind bending the taller grass at the edge of the mowed field. From far away it looks like rows of long-haired men being blown backward. Nana would say it's an omen, but I don't see signs like she did. I don't believe in signs.

"What do you think are the chances of us being found on this planet by an ally ship or rescue bot?" I ask. It's a leading question. I know he doesn't know the answer.

He shrugs, the nonchalance just dripping from his shoulders. *Who can know?*

"Given the time of the attack and the proximity of the outpost to the next Republican allied base and the likelihood of survivors based on the hostility rating of the reb—I'm sorry, the Sueronese, our chances of rescue are approximately three million and twenty-four thousand to one, decreasing by an additional ten or twenty thousand every Sueronese hour," I say.

Interesting, he replies, as if I've just spouted the scientific names of all the visible native flora and not our imminent demise.

"My point is that out here it is us versus them, and it doesn't matter how rich their traditions are or how beautiful their music or food culture may be. They are the enemy and we are the good guys."

Do you feel like a good guy? he asks. I pause and take in those scrutinizing eyes and the curious half smile and know he'll use my answer to further analyze me.

I blink hard and stumble forward as a strong feeling of déjà vu blooms across my skin.

He catches me. Our helmets clink a bit, and the pressure of his fingers against my suit seems grossly intimate. One second it feels like I've known him forever; the next I'm faced with a stranger and my stomach trembles with anxiety. I press my lips together and straighten myself back up to stand.

This guy is in the spy unit. He's literally in my head. And I've been talking far, far too much.

35
FAYARD

SHE DOESN'T LIKE ME VERY MUCH, OR IT'S THE FACT that she doesn't like being vulnerable around me. Whether it's personal or general, I don't know. It doesn't matter.

She is strong.

I like strong.

The quiet presses down on us the farther we wade into the grasslands. I feel the silence like a person standing too close, holding their breath—waiting. The ringing in my ears has stopped now, and though the pain is still there, I realize that something is very wrong. I can't hear myself swallow. I know my heart is still beating only because I'm still moving and the monitor on my helmet tells me so. I don't need to be a doctor to comprehend that the damage is significant.

She dances when she moves.

Gravity levels are adjusted on base, but the standard g on Beta-Sueron isn't that substantial, so there's a certain way you have to walk to keep your pace without wearing yourself out. The Sueronese, obviously, don't have to worry about that with their massive height and weight, but I'm struggling. She's got it down. The sway you need to swim on land.

"Try to keep up," she says.

I might do better if I knew where we were going.

She nods her head into the distance. "There is a copse of rock formations just over that hill. I want to make it there before the suns rise. We'll be less exposed, and the elevation might help us avoid the interference from the grass," she explains.

I don't understand.

"Sorry, I forgot you can't hear it. The wind blows harder at night and makes the grass sing. With the storm coming in, it's pretty loud. Shame you're not able to listen. It can be musical."

I'm about to tell her about the bottle trees on my home planet, where the aunties hang bottles on the branches to catch wayward souls. When the wind blows, they clink like chimes. But then she holds up a fist and my back stiffens. I feel it, a vibration in the ground beneath our feet. We both drop to a crouch and I crawl closer to her. Even though I know she'll hate it, I take her six, positioning myself behind her while she sifts, frantically, through her bag.

Hold your breath, she broadcasts, not risking speech out loud.

I don't ask any questions. I swallow air as she detaches my helmet for the few seconds it takes to slide a thin metal stick across my neck, just above my chain. It's cold, but my blood heats at her touch. Her lips spread into a sweet, almost innocent smile, and in this moment it's hard to ignore the effect my cryo dreams have on me. I've been trying to fight off the feelings of recognition, the hallucinations that I've always chalked up as nonsense. This time it feels different. It's her, not some random girl's face but a real, living and breathing person instead of a dream, and my body is reacting.

In the entrance exams I found out I had the eyes of a sniper. I can shoot anything, but I don't have the heart for combat. I'm too emotional. And it's my feelings that are getting in the way now—the overwhelming sense of desire now that I'm breaths away from her mouth, close enough to touch. I swallow and clench my fists as she closes my air seal again. This is not the time to wish for a romantic moment.

I need your DNA signature, she says quickly. Her eyes linger on mine for a beat longer than if I were just another soldier, or so I think. A second later she's back to business.

Her fingers fly so fast I barely register what she's doing, but from the way her teeth are digging into her lip and the rattle of the ground below, something big is getting closer. Her face lights up like the desert sunrise as she finds what she's looking for. It's slim like a stylus, with a trigger. She raises it high above her head, but her arm doesn't reach above the grass line. It doesn't matter. She squeezes one eye shut as she focuses and shoots. A puff of yellow air dissipates in a second, and then I feel her hand press hard against my chest.

Breathe, she says, much more calm than she seemed to be a few seconds ago.

For a split second I can't remember how to draw breath into my lungs.

It'll tingle at first, and then it'll feel like you're running full out. It helps if you hum.

I blink hard. I want to ask her if she's serious, but I know she is. She's a field soldier.

What's the melody? I ask.

She sings a bit. It doesn't make much sense, but the rhythm is easy enough. I get the hook after the third repetition, just in time for my blood to heat as she said it would. It feels like lightning in my veins, and suddenly the grass seems bluer than blue and the few peeking rays of sunrise break through the sky before the explosion.

Tap the beat on your chest. Your heartbeat will sync with mine.

". . . these expensive, these is red bottoms," we sing.

I don't stop the melody in my head. The ground is rocking so badly we're knocked backward. Even through the grass I can see the Sueronese warrior above us. He's maybe three meters, short for Sueronese but still big enough to crush either of us. His hands are over his ears and his eye is bleeding. My heart is beating faster than I've ever felt it beat before.

Hit the store, I can get 'em both! she shouts in my head, repeating the lyrics.

I shout too and pound my fist across my chest to the rhythm. If we can keep the rhythm, we can control our heartbeats. That's how sound missiles work: they send out a pulse that your heart connects to and then keep accelerating it until it explodes. I've heard that some soldiers hack theirs to songs, so they ride the pulses instead of being overtaken by them, but hearing and experiencing aren't the same at all.

The Sueronese warrior opens his mouth wide and I know he's wailing. Tamar's hands fly up to her helmet and she stops singing. It's the Sueronese death cry.

I pull her close to me just as the warrior falls to his knees. I grip her hands in mine and fold my fingers over hers to bring them to her chest. I yell as loud as I can to guide her back to the rhythm, to bring her heartbeat down and out of danger. If I can't get her to sync with me, her heart will explode.

"Focus on me!" I shout.

She's shaking. Her body feels small tucked under mine and I want to fold myself around her to keep her safe. She'd probably kick a mudhole in my chest if I tried, but the instinct is there. I keep the rhythm until the final tremble when the Sueronese soldier plummets to the ground. I wait two full minutes before I reluctantly let her go. Her heart rate is still elevated, but I don't want to put her off. To my surprise she doesn't scramble to get away from me. Years seem to pass before either of us speaks.

"That's an interesting meditation device for a death screamer," I say.

"Songs are easier to remember than calculations," she replies.

"I don't think I'll be able to forget that one," I say, trying to take in the fact that we were almost toast.

"Are you taking a jab at me?" she asks. She jumps to her feet and rolls her neck as if she's just been out for a run.

"You could have died, you know? Screamers are banned for a reason," I say, not wanting to dwell on this any longer, except she scared the crap out of me.

She shoves a hand into her pack and places something into my hands.

"A knife? Eh? Analog," I say, trying to put a little levity into my voice.

"It's small, approved for transport, and can cut through bone. Let's check out big boy."

The warrior is still breathing when she severs his head with a much bigger blade she assembles from her pack. She does it quickly and without commentary. The cut is clean and my mind says that this is a kindness, that to leave him here to die slowly and alone would have been more barbaric, but I'm not completely convinced. He didn't attack us; he was just in the wrong place at the wrong time. Does that have to be a death sentence?

Her eyes flick over to me as she cuts the locator from his embroidered chest plate.

"This will help us navigate our way back to base camp," she explains. "From the look of his boots I'd say he was on foot, so there's no chance of any transport. Help me get his boots off."

She drops down to her knees and tucks the locator into her bag.

"His people will come looking for him soon. Those stones set in his nose bridge means he's betrothed. His partner shouldn't find him like this," she replies.

I didn't think she'd want to take the time to do this for an enemy, but it does ease my conscience a fraction. She stands and chews her lip for a moment like she's thinking, and then bends again to start to unlace. It takes longer than I thought we had time to spare, but the laces are intricate and her slim fingers far more deft than mine.

"Do you play an instrument?" I ask.

A smile ticks at the corner of her mouth before she drops it.

"Not anymore. I played pinalyn for six years. I had an opportunity to take the exam for the Interplanetary Oirchestra, but my chances weren't high. Why?"

"Your fingers. They look . . . like musician's fingers," I say.

She doesn't comment. Whatever emotion she has, she's keeping it for herself. We work in silence for a few minutes, but I know she's thinking about something. Her brow furrows in a way that tells me it isn't just the laces she's concentrating on.

"When they called us up to fight, did you know I was a girl?" she asks.

"I had a suspicion."

"Did you go easy on me?"

"No. I had a cracked rib. I couldn't afford to be gracious. Besides, I didn't think a girl who'd won her last two matches would appreciate something like that. And while we're on the topic, thanks for going easy on me."

"I didn't go easy on you."

"You knew I had a cracked rib. You could have done some real damage," I add.

"I was just being . . . fair."

When we finally get the boots off, our helmets adjust to level-six filtering. The smell must be pretty bad.

"We'll set them here next to his head. I've seen it done in observations, although I'm not sure why," she says.

"They believe you can't walk into the afterlife with your boots on. Ideally, a family member would remove the boots; there'd be a ceremony," I tell her.

"We don't have time for that, and who knows how long it'll take for them to find him without his locator. This is better," she says, her mind made up.

"If they can find him without the locator, they can find us. Can't they?" I ask.

I can tell she's drawing in a deep breath by how her chest rises. "Yup. Sucks, don't it," she says. Then she crouches down and waves for me to follow her before sprinting into the grass.

I don't hear the dart—I can't—but I feel it, sudden and sharp as a snakebite, with venom so potent I don't even get a chance to turn around.

36
FAYARD

I SMELL THE RIVER BEFORE I SEE IT, MOVING WATER THAT reeks of life and death. When I open my eyes, it rushes below me at the bottom of the hill, gray like the sky above it. Glass explodes nearby. Soon the scent of the river gives way to char. My nose stings from the fumes, and I see smoke rising from a city in the distance. I don't recognize it. Too much wood, too much stone. The architecture is all wrong. Uneasiness and disorientation steel my spine, and I try to stand, but a dainty gloved hand holding a pair of delicate binoculars presses down on my thigh to stop me.

It's Tamar. Her biosuit is gone, and she's in a purple dress with a high collar and small buttons trickling down from her neck to her chest. She's holding a white lace umbrella over her head in the other hand.

"Where are we?" I ask.

The corners of her mouth turn down in a frown as she adjusts the binoculars and considers something in the distance.

"Paris, 1789," she mutters. "Earth."

"Earth!"

"*Oui, monsieur.* There is about to be a revolution. See?"

Her dainty hand points to a couple across the river. They're arguing.

"The boy in the plum-colored waistcoat and stockings is you, and the girl in the periwinkle frock is me. He's trying to convince her to come with him to New Orleans."

"She doesn't look too interested in the deal," I say, beating back my confusion to follow the thread of conversation. I look behind me, under the bench, lift up my feet to test the gravity, anything to help me determine whether this is a dream or a simulation. Nothing gives me anything to go on.

"The Civil War is nearly seventy years in their future. Louisiana is notorious for its treatment of slaves, *the gens de coleur* as well if you consider the Knights of the White Camelia. A Paris in flames might be better than all that. There is also the opportunity for her to train under the famed composer Joseph Bologne, Chevalier de Saint-Georges."

"Long title."

"*Oui.* He was one of the queen's favorites, as close to the nobility as a Black man can get, back when that meant something. He's in London at the moment, so chasing that dream is a bit reckless."

"But—"

She places a gloved finger to my lips, and my mouth vibrates from the contact, like it's a button that she knew just how to push.

"Wait. This is the good part."

The guy, or the other me, gets down on one knee. I can't hear what he's saying, but I can assume by the way the other Tamar wraps her arms around his neck that he's gotten her to agree to whatever request he's made.

"Ah! Young love," Tamar says.

"Great. Happy ending. Can you tell me why we're here? What all this is?"

She looks at me, eyes full of laughter, like I've just told her a funny joke. "Happy ending? Silly boy."

I pull her hand from my cheek and hold it in my lap. She's acting very strange in what is disconcertingly an even stranger situation.

"Why are we here?" I ask, my voice soft, my gaze searching for an answer hidden in her expression. I've heard of mind worms that can extract information from your subconscious. Make you see things that aren't there. This isn't like any dream I've ever had. I've never watched myself from the outside.

"I don't know," she replies with sincerity.

"Is this real? A vision? A dream?"

"A memory, maybe," she says, her eyes looking past me to something I cannot see. Then she shakes her head. "I don't know."

"What do you know?" I growl, suddenly angry but trying hard not to scare her.

She leans close as if she's going to tell me something, her expression shining with a secret. "You need to wake up."

"What?"

"WAKE UP!"

My body jerks as I sit up straight, eyes wide open. Restraints bite into my wrists, and my stomach roils with the aftereffects of what I can only imagine is poison.

They got us.

I knew the moment she looked at me that something was wrong. Maybe if I'd heard it, I could have known they were flanking us, I would have known where to run. But as my commander would say, if wishes were fishes, we'd never starve. They hit us both with tranquilizer darts. If they were bullets we'd be dead; synth lasers and there'd be nothing left of us but bones.

They've dragged us to some hidden rebel outpost. Who knows how long we've been out or how far they've dragged us from our original location. A Sueronese woman, tall and lean with skin the color of bellflowers, pushes a communication device in front of me.

"It won't work," I tell her, trusting that the old tech is translating correctly. It's not a Republican design, but I've seen some similar to it, if a little bit newer. "My ears are injured."

She shakes her head and says something in return, but I can't make out the shape of the words; her lips are hidden behind her beaded headdress. The communicator lights up, but the translation is jumbled and the grammar is off as it scrolls across the screen. I'm getting frustrated, and by the way she kicks the dust in front of me, she's downright angry.

I switch to the little Sueronese I know, rolling my *r*'s and hitting my consonants extra hard. I lower my pitch at the ends of my sentences to show deference, and grant her the honorific of "grandmother," though I am sure she's still a maiden by her people's standards.

"Grandmother, I beg your forgiveness for my existence. My sister and I are only travelers."

She stops in front of me, but I don't look up. I keep my eyes planted on her toes, stained an even darker shade of blue from walking barefoot on the mowed grass. Her large hand grips my chin and thrusts it upward.

"Speak, child," she says, or possibly, "Confess, insect," or some other combination. The words light up and scroll very quickly. The vines are digging into my wrists, and Tamar is still unconscious beside me. At least they've turned her onto her side so she won't choke on her own vomit.

"I am of low standing, Grandmother, a missionary. I cannot hear well, and my sister has only accompanied me in order to avoid the war on our home planet."

She spits in Tamar's direction. She's aware I'm lying. I lean forward and dip even lower so that my medallion peeks out from my undershirt. It glints in the firelight so I know she can see it.

"Priest?" she asks.

I can *hear* the question even if I'm not sure what she's asking. My ears have stopped ringing so loudly and words, low as they are, are finally getting through. I force myself not to jerk in Tamar's direction as she comes to. She groans and begins to cough and spit. Her brain is a jumble of sounds and half-formed questions.

You were hit with a seeker. We are in a cave compound, I say into her mind.

Escape routes? she asks.

She's still coughing and spitting, but her telelink is strong, maybe too strong. I'm not just getting sounds; I'm getting images. It's the chemicals in her blood.

None that I've seen so far. The compound is surrounded by an invisi-shield. It blends into the landscape. It's so good the rodents smash into it every so often. When they pile up, they send someone out to clean up the mess. They'll have to let us out if we want to get out, I say quickly.

She retches hard and gasps for breath. I move closer, but Grandmother presses a finger into my forehead, scratching a nail across the skin until it breaks. I suck in air and clench my teeth. I hear her through my connection with Tamar.

"Your people live on lies. This will tear the truth from your tongue," Grandmother says, like a curse.

The paste she rubs into my forehead wound is cold, reminiscent of the numbing agent they poured on my leg before it was severed and replaced with a prosthetic three years ago.

I nod in Tamar's direction, more than a little concerned that she can now hear my inner thoughts and not just the ones I push toward her. I'm not sure what chemicals they've already flooded into our systems.

Are you okay? I ask.

I'll be fine. What is she doing to you? she says, scared.

Bush magic. A hallucinogen. She thinks it will force me to tell her the truth.

Will it work? she asks before she coughs again. Yellow bile spews out this time.

Grandmother mutters something to the guards I can't make out—not that I've been able to understand her anyway. They're posted on the other side of the veiled partition that makes up the "room" we're being kept in. A guard comes in with rags and a bowl of water to clean up Tamar's mess. Without my helmet my senses are heightened from the previous suppression. The stink is ten times worse than it should be. My face doesn't show my disgust. My training and my respect for Tamar keep my reactions in check.

They lace the food of all the intelligence recruits with poisons to build up our immunity, I offer. Tamar's smart. She'll be looking for signs of whether I've been affected like she has. Most people don't know what counterintelligence training is like. It may not be combat forward, but it isn't a walk in the park.

She's shocked. She doesn't say it, but I can . . . feel it. And I can see it: a yellow-orange ribbon like smoke erupts from Tamar's skin. Her emotions look like colors. Synesthesia. The poison is having an effect. This is not good, not good at all.

Whatever I say. Whatever they do. Do not negotiate. Do not make deals. A translator won't help you with the language. Words have triple meanings here, based on who says them and how they say it. You are the meek and chaste sister to a young priest. Repeat it, I say, my voice calm but serious.

I'm trained in seven martial arts forms. We're getting out of here. Where are the bags? she retorts.

Don't, I repeat.

If they wanted to kill us, we'd be dead already, she argues.

I'm starting to see . . . things I shouldn't, I confess. *The agent she gave me is topical. It shouldn't last as long as—*

She shakes her head slowly. *You can't see what I see. That gash is deep. You're bleeding into your eyes. It's fear talking,* Tamar says.

"Do not insult me," I mutter through clenched teeth to emphasize the point, the pain taking over the shred of control I held in my voice.

"Stop insulting *me*. We will *not* die here. I'll make sure of it," she whispers out loud.

Our eyes are locked in a battle of wills; maybe that's why we don't notice the child until it is too late. She must be Grandmother's novice, an adolescent just barely six feet tall with a shaved head and animal-hide boots that soften her walk. Recognition catches me off guard.

It's the girl from the cave.

When she breaks the clay jar in front of Tamar and me, I instinctively hold my breath. A second later my eyes clench shut, but Tamar is too sick to do the same. Grandmother chuckles, a deep throaty vibration that rattles the ground. I try to apologize again, to make one last plea, but my brain won't cooperate. I have no choice; I need air. The oil smells like dead leaves and chrysanthemum tea. It smells like the old and the unknown. I'm losing my grip.

"Grandmother, please . . ."

"Save your strength, spy. You will tell me your truth in time."

37
TAMAR

STARE AT THE SUERONESE GIRL, WATCHING HER FACE quiver and fade as my lungs grow ice cold from whatever gas they've given us.

I blink and she's gone. Every pain I was feeling is gone too.

Something soft presses against my shoulder, warm and wet. A giggle escapes from my throat. It surprises me. I haven't giggled since I was ten years old. Spiced smoke tickles my nose—incense, sharp and thick. I open my eyes and expect to see the girl; instead I see Fayard staring up at me, his hair cut low, scars across his cheeks. They look tribal. Fayard's nose grazes mine as he presses my forehead against his. He moves his lips to my ear and kisses the upper lobe, whispering something.

"Hmm?" I ask.

He pulls back, his face switching from delighted to serious.

"Open. Your. Eyes."

I draw in a deep, centering breath and shake the vision from my mind. It's not real. Even if it feels like a distant memory, it's not real.

I am a prisoner. I am a soldier in the New Republic Army. I am eighteen Earth revolutions old. I am the daughter of Morana and Sincere. I am an orphan. These things are true. But the wind in my braids as I watch myself ride my favorite horse, Fay's smile as he gallops ahead of me on his, *feels* real.

Truth: I have been poisoned and all these so-called memories could be a nasty side effect of the psychedelic drugs. Except they don't feel like a lie. They feel as real as my own heartbeat. I'm back in the cave again; I look over to my left and see Fayard, eyes closed and unmoving, save for the subtle rise and fall of his chest. At least he's breathing.

The younger of the two Sueronese women picks up the translator; she adjusts some of the settings and then drops it at my feet. The room is small, with no windows. The earthen walls are inorganically smooth and curved like they've been hollowed out by an ice cream scoop, pockmarked with shimmering bits of stone shot through with veins of precious metal, some as small as a child's hand and others as large and wide as a man's torso. There's no way that our transmitter can be detected here.

"We have adjusted the oxygen levels to accommodate you. The gravity levels have been modified for your benefit as well," she says.

I take a look around the room, which is little more than a hollow dirt cave, and nothing makes sense. How they are able to adjust gravity and oxygen levels is problematic. The Sueronese are supposed to be a level-three society with little technology and little interest in the modern tech trade, and Alpha 9 is classified as an energy desert with next to no means of electricity. The ability to adjust anything means our intel is either wrong or has been purposefully obscured. I do not know who I'm dealing with.

"Are you impressed?" the older woman asks as she walks over to a wall and pushes the surface back with her hand. In seconds, small vines begin to burst through the rock face, twisting and blooming into glowing vials and platters. Table legs form from roots, and flowers sweat a liquid that instantly hardens into a glasslike tabletop. Luminescent berries descend from the ceiling and cast the entire room in a warm glow. I'm momentarily stunned as she plucks one and eats it, her cheeks flaring for just a second before she swallows. She pulls a small ovule from her apron and drops it into a hole in the table. She smiles as a 3D rendering of Earth appears just above the table's center. None of this is supposed to be possible. Plants can't be manipulated to form furniture. Vines don't grow into lab equipment. I must be hallucinating, but I can't deny what I'm seeing with my own eyes.

"Earth is a young planet. Much younger than Alpha 9, just as humans are much younger than the Sueronese. We reached out to your people early on, worked with you on architecture so that you could form your pyramids, and we occasionally visited to monitor your progress. But there is a fundamental flaw in relationships with humans. You seek to dominate, to conquer, and eventually to destroy. After all this time, you cannot help yourselves. Born thieves, like this one here."

Her eyes fall to Fayard, and I'm hoping she doesn't inject him with anything else as punishment.

"We have hidden ourselves to prevent unnecessary bloodshed. It is not our custom to fight mindlessly, but there is a limit to what we will allow to be done to us, and the Republic has crossed that line. The destruction of our surface cities, the biosphere, and now thieves sent to pilfer our most sacred artifacts."

She tears a thorn from a vine, and what looks like a glass vial from a dripping spiked flower. A few twists and splices with a small knife and she holds up a syringe. I swallow hard, willing my body to cool down so they can't see me sweat. The girl waves her hand at the older woman and kneels down before me.

"I am Shulat," the girl says. "Now you will tell us your name."

I don't dignify her demand with an answer. The older woman smiles and turns back to her bench to work steadily on something I can't see from my vantage point. "He has not told you," she says as she works. "Maybe he does not know himself."

Shulat walks over to Fayard and lifts up the gold chain peeking out of his suit. She runs her thumb over the emblem, a bird reaching behind itself. It's one of those ancient religious symbols some of the older colonies use: a sankofa bird. She shakes her head. "The goddess is mysterious in her ways."

I don't know what she's talking about, but I'm getting worried about Fay. A thin coat of sweat has broken out on his face and neck, and he seems to be shivering even though it's sweltering in here.

"The soul that sits there, resolute in his mission, is not a priest or a soldier or any of the things that he may have told you. He is far more dangerous than that," the older woman says in a sinister tone.

Shulat whispers something to the older woman—her commander, maybe? She takes her eyes off me to lean down to listen, and I use the distraction to inch closer to Fayard.

Fayard? Fay, are you okay? I push my thoughts into his, but it's like he's put up a mental block.

Shulat's eyes flick over to us; her piercing stare forces me to look away.

"Shulat tells me our time runs short," the commander says. "Not all of my people believe in the old tales like I do, and the storm is raging. Prophecies are wasted on those committed to war, but I have faith that this will change their minds." She turns around to reveal twin syringes glowing with a golden liquid that moves inside the chamber on its own.

I call on my training and remain still—I don't so much as flinch—but my heart can't help but race at the sight of it. I don't know how long I've been here, but I know that our window for rescue is closing. Even with rested bodies, we had a ways to go. Badly injured we might never make it. I pull at my wrist tie again, and though it bites, I feel the smallest bit of give. I struggle, but I'm able to slip one hand free and then the other. My mind scrambles with scenarios. Disarm the commander. Plunge the syringe into her eye, drive my boot into her large gut, use the leverage to twist my body, somersault, and grab the girl's chin in my right hand and her ear in the other, then jerk on my way down, snapping the two thin spines in her neck. My eyes flick to Fayard. He's in no position to move and I can't carry him.

I could leave him.

The thought slips into my mind and falls away just as quickly. Every soldier in the army knows there are situations where it is most advantageous to leave a comrade behind. It was one of my favorite debates in Military Strategy 101, but that was a place where sims on a commscreen represented real people and all the blood and death was digital. This is real life, and I'd rather die than leave Fayard behind. The certainty of that revelation surprises me, but the feeling is sincere and concrete and scary as hell.

The commander walks gracefully toward us. She stands directly in front of me before she squats down, crossing one ankle over the other as she sits. Shulat shakes her head and tries to whisper something into her ear, but the older woman raises her fist in silence. Shulat stiffens and presses her lips into a straight line, then takes a few steps back.

"I want to tell you a story," the woman begins. "You are so ignorant it seems unfair to keep you this way. Especially if my test confirms what I am almost sure it will. I am three and forty summers old. Young for command. Younger still for high command, by almost ten summers."

"Congratulations," I say bitterly.

"Unlike me, you are not high command. You have no knowledge of whom you kill or why, yet we are called barbarians. You have little knowledge of the planet from whence your people come, and even less desire to acquire that knowledge. You have no idea who you are and what your purpose is.

"I am my brother's companion," I say, seeing if I can keep Fayard's act going. But I am a terrible actress. I can tell by the cough the commander gives that covers up her laugh.

"So, you are a follower of the Path, then? Tell me, young sister, what are the seven pillars of the faith?" the older woman asks.

"I am unworthy to speak on such matters. My brother is the evangelist," I reply.

"Your brother is a thief and a criminal who came here to find Sueronese artifacts and then sell them on the black market," Shulat spits. She walks over and pulls off one of Fayard's gloves, revealing a thin red line of broken skin. He's been handcuffed—recently, if the angry, not-yet-healing scars are any indication.

"He was brought in to decode one of our sacred cave texts, and I watched him lie about the translation. He deliberately obscured the coordinates so that he could return to find the artifact himself," Shulat says. She turns her head, eyes pinned on mine, waiting for some change or confession.

"You must be mistaken," is all I can think to say.

"You should be grateful that we found you. The penalty for violating treaty law is death for your people, is it not?" she asks, not looking at me anymore.

"You must be mistaken," I utter again.

"Do you know the story of how the world began? It is a love story, after all," the commander says as she hands the syringes to Shulat.

I shake my head.

"In the beginning, the great sky goddess became pregnant with an idea and birthed the world. She had many ideas after the first, and together they became the known universe. She gathered them into her hands and blew on them with a breath of fire, and they burned bright for her. When they began to cool, she cried over them to create oceans. She plucked out her teeth to form the mountains, and the land became lush, but there was little drama on the face of these planets. It was then that the great sky goddess decided to entertain herself, so she made human beings out of the finest mud at the bottom of the deepest ocean. Of course, her earlier projects had used finer materials—stone for the Sueronese, silica for the Camians, and so on—but Earth and her human beings were unique.

"She created the allfather first. She gave him laughing eyes and a trickster spirit, the ability to find the most interesting way out of any situation. She spent a millennium watching him age and die, resurrecting him after each death, perfecting her design until—"

She stops and sniffs, breathing in deep. I smell it too: a sharp, mineral odor, like spilled blood. I look over to the now-overgrown wall of foliage and watch as small green buds grow and burst from cobalt vines that snake along the ceiling. The commander stands quickly and rushes out of the room. As soon as we're alone, I check on Fayard. He's shivering. Sweat is beaded on his face and neck, and while the gash on his forehead is no longer bleeding, I can tell it is very deep.

The light in the room is dim, but my eyes have adjusted, and it's not as small or as sparse as I once assessed. What I thought was a flat wall is really a stack of large cubes. I crawl over to it and find one stuffed with our helmets and go bags. I'm sure they've already searched the bags and confiscated anything useful. It's the first thing I would have done. I'm still searching when I feel someone behind me.

"Find what you were looking for?" Shulat asks, and I freeze.

38
TAMAR

SWALLOW HARD AND TURN AROUND. SHE'S TALLER THAN me and Fay, so I have to look up at her. Without the commander in the room she stands more confidently, and I brace for whatever this newfound conviction emboldens her to do, but she backs up and then walks over to the table.

"Lyn Walmat is a formidable leader. She is speaking to the Congress of Elders to stop what has already begun. She believes she's found proof of the one true religion." She pauses and turns around to stare at me, looking intently for something, but she must not find it, because she relaxes and turns toward the table she and Lyn, their highest religious leader, have been working at. "Sit down. I'm not going to hurt you. Not that you will believe me."

I do as I'm told and watch her press a button on the table. A stone egg pushes through what looks like packed dirt, while something circular, maybe a ring, pushes through a slim slat in the wall behind her. She picks up both, dusts them off with a frond of greenery she snaps from the growing table, and then slides the ring over the stone. It snaps in place with a small click.

"My people have been warring with one another for a century. Sister against sister for one hundred years without resolution. It is a debate that cannot be settled. This timeline is no good. I know that now, but the commander, she still has faith. She still believes in the prophecy."

She holds up the stone. "This device is priceless. I say priceless because a Tilibine general was rumored to have stolen one and held an auction for it. He sold it to the Old Republic for the bargain sum of an entire planet."

"But Tiliba earned its independence after it was classified as a level-six planet. Their technology and state relations progressed so fast the five councils had to recognize their right to self-govern," I say.

Shulat laughs and turns the stone over in her hand. "Since you are fond of repeating your school lessons, consider this. When has anyone ever *earned* their independence? Freedom isn't given; it's snatched from your oppressors' bloody fingers. The Republic gave up the planet for this. The first people called it the Goddess Star."

A puff of air escapes the table and Shulat sets the stone above it, where it begins to hover, suspended by the air flow.

"What does it do?" I ask.

The table starts to shift and grow, bleeding sap that hardens into petri dishes and cracking open to burp flames for vials that squeeze through the walls behind her. The ceiling still crawls with the budding vines, creating a constant swish-swish chorus of leaves rubbing upon leaves in the background.

"We believe it resets time," she says.

"You don't know?"

She shakes her head and sniffs the air as one of the buds on the ceiling bursts, releasing a scent not unlike roasted corn. She nods her head and goes back to building what is beginning to look more and more like a wet-lab station. The kind used for examining specimens under a microscope. My nerves twitch.

"Legend says it was created to correct grave mistakes, but manipulating time is dangerous business. Stop a flood and cause an avalanche. There is no way to know how our actions play into the goddess's plans. Who can know the difference between fate and folly?"

"It must be very rare," I say, and scrutinize the ceiling. The vines might be an olfactory alarm system. Quiet and decipherable only by your own people. Genius-level tech. I tear my eyes away and fix them back on Shulat.

"Not really. Stars are usually given to children at the time of their first bleeding so that they understand that their actions have great consequences."

"What happens to the people who use it?"

"They disappear, never to be seen again."

"So for all you know it could really be a weapon and doesn't correct anything at all."

"That's a question of faith. Something you should discuss with your *brother*."

I bite my lip so I don't confess that he isn't my brother. Shulat's eyes twinkle. She, too, knows the truth, but to what extent I don't know.

"He is a great man of faith. He would not have attempted something so foolish unless he truly believed in the legend. It is unfortunate that you do not share this belief. It would make what is going to happen easier for you to accept." She pauses, probably waiting for me to ask some question about the legend or her, but there's no need to talk anymore. I need to listen. From everything I've seen, these walls aren't as solid as they seem. I've got to be smart, and smart people keep their mouths shut.

She picks up the two syringes Lyn left on the table in one hand, palms the star in the other, and walks over to Fayard. My heart jumps to my throat.

"Don't!" I yelp, and she turns to me.

"Don't what?" she says, and looks at me curiously as she slips the stone into one of the pockets on his suit. "He risked his life for this," she says, and wipes his face with the edge of her apron. "It's easy to use. You slip on the ring and say the words, and then— poof—you're gone. It only works once, though. You would have to be sure."

"Why are you telling me this? Why would you give it to him?"

"Because he earned it. A kindness for a kindness. Besides, you're going to need it. You're not who my commander thinks you are. You're not the fulfillment of some prophecy or proof of some grand cosmic love story. Her petition to stop the destruction of the planet will be denied because our people love war more than they love truth, much like you humans. Right or wrong. He's just a thief and you're just a soldier," she says dreamily. Then, quick as wasp stings, she plunges the syringes in our thighs.

39
FAYARD

A TRUE ACOLYTE CAN WITHSTAND HEAT, COLD, THE lightest touch upon their exposed skin, and bones broken without flinching. They compartmentalize. After years of training, prayer, and meditation they learn how to separate their minds into distinct rooms. One room is for pain and sensation; one room is for dreams, another to sit and wait for the goddess. They can move from room to room and lock the door behind them; they leave the world outside and keep their reactions, and bodily functions, within. I am not a true acolyte.

I know someone has stabbed me in my thigh, almost touching bone. I can't feel it; that pain is locked behind a door I've lost the key to. I know someone has also cut my wrists free. I'm not a priest. I'm not a soldier. I'm a spy getting by on a little bit of faith and a year of religious training. Still, I did learn enough to build a few rooms. The problem is getting out of them.

I hear Tamar's voice—not screaming, pleading. It is muffled, yet all around me, not as if she is behind a door, more like the alarm system during a fire.

"... *Fayard.*"

"... *Fayard!*"

She's calling me. I need to get out of *here*, but here isn't a real place. I *need* to wake up. I need to—

"... MOVE!"

My eyes spring open and sting with whatever she's thrown over my head. I draw in a deep breath and cough, barely able to keep myself upright. She grabs my arm and hauls me to my feet with more strength than I would have ever given her credit for.

"We gotta walk! Can you walk?"

I hear the question and nod dumbly, trying to take in the chaos around me. She's yelling, and through her I can hear the horns blaring in the distance—an alarm. The ground shakes.

"What's happening?"

"We have to move," she says. "There!" she says, and points to a carved-out shelving unit in the rock face. When she lets go of my arm to retrieve our bags, it feels like I've lost my limb. It takes every muscle to pull myself together and lean a hand against the wall for support, but I have to snatch it back because the vines start looping around my wrist.

"Can we make it?" I ask.

She doesn't look at me. She doesn't answer, which is an answer in itself. We stumble out of the room and up a staircase. I blink hard, trying to get my eyes to start processing visual cues again. They slide uselessly from side to side, searching for outlines, colors, remembrance. I had to go deep to keep the drugs from tearing secrets from my throat. I have no sense of time when I'm closed off, no sense of anything. I can't feel, see, or really hear inside the rooms, but when you come out, everything is triple its original brilliance—every light, sound, and touch is electrifying.

Our heads pop out on the surface minutes later, just in time to see the ground split like the opaque glass of a snow globe, revealing the hidden capital city of Sueron underneath. Kilometers of buildings push through the ground, exposing stone apartments inlaid with mother-of-pearl domes, grand fountains bubbling over with rivers of water that flood the polished streets. Trees, so thick and sturdy their branches contain homes. A small laugh escapes me. They've hidden from the Republic all this time.

"Let's go!" Tamar shouts, and tries to lead the way across a field, but it starts to crumble so that we're left stranded on a hill surrounded by a city that's being abandoned. Pods, sleek and egg-shaped, are detaching from rooftops and tree branches by the hundreds and then disappearing before our eyes like soda bubbles.

"They're using their stars," Tamar says with a panicked voice.

"What are you talking about?"

She dumps the contents of her go bag onto the ground in front of us, but there isn't much in there.

"The commander's story about the allmother, us, they didn't buy it. They're abandoning the planet. This is an evacuation. They took my transmitter," she says pitifully. "We can't call for help, and we won't be able to make it through the city to base in time. If there's even a base to make it back to."

Her eyes are wild and wide with hysteria.

"Try to stay calm. We'll figure this out."

"'We'? Is it 'we' now? You tried to steal from them. How do I know that thing in your pocket isn't just a quick death for a criminal and his accomplice?"

I slide my hand across my thigh and feel a bulge.

"How did you?" I ask, barely able to get out the words.

"Shulat gave it to you before she stabbed us both in the thigh with who knows what!"

"It's pheromones. It'll allow us to use the star. I can't believe she—"

Realization cuts off my words and steals my excitement. There's only one reason Shulat would have just given me what millions of seekers have lost their lives trying to find. She knew I'd never be able to trade it. I'd have to use it.

"We're not going to die here," I say firmly, but my words are crushed by the sound of buildings exploding in the distance. Much closer to us, one of the tree houses collapses, flattening everything in its path and shaking the ground so hard, we tumble to our knees.

Tamar's fingers dig into the kinograss and her head shakes from side to side. Her shoulders shudder, and even though I can't see her face, I know she's holding back tears.

"I—I don't have a plan," she says in an almost surprised voice. I'm not sure if she's talking to me or if she's admonishing herself.

"No one expects you to," I say, and another building cracks open and disintegrates nearby. A moment later the sky begins to blacken. The storm is coming. Tamar seems to regain her composure and points down into the city. There's a pod on the roof of a building. The windows have been blown out and the street looks empty. No one has claimed it.

"We can slide down this hill. It's a little steep, but we could make it, then make a run for it," she says as she looks at me for confirmation. I'm prepared to nod, but thunder begins to roll again and a shower of lightning erupts, setting fires all over the city in a matter of seconds. Even if we make it to the building, we'll have to scale the sides to make it to the roof, and I don't think I can do it with my leg. The only other option is to take our chances inside, but if some rogue Sueronese are still there, we might not survive the battle, and that's if the building doesn't just collapse on top of us.

"We're not going to die here," I say again, more forcefully this time so even I believe it. I pull the stone from my pocket, letting my thumb rub across its etchings, becoming fully aware that none of this is coincidence.

Tamar sucks in a disgusted breath of air. "I'm talking about strategy and you're suggesting an untested alien technology that could be just a bedtime story."

"We are in a life-or-death situation. This isn't a war game."

"That's right, because in a war game there are rules; supernatural bullshit isn't part of any training exercise I'm aware of. That back there was a brainwash attempt. I'm not falling for it, and you *would* have if I hadn't gotten us out of there."

"None of it sounds plausible to you?" I ask.

A pitying smile breaks out across her face. "You really are a zealot, a true believer, just like she said."

"I'm a thief."

"So she wasn't lying," she replied.

"No. But it's more than that. My mother forced me to join, and I am being trained in intelligence, but I am also on a mission for my colony. My home planet is starving, and the Republic has started drilling new mines that will poison what little water supply we have left. This could have saved the lives of millions of my people."

Tamar shakes her head, ash falling over her helmet like snow. "It's a fairy tale."

I pull the stone from my pocket and roll onto my side to face her. It's small and etched with several languages on its surface.

"This stone is worth more than the GDP of my home planet times a thousand. It's worth more than my life."

"It's useless if we're dead, and it's a death sentence for underground trading if, by chance, we don't die and you're caught."

"That's just it. They did catch me, Tamar, in a restricted area, with stolen dig equipment. I was being arrested when the sinkhole caved in. I ran. There's no record of my arrest because all the servers are under a pile of rubble right now. I should be dead. That we're here, still alive, with *this*, is fate!"

She leans in, her eyes full of fire, about to say something, but suddenly the ground stops shaking long enough for us to stand. In a blink she's sliding down the hill with me right behind her. I tumble a bit at the bottom, but I make it to my feet and fall into a jog, gritting my teeth as the pain in my thigh radiates like a fire bomb across my entire right side. We don't talk. We just run until she skids to a halt and holds up her fist.

A Sueronese family is loading into one of the last remaining pods, carrying a body. We wait and watch as the sky lights up with streaks of lighting, and ash and dirt begin to gather and swirl into mini cyclones along the lanes. The pod door closes, and within a minute they blink out of the sky. Then, as if they've cued it, the rain comes in hard gray sheets, turning dust into slick mud. We run again, but the downpour is so massive we can't see two feet in front of us.

"We're not gonna make it!" I yell.

"Only if we don't try!" she yells back, and I tackle her. She didn't see the tree falling right in front of her path. It hits the ground and seems to trigger something underneath the city: The buildings begin to crumble again; the streets start to buckle.

"We've got to go!" I shout over the noise.

She nods. "I know!" she shouts back, and tries to stand, only to be knocked back down by the quakes.

"That's not what I mean. You didn't train for this! This isn't a normal life-and-death situation and you know it." The rain slows to a mist for a moment, clearing our line of sight, but the sky groans with thunder, and the internal skeletons of the buildings continue to shriek as they bend. Still, it's a bit quieter than it was minutes before. A moment where she might listen. Our time is running out.

"Do you dream of me?" I ask.

Her shoulders straighten as she swipes mud from the face of her helmet in silence. I know before she says it that she does.

"Hallucinogens. Biohacking—"

"You want a scientific answer for a supernatural phenomenon and there isn't one. You and I are meant to be on this planet. Right here. Right now. With this . . ." I dig in my pocket and pull out the stone again.

Tamar opens her palm.

"Give it to me. I'll tell them I found it once they find us. They'll put it in a vault somewhere or use it to negotiate with Sueronese on another planet or put it in a museum. I don't care!" she says, her voice a fever pitch.

"Tamar, you don't get it. No one is coming. The Sueronese are destroying their own planet, and who knows where or when they'll appear again."

We don't have to die, I say over our link.

Thunder rolls and the rain has frozen into a shower of foot-long, razor-sharp icicles. We duck into a building, knowing that we can't run; we'll surely be crushed if the building falls.

Where will it take us? Tamar asks weakly, finally giving in.

It's not just a question of where, but when. It's not a machine. It's a tool of fate.

The building across the street cracks down the middle like it's been split by a giant ax and moans like a dying animal as it begins to shatter. I turn the ring around the stone until it clicks and begins to glow.

Tamar shakes her head. "Don't do it. If it's our time, then that's it. It's our time, Fay. What if we're pulled back to the paleolithic age? What if we aren't us?"

"So we just give up?" I ask.

"No, we take control. Why does fate get to decide?"

"Fate says we die here in the next sixty seconds. We can decide not to die. We give ourselves a chance at life. Do you trust me?"

"You're a thief and a liar," she says half-heartedly, and a manic kind of wispy smile appears on her face.

I inch closer so that we're just a hand's width apart. That nervous feeling in my gut fires up, and I can only hope that she feels the same. In the corner of my helmet I can see my heart rate jump ten points as the butterflies in my stomach amplify through our telepathic connection. We're both vibrating. Eye to eye we're beat and rhythm, electricity and feeling.

"You've met me before. You've grown to know me in your dreams, in all those other lives you've watched play out in your mind your whole life. I know you have because I've seen them too. We're together. Always. You trusted me then. Do you trust me now?"

Her fists clench as she tries to deny what's between us. "I don't know you," she wails, uncertainty in her eyes. Tamar does science and facts, a hard fist and bombs. Not myths and fate.

"You know me in here," I plead, pressing my palm to her heart. "Trust me."

Something above us cracks, and the door to the building slides closed. There's a deafening roar from the sky, and a shift in the ground knocks me to my knees. The lights in our helmets click on, and it takes all my strength to crawl the few feet so I'm next to Tamar. I grab both her hands and drop the star into her right palm.

If we do it, we do it together.

I hold up the stone and begin to recite the words on its surface. It's simple Hebrew on the first line and then Latin on the last two. I say the words over and over until she's got them down. Then I hope with every fiber of my being that this works.

A blessing to live but a curse to die if only love
the heart does find.
On the wind of chance does the goddess climb,
To turn the many-faced head of time.

40

TAMAR

STARE AT THE CLOCK ON THE WALL AS THE SECONDS TICK by loudly in my hospital room. I'm lucky. At least that's what they tell me. There was a malfunction on a plane, or possibly a terrorist attack; they're still investigating. But whatever it was, it nearly leveled Columbia Metropolitan Airport. No survivors, save for me and one other person.

Ms. Collins says it was front-page news in the *State* for two weeks, which is supposed to be impressive. I *try* to act impressed, but feeling anything makes my chest hurt. I have two broken ribs, a sprained wrist, three toe fractures, a punctured lung, and "more bruises than you can shake a stick at," as she likes to say, and that's on top of my traumatic brain injury. It's what's causing the amnesia. It's also why my instinct is to call her Ms. Collins instead of Auntie O. I don't remember that she's my auntie. I don't remember anything before two weeks ago, when I woke up in excruciating pain.

It's a miracle. The FBI, CIA, state police, and all the other alphabet people don't believe in miracles, so there is an investigation.

I turn the picture of my sister, Aabidah, over in my hand a few times before I place it back on the side table. I've been staring at it, trying to remember the beloved sister I've lost, but I keep coming up with nothing. A part of me doesn't want to remember. I think I'd rather avoid the grief. Then I wonder if the grief is better than this emptiness.

A soft knock on the door interrupts the murmuring voices of some entertainment program on the comm . . . no, the television screen.

"Tamar? You have a visitor," my nurse says.

Behind her, a smiling, tawny-skinned woman with a bouquet of flowers and a large paper bag walks into the room and waves at Auntie O before coming closer. She knows me. Her smile is infectious, so I smile back, but there's this niggling sense that somebody's playing a trick on me—a paranoia, like someone is standing right behind me, waiting to pounce.

"You don't remember me, do you?" she asks.

"I'm sorry."

"That's okay. My son, Fayard—we call him Fay—he doesn't remember me either. I'm Silvana Daniels. Lord knows I did work a lot, but not enough for my only son to forget all about me." Her laugh is dry and humorless, but she doesn't stop smiling. I can sense the barely contained tears behind her eyes.

"That was an amnesia joke," she adds.

"Oh," I reply, unsure of just how to respond.

"I wanted to come by and bring you a few of your favorite things. The doctors say it might help jog your memory."

She pushes my empty breakfast tray to the side and lays the flowers on one of the plastic chairs.

"Ranunculus. Fay always said they were your favorite. There are Reese's Peanut Butter Cups in there. I froze them last night and ziplocked them in ice so they should still be nice and cold. Also, I went to Sandy's and got you two chili dogs with extra mustard for lunch, and then there's this."

She pulls out a gray metallic box with black square buttons and dials from the bag and sets it on the bedside table.

"Ta-da!" she says.

"What is it?"

"It's your beat machine. It arrived at the house a few days after the accident. You must have mailed it the day you went to the airport."

I turn the thing over on my lap with my good hand. It's not heavy, but not insubstantial, either. The large buttons light up once she plugs it in. "Is it a weapon?"

Auntie O laughs from her perch in the corner, but she doesn't look up from her Bible.

"Nooooo, you make music with it," Ms. Daniels says.

She presses one of the glowing buttons and a rhythm spills out. She presses two more in succession and it makes a sound; she presses two more together to add even more sounds.

"You try."

I press the keys. One, then all of them. She's right. It does jog my memory, but in some other place inside me. I've done this before. I know it because I tap out a rhythm, save it, and lace it over another without even knowing what to call what I'm doing. I feel possessed.

"Well, it looks like you're gonna do just fine." Ms. Daniels studies me for a moment. "Wow! You look so good," she says.

"Really?" I say, my eyes lingering on the casts I'm sporting, but I can't help but notice the look passed between her and Ms. Collins.

"Eating everything they put in front of her. Put on twenty pounds, just like that. All that scar tissue? Gone. Damnedest thing they ever saw," Auntie O pipes in. Ms. Daniels shakes her head as if all this new information is too much.

"If you don't mind, I'm going to send Fay over here tomorrow to, uh . . . hang out with you. Maybe being together will help. Maybe it'll even be fun. Would that be all right?"

"Yes. I mean, yes, ma'am," I say, remembering at the last minute to add the honorific. Just because I'm in the hospital doesn't mean I should forget my manners.

"Great!" she says sunnily.

I don't notice her leave. I continue to play, letting the rhythms pour out of me by muscle memory.

Fayard's mother forgets to close the door, so I can see the parade of people walk by as I work. Parents, grandparents, nurses, doctors, other patients on crutches, in wheelchairs, hobbling by, leaning on rolling IV stands or pulling oxygen tanks. They're all fine, background noise, but it's the men in the black suits who disrupt the flow—brassy, discordant notes that stand out. They all have names like colors, Mr. Black, Mr. White, and they share the same face on different bodies, asking questions I don't know the answers to.

I find a backbeat and play with a few chords. Bass. I'm in a bass mood, I realize, as I filter through the options on the machine. I think I've got something brooding and erratic, something to illustrate this moment, when Mr. Black comes in.

"Good afternoon, Ms. Collins. Tamar. I'm Mr. Green."

Auntie O and I nod in greeting. Auntie's got her large purse clutched on her lap and a scrutinizing eye to add to her greeting. I don't even have that.

"I met a Mr. Black," I say.

"Ah, yes. He's my colleague. We work in the same department. We wanted to see if you remembered anything yet?"

"Today is the same as yesterday," I say. My eyes fall back to my beat machine, and I hold my body tighter. It seems colder in the room with him here.

"I wanted to show you some photos. May I?" he says.

I let him slide the pictures across the tray that swings over my bed as I continue to play. There are ones of a girl—me, in a BLACK LIVES MATTER T-shirt. I'm smiling next to another girl holding a sign that says ABOLISH ICE.

"This is you and your sister," he says.

"Okay."

"Do you remember attending this protest at the airport last year?"

"Sir, I don't remember last month."

"Fair enough. It was a protest against changes to the administration's immigration policy. We have some propaganda we uncovered, and I must say the language is a bit coarse."

He hands the paper to Auntie O, and she has to pull out her reading glasses and hold them up to her face to get a good look. She takes a minute but then she laughs, a short cough/chuckle that flies out of her throat. "This is an essay for her Current Affairs class in high school. She got an A-minus, I see. Not your best work, Tamar."

"I'll try harder next time," I say flatly.

Mr. Green slides another photo over to me. Me and a boy. He's kissing my cheek, his eyes cutting to the camera. It's a night shot with blurred circular lights in the background. I'm eating something covered in powdered sugar. Another image. It's the same guy in a hooded sweatshirt; he's got both middle fingers pointed to the sky and a scowl on his face, but he can't hide the warmth in his eyes, no matter how much of a front he's putting on. He's got a stack of cash held up to his ear like a phone. He's with a bunch of other guys who are doing the same thing. Next picture. The same group of guys, but they've got their fingers twisted in a weird configuration. Another looks like a passport photo.

"Does this jog your memory? How about this one that looks like a mug shot."

"Looks like a driver's license photo," Auntie O says.

I shrug. "Fayard, right?"

"So you do remember?"

"No. His mother just left, and he's the only person who survived the crash with me, so I'm assuming you would be interested in him too. You haven't shown me any pictures of Auntie O, or any class pictures. I'm not dumb."

"No, you're not, and you don't seem to be the kind of girl to get swept up with the wrong crowd, either. I don't want to take up too much of your time. I'll leave these with you to help jog your memory. You're a very lucky girl, Tamar. I wouldn't want you to squander any second chances."

He pauses. "Last thing." He drops a brochure on top of the pictures.

"It's a pretty good program. The one you were looking into. Try not to give up on the girl you used to be too quickly?"

"Okay," I say, and give him a sarcastic thumbs-up, hoping he'll leave.

I press the button to cue up a trumpet and blare it loud and long for Mr. Green as he walks out.

Auntie O sucks her teeth and gets up from her perch to pick up the photos.

"Wrong crowd, huh? Fay's in a Morehouse sweatshirt in this one. Probably 'cause it was cold. Does he look like a suspect to you? *Please*. I know this game."

She brings the photo with all the guys together closer to her face.

"Fayard and his robotics team. They were state champions, two years in a row. See, number two and the other hand a number one. Dumbass. Probably thought it was gang signs. Baby, people like him see what they want to see. You're hittin' this world brand-new again. I don't want you soaking up any of that crap about so-called dangerous Black boys from those Crayola men, you hear me? And if you want to keep protesting, you do that. World changes 'cause kids like you and Fay change it."

I nod and drop the horns. My mind isn't the only thing that's trying to play tricks on me. I pick through the paper bag Fayard's mom left and inhale the two chili dogs, then top them off with the candy cups. They're so delicious I groan.

"Nothin' like a Sandy's dog. I'm surprised you didn't lick the wrapping. Didn't mind those onions on the dogs, did you?" Auntie O asks.

"No? Why?"

"You used to hate onions. Used to gag on 'em. Hmmm."

She regards me with a scrutinizing eye, like I'm a cake she's not sure is done yet.

"Do you want to try a few things? See if there's other foods you might like?"

I nod, appreciative of the goodwill. But as soon as she leaves, I get another unwelcome visitor.

I need a break.

My therapist, Dr. Gupta, is a petite lady with small wide-set eyes, almond-colored skin, and shoulder-dusting earrings. She's painted her toenails bright red today, and she keeps tucking and untucking them in her sandals. I wonder if she likes her job. She looks like the kind of person who prefers solitude and appreciates the nuances between Lady Grey and chamomile tea.

"How have you been sleeping?" she asks politely.

I nod my head from side to side. "I'm on meds," I say apprehensively.

I don't really trust anyone just yet, least of all this therapist. One wrong statement and I'm certain they'll put me on more drugs, or, worse, they'll write a report giving them carte blanche to do whatever they want to me. No, thanks.

"Any dreams?" she asks. "I'd like you to be honest with me. There is no judgment here. You've had a significant amount of trauma inflicted on your body and brain. Some side effects are to be expected."

"A few."

"Good dreams or bad?"

"Both." It's hard to explain how a boy I've never met can make me so happy that I wake up breathless and covered in sweat, and how that same person can make me so angry I wake up breathless and covered in sweat. Do I describe how his eyes dance after we kiss? How I can still smell the hay from the barn we snuck into or smell the smoke from my last nightmare where I died screaming his name? Or the smell of the seawater before I drowned, tossed from a huge wooden boat in the middle of an ocean?

"Do the dreams make sense or are they abstract? What I mean to say is do they seem like memories or are they things that could never happen in real life?"

I swallow hard. *Don't cry. Don't cry. Don't cry.* Damn it!

She hands me a tissue.

"I'm here if you'd like to talk about it."

"There's nothing to talk about. They're just dreams. I'm there and then I wake up just before I'm about to die. It's normal to dream about dying when you just survived a near-death experience, right?

What I don't share is that they don't feel like dreams, though. They feel like memories. I can't say that. If I admit that, I'm sure there will be consequences.

"Is it every night?"

I nod.

"I'm going to write you an antianxiety prescription, okay? It will help you sleep a little better than some of your other medications. The next time I see you, I'd like to hear more about those dreams.

There's a notepad in your side-table drawer. It might help if you wrote down what you dreamed of as soon as you wake so you don't forget."

She pats my hand with hers.

As soon as the door closes, I take out the notepad and I write.

41
FAYARD

THEY SAY I'M LUCKY. OVER 60 PERCENT OF MY BODY WAS burned. The tendons in my right knee were torn at such an angle that I'll never walk straight again, and I've lost all memory of who I used to be. But I'm alive. That's something, right?

The woman who says she's my mother (and who am I to dispute her?) comes back with a beatific smile on her face.

"Did it work, Mamá?" I ask as I turn the rosary beads over in my fingers. It's something I like to do when I'm nervous, which seems to be all the time.

"Yes, baby, it did. And I've told you, you usually just call me Ma."

"Yes, uh . . . ma'am."

All the women like to be called ma'am. I think I will just keep to that from now on. My doctor, a squat man with an impressive build for his age, gives her a reassuring smile.

"Don't take too much offense, Ms. Daniels. The brain takes time to heal. Some memories will take longer than others," Dr. Swafford says. He doesn't say how or when this feeling like I've been cut and pasted into someone else's life will leave.

"Well, he seems to be fleecing you just fine," she quips. It's meant to be a joke, but there is a little sour with the honey. Dr.

Swafford winces along with John and Mack, the two orderlies sitting at the makeshift poker table I've cobbled together from three abandoned lunch trays.

"How much are you down?" Ma asks.

"I'm embarrassed to say," Doc says, and laughs. "We started with five-card stud, but it only took him one round to come out ahead. Then we switched to Texas hold 'em, and I felt like the sage for all of twenty minutes. It's the most amazing thing I've ever seen, and I'm a neurosurgeon."

I surreptitiously close the drawer holding my winnings. It began with packs of snack foods—cream-filled cookies and colorful chips—and eventually I traded the snacks for cash. I know without being told that my mother doesn't completely approve. She shakes her head as she sets her purse down in the lounge chair she's made her bed for the last two weeks.

"If I didn't know any better, I'd say he was hustling you. He's a card shark. I told you not to bet anything of value, but look at ya. All of you have that glassy-eyed look of straight-up gambling addicts. I thought you were professionals."

"I'm on break," Mack, a pug-nosed man with an affinity for cartoon-covered scrubs, counters in mock offense. "I'm doing double shifts, trying to get overtime before the renovations start."

"And losing all your overtime pay right here in my baby's room," Ma chastises.

"All right, guys, Ms. Daniels is absolutely right. Fayard needs to recuperate," Dr. Swafford says.

They all make a big show of getting ready to leave, but when John knocks an unopened pack of cards onto the floor he whispers, "Gin rummy. Tomorrow, right after lunch." The lunch trays disappear, and I roll my wheelchair behind Dr. Swafford as he makes his way out.

"I want you to write down as much as you can remember about your stay here," he asks.

"I'm not doing anything but sitting, maybe rolling down to the game room."

"Yes, but you're meeting people, eating foods you can and can't remember. Write it all down: the smells, tastes, sounds, all of it. It's very important. Describe your mother to yourself as if you're writing to someone who has never seen her."

"I picked up a blank journal in the gift shop downstairs," Ma replies.

"Good," Doc says to her, and turns back to me. "Just a few more days and we'll get those bandages off. And as soon as you feel ready, try using those crutches. I'll talk to the nurse about getting you extra sessions with the physical therapist. Don't worry. We'll have you up and about in no time."

I nod my head, but I can smell the fear and uncertainty wafting off my mother as keenly as if she'd stepped in it. I would smile to reassure her, but she wouldn't see it. They have my face wrapped up pretty good and I'm drugged up even better.

"Do you want to watch some television?" she asks.

The question sounds muffled, like she's standing behind a curtain. I shake my head. I'm thinking about the girl. I'm nervous and I feel stupid for being nervous about meeting someone I used to know, who used to know me. We are essentially strangers, but realizing she's on the same floor fills me with . . . curiosity? Longing? How can you miss something you don't even remember having?

. . .

I can't look at her. Not that I'm physically incapable—there's just something else holding me back. We decided to meet in the teen area of the children's wing instead of in her room so my stilted conversation wouldn't be the only entertainment. The game room at the hospital is pretty large, made to fit a whole horde of sick children, but there are just a few of us here. Bright colors swirl along the walls and meld into a yellow ceiling cut at an angle so there are more corners than there should be. I assume the design is supposed to keep our minds off the pain coursing through our bodies. There are large televisions affixed to two walls, one for watching and one for gaming. Since the younger kids keep an endless stream of fairy tales in queue, gaming is where the action is.

I get there first, and when she arrives, I'm able to ask her mundane questions over my shoulder instead of trying and failing to keep her from staring at the bandages on my face. There's a couch, yoga balls, and a love seat, all facing the gaming console with space for wheelchairs between. I've taken up residence in one of the love seats nearest to the window, but with a view of the hallway and exits. I get nervous when I can't see the exits. Her nurse, a slim guy named Hassan, rolled her in and parked her almost directly behind me. I keep my voice light, using all the effort I have to keep it from shaking or breaking like a tween's, but that's how I feel: an awareness waking up inside my bones, vibrating and lighting my skin on fire . . . again.

Her voice is like music.

"My cousin Letitia said you came to say goodbye to me at the airport. I'm sorry. I know I don't remember asking you to come, but you might not have gotten hurt if you didn't, so I, uh . . . wanted to say that."

"It was my decision. Nobody knew what was going to happen. I'm sorry about your sister," I say.

"Thanks. I . . . don't remember her."

"I don't remember my mother. It's awkward," I add, and when she replies, I can sense the smile in her voice. At least we've got camaraderie born from a similar situation.

"I know. I'll say something and people think I'm being rude, or they'll touch me in a familiar way and I'll jump 'cause it's a stranger stroking my arm. Then they'll look at me like I've just spit in their coffee," she says.

"I stopped talking as much. My mother keeps staring at me like there is some stranger underneath the bandages who is impersonating her son," I say sadly.

There's a pause. My heart skips a beat from the tension. "Have you seen what you looked like without them?" she asks.

"I've seen pictures, but I don't recognize that person," I reply. He feels like a stranger whose life I inherited.

One of my hands is completely untouched by burns, so I was able to use my thumbprint to log into my social accounts and get on my phone. I try to spend at least an hour a day scrolling through pictures of myself with friends, family, trying to jump-start something in my head. Some pictures are more private than the others. I saw her naked this morning. Not completely, but in parts, like a wicked puzzle in my photos folder. A thigh here, a belly shot there. More.

I won't mention the pictures. Maybe that other guy won't ever come back, and I want her to like me for who I am now, not some memory, or out of obligation. Plus, who knows what I will look like once I'm unwrapped. I don't want to get her hopes up. I don't want to get *my* hopes up.

"I don't like dresses," she says firmly, as if she's just made a very important decision that needed to be announced.

I'm not ready to turn around completely, but I can see her leg, a lean brown velvety limb, jutting out from her cast and covered in a gauzy purple flowered fabric. *I* like dresses, this dress, even if she doesn't, so I don't respond.

"I think the girl I used to be liked them, but I don't. There's too much air breezing against my legs, not that it can be helped in this wheelchair."

I want to be that air. Wow! I have got to get myself together. I clear my throat and adjust myself in my seat, staring at the little dinosaur on the screen as it burps flames.

"Is there another game on here?" I ask.

Corey, a bald boy with cracked lips and a filthy sense of humor, switches to another screen. He can't be more than fifteen, but acts like he's thirty. "I know your bag, Torch. You want a first-person shooter. I can tell."

I am so desperate to do something with my hands, distract myself in some small way, I forget to tell him not to call me Torch. "Uh, sure. I would like a first-person . . . shooter. Um, what exactly is it?"

"It's really self-explanatory. *Apocalypse Moon.* You see something, you shoot it."

A minute later the entire room is filled with the sound of gunshots; animated gore splashes against the screen, and it does the trick. I can't say that I like what I'm doing, but it is immersive, and then I remember that this is supposed to be a light chat, a chance to meet an old friend and make a new one. I grit my teeth and turn to face her.

"I'm sorry. This probably isn't the kind of thing you want to see right now, after what happened."

Her head tilts a bit as she considers me, and her mouth lifts into a slight smile. She looks exactly like the girl in the photos, but she's got this unexpected strength, a sharpness like the key lime pie they served for dessert last night. The girl in the pictures seemed softer, sweeter. Neither one better than the other, just different.

"I got next."

42
TAMAR

EXPLOSIONS ERUPT IN QUICK SUCCESSION. MAYBE I should be a little unnerved by them, but I gotta say, now that gaming has become part of my daily routine, it's kind of comforting. I like that I'm able to complete something that doesn't require memory or the use of my healing body. I only need my thumbs here. Physical therapy leaves me in tears, and the doctors don't know yet if I'll regain full use of both my legs. There's still a lot of swelling, but in the game none of that matters. The rumble and cacophony of noise soothes me from the silence.

"Did guys in suits come and ask you about the accident?" I ask Fayard. Turns out Ms. Daniels was right. It didn't take more than a day for Fay and me to fall into a comfortable rhythm, friends. It would be hard to explain how or why I feel so at ease with him—I just do.

He's furiously punching buttons, his focus completely on the TV monitor. He's wearing shorts today and a BENEDICT COLLEGE TIGERS T-shirt that he ironed so fastidiously the crease is plainly visible down the sides. His head is still bandaged, but I can see the hollow of his collarbone, the outline of his calf muscles in his good leg, the taper of his fingers . . .

"Hmm?" he finally replies.

"Oh, I said, have guys in suits come and talked to you?"

"How did you know?" Fayard turns quickly in my direction and does a swift survey of the room, probably to make sure we're alone. He avoids looking me in the eye. Maybe it's the bandages that make him insecure; maybe it's just me. I don't judge him for it. I like that his face is obscured. He looks like I feel: hidden behind a mask.

"They've been coming to see me, too. This last time they let slip that they think the bombing was some assassination attempt. One of the president's senior cabinet members was supposed to fly out that day, but he missed the flight because of a car accident."

"Really? They told my mother it was a terrorist attack. Really scared her. They never asked me anything directly; Mamá wouldn't let them past my bedroom door."

"I don't like it. It feels as if they're trying to pry information from us. Like we have some connection to all of it. You don't remember anything, right?"

Digital explosions rock our corner of the game room and light up the screen with scattered debris. Fayard shakes his head.

"They give me a bad feeling," he says. "But as long as we're in the hospital we'll be fine. There are cameras, people. Once we're released, though, who knows what will happen. I've been watching the news. You would think that an attempted assassination or terrorist threat that hasn't been solved yet would still be relevant, but there is almost nothing about it. It's like it never happened."

His voice switches in and out of this weird accent. He'll start a sentence and then catch himself, like he's pretending to be someone he's not or he's remembering who he's supposed to be in bits and pieces. I know the feeling.

"You sound almost happy," I say.

"I am happy. I'm alive. You're alive. That's enough to make me happy."

I can feel the heat bloom across my cheeks. And now I feel stupid.

"Is there anything wrong?" he asks, fingers jamming the controller as fast as a hummingbird's wing.

"No," I say, a little too loudly.

"Are you sure? You seem distracted. You never let a troll get by you, and three just slipped past your sniper site."

"Oh, sorry. Um, can we stop?"

His fingers pause over the controller.

"Sure. There's a few other games here." Fayard stops the play and switches to the main screen to scroll through our options.

"I don't want to play a game anymore. I want to talk," I say.

My stomach flutters, but the antinausea meds I'm on pretty much guarantee I'm not going to throw up.

"We were together, right? Like more than just friends," I start.

Fayard takes in a deep breath. I can tell from how his chest rises before he hobbles over to brighten the lights.

"Yes, definitely more than friends," he adds. His back is turned. "Do . . . do you feel anything when you look at me, when we're together?" I ask. He still hasn't turned around to face me.

"I don't have any memories of us, but . . ." He pauses to adjust the light switch.

Everything becomes bright, and it feels like the floor falls out from beneath me as embarrassment crackles hot and fierce in my chest. "But?" I prod.

"But I have these dreams. Immersive, more vivid than these games, dreams where I live whole lifetimes . . . with you," he says softly.

I swallow hard.

"We're in different places, but I'm the same person, or I feel like the same person. It's hard to explain," he says in a rush.

"Okay," I say slowly, trying to keep my voice even, which is difficult because my throat is as dry as the desert I walked through in one of my own dreams with him.

"Last night I was—I mean, *we* were on a train. I worked there and I ran a numbers game. It's like gambling. I made money and got into some trouble. I was running, or at least trying to. My leg," he says, and taps his cast. His eyes have a far-off look as he explains, like he's back there. I must make a face, because he laughs.

"Yeah, in every life my leg gets broken or severed or something. But you're always there. We meet and I fall for you and . . ."

I break eye contact. I can't risk him seeing an understanding in my gaze. If he looks deep enough, maybe he'll see the life *I* lived last night in Mali. I know, because I woke up in a cold sweat and asked the night nurse if she'd ever heard of Mansa Musa. It was just my luck that she'd minored in ancient African studies, because she talked to me for nearly an hour about how he was the richest man on Earth and how famed his pilgrimage to Mecca was. I didn't breathe a word to her about how I watched myself live as a slave, how I fell in love with a soldier wearing Fayard's face. If I close my eyes, I can still taste the dates he fed to me.

He puts the controllers away and gingerly grips my wrist. I stop breathing when he lifts his hand to pull away. I turn my palm up and take the plunge, lacing my fingers in his.

"Are you okay?" he asks.

"I'm fine," I lie.

"No. I'm scaring you. It's weird, I know. I told my neurologist, but he suggested I talk to a therapist specializing in head trauma."

Warmth floods through my body, and I ease my hand back so I can fiddle with a button on my dress.

"I see a therapist."

"Do you think I'm crazy?" he asks, worry lacing his voice.

"I didn't say that. We're in the same boat. Trying to figure things out with bits and pieces of a broken picture."

"Right," he says. He sounds disappointed. I feel guilty about not corroborating his story, but I need more information. I need to get this new life in order. My mind is playing tricks on me, just like his is playing tricks on him. We don't need to get caught up in some shared delusion.

I take a deep breath. "But those are dreams. What about now? What do you feel when you're with me . . . here?"

"I feel *something*. Not physically. Well, not entirely physically, but like I'm supposed to remember you. Everyone else seems like a stranger, but not you. I can drop my guard when I'm around you, but I can't make sense of why that is. Why do I feel so comfortable if I can't even remember us being together before the accident?"

He meets my gaze for the first time all morning, and my heart catches. That simmering energy between us that makes me want to touch him suddenly boils over. He keeps his eyes on me for just a moment longer before he turns and presses a fist to his chest, rubbing it in small circles.

"Are you okay? Should I call for the nurse?" I ask.

"No, no. It's just . . . you make me nervous. No, that's not what I mean. Sometimes I think English isn't my first language, but I can't remember what that language was." He sighs. "I try to find the words to explain what it's like when we're together, but I can't. Does that happen to you too?"

I shake my head. "Not really, but I do feel out of place." *And out of time*, but I don't add that. Instead I change the subject. "I'm supposed to love carrots, but I finally tasted carrots a few days ago and I hate them."

"When they told me what the chili dogs were really made of, I almost vomited," he says. He looks like he's about to gag just thinking about it.

"I inhaled them. They were delicious. What are they made of?" I ask, a bit scared of what he's going to tell me.

He shakes his head and laughs with his mouth wide open. "You do not want to know."

"No, I do. I want to know. I want to know everything, even though I can't wrap my head around the simplest things. Food should at least be simple."

"You guys need Google."

We both turn our heads toward the voice. It's the boy with the oxygen mask. I'm ashamed I still don't know his name, and I've seen him too many times in the game room to ask.

"Who's Google?" we both ask in unison.

He wheezes, and his voice comes out as thin as a paper gown.

"It's a what, not a who. Has anyone put you guys in front of a computer yet?"

Another kid in a wheelchair, but with two working arms, wheedles in on the conversation. "They keep the brain-damaged kids away from them. Something about agitation."

Mask boy rolls his eyes dramatically. "Follow me."

We trail him down the hall into his room. It's larger than mine and empty. Auntie O hasn't left my side, so she's become a fixture in my tiny space, sitting quietly under a soft lamp I'm sure she brought from home. The sickly-sweet scent of fresh but soon-to-be-rotten ranunculus fills the air, and the hospital-issue blankets have been supplemented by hand-sewn wax-print quilts that smell faintly of nag champa incense.

His room is barren, with only the scent of antiseptic and the glare of the afternoon sun as its complements. My breath sounds too loud in here. In the corner there's a glowing screen, smaller than a television, but larger than the phones I've seen people carry.

"All right, so, uh . . . what's your name? I've been calling you Bomb Boy in my head, but my mom would say that isn't polite."

"Fayard. Her name is Tamar, not Bomb Girl," Fayard says before I have a chance to defend myself. "And what should we call you?"

"P-Nasty."

"Excuse me? You want us to call you P-what?" I say in disbelief.

"P-Nasty," he says to me with a straight face, and then turns to Fay. "Oh, she wasn't Bomb Girl. It was Hot Angry Chick."

"I'm not angry; I'm just opinionated," I mumble, more concerned about this Google business than my hurt feelings.

"So, you open up the browser and type in anything you want to know more about. You sit here," he says to Fayard. "Before you tell me how girls can do it too, he's got two working hands with all the functioning fingers," P-Nasty says to me.

I'm about to tell him where to go, but he's right about this one. My thumbs are fine, but I don't think I'll be able to type. My competitive side suffers though. Ever since he mentioned girls being less aggressive during game play, I've been extra attentive to my kills in the *WatchKiller Dogs* game we play with the Busan team online every other night. I've surpassed his kills by nearly two to one, and I've only been playing for a short time. I turn my attention to Fayard, whose fingers seem to fly across the keys like he's in some kind of trance.

"How do you know what keys to press?" I ask, and he just shakes his head.

"I bet it's sense memory. I'm pretty sure you've played video games before, too. You wouldn't be half as good if you were just picking it up." He turns to Fay. "You want to look up the accident? Probably the best place to start," P-Nasty replies.

Fayard starts typing and a flood of conspiracy theories associated with the event pop up on a few newspaper websites and forums, this mini-journal online conversation lounge where you can only write a few sentences, and this video forum where people have posted clips of the explosion. We should be dead. The blast radiated in all directions, and what was once a beautiful feat of architecture is now just rubble. A tiny red *X* superimposed over a cloud of ash points to where Fay and I were found, almost as soon as rescue efforts commenced. Fay plays a short clip from a local news station. A man in a shirt and tie stands outside the airport gates.

"A seventeen-year-old boy and a girl the same age were found in the rubble, almost as if they'd been dropped on top of it, clasped hand in hand. Some are calling it a miracle, others the second coming, and still more don't know what to think. Extra security has been ordered at the hospital to keep away well-wishers and worshippers alike."

Fayard stops the clip. "Why? The investigators have nothing to go on."

P-Nasty shakes his head and takes a second to catch his breath after getting out of sync with his oxygen machine.

"*Au contraire.* It means they want your bandaged head on a p . . . pike," he wheezes. "Have you looked outside lately?"

I peek out the window to the parking lot below. I haven't paid much attention to it these last four weeks. There are six police cars parked along the walkway into the building, and two larger black SUVs flanking the lot's exit. Blue and red lights flicker from inside their front windshields. There are even a few military vehicles parked along the street, though they are farther away.

Fayard has upgraded his wheelchair to a boot, so he hobbles over to look out as well.

"That's a lot of security for a children's hospital," he says quietly.

I nod.

P-Nasty leans back to explain further. "You can tell who's really coming to visit somebody and who's just snooping. It's in the walk. All the parents move fast, eager to see their kid because their labs came back positive or wanting to soak up every last minute with them before kickoff to that old soccer game in the sky. It's the ones who are strolling, like they've got nowhere to be, that are the problem, and don't rule out the staff, either. If either of you gets a new nurse on rotation, or a doctor you can't verify online, don't trust 'em,"

"You're handing out all this advice for free?" I ask, suddenly suspicious.

He shrugs and takes another labored breath. "You guys are my entertainment. It's like a telenovela. Amnesiac lovebirds infiltrate underground CIA network. It's better than daytime television."

Fayard hobbles back to look through the news listings, and a slew of images fills the monitor, but one in the upper right-hand corner leaps out at me and I nearly scream. It's a drawing of a small egg surrounded by a metal ring. I stab the screen with my finger; Fayard clicks on the video and hits play.

A dark-skinned woman, hair up in a high bun and wearing a beige trench coat, begins to speak. "I'm Sarah Jackson-Hyatt and we're outside the Smithsonian National Museum of Natural History with Dr. Carl Little Feather, curator of the Lost Ancient Rites exhibit, where a priceless artifact has been stolen. Dr. Little Feather, can you tell us what the artifact is and how you discovered the object was missing?"

"The piece is an intricately carved agate stone surrounded by an osmium ring, believed to be at least five thousand years old. On its surface we've identified sixteen different languages, each with its own unique alphabet or hieroglyphics. Two of the languages we know, Tamil and Hebrew, but the stone itself predates the languages. It is arguably the most significant archeological find of our times."

"And it's been stolen," she adds.

"Well, yes. We opened the exhibit to school visits in March, so that people could see the results of the excavation process firsthand. We had a good idea of the kinds of things we'd find in regards to pots, and clothing items that you usually find in this sort of dig, but we couldn't know just how different this dig would be as we began to excavate the burial grounds near the new convention center."

"You're referring to the unmarked cemetery of newly freed African Americans found in Queens, New York, late last year."

"Yes, the excavation is a joint effort by the Smithsonian and the Weeksville Heritage Center. The excavation finds don't even belong to the museum alone. The Heritage Center trusted us with the stone, and we assured them that our facilities were secure. The FBI is now involved. They've reviewed the tapes, and we've closed the exhibit until further notice, but the stone needs to be returned immediately. It has a very unique radiation signature. It's not meant to be held bare-handed," Dr. Little Feather says.

"And why do you think a person would steal something like this? Is there significant value on the black market?" the reporter asks.

"We couldn't begin to put a price on a find this rare. So little is known about these ancestors. A few small tribes in Guinea-Bissau have tales of an invisibility talisman that can grant the wearer the ability to fly that fit this description, but how this artifact would have shown up in New York and remain hidden all this time is a mystery. I can't imagine there would even be collectors yet. Stealing from a museum is a federal crime. Who would risk years in prison for an unspecified payday?"

"Well, let's hope someone out there will be able to provide some clues. Anyone with information is asked to contact the museum immediately."

The video stops and switches to an advertisement for toothpaste. I have this nagging sensation that there's something important I'm missing from the video, but I am unable to connect the dots.

I think Fay got the same impression too, because he's up and out of the room without even saying goodbye.

43
FAYARD

MAKE SPACE IN MY DUFFEL BAG SO I CAN PACK IT TIGHT.
Two pairs of basketball shorts, socks, underwear, deodorant and
solid cologne, a hairbrush and mouthwash, an unopened pack of
playing cards, two pre-paid phones and chargers, dice . . . and a
small plastic bag. I pick up the bag and open it, dumping its contents next to everything else. It hasn't been opened since I woke up.
It's probably only been touched by the emergency-room staff and
me: one wallet, blackened and singed, one school ID, and a rock.
But it isn't a rock. I walk the stone over to the sink and rinse off the
soot and ash with antibacterial soap and watch with dread as each
language etched upon its surface leaps to life under the rushing
water.

I jump at the two knocks at the door and drop the egg-shaped
stone into my left pocket before the door swings open.

"Hey, hey, there, soldier. Am I interrupting anything?"

"I . . . uh . . . I'm just washing my hands," I say, and shut off
the water.

It's Mr. Sato, my homebound teacher from the high school.
He checks in every week now that we're nearing the end of May
and brings me my last few assignments so I can graduate without
repeating the year.

"Good habit. I still wear my mask at the movie theatre. Since the pandemic, it's just become something I do. I was visiting one of my other students on the maternity ward, so I thought I'd drop in to see how you were adjusting. Huge baby. Cute, though. You'll be coming home soon, I heard," he says as he settles himself into one of the only comfortable chairs in the room.

He's got a full head of gray hair but a young face, which makes it hard to tell just how old he is. But his ubiquitous khaki pants and school-issued polo shirt announce his profession pretty loudly.

"Uh, yes. They're going to check my bandages soon and then I'll know."

"Good. Good," he adds.

Mr. Sato's not a very talkative man. He mostly smiles and nods, with the occasional little-known history fact thrown in for good measure.

"I know you don't remember this, but after our class trip to the Smithsonian, I talked to my buddy at Howard University about your interest in Africana studies and archaeology. Now, I know you were looking for something with a bit more earning potential, but he said that with your test scores there may be a scholarship if you double major. You were thinking physics, right?"

"We were in DC?"

"Sure were. You were obsessed with the Weeksville exhibit. I thought they were gonna close the place down with you in it. Anything jogging your memory?"

"No, uh . . . I just saw something about it on the internet."

"Oh yes, it was all over the news for a good while. It's crazy that we were one of the last groups to ever see the SOTA egg in person."

"SOTA?"

"Star of the Ages. There are some scholars who say it's supposed to be called the Goddess Star or God Stone. No one is certain. Ancient cultures are so fascinating. There is some online footage of a Temba tribal elder in Togo retelling the story of the stone and how it chooses to grant its power of invisibility. Apparently, you can't just hold it. But there are conflicting stories. While a stone egg isn't mentioned, there is another tale I've heard among the matriarchal Bribri people in Costa Rica where a goddess transforms into a bird and is reincarnated by laying her own egg. And then there's the Ghanaian sankofa bird, the adinkra symbol, which is everywhere. Very, very interesting stuff."

It feels like the ground has dropped out from below my feet, and I'm about to fall flat on my face. I have to hold it together.

"Reminds me of those mysteries, like *The Thomas Crown Affair*," he continues. "Maybe we saw something that day in the museum and we're not aware of it. We could be material witnesses."

"What would . . . the . . . charges be for something like that?" I try to say as casually as possible. I slowly put my clothes back into my duffel bag just to have something to do while I hide my shaking hands. A glance out the window and I could swear that I saw one of the guys in black suits looking right at me. I blink and he's chatting with an officer in the parking lot.

Mr. Sato whistles real high, like he's calling the truth back to him after it's gotten away. Then he takes his glasses off so he can clean them with the bottom of his shirt. "I dunno, kiddo. It's a federal crime, so even if the time served isn't that long, the implications will last forever. You'll never be able to vote or travel outside the country. If the person who stole it is younger, they can forget financial aid for school and if they're older, they are pretty much locked out of gainful employment in a ton of fields. It's really unfair, if you ask me. If you've paid your debt, you've paid your debt, you know."

My mouth goes dry and I grab the cup of water resting on my small side table. I drink until it's empty, then refill it and drink again. "Could the person possibly just return the stone?"

"I mean, they could, but if I were them, I'd do it anonymously. Better yet, I'd return it the same way I stole it. If they didn't catch him going out, they probably won't catch him going in. Or her. Or they. I don't want to be sexist."

If the room isn't spinning, it's definitely off-kilter.

"You okay there?" he asks, looking a bit concerned.

I nod and take a seat on the bed to steady myself. I need to snap out of it.

"Hey, the reason I actually came by was to tell you that I talked to DeAndre, and he said you turned down the Morehouse scholarship. You guys talked about being roommates if you decided to go with the House," he says, not hiding the disappointment in his voice.

"I don't remember, but I must have," I say quickly, eager to get Mr. Sato out of my room.

"It's not my place, but I need to say something. About you and Tamar."

Too many thoughts are swimming around in my head; I've only been half listening to what Mr. Sato has to say. My priority right now is what I should do to get this thing out of my room. But when Mr. Sato says her name, I stop. He's got my full attention.

"I know you love her," he says, and glances at me, gauging my reaction. "Right. You kids don't like that word, but whatever you call it. You did before the accident, and now that you're here together, it's probably just a matter of time before you fall into an *entanglement* with her again. You were devoted, which is admirable, but you're both so young. I don't know if she's still sick or not, but it doesn't matter. Some people are masters of focus. You're like that. You set your mind and make it happen. Your focus used to be on getting a full ride to college, and then it was like you changed the channel and it was all Tamar all the time.

"What I'm trying to say is that you'll graduate soon, and when you're as bright as you are, your world is supposed to expand with age, not contract. There is so much to see and experience if you just take the time to look around."

"Okay," I say, needing this conversation to be over. I know Mr. Sato has good intentions, or at least I think he does, but he's making a lot of assumptions, and I've got bigger things to think about right now. Tomorrow is as far into the future as I can wrap my head around. The rest of my life can wait a bit.

"Okay? Great. That's the end of meddling Mr. Sato. Break out those cards I saw you pack away. I've got a poker game this weekend and I need to brush up on my poker face," he says with a big smile.

So much for getting him out of my room.

Later on, in the game room, I struggle to come up with a reason I've been cutting my time with Tamar short this week. It's hard to push all my plans to the side and just focus on the game, focus on her. My brain is filled with scenarios: how to get into the museum to return the stone, what it's going to take to get the men in suits to stop hanging around, how I explain, and get that person to believe me, if someone finds that I have the stone before I've had the chance to return it. All of these what-ifs are swirling around, and the only person I want to talk to about it is her. I'm not sure I can lie, so I figure it's best to keep my distance.

"Don't tell me you're focused on your schoolwork, because I finished a month's work of assignments in four days," she says. "And from what Mr. Sato says, your grades were better than mine."

"You talked to Mr. Sato?" I ask. I should have realized he was checking in on her too.

"He came to see me this week, and I had to pry the information out of him. He mentioned some scholarship you had," she says.

"That's not his business to share," I say quickly, upset that Mr. Sato is meddling not just in my life but hers.

"Why not? That's fantastic! I have no idea what I'm going to do. The other Tamar—it's what I've decided to call her until we can come to an agreement where she gives up her memories in exchange for my sparkling wit," she says with a sly smile. "The *other* Tamar was so sick she didn't really make any plans for the fall," she adds sadly.

"She must not have thought she'd be there to see it," he replies.

"Well, I'm here now, so I have to help her or *me* make a decision," she says. There's a determination in her voice that I haven't heard yet when Tamar speaks of the future.

"What are you leaning toward?" I ask, trying to keep the

desperation out of my voice. The truth is I can't see a future without her in it, but there is no way to tell if she feels the same way. I already shared too much when I told her about the dreams. Showing your cards too early is a cardinal sin of poker, and if I lose with her, I'll be out more than a few dollars.

"I want to show you something," she says while she twists around in her wheelchair to dig into her backpack.

She's wearing a long dress today, with a black-and-white geometric print that flows down to her ankles and long black leg warmers. Someone painted all her toes dark purple, and they wiggle as she struggles to find what she's looking for. It's almost too cute.

"You cut your hair," I say, glad for something else to talk about other than the thing I'm completely avoiding explaining to her.

"I did! I was just looking in the mirror at this other girl's face and I asked Nurse Lesli for some clippers and shaved off the side. Auntie O nearly had a heart attack. She called in my cousin Letitia to make it look like something," she says, and laughs.

"So, you're telling me she likes it."

Her smile widens. "Oh, she loves it so much she asked my therapist to come a day early. Ah, found it."

She raises her new phone above her head like she's won a prize. "The other Tamar made music. I can access all the old songs in something called the cloud."

"I know. I found some videos on my phone. There's also an album of songs. There wasn't a name on it, but I think it's you. Her voice sounds like yours," I say.

"You never said anything," she says, a questioning look in her eye.

"I didn't want you to know how much time I spent looking at

photos of you and listening to you sing," I say, hoping this confession won't dig me further into a hole.

"Well, you don't ever have to be embarrassed with me," she says sincerely. I'm sure she notices how awkward I'm getting even though I'm trying as hard as possible to keep my cool. I wish it weren't so hard to discern what's too much to share.

Our eyes meet, but she pulls hers away before the moment can deepen. "Well, I thought, if she could make music, so could I, so . . . I wrote a song," she says, and clears her throat, a little bashful.

"Let's hear it, Sniper!" Leo says as he rolls into the room. I told him that I just couldn't call him P-Nasty to his face so he reluctantly gave up his real name—after I beat him in three rounds of *Apocalypse Moon.*

"I do have a name," Tamar chides, but lightly. I think she secretly likes the nickname.

"Yeah, but Sniper's much cooler than Tamar," he says with a smile, proud of his nickname for me. "Play the song. I wanna hear."

"Okay, but you guys can't be too critical. It's my first try. I had these lyrics that were just floating around in my brain, and I needed to get them out," Tamar says.

"Just play the song, already," Leo groans. "I'm getting older waiting."

She hits play and the lyrics stab me in my chest.

> A blessing to live but a curse to die if only love
> the heart does find
> On the wind of chance does the goddess climb
> To turn the many-faced head of time

My entire body goes cold. My head begins to swirl like I've fallen backward in a pool and can't figure out which way leads to the surface. My vision fogs and then it's all crystal clear.

I remember.

44
TAMAR

HE LOOKED HORRIFIED. THE SONG WAS UNFINISHED, but I didn't think it was that bad. Leo liked it, but I'm not sure if Leo's opinion really matters. Leo likes peanut-butter-and-pickle sandwiches, so there really is no accounting for taste. For the second time in a week, Fay has left me in a room with Leo, forcing me to wonder if I've done something wrong. I'm over it.

"The school band sent those flowers over there as a graduation present," Auntie O says as I roll into my room. "You should thank them. Peonies are expensive, my dear. Lord knows where they got them from this time of year."

They are beautiful and they smell even better. Nurse Lesli walks in as I'm admiring the flowers and joins me.

"They're going to let you out of here soon, girlie," she says with a smile.

"I know."

"You don't sound too excited."

"I am. I guess I've just gotten used to the place," I reply, which is true. The hospital has clearly defined roles. Tamar is a patient. But when I get out in the world, who am I? There are no easy definitions, no plan.

She beckons me over to the bed so she can check all my vitals. Again.

"Oooh, honey, don't say that. This place is just a holding cell. Life is outside these doors. Don't ever mix up the two. You think you might want to try to attend your graduation ceremony? It's a rite of passage," she says with pride.

"I don't remember passing through anything, so I think I'll skip it," I say.

"Auntie, what do you say to all this?" the nurse asks, directing her attention to Auntie O.

"I say it's good to start putting energy into making new memories, preferably with a wig on," she says with all the snark she can muster.

The nurse bursts into a fit of giggles, though when she sees the look on my face, she kind of apologizes. "I like the cut. I do. Really," she adds.

I just smile, because I don't care whether she does or not.

"Oh! I almost forgot," she says, now excited. "We found your personal items from the day you came in. As you can imagine, the ER was a madhouse that day, but we were able to dig through and gather your things. The clothes were a mess and tossed, but everything in the bag you were holding is in there."

"Uh . . . okay."

She rushes out, and I catch a glimpse of a man in a dark suit standing just outside the door, but when it swings back open again, he's gone. My nerves, already on edge, sharpen just that much more when the nurse comes back with an oversized plastic bag. I immediately dump it onto the bed to see what secrets the old Tamar wants to share. There's a binder with sheet music that looks like original compositions in pencil, ruined lip balm and three lonely earrings without matches, cloth sanitary pads in jewel-toned fabric, and an oval metal ring wrapped in a piece of muslin. I swallow hard and finger the delicate thing through the cloth. Recognition grips me. I've seen this before.

"We can call between rooms, right?" I ask.

"Sure. You just need to know their room number," she says.

I consider it, and then I'm releasing the brake on my wheelchair and out the door.

"We need to talk," I announce.

Nurse Matthew, Dr. Taylor, and Miss Cynthia, who sometimes reads stories to the younger kids, all look up at me like I've grown another head. Fay chews his bottom lip and nods.

"Yeah, uh . . . game over."

"But I need a chance to win back that last fifty," Miss Cynthia groans.

"I'll make it up to you guys tomorrow. We'll switch to high Chicago instead of five-card stud," he replies.

The adults grumble, but they get up to leave, some with more sheepish looks on their faces than others as they pass by me.

"I was hoping you would come to it on your own," he says hesitantly as soon as I close the door. "I didn't know how to tell you or even if I should tell you. It's not really something that makes sense, you know?" Fay drops down into a chair and props his leg up on a stool. He blows out a big breath of air before both hands slide down his face. Then he smiles, bright and sharp as a squeeze of lemon. "I'm so glad you're here."

"So you're a thief?" I ask.

"What?" he exclaims.

"Or we're both thieves." I roll over to him and hand him the silver ring. "They just returned my items from the blast. This was in it. I remember seeing it on the internet. Right before you stormed out of Leo's room. This is why you've been acting so strange, isn't it? You remember."

The smile on his face is gone, replaced by confusion in his eyes and other emotions I can't really name because his face is still partially bandaged. He opens his mouth and then closes it. Stands and then sits back down.

"Do you remember us stealing this ring?" he asks. "The stone?"

"You have the stone?" I reply.

He nods. "But that doesn't answer my question."

"Well, no. But we've got to tell someone," I say.

"We can't. We can't explain what we did. We don't remember if we did anything. Who's to say we aren't unwitting members of some criminal conspiracy? And . . . and ignorance of the law does not absolve you of its consequences. I looked it up. This stays between us. We fix it ourselves."

"How?"

"I've got a plan, but are you sure you don't remember anything?" he pleads.

His eyes bore into mine, looking for something, any recognition at all. But there's nothing. I feel exposed in a way that even the sponge baths the nurses give me don't make me feel. I wheel a few inches back.

"You're right. The Crayola men aren't letting up, and I don't want to give them any more reasons to ask me any more questions," I say.

"Crayola men?"

"Mr. White and Mr. Green. The men in suits who've been watching us. They showed me pictures of you. Tried to make it seem like you were up to something."

"Do you think I'm up to something?" he says.

I pause. Whatever I'm about to say next will determine which way our relationship will go. It's an ask for trust. For all intents and purposes, he is a stranger, but I'm a stranger to myself. I know as much about him as anyone else on Earth right now. Trusting him is a leap of faith, and in the end, faith has to do with the heart, not logic. If I ask myself who feels more like family, like safety, like someone I . . . love, then he's the answer.

"No. I trust you," I say, and I hope he can tell that I mean it.

"Good, because this only works if we're in it together. All the way."

Music therapy is much more enjoyable than therapy therapy. The former, I'm in control, and the latter is like a car flying in reverse with a blindfolded driver at the wheel, or at least that's how I picture it in my head. I'm visualizing it right now: Dr. Gupta in the front seat, calmly taking notes, a silk bandanna covering the driver's eyes as we hurtle down a crowded city street; she's completely unaware of or indifferent to what's coming next, while I grip the leather beneath my legs and pray for the ride to end.

"You don't know him," Dr. Gupta says flatly.

She's a good therapist. There's no judgment in her tone. It's just a fact, one that's true and not true at the same time.

"But I trust him," I say, just as simply.

"More than you trust your doctors or your aunt," she adds. It feels like she's trying to bait me.

"I feel like I've known him longer," I reply.

"Yes, but feelings are not facts. Our bodies store memories. There is research that emotions can live in muscles and bones. There are people in my yoga classes who've told me that they've had past trauma revisit them as they come to master poses." She pauses. "What I am trying to say is that your body is healing, and as it mends, old emotions may arise unprompted. Feelings like love, devotion."

"What's wrong with that?" I say, unsure of where she's going with this.

"Because those emotions can be confusing. And with your current medication regimen, there is no way to rule out the delusions." Before I can even open my mouth, she adds, "I know. I know you don't like that word, and I have respected your request not to include your neurologist in these discussions *yet* . . . but I am concerned that these . . . dreams are getting worse despite your course of sedatives."

"You're trying to say that how I feel about Fayard isn't real?" I ask, my body going stiff, not with betrayal, but with something that feels too vulnerable, a feeling that makes me wonder whose side Dr. Gupta is on, the side of logic and data, or mine.

"I'm saying intense feelings can seem real, which makes them destructive." She looks down at her notepad. "Have you taken another look at accepting your place at Spelman? Your aunt says that you're a legacy. Generations of your family have attended the school. Being there may help you connect to other parts of yourself that are still closed off. You are part of a family with a rich history."

I shake my head. She wants me to choose between the known and the unknown.

"There's a new music therapy program at Florida A&M University," I reply. She's now flipping through my dream journal but still holds the thread of the conversation.

"I've heard of FAMU. You'd have to wait until spring to attend. Spelman would have you on your feet in the fall."

"Have you been talking to Mr. Green?" I ask, my eyes narrowing. I wonder, if I look hard enough, will I be able to see the physical manifestation of her duplicity, like some kind of traitor's mark?

"Who is that? Does he work for the hospital?" she asks, no hint of recognition on her face.

"He's not a doctor, if that's what you mean. He comes and asks questions. Sometimes it's a Mr. Green; other times it's his partner, Mr. White. It doesn't matter; they're both the same person, really. I think they work for the airline or maybe the government? Police?"

Her face is blank, and I realize just how paranoid and ridiculous I sound. I roll my right wrist, getting used to how it feels without a wrap. It's healed, finally. I'm getting better, feeling more like a real person and not a shell. I just want to leave, to be done with all of this.

"Your birthday wasn't that long ago," she says, changing the topic.

"And?" I say, glad that I spent said birthday with Auntie O and a dinner plate from Lizard's Thicket instead of a big to-do.

"Turning eighteen is a big milestone. Many people have anxiety around that. Some people even dread it."

"Why?" Of all the things to fear in this new life, turning eighteen isn't one of them.

"Transitioning from childhood to adulthood can be extremely difficult for some people, especially those who've experienced past trauma. There are also some very interesting studies in epigenetics, which has to do with genetically inherited trauma. Have you considered that the dreams may have something to do with that?"

I've reached my limit. Talking isn't going to make her get to know me better, and nothing she's said has offered me one shred of peace or understanding. I am still the same confused girl I was when I woke up without a memory over a month ago. I pluck my journal from her hands, as politely as I know how, and slide it back into my side table. Dreams aren't real, I know that. But they feel real, and sometimes they feel more real than what I wake up to every morning. Sharing them with her feels like I'm opening my brain up for exploration.

"Tamar, I thought we were past this," she says sadly.

"Dr. Gupta, I'm not being aggressive or combative. I've just decided to end our session early. As per our agreement, I have that right, yes?"

She nods, though I can sense her disappointment.

"Just think about what I said, please, and take a good look at Spelman's program online. The Children's Foundation just donated three gaming PCs. You can use them in the game room if you can avoid *War Dogs* or whatever you call it. You have a future, tend to it. Record how you're feeling. Writing can be extremely therapeutic, as you well know," she says.

"*Thank you,* Dr. Gupta!" I say brightly, as Auntie O breezes in with an aromatic takeout container. Thank God.

45
FAYARD

A FTER I DISCOVERED THE STONE, I GAVE MYSELF TEN days. Long enough to get some money together but not so long that I'd get comfortable in this borrowed life on borrowed time. I could be released from the hospital any day now, but it's a risk I had to take.

My days form a rhythm. Breakfast with Ma from seven to eight, teleconferences with the pro bono lawyers Mr. Sato got me from the ACLU until nine. He didn't ask too many questions about why I needed to talk to them, and I didn't give him any answers. Lunch, gaming, then dinner alone so I can research until lights-out, and then poker. Tamar doesn't remember anything else, and I don't reveal that I know any more than she does about the stone. I try to bring up more about the past memories I've had. No, that's a lie—I don't try; I *think* about trying to say something, but I never do. Maybe I really did lose my mind, and if that's true, I'm going to keep this to myself. But that doesn't stop me from looking up names, dates, birth and death certificates, and census data on ancestry sites. I remember everyone, all of my mothers, every best friend, every slight, every injustice.

I sleep maybe four hours at night; the rest of the time I'm hustling. Dr. Swafford still nips at my heels, but the online pots he suggested I look into are larger and anonymous. A week later I've got ten thousand dollars in bitcoin and other currency in my account and a very contrite burn doctor clipping away at my bandages.

"We've talked about expectations, but I want you to be ready for the changes. Okay?" he says, patiently.

I nod. The face in the pictures is some other kid. Some kid who was blown up in an airport explosion. That kid is dead. Whoever I see in the mirror is me now.

"Don't be nervous." Tamar's voice is steady and clear. It's a statement. Maybe a bit of a command. It's comforting. It helps.

"I'm so glad you're here, Tamar," Ma says, but she doesn't mean it. Of course, she knew Tamar before the accident, but she says she's totally different than she used to be. She says the old Tamar was submissive, almost to a fault, and more feminine, though I can't make out much of what that must mean. It worries Ma that a personality can change so much and that she may have lost her cupcake-competition baking partner. Ma's hopeful for me, I think, but anytime Tamar is around, her smile gets just a bit tighter.

The air feels cool against my skin as layers of warmth are peeled away. I work my jaw left and right, opening my mouth, sticking out my tongue, loosening what has been stiff, experiencing for the first time what it's like to sit without a mask.

Dr. Swafford's face, which was set in a schooled, concentrated glare, breaks into a smile. "Now, there's a handsome guy," he says before handing me a mirror. "You've got a bit of scarring, and we had the plastic surgeon do a rhinoplasty, so your nose won't look exactly the same, but I'm happy. Very happy."

I can hear Ma draw in a shaky breath as I turn around and then blow it out quickly. She looks sad, shoulders drawn in as she stares. I flick my eyes to Tamar, who's wearing the biggest smile I've ever seen.

"You look so . . . good . . . but different," Ma says on a breath. "So, so, so different."

Dr. Swafford takes her by the hand as the tears that were just swimming in her eyes a second ago begin to fall in earnest.

"Let's take a walk," Dr. Swafford offers, rubbing his thumb across the top of her hand affectionately.

As soon as the door closes, Tamar relaxes and leans forward as much as she can in her wheelchair. "You almost look as good as me," she says, and smirks.

"Now I'm really scared to look. I might be blinded by my own beauty."

"I have to wonder if all that charm is a personality quirk or if you really mean the things you say when you're flirting," she adds.

"Is it flirting if it's true? My mother says her psychic told her I'd die young. I don't think she really believes I cheated death, not just yet," I say.

"Quit stalling and look," she urges.

She's right. I've been stalling, even if it's just a few seconds. "Right."

I don't realize I'm holding my breath until I blow it all out at once as I raise the hand mirror.

"Disappointed?" she asks.

"No . . . just, I thought that maybe—"

"You would recognize yourself?" she interjects. "I could have told you not to dream that big. I still see a stranger in the mirror. It doesn't change anything," she says, and frowns.

"It does for her." I point my chin to the door. I can still see my mother's back retreating down the hallway.

I leave a note for my mother on my bed and at Leo's request get chili dogs delivered to the game room for a Sandy's versus Rush's restaurant showdown. The competition delights everyone on the floor and ignites a debate that leaves no one the winner. It's excitement and distraction—exactly what I need. Once the last votes are in, I ask the night nurse for a little fresh air alone. He doesn't so much as blink an eye, just nods and keeps staring at whatever charts he's scouring. I don't have to explain the duffel bag across my shoulder, which irritates me just a little bit because I came up with a really good story. It's shift change and the NBA finals are tonight. Everyone with a screen is glued to it, and even the suits are caught up in the hysteria. Basketball. It's the universal language.

As nervous and as prepared with excuses as I am, it's all unnecessary. The ride-share is already idling when I walk out of the employee exit of the hospice wing and I'm barely in the car when Tamar rolls out a minute later from the opposite building.

"You look good!" I shout from the passenger window before getting out to help her into the back seat. The driver, a sunburned Carolina fan, as evidenced by his well-worn baseball cap, folds her chair and slides it into the trunk carefully, along with her crutches.

"Thanks. You do too," she says. I feel the excitement floating off her skin in invisible waves. Our feelings are mutual.

I'm nervous, too nervous to chat during the ride, and now that we're at the train station waiting to board, I still can't find much to say.

I know what happens when she and I are alone. I remember every look, kiss, and touch. But she doesn't, which means I have to keep my mouth shut and my hands to myself.

I'm just happy she's coming with me. That has to count for something.

And right now, it's damn near all I've got.

46
TAMAR

FAYARD FOUND AN ARCHIVE OF OLD RACE FILMS MADE by Oscar Micheaux in the twenties and thirties and downloaded them to his new laptop. We spend hours watching stuff like *Murder in Harlem* and *God's Stepchildren*. For some reason they feel more relevant than the recent stuff we can stream, like we're rewatching them instead of seeing them for the first time. I write as much in my journal, wondering if I'll ever see Dr. Gupta again to deconstruct it all.

Fayard charms the staff in the same way he did at the hospital and barely sleeps as he pulls in new poker partners at every stop. We change our names every time we meet someone new and laugh until our sides hurt, but there's something he's not telling me. I hear it behind every joke and see it lurking in the corners of his eyes whenever he holds my gaze a bit too long. I've noticed how he's avoided touching me. He hasn't so much as brushed up against my arm since we boarded the train.

"We aren't exactly keeping a low profile," I say as we sit down for breakfast in the club car. We got the deluxe accommodations, a private compartment with two tiny beds that pull down and three meals a day. The cheapest tickets just get you a seat and you have to eat what you bring. The small tables are difficult to fit into with my crutches, but the waiters are exceptionally helpful, even if they do sometimes sit other travelers with us in a nearly empty car. Today we're lucky to be alone. Apparently, meeting people is supposed to be part of the fun.

"We're hiding in plain sight. People don't make up stories about people they've met, but they'll construct entire lifetimes for people they watch from a distance. Plus, it's fun. Why be yourself when you can be anyone you want to be?" Fayard says.

I roll my eyes and hold in my irritation when the waiter sits a girl and an older woman in our booth. My smile is tight as Fay introduces us to Miriam, a girl with a thick cloud of curly hair that surrounds her head like a crown. She's traveling with her great-aunt, who doesn't bother to smile or say hello; she just nods, wisps of gray hair framing her preternaturally unlined face.

"So where are you guys from?" Miriam asks.

"Chattanooga," Fayard lies, and tacks on friendly small-talk questions I ignore. My eyes are fixed on the old woman. She hasn't said anything, but she's paying attention. A few times I catch her scrutinizing Fayard's face before sliding her gaze back to the window to watch a field of sunflowers roll by.

"My aunt and I are relocating. Our family had a shop right outside New Orleans for, gosh, how long, Tante?"

The old woman just sips her coffee and Miriam has to compensate. "Seventy-five years."

I think about Auntie O reading my letter, hoping she'll hold off on calling anyone to look for us, like I've asked.

Fayard presses his lips into a short whistle. "That's pretty long. Why'd you pull up stakes?"

"Everything comes to an end. Too many bad memories. We needed a new start," she says with excitement.

"What did you sell?" Fayard asks her.

"Readings. Our family is full of astrologers, mystics, a couple of astrophysicists, and one astronomer who may or may not work for NASA."

He laughs. "You're psychics?"

"Some people call us that, but I don't like that label. We see things other people either refuse to see or cannot see. It's much more scientific than people think, and more spiritual than some want to admit."

"Sounds expensive if it's both science and . . . spirit," Fay says with a hand flourish. Miriam laughs. She's hooked. I'm not jealous. Everybody gets hooked on Fay eventually.

"Now, we do provide pro bono services if the spirit compels us," she says, and grins.

"But I'm sure that is rare," Fayard replies, laying the charm on thick.

"Most people aren't as special as they think they are," she teases.

I order pancakes piled high with strawberries, and the waiter perches a pot of coffee on the end of the table along with four ceramic cups.

"Well, now that you've insulted me, I'm going to give you a reading free of charge, just to shut you up," she adds.

I've lost the thread of the conversation, but this proclamation snaps me back to the present. The old woman seems to feel the same, because her back straightens as she utters the first word I've heard her say all morning.

"No."

Her niece looks at the woman as if she's grown another head.

"Tante? Why? Just a short reading," she says, and turns back to Fayard. "Hold out your palm."

The old woman pulls her niece's outstretched hand to her side of the table and shakes her head.

"Auntie, you're being rude," Miriam says before she launches into a flurry of what sounds like French but isn't. I look at Fayard, who glances back at me with an amused look in his eyes. He likes drama. I know before it happens that this argument will be the story he recites before we go to sleep tonight, the story he'll perfect before retelling it to whoever shows up for his midnight poker game. The human condition. It's his drug of choice.

The old woman slams her hand on the table with finality, shutting up her niece, whose mouth has disappeared into her face, angry red blotches now snaking up her neck and onto her cheeks.

"Give me your hand," the old woman says roughly, eyes trained on me. I blink, taken aback by her bluntness and surprised that she'd even ask it.

"Why me? He's the one who wants the reading," I say.

"It must be you," she says quickly, her words sharp and quick as bites.

"Go on," Fayard urges, as if this really is just a fun psychic reading with new friends over breakfast, but he's interpreted the room wrong. It's clear this woman needs to prove a point, and I'm not sure I want to be at the center of it. Still, I reluctantly hold my hand out. She grips my fingers in her gnarled ones and presses a thumb into my palm as she closes her eyes. I can see her irises move from side to side behind her lids, as if she's reading, slowly at first and then quickly. I try to pull my hand away, but she grips it harder.

"You are a traveler," she says.

"We're on a train," Fayard snarks, and I cut him a withering glare. He holds up a hand in apology.

"You are . . . not who you say you are. You travel together on a long journey, and what you seek you have yet to find, but time is a jealous god. You have escaped your fate. Destiny finds you again, as it always has, leading you on a path to the same destination."

This wipes the smile from his face.

"You should not be here," she continues, "Your story . . ."

Her eyes flutter open and she stares into my eyes, seeing and not seeing.

Fayard laughs nervously. He laces his fingers into mine with one hand and calls the waiter over with the other. The waiter nods, and after rummaging in his pocket Fayard immediately places a few bills on the table.

"Unfortunately, we have to go," he says, as amiably as possible. "Uh . . . thank you, Miriam. Madame. It was a pleasure."

"But you haven't even finished," Miriam blusters, unobservant of the charge in the air. Fayard ignores her. He's already standing when she launches into an apology for her aunt, or maybe the reading itself, but he doesn't care.

My mobility is compromised, so it takes quite a bit of maneuvering to get me back to our room. No one could call what we did a smooth exit. As soon as the doors to our small car slide close, I let him have it.

"She scared you. I know she did. You're going to tell me what you're hiding. Now," I demand.

"Tamar, you don't understand," he argues.

"Then make me understand. I'm essentially a runaway with a would-be, could-be, might-have-been, and may-still-currently-be criminal. You've got something tucked away and you don't want to tell me. Tell me!"

"I . . . ," he starts.

"Tell me now or I swear to God I'm getting off at the next stop and calling the FBI myself! Tell me, Fayard!"

"We're . . . we're dead."

"What?" I ask, confused, fear and anger warring for dominance inside me.

"You and me. We've lived before, died before. God, this doesn't make sense. Okay, this is going to sound crazy, but you and me, we're supposed to be together, like fated to be together, and we are, in every life we've lived, but then we—"

"Are you having an episode? I . . . I need to call your doctor. I'm sorry I yelled at you. I'm just worried. I shouldn't have said those things." I'm babbling as I search for my phone.

"I don't need a doctor. Tamar, look at me."

I stop searching and look up.

"Just before I tell you everything . . . you have to be honest with me. Have you really never dreamed of us?"

I'm frozen. I can hear every beat of my heart rushing past my ears. I should tell him. *Yes. It's easy. Yes, I have.* All I have to do is open my mouth.

"'Dream' isn't really the right word," he continues. "'Vision' is more like it. Have you ever gone to sleep or gotten lost in your thoughts and seen yourself, but not the person you are right now, alive in an entirely different life?

My lips remain sealed shut. I wish I could lie and let him live in this delusion alone, but I can't admit it to him either. It's like as soon as I say the words out loud, they'll be real. All this history between us will have really happened.

"I'll make it easier for you. I'll tell you about a life I've watched us live. If you remember, just nod your head."

Maybe I move; maybe I don't, but I feel frozen. My heart is beating too fast and too loud for me to focus on much else.

"We lived in Florida. I met you at the Excelsior Hall, where your mother made costumes and I worked as an assistant for Buster Brown on the vaudeville circuit. The first time I kissed you, I was so nervous my whole body shook. You gripped my arm and danced with me as Scott Joplin played 'Please Say You Will' on the main stage. It's one of my favorite memories, but I don't dream it often. The older lives come more frequently. You were always Tamar, but in Al-Kawkaw my name was Fayid. I fell in love with you at the stall of a honey merchant. You were a slave, and I wanted to make you my wife."

I will my head to move and acknowledge that what he's saying is real and true, that I've seen this too. The relief in his eyes is a holy thing, vulnerable and naked.

My lip quivers. "Are we crazy?" I ask, my voice cracking.

His arms enfold me, his lips press against each temple, his thumbs wipe away the cascade of tears.

"You're not crazy."

And then he kisses me, softly at first and then so deeply it shakes the memories from my bones and sets every reservation and fear on fire.

"I could sleep my entire life away with you," Fay whispers into my ear as the sun sets. The train is rocking us into a blissful sleep, but there's just too much to talk about.

"I remember what it felt like to be sold away from my mother in Charleston, how good fresh rattlesnake tastes on a wagon train, and how safe I feel when all of your weight is pressed against me," I say. "How long have you known?"

"Not long. I thought I was losing it, but it felt too real and the dreams kept coming. I didn't want to scare you, so I held it in. I'm sorry I wasn't honest about all of it sooner."

"I'm sorry I didn't tell you the first time you asked. I didn't want to believe it was possible. I thought it would all go away once I healed, once we left the hospital. I never know what will trigger another story, another us. Most of the time the memories come when I'm sleeping, but sometimes it's a smell, or a song."

His breath is hot on my chin, my face, and I think he's going to pull back, but he leans in for another kiss. This time it's soft and slow, and instead of a raging waterfall of images there is a soft lapping of waves, in and out. There is laughter and kindness and . . . music, of all kinds.

"You're talented," he says before he rolls over and falls back on his elbows. "Flute, guitar, piano. Music's a theme for you. I could reach out to DeAndre. He called me the other day. We were really good friends, and he's been doing our YouTube channel without me. If we did a series on you, maybe that might help you get your music out there."

"Do you ever see us grow old?" I ask.

"No. I figured we could only see as far as our present age. We'll probably get new memories, new visions as we get older, right?"

"You can't be so nonchalant about all this," I say with a growing uneasiness in my belly. Sure, we could be reliving our grand romance over and over. It's possible. But something doesn't feel right. I've trusted my gut this far. I'm not going to stop now. I chew the corner of my lip as I think, staring out the window and letting the corn meld into a blur of green.

"I love you," Fay says, and snaps me out of my thoughts. I forget to breathe. My brain shorts out from the weight of the words because I know he means them. This isn't Christmas card, Valentine's Day love. It's I'll-die-for-you love.

Maybe he already has.

47

Gao, Mali, 1325

TAMAR

FAYID SITS SMUGLY ON HIS STOOL AS IF HE'S GOT EVERY-thing figured out, as if he knows my mind so well he doesn't even have to consult me before a decision is made that will change both our lives. He wants me to trade one form of slavery for another. I cannot.

"I do not need a man who believes my best quality is my ability to endure pain and disrespect. I do not desire another master," I say bitterly, my voice breaking on the sharp edges of each word.

He flinches at the word "master" as if I am the person who has any power to hurt him.

"I am securing your freedom. I would never be your master and you would not be my slave. You would be akin to second wife. Honored in my heart, if not in name," he says with kindness.

I shake my head, realizing deep in my bones that this will not work. Hating myself for being unwilling to share him. Is what he is proposing so unreasonable? I've seen happy families with as many as seven wives. I have also seen second and third wives treated worse than worm-ridden dogs, footstools for the first wife to tread upon, walls of flesh for the first wife to beat until her fists bleed, while her husband goes out in search of yet another girl to amuse himself with for a time.

"When I told my father about you and me, after the feast, he said that you would not submit. He said, 'A girl like that wants to run beside a man and not behind,' that you would not know how to be a wife. I said he was wrong." His eyes are pleading. He wants me to assure him he was right.

A voice slices through our small universe. "Your father is a wise man."

My head snaps to see Iyin in the doorway. She has dressed herself, and it shows. Her headwrap is tied too loosely to hide the thinning hair at her scalp. She's trying desperately to look regal as she strides across the floor, her steps slow so that she can breathe deeply enough to keep her lungs from rebelling.

I leap from the chair and watch as she gingerly takes my seat. I reach out a hand to steady her, but she refuses me. Fayid smiles with all his teeth, surprised at her arrival.

"*Hayati*, what a delight to see you so early. I had hoped to delay our meeting until this afternoon so that you may rest," he says.

"It is not necessary. I had hoped you would call upon me today, and I see that you have. I am grateful to Tamar for entertaining you until I could prepare myself for visitors."

If he's confused by her lie, he does not let it show.

"I—" he begins, but she holds up a thin hand to stop him.

"I have heard your amended marriage proposal, and I would like to offer one of my own. I am not prone to jealousy, so you should never fear that from me. I am my father's daughter, and I am nothing if not practical. I had resigned myself to being second wife or even third after it had become clear that so many men of acceptable quality had been killed or captured, or had fled the city.

Now I see an opportunity, and I believe you do as well. You would like to marry Tamar, but my father, shrewd businessman that he is, has persuaded you to take both of us. You also ask for her consent to become your second wife, but I must tell you that she cannot consent. She is a slave, *my* slave, willed to me by my mother before she died, and I will not allow you to purchase her freedom. You cannot buy what is not for sale." She says this as if I'm nothing more than an expensive chair that has caught his eye in the market.

I lose all feeling in my legs as the words spill smoothly from her lips.

"Surely you—" Fayid begins again, but her hand, like a small flag from a conquering ship, goes up.

"My father has no sons. I grow older as tumult in the city increases each year. If you love Tamar, if you want to be with her, you will marry me and take no other wives. Any children she births will be raised as our own, and she will never take your name. Not while I still draw breath." She pauses, in the same way one would break in the middle of slaughtering an animal, bracing themselves for the final blow. The servant in me, my worst self, wonders if she needs water, so attuned am I to seeing to her needs. I clench my fists tight. If my dreams are to be murdered, I should at least bear witness.

"If you choose not to agree to my proposal, I will sell her to a brothel of the lowest quality tomorrow. You will never see her again, and you can go to sleep every night assured of her unending suffering."

His mild annoyance, characterized by the small nods he was giving her while she spoke, recedes to something much darker.

He crosses and then uncrosses his legs and places his fist upon his knees.

"She has been your closest ally and servant for nearly her entire life. Your father has said as much. He told me you were as close as sisters. You would do this?" he says, astonished.

She does not hesitate. "I would."

In a flash I see my life play out before me. Iyin as the first wife, the honored wife, who sits across from Fayid at feasts. She orders the servants to manage her household to her liking, making adjustments to the dishes so they suit her tastes. Suggesting that this or that rug be replaced, that Fayid wear a brown bou-bou instead of the scarlet. She would be the best of the noble wives, retiring early every night to her own rooms, weary from a day of ease. I would fall onto my cot in a small room kept for me, where Fayid would visit me at night, and when the children come, they would become hers, just as I am hers, and he would say nothing.

His eyes search her face for some weakness, or maybe he is trying to discern what kind of demon has possessed her, to make this frail girl such an evil monster. When he does not find what he's looking for, his eyes fall on mine and I see the resignation.

Hatred courses through me.

"I will do as you ask," he says solemnly.

Iyin claps her thin hands and smiles. "Binta! Call Father inside. We are a blessed house. I am a blessed woman," she cheers.

Like a nightmare come to life, Fayid embraces Iyin's father like a son, and I fade into the kitchens.

The knife I choose I sharpen myself. I am not sad as I contemplate its gleam. I have had more joy than most. I have lived longer than many of the house girls I've known.

If God is merciful, I will live again. I have done this life wrong. Where I am going, I don't need any solutions, because there are no problems.

FAYARD

HAVE THE FIRST DREAMLESS SLEEP SINCE I WOKE UP IN THE hospital. The first thing I notice is that the train has stopped. That smooth rocking that helped loosen the memories from Tamar's brain is gone. And then I realize that she's gone too.

I must have slept like the dead, because she can't get around without help, but her collapsible wheelchair is gone, her bags, everything. For the slimmest of seconds, I consider that all of this is just a figment of my imagination—the dreams, even Tamar—but then I catch my reflection in the mirror and taste her cherry-coconut lip balm on my lips.

I pull out my phone to see if she texted or called and see a missed text from Leo. It's a link to a video from one of his social media feeds. The screen fills with the bright colors of the children's lounge in the hospital. Police in riot gear and strapped with long guns are rushing through the hallway. A German shepherd on a leash rushes right up to Leo and sniffs the hidden camera attached to his oxygen tank and then trots off. Screams erupt in the background, and I see my favorite nurse get into a near fistfight with a police officer.

"We're all being moved. The pigs are shutting the entire hospital down. Full riot gear, people. I'm having some trouble making out the letters on their chest plates, but it looks like DHS. Some are

ICE. If my theory is correct, they're . . . alien . . . Area 51 . . . they're getting close. Share this post!"

The camera buckles as he starts wheeling himself at top speed away from the melee.

"We're American citizens!" he shouts as much as he can with his limited lung capacity, and then the video cuts out. I'm not sure what I'm seeing, so I reload the page and get an error message.

I flag the porter.

"Where are we?" I ask as I hold the door open with my shoulder.

"Pulling into Washington, DC."

"Did you see my girlfriend get off? Shaved head, wheelchair?"

He winces. "I've been working a few cars. I'm not sure I could . . ."

"Sorry. Let me stop you. Do you have mobile payment service? MoneyApp? I hate to tip in cash. You never know what the tip share is gonna be, and you've really helped us out with her wheelchair and everything. The room service. Top-notch. Really."

The guy brightens up a bit and gives me every detail of her departure. A minute later I've transferred eighty dollars into his account, and when I ask where Tamar is the second time around, he's happy to let me know she got off at Quantico. He makes a quick call to a buddy who just happens to be a ticket agent at that location, and I've got the name of the only wheelchair-accessible ride-share company that will drive from Quantico to DC.

I must have said something—no, I did something, but I can't think what it is. Shit, this isn't my fault, or hers; this whole situation is just too weird. Maybe it was too much for her to take. The sun has baked off the dawn fog, but it's still early. I'm getting into the ride-share when my phone buzzes.

Tam: I'm sorry.
Fay: R u ok
Tam: Fine. I . . .

I stare at the screen as she writes and rewrites something. Those three dots are a held breath, a pause where my entire life dangles in the balance. What is there to say to reassure her? I got nothing. But when all else fails, you stay the course. She has the ring. I've got the stone. We still have a job to do.

Fay: I'm going to make the drop. I got us a room at the downtown Marriott. We can talk after.
Fay: I'll never leave, okay? Even if I'm not sure about anything else, I'm sure about you.
Tam: . . .

The three dots sit there for another minute and then they disappear. A seed of dread starts to root in my gut, and a thousand doom-filled scenarios emerge like a cloud of locusts. I can barely see straight.

"Uh, kid? The ride says you want to head downtown to the Smithsonian. You sure you want to do that today? With the protests on the National Mall and all?"

"I need to drop my bags at the hotel first. What protests?"

After that first Google search about the airport blast and then the stone, I haven't been so pressed to check the headlines. The plan is to make a smooth drop-off during visiting hours. It's a weekday. There shouldn't be any problems getting in, but I should have known fate would throw a wrench in all this.

We pull onto Constitution Avenue and hit a wall of people, some dressed in scrubs and white coats, others with T-shirts that read REMEMBER THE DEAD, and a few have painted their faces to look like skeletons.

"It's a health care thing. The Mall ain't a stranger to demonstrations, but this is the biggest one I've seen in a while. Aggressive, too. Reminds me of the ACT UP protests in the nineties. AIDS activists, you know? They used to throw the ashes of their dead lovers on the White House lawn. You believe that?" the driver says.

I stare wide-eyed at the crowds, trying to calculate my next move.

"But who am I to judge strategy, right? They got what they wanted. It made people pay attention. Anyway, I'm just warning you. The boys in blue might come in hard on 'em if things get heated. I don't want you caught in the crossfire. You sure you still wanna go?"

My head nods yes before I can get my mouth to work.

"All right, it's your funeral," he replies. "We'll have to wait while we work through the lights."

I can't wait. I take a chance and get out of the car and pay him extra to loop around museum a few times before picking me back up to ride to the hotel.

I feel like I'm swimming upstream as I make my way to the museum. There's an electricity in the air that I would probably find energizing on any other day, but today I'm more nervous than anything, pulled as tight as a kora string. The driver was right: The crowd is aggressive, chanting loud with fists in the air, mouths pulled into angry grimaces that look all the more ominous with the black-and-white makeup. I blink and they're just people. I blink again and they're an angry chorus of the dead, a legion of demons sent to steal my soul. The stone feels heavy in my pocket, and getting heavier with each step I take closer to the museum doors. It's hot out, nearly ninety degrees, and I feel every degree as I stand in line to get in. All I have to do is buy a T-shirt, wrap the stone in it as I wipe off my fingerprints, and drop it at lost and found. Simple. Then Tamar and I can talk and figure the rest of it out. Everything else will fall into place after that. I hope. I take another step and hear a pop, then a scream. Next thing I know, it's total chaos.

It's dark and cold, much colder than I thought it would be, when I make it to the hotel. For a few miles I was sure I was being followed, but I chalk it up to paranoia. My eyes still burn a bit from the tear gas, but I'll live. It's my stomach that needs attention. I haven't eaten anything in hours. The front-desk agent can hear it growl, and while her face remains neutral, I can see her eyes dart to the side at the sound. She hands me my key card, but lets me know the room won't be ready for another hour.

"A girl was here. She tried to check in earlier."

I draw in a breath of relief. "Where is she?" I ask as I look around the empty foyer, but she directs me to the restaurant next door, a tiny place called the Last Chance Diner.

It's one of those local places, I guess, with a bright neon pie plate for a sign. The glow gives the street an otherworldly feel. All the other establishments on the block are sleek and modern, with small tables on the sidewalk, but this place looks quaint in comparison. I have to wonder how they stay in business.

A bell dings when I open the door, and everyone looks my way.

"It's your last chance, traveler!" a waitress behind the counter sings brightly, and a couple of people groan. The smell of coffee and something smoky and familiar assaults me as soon as the door swings closed.

A man, possibly the manager, if his button-down shirt and name tag are any indication, slaps the counter angrily with a dishrag. "Stop saying that every time somebody walks through the damn door, Patience."

"But it's our tagline, Daddy," she says sweetly. "You'll see. It'll catch on. Sit anywhere you like, sweetie!" she calls out.

A boy no older than ten is in one booth, copying something from a textbook, while a pair of twins who look like models sit at the small bar. A man who is either suffering from a fatal case of bad taste or makes his living as a pimp is squeezed into a booth with a few folks in dirty jumpsuits. All of them are staring at a large television screen installed behind the bar, where the news is playing.

I scan the faces in the low light and then switch tactics and scan the feet of everyone in the crowd, looking for wheels. My stomach sinks when I realize there isn't anything shining. The prepaid phone slides inside my fist on cold sweat and then I see them. Crutches, glinting at the edge of the crowd.

"So what was the point of leaving me if we're going to end up in the same place anyway?" I say as I slide into the booth.

"I knew you'd find me once the hotel clerk let you know the room wasn't ready. I just needed some time to think."

"You couldn't think in the club car while I was sleeping? You didn't have to be sooo—"

"If you say 'dramatic,' I'll throw this coffee in your face," she says, but she's not angry; she sounds tired. Somehow that makes my heart sink more.

The waitress comes over and asks if I want anything. I tell her I'll take the special. I don't care what it is.

"Anything more for you, sweetheart?" she asks Tamar. I can barely hear her over the jukebox playing "Where Is the Love" by Donny Hathaway and Roberta Flack. I know this because the cheetah-print-suit guy in the next booth over announces it, along with the release date, as soon as the track starts, like we're playing some kind of trivia game.

Tamar shakes her head.

"How about a piece of pie?" the waitress tries.

"No, thank you," Tamar protests.

"You should eat. How about some chicken soup? Ooooh, or some of our Tennessee hot chicken. It's my grandma's recipe. I guarantee you'll love it," she gushes.

"Patience!" Tamar snaps. "Really, I'm fine."

The waitress is still for a breath and then tops off Tamar's coffee. "I'll bring you the pie."

"She's aggressive," I say.

"She's been that way since I came in. The manager, though, has been staring at me like I'm going to rob the place since the moment I sat down," she says, shifting her body.

I take a look at the guy. He does look angry. He also reminds me of someone.

"So, you gonna tell me why you left?" I ask.

I hold out my hand, palm up, until Tamar places hers in mine. I squeeze it, anchoring us here.

"Do you feel like there's something we're supposed to do?" she asks.

"Well, the first thing that comes to mind is getting rid of this thing, whatever it is," I reply.

"Yeah, and how did that work out today?" she asks.

"A minor setback. We'll try again tomorrow," I say as optimistically as I can muster.

"Tear gas and rubber bullets aren't minor. When I was trying to make it to the Mall, it seemed like the world forgot how to drive. There were six car accidents, and then when the driver got out to get my wheelchair, the first tear-gas can erupted. I slammed the car door so the air couldn't get in, and then someone ran over my chair," she says, her voice shaking.

"Damn."

"Yeah, damn, or, better yet, damned," she replies. She shakes her head and squeezes my hand harder. "I have this feeling, like déjà vu mixed with dread. I've had it since I woke up six weeks ago without even remembering my name, a feeling in my gut like there's something I'm missing. I feel better when I'm with you, but I also feel like it's getting stronger."

"Like you're running out of time?" I ask.

"Yes!"

"Maybe we should just go back, then. Mail the rock and the ring anonymously. I know Spelman is your auntie's thing, but there's a music program at Carolina. Instead of Morehouse, I could enroll in the linguistics department there."

"I thought you were interested in history, or even physics," she says.

"*He* was. I've been thinking about the Air Force, really. Can't get the space program out of my head for some reason."

She frowns and pulls her hand back.

"Don't change your plans for me," Tamar says sadly.

"But I want to. I want to be with you. It's the only thing I'm sure of. Nothing else seems familiar, not these clothes, not the food I eat, not even how my body moves. It's like there's too much gravity. It all feels wrong. But when I'm with you, the world and my place in it click," I say, wanting to tell her everything I feel, put it all out there.

"That's just it. I don't think it's supposed to," she says, her voice low.

It's quick. The sirens. Given how dark it is outside, I should have noticed the lights coming.

Floodlights pour into the diner from the outside, and a voice breaks through Donny Hathaway's "You Were Meant for Me," 1972.

"Time's up!" An oddly robotic voice booms from outside the glass windows, so loud the mugs and wineglasses shake inside the restaurant. Every head in the diner turns toward us, and my gut churns. Red and blue lights spill into the diner. It's over. I know without having to look that on the other side of those windows are our Crayola men.

"Exit the diner slowly!"

I slide out of the booth and make my way to Tamar's side to help her with her crutches.

"One at a time," the megaphone voice continues.

Tamar shakes her head.

"It didn't happen like this last time," she says.

"What are you talking about?" I ask, not understanding what she means. I've never been in this diner before.

"Last time. We had more time last time," she says, upset, searching for something, or perhaps someone, in the diner.

"You have ten seconds to move or we're coming in!" the voice booms.

"I've got to go out there," I say.

She shakes her head. "Don't go."

"Ten!"

"I've got to. Let me go first. We'll work it out. Those lawyers I talked to will help. We'll be okay."

"Seven!"

A frustrated tear runs down her cheek as she scoots herself back into the booth and rests for a moment, trying to make herself smaller, her teeth biting into her bottom lip. She starts to move toward her crutches.

"Four!"

"It's fine," I tell her, and start backing toward the door, unable to let her out of my sight.

I open the door and put my hands into the air as I turn around. My shirt rides up, and I get a hit of the cool breeze right before a voice yells, "Gun!"

I don't feel the shots, I hear them, and it's weird that everything doesn't fade to black; instead it all just gets brighter.

49

TAMAR

MY BODY IS VIBRATING, LIKE SOME STRING HAS BEEN plucked inside and my nerves won't calm down. I jump at loud noises and flinch at loud voices. If the wind blows too sharp I freeze, absolutely sure I'm being followed by someone dangerous. I stop into a restaurant bathroom and sob for ten minutes, a loud ugly cry that I can't explain.

Trauma. This feels like what Dr. Gupta prepared me for when we had our first meeting, except the paranoia, unexplained tremors and nervousness she said would come never happened. I don't know why it's suddenly hitting me now, but it doesn't feel like it has anything to do with the blast. This isn't a body hurt. It's deeper. Although, I could definitely be wrong. What I do know is that somebody, somewhere has it out for me.

I know because I've tried everything to unload this stupid ring at the museum and I just can't make it happen. The first ride-share driver was fine until he got lost. I got out and ate lunch at Ben's Chili Bowl. Why did I run? I wasn't sure. So I didn't say anything. Then I tried the bus, but the crowds got too thick for the bus to cut through, and then there was that sinkhole. When has there ever been a sinkhole in Washington, DC?

There are Crayola men running everywhere. I've called Fayard ten times, but he's never picked up. Dread curdles in my stomach, and I have to use the paper bag from my lunch leftovers to throw up.

"You okay back there?"

I nod to one of the ladies on the bus, an older woman in bright pink scrubs and rubber shoes. I wipe my mouth with a ketchup-stained napkin and ask her how to navigate my way to the hotel where Fay made reservations ahead of time. I'm almost out of the cash I *borrowed* from him, so I don't have much choice.

The hotel is on a quiet street, but it's clean when I roll in. Unfortunately, the room isn't ready, so the desk agent suggests the diner next door. She recommends I have the soup, and if I can't keep that down, they've got ginger ale.

The bell dings overhead and my gut roils. I feel lost, like there's something I'm supposed to know or perhaps do. A song, mournful and soul-stirring, plays on the jukebox; then the smell of incense in the air, thick and out of place, wakes me out of my daze. Odd choice for an air freshener. It's like an Old West disco inside: polished wagon wheels sit alongside pictures of a family of Black cowboys that spans decades, maybe a century. Each face appears, ages, and then disappears, only to pop up farther down the wall with a slight change here and there. A larger nose added to the mix, or a pair of dimples.

A boy in a red hat waves at me as he dips a paintbrush into a cup of dark liquid. He's painting the front window. My arms feel heavy as I roll down the aisle, and every eye is on me, but not with the usual furtive look people give folks who use mobility devices; it's something else. A set of twin brothers sitting on slim wooden barrels at the bar unnerves me the most. They don't speak, just stare, and I don't have the energy to teach them manners, so I roll on.

"No one wants to hear any more of that old stuff, Mr. Lucky. Play something else," the boy calls over his shoulder.

"This right here is your musical education, Ralphie. Listen up! The closer I get to yooooou," he croons, and snaps his fingers to the beat.

A waitress bursts through the kitchen doors to sing along with him. "The more you make me seeeeee," she trills with her eyes closed, both hands and arms covered with plates full of food. She nearly crashes into me before she opens her eyes and stops short. "It's your last chance, traveler!" she says, and winks. "It's our tagline," she adds after I give her a look. "Says so right on the window."

I turn around to see the sun setting just behind the mural on the front window. "Uh . . . okay," I say.

"Go on and take a seat. I'll get right to you, sweetheart."

I settle into a booth and try to shake off the nausea I've had since I left Fay on the train. I just needed time to think. I can't get my thoughts straight when I'm around Fay. At least that's what I'm telling myself. I'm not scared. I'm not. I just want to figure some things out on my own.

The waitress comes back and sets a glass of ginger ale on the table.

"But I didn't order anything," I tell her.

"Oh, I know, honey. It'll help settle your stomach. Want anything to go with that? You should eat. How about some chicken soup? Ooooh, or some of our Tennessee hot chicken. It's my grandma's recipe. I guarantee you'll love it," she gushes.

I grip the table as the nausea grabs me.

"What did you say?" I eke out.

"I'll bring you the pie," she says, and taps the table, singing as she makes her way back into the kitchen, "Your love has captured meeee. Over and over agaiiiiin . . ."

"Patience, will you stop that noise," a man bellows as he passes her. He must be the manager. There's a little placard next to the kitchen door with his unsmiling face on it. Joseph Williams.

"Are you gonna sit there all night?" he barks at me. "We close soon."

"Daddy!" I clap my hand over my mouth, embarrassed. Why did I call this complete stranger Daddy? "I'm sorry. Um, sir. I . . . uh . . . I just sat down," I protest. "And it's only six o'clock."

I point to the clock on the wall with the over-easy egg in the center. I noticed the butt-ugly thing when I first rolled in, but what I didn't notice is that it's moving much faster than it should be, and backward. I blink and realize the sun has set so fast it's pitch-dark outside. My heartbeat quickens with worry. I squeeze my eyes shut and take a deep breath. I look down at the table and have to cover my hand with my mouth so as not to scream.

It's filled with plate after plate of half-eaten cherry pie.

"Oh, hey!" a voice calls over to me.

I look up and see a familiar face, but it's a memory from a life that doesn't feel like mine. *Her* life. "Rose?" I say, and the woman shakes her head.

"No. I'm Iris. Though I do have a cousin named Rose. A sister named Clover, too. Nana loved her flowers."

"Oh, I'm sorry. I thought . . . Never mind," I say like a confused fan who just approached the wrong celebrity for an autograph, but then I catch myself. Iris spoke to *me.*

She's copper-haired, with dimples, wicked eyeliner, and a kind of old Hollywood glamour about her. Beautiful iris tattoos bloom from her forearm to her shoulder.

"Mind if I sit with you until my date shows? Those stools at the bar just won't do."

"No, please," I say, because she's right. The seating options for bigger people aren't really that great here.

"You okay, hon? You look a bit squeamish."

"I think I might have a bit of motion sickness. I'll be fine," I say quickly. She doesn't need to hear about my PTSD.

"You know what you need? Some tea."

She raises her arm to call the waitress over, and before I can object, the pie plates are gone and there's a steaming cup of hot water in front of me. I stare at her as she tells me all about this band she's supposed to go see tonight and watch as she takes a small tin filled with pouches of loose tea and a strainer spoon from her purse.

"Loose tea is always better than prepackaged. Half of what you get is no better than the stuff that comes out of a lawn mower."

She's about to dump the tea into the strainer when I put my hand over my cup. Our eyes connect and she smiles warmly, too warmly. She's got an ease about her that you just don't have with a stranger.

"I think you're lying," I say.

"About the lawn cuttings?" she says coyly.

"No, about the tea and about not being Rose. You *know* me."

The entire diner becomes eerily quiet. The hiss from the dishwasher stops; no one tinkles the edge of their coffee mug with a spoon; there's no laughter, no chatter, just the pop of the speakers from the jukebox, amplifying nothing. I can feel everyone's eyes back on me, but I don't take my gaze off Rose. I think she's going to protest, but she winks and settles herself back into the seat, completely letting her guard down and her posture with it. The track changes on the jukebox again.

"'Les Fleur.' Minnie Riperton. 1970! She that *SNL* girl's Mama. Uh, what's her name? Maya," music-historian guy yells, and his party bursts into conversation again.

"You are smarter than you give yourself credit for," Rose tells me.

"What is going on here?" I ask; nothing is making sense anymore.

"Well, you're right that *something* is going on here, and wrong that I'm Rose. I look like her, but I'm not her, not in this timeline anyway. It can get real complicated," she says matter-of-factly.

"Am I Tamar?" I ask.

She laughs and pours herself a cup of hot water from the pot the waitress left on the table. "You're always Tamar. That's the cool thing about people like you."

"People like me? What am I?" I ask, officially frightened.

"I'm not sure. All I know is that most of us live just one life and that's it, but there are people like you who live over and over again. And there are people like me who kind of hop around."

"I want to stop it. I need to stop it," I beg.

"There are worse things than being a perpetual teenager," she says.

"I'm not a vampire. I don't get to live forever. I get to live and . . . die," I whisper. Involuntarily, I rub my hand over my belly, gingerly pressing my fingers against a mortal wound that isn't there. I take a deep breath. We're not seeing ourselves get older for a reason. "I die, over and over again, or he does. That's a form of hell. Fay thinks that we're caught in some eternal love story, but he's wrong. This life is wrong," I say bitterly.

"Well, then, obviously, there's something you're not learning, and the universe is sending you back for a do-over. Over and over again."

"You're a psychic. I mean, you are a psychic, right?"

She blows on her tea and gives me a small smile. "I am."

"Why don't you just tell me what I'm supposed to learn, then?"

"It doesn't work that way. The most I can do is guide you. We're like the church, or more like angels and demons in that movie with Keanu Reeves. I can't remember the name. Jesus, that's gonna bother me." She frowns. "Anyway, we can encourage or discourage, but we can't make things happen or stop them from happening. We don't have that kind of power."

"Then why are you here?" I ask. I grip the cup so hard and long that it starts to burn.

"The same reason you are. The universe has led me here. I really am meeting a date tonight. I can't see everything, and even if I could, you still have to make a choice. You have to turn left or right, and they both lead to infinite possibilities, infinite realities. Maybe I'm here to help you see that you actually *have* a choice," she says. "Think hard. Is there something you haven't done, or something you keep doing that maybe you shouldn't? Where are the forks in the road that you keep turning down that lead you into a ditch?"

We sit in silence for a few minutes, Iris bobbing her head to the music and me trying to think of the right questions to ask her and coming up empty. The bell dings over the door, and her smile brightens. Even knowing what I do about each life I've lived, even with the coincidence of meeting a psychic from one of my previous lives hundreds of miles from home, I still have a sliver of doubt about destiny and fate in this world.

Until Dr. Carl Little Feather walks into the diner and right over to our table.

50
FAYARD

THE BELL DINGS AS I WALK INTO THE DINER AND I IMME-
diately get the sense that someone is right behind me. I turn
around and look up and down the empty streets. The hair
on the back of my neck stands up; the bubbly déjà vu feeling hits
me like a bad odor and then passes just as quickly as it came.

"It's your last chance, traveler!" a waitress sings to me as she
pours more coffee for a pair of twins at the bar. Both men, Black
but red-haired and freckled, turn toward me. They're older and
remind me of someone, but I can't remember who. The staring
contest gets weird, so I focus on finding Tamar. The desk agent
at the hotel said that a girl in a wheelchair checked in earlier and
I might find her here. Sure enough, I see her sitting at a booth,
talking to a man I do recognize.

"Dr. Little Feather?"

The esteemed archaeologist from the museum news clip turns
toward me and thrusts out his hand. "Yes. And you are?"

I take his hand and shake it, almost expecting him to accuse me
on the spot of stealing his precious artifact, or make some sort of
citizen's arrest, but he just smiles as I introduce myself. His hand is
warm and dry, and he really doesn't pay much attention to me. His
eyes are glued to the woman sitting across from Tamar.

"I'm Iris," she says, and I shake her hand too. "Oooh, Carl, there's a booth opening up. Let's grab it and let these two chat." She smiles, and the couple slinks away. I settle into the warm space Iris left behind.

"Is this why you left? To find Dr. Little Feather?" I ask.

"I'm amazed you think I have that kind of foresight. No. Iris and Little Feather are here purely by coincidence."

"I'm not so sure I believe in coincidences anymore. Not with what I know."

"But that's just the thing, Fay. How much do we really know?" she says apprehensively.

"We know we love each other." I slide my hands across the table, and she laces her fingers through mine. "We know we belong to each other."

Her brow wrinkles a bit like I've said something insulting.

"Looks like you loved that cherry pie," the waitress says.

"But I didn't order any pie," I say, and look down at the table, where two plates of gutted pie slices remain.

"You are funny and cute. Now that you've had our world-famous chili, you've got to try our cheese fries," she chirps. I'm about to protest again, but Tamar hands me a napkin and motions for me to wipe the chili sauce from the corners of my mouth.

I blink a few times, unsure if I'm blacking out and if the waitress will still be there when I look up, but she is.

"Pie?" she asks.

"Sure," I say, realizing it may be best if I just go with the flow.

I look over at Tamar, and while her hands still feel as solid and real in mine, she looks different.

"When did you get braids?" I ask.

"What? I've always had braids. You sound . . . strange." She holds the last word, and I can see, clear as day, that she's worried.

I look around at the patrons in the diner and everything looks just as it did when I walked in, but Iris catches my eye, and I notice that her dress is white with green polka dots now, instead of red. She nods at me like we've shared a secret, and I turn back to Tamar.

"Something is going on in here," I tell her.

She nods ominously. "I know, but I can't figure out what. I think . . ." She pauses, then squeezes my hand. "I think we're doing this wrong. The plan, our lives . . . us."

"What do you mean?" I ask, and I work hard to try to tamp down that sunken-belly feeling that something bad is about to happen.

"And here you are. A good cup of tea. Your friend over there said it'd help settle your stomach," the waitress says, and points a slim finger over at Iris's table. The aroma from the tea is strong. Licorice and rose.

"Now, she said it's best to drink it hot," the waitress says before hopping over to see to someone else's needs.

Tamar pulls her hand back, and she seems more than just a table away—miles, lifetimes.

"You say we belong together, that you remember us, that we always find each other," she says.

"Right," I reply.

"But you don't remember everything, do you? You don't know how all our lives end."

"So what?"

"So that's the problem."

I think she's being a little paranoid. So what if the memories stop? We have the rest of our lives to watch them unfold. I take a sip of the tea, ready to launch into my argument and reassure her, but as soon as I swallow, the warmth rolls over me like an ocean and the diner drifts out of focus.

"Tamar? T!" I call. I'm yelling her name until I realize I'm not yelling. I'm not even speaking. I've got no voice at all.

Durham, North Carolina, 1924

Tamar rushes to put her things into a suitcase. I take a minute to just admire her: no makeup, pin curls in a hairnet, and a cotton nightdress that can't hide what God made. I'm broke, jobless, and more than a little beaten up, but I still consider myself lucky. This angel's gonna conquer the world with me.

"Almost done," she whispers, her smile digging out a hidden dimple in her cheek.

"I guess that's a yes," I laugh, and turn back to the melee below. Dawn hasn't sliced open the night just yet, but Tamar's would-be father-in-law has made it outside in his robe and slippers. A pregnant girl and her shotgun-toting daddy have come to call. It's the perfect cover for our getaway.

"We gotta get going while they're still caught up with Norman's soon-to-be betrothed. Oh-ho-ho! Daddy Norman is bolder than he looks—he's going for the rifle. Wild, I—"

Tamar's bent over. She doesn't see. Honestly, I don't either. I only hear. A shot. Shattering glass. I tumble back. I open my mouth to say her name, but I can't. She screams, pouring out the pain I can't voice as my shirt soaks through with blood flowing so fast . . . so very, very fast.

Her words jumble as I gasp for air.

"Fay! Breathe! No! Don't—"

"Breathe!" Tamar urges, and I blink and then open my mouth to draw in huge gulps of air. I push the teacup so far away from me and so fast that it crashes to the floor.

The waitress rushes over to clean up the mess. "Oooh, don't worry, dear. I got it."

I have to grip the table to orient myself back to reality, or what is passing for reality in this place. I close my eyes and do what Tamar asked me to do—breathe.

"We die," I say flatly.

"We die," Tamar agrees, as if she's known this all along. And here I thought we were acting out some grand love story across the ages. As soon as my heartbeat settles down to something like normal, I open my eyes. Tamar's eyes meet mine, but they aren't worried, just sad.

"You were the first to realize what was happening to us, that the dreams weren't fantasies but memories. You woke me up and forced me to see what was really happening. I have trouble voicing my feelings. For whatever reason I keep them locked up behind a wall, and no matter where I am in time, you find a way to scale the wall or blow it up entirely. I love you and I'll always love you." She pauses, and I think back to every one of our lives together. She's never told me she loved me. I knew she did, but this is the first time she's said the words.

"I've loved you more than my future, and at times I've loved you more than my own life. That love is as real as my own heartbeat. But . . . I think it's my turn to wake *you* up, Fay, so you can see that we're stuck. We need to turn left when we've always turned right."

"I don't understand," I say, and notice how quiet the diner has gotten. The lights seem dimmer, and that déjà vu feeling is completely gone. This moment is new. This isn't a memory or a replay of something that's happened before. I close my eyes. I take a deep breath and watch every smile, first kiss, brush of the shoulder, and death play behind my eyes.

"We're in a loop," I say, and she nods.

"I keep choosing the easiest path," she says, "and because you're there it makes it even easier. If I hadn't stolen your money on that train from Philadelphia, you wouldn't have had to chase me, and you wouldn't have been shot. I would have figured out a way to get to Spelman and we could have written. In Al-Kawkaw, I could have buried my pride and become the concubine and then bided my time. Iyin would have died eventually, and probably much sooner than I would have hoped. Instead I killed myself. There are countless other lives we've lived where I had a chance to put myself first, put my life first, and *then* pair it with yours. But staying with you, or focusing on you, on us, was the path of least resistance. I love you, but first I've got to love me. I need to start making my own decisions, thinking about what I want to do with this one good life I have."

I lean back in the seat, unwilling to let go of her hands, but blown away by everything she's saying.

"You love me?" I ask.

"For all time," she says, and smiles. "What would you have done in any of your other lives if you weren't loving me?"

I think about that and wonder if I was using Tamar as an excuse. I remember what I was running from in Philadelphia and realize that while I found Tamar, I was really trying to avoid having a steady job. Uncle Max was everything I didn't want to be, but I didn't put any real effort into finding my place in the world. I could have let Tamar go with the money. I would have made it back. In Al-Kawkaw I was just being reckless. I could have put my foot down, but I didn't want to make waves with my father. It seemed easier to let the decisions be made for me.

"I would have grown up," I say, more to myself than her. "It's been easier to put all my attention on you than to make a decision about what I really want to do and be. I don't even consider any other possibilities where we're not together."

"But those might be the best possibilities. There are no coincidences, right?" she says.

"Right."

Tamar lifts herself up and grabs my shirt so that I have to lean over the table to kiss her. She tastes like ginger and cherries and I can feel every kiss we've ever had, the shiver of the ocean breeze on my skin and the smell of the smoke from the midwife's cook fire. I'm everywhere we've ever been before, and when we break, my heart breaks too, unsure if we'll ever be there again.

"What do we do now?" I ask softly.

She reaches into her shirt and pulls off a necklace.

"I looped a chain through it so it wouldn't be suspicious when I went through the metal detectors at the museum."

I take it from her and sniff it. She bursts out into a huge laugh. "Gross."

"I'm a guy. What can I say?" I say with a smirk.

"Take this and the stone over to Iris's table. She said Dr. Little Feather is a friend and he won't ask any questions."

"We still don't know what it is," I say. "I've got memories that don't fit anywhere else, some visions of us that feel out of place, but they're fuzzy, like someone erased the useful stuff and left the rest. Maybe the stone has something to do with it."

"It doesn't matter. But I think your subconscious was right—we need to get rid of it."

"And then what?"

"Then we both head home and start planning our lives," she says. There's a smile in her eyes, but it doesn't light up her face. It looks a lot like resignation. Or it could be relief.

I shake my head. "I don't know if I'll be able to keep away from you," I whisper.

"I'll make you a promise. Since neither of us believes in coincidences and fate is a cruel but consistent bitch, we'll know that if she brings us back together, it must be inevitable. But we have to put in the effort. We have to be selfish, make hard decisions, do the things we want and need to do. It's the only way we'll know for sure."

"For sure about what?" I ask, not knowing what meeting a few months from now will change.

"That us being together is a permanent thing and not just a cosmic mistake." A tear rolls down her cheek and she brushes it away.

I get up from the booth and kiss her one last time, not caring how we look, wishing we were alone so that my lips and hands in hers could say that even if time stops and the world starts over, I'll still love her.

But if my leaving her is what she needs, it's time to make my exit.

I break the kiss and turn around so she can't see the water in my eyes. I walk over to Iris. Her smile is warm, her eyes knowing. She takes the bag without a word and enfolds me in the conversation she was just having with the doctor. It feels like I've only just sat down when I look over at Tamar's booth. She's gone.

I blink and the waitress clouds my vision as she slides a piece of cherry pie in front of me.

"Here you go, sweetie. It's the best thing for a broken heart."

51

Cape Town, South Africa, 2032

FAYARD

THE SMELL OF GRILLED FISH, SMOKE, AND HOT PEPPERS wafts around me as I dip my head into the tent. Before my eyes can adjust, everyone at the table bursts into a rendition of "Happy Birthday," the Afrobeat version.

"Surprised?" Femi asks when the song's over, eyes shiny from starting the celebration a little too early.

"Yes. Grateful, though. You know I don't do anything for my birthday," I say.

"I know. That's why we had to do it! You're the head of the company. We can't let your birthday just slide by without acknowledgment. Besides, it gives me a chance to one-up the Busan office."

"You can't still be worried about that Korea bid?" I ask.

Immediately I wish I hadn't said anything. Femi's hell-bent on exclusivity, and he just can't shake the fact that another commercial exploration company beat us out for the international streaming rights in South Korea. The US government won't fund space-exploration projects anymore, so we went to the private sector. Lunar travel for a price.

"Think of it this way: we'll be able to share more of the profits on the ground, in emerging markets in South America and Central Africa, which is why we're here. Relax. It's my party. I order you to," I say in a stern voice, even though it's clear I'm joking.

"Fine. Fine, I'll let it go. If and only if you share some cake with one of these lovely ladies," he urges.

"C'mon. You can't be—"

"I *can* be and I *do* be. You are single, and that cute girl at the hotel said her cousin played in the band Sniper," he says eagerly.

The name of the band makes my blood run cold, and immediately my back stiffens.

"You're kidding."

"Nah, man. How else do you think we got into this underground restaurant? Nobody knows where this place is. It's like a myth. I can't even tell you the things I had to promise that girl," he adds, then tells me the things he promised that girl. I don't follow because my eyes are busy scanning every face in the tiny tented yard. It doesn't take long.

She's older. Her hair is cut in a kind of new punk style and she's put on weight. I like the weight a lot. My hand flies to the early-onset gray at my ears. I knew I should have colored it, but Femi talked me out of it. I should have fired him. I would not be here looking at her again if I had fired him like I wanted to.

There's a crew of people around her, including a huge guy with a mohawk, who must be her bodyguard. I inch my way closer, with Femi trailing behind me, oblivious to what I'm doing.

What am I doing?

We don't know each other anymore. Maybe she's forgotten all about me. No, that's not possible.

Damn, I haven't been this nervous in years. I'll just say hi. No, I'll just catch her eye and raise my glass. I'm still debating the possibilities when a girl with a massive afro and laughing hazel eyes walks right into my eye line.

"So, Fay, this is Tiana. She knows the owner and got us the reservation. I told her all about you."

"Oh . . ."

52
TAMAR

THERE WAS A CHANCE THAT I'D DREAMED EVERYTHING up. I went to countless therapists, two hypnotists, and a quack psychic who tried to sell me a thousand-dollar crystal to restore my true memories. I never could find Dolly's Mirror again, and after my last breakup I was starting to believe that maybe I had made all of it up.

"Cheer up," Danny says, trying to get me in an after-party vibe

"I'm cheery. I always get like this at the start of a tour."

I'm about to give my standard reason why I'm not in the mood when I see him. Like magic, a decade in the making. *Poof* and he's there.

Laugh lines around his mouth. Broader, maybe even taller, and starting to gray just the tiniest bit at the temples. I like it. A lot. He's talking to some girl. She likes him. He's being polite, a little standoffish. He really has changed. The old Fay was an incorrigible flirt.

"Why don't you just summon him?" Reina, my manager, jokes, and I flick water at her from the sides of my glass. "He is cute," she offers.

"I know him, from when I was younger," I tell her.

"Isn't that like now? Since you're turning back time and not allowing us to acknowledge your real age," she says, and laughs.

"You know the paparazzi keep track of all that. No pictures," I warn her.

"Booo. Why can blast-from-the-past have a party and not you? It's your third world tour!" she yells excitedly.

"Excuse me," I say to them, and start to make my way over to him. "Danny, don't follow me, okay?"

"It's dangerous," he says in his uncharacteristically high voice. Must be all them damn steroids. I told him to lay off that crap. I put a hand on his chest when he tries.

"Really. It's fine," I say, reassuringly.

Like always, eyes follow me when I wade my way through the crowd. I've gotten used to the attention, but I think it might be time to focus on songwriting instead of being out front. It's not a question of money anymore, and I've seen every corner of the world. I'm not too old to change things up. I'm not too old to make a different choice. I'm ready.

I tap the shoulder of the girl he's with and watch as her eyes bug out of her head. She stammers over herself, congratulating me on my latest Grammy. I hear her, but my eyes are on Fay. No ring on his finger. Good. That little bit of fear is dropped, along with any apprehension I had about what I was going to say.

"You see that big guy over there? He's my bodyguard and he thinks you're cute. Can you go talk to him? For me?"

The girl looks a little confused. If I had to choose between Danny and Fay, it'd be Fay all the way, but I asked, so she trots off.

"Does he really want to talk to her?" Fay asks.

"No. But you didn't want to talk to her either," I reply.

"What makes you think that?" he asks, and offers me a slight smile.

"Because I know you," I say.

"Yeah, but I need to get to know you. I followed your career for a bit. I've got all your albums," Fay says.

"Even *Gemini's Tale*?"

"Uh . . ." He quickly looks down.

We both laugh. *Gemini's Tale* was horrible. I'd just broken up with my fiancé and I was really on a single-and-sever-all-ties kick.

"At least you're honest," he says lightly. "You know, I wrote you a letter after everything that went down at the diner. I bet your aunt got to it before you were able to read it," he adds.

"No, I got it. I . . ."

"Oh. I . . . uh want to apologize for it. I know it doesn't mean a lot after all these years, but it was too much. I was doing *too* much. I just loved you, completely, and I couldn't bear to let you go. Over the years I realized that I was suffocating you. You were right. You knew better." He seems relieved to have finally been able to say this.

"I didn't know better. I was just scared. I thought I had to cut you out to get what I wanted, but I didn't even try to bring you with me. I still have the letter," I say.

He blinks hard. I've surprised him.

"My cousin Letitia has it locked up with some of the special things I don't like to move between homes."

"Homes. Wow!" he exaggerates.

"Shut up. Doesn't look like you're doing too bad for yourself, Mr. Designer Shoes."

He kicks up a leg and turns the expensive sneakers from heel to toe so I can get a good look.

"I run an exploration company," he says in mock offense.

"I know. Skyward Dreams. You're not the only one who can use the internet."

He reaches out and takes my left hand, and that electricity, that feeling like I've had a shot of espresso and the light's just been turned on, ripples throughout my body. I moved on. I did. But this was missing.

"No ring?" he says, and I shrug.

"No ring. I got this, though." I pull up my sleeve and shake my bracelet. It's silver with tiny diamond guitars, a cello, a small platinum spaceship, and other charms. It's cheesy, completely anti-thetical to my eclectic-but-sexy aesthetic. My stylist hates it, but it's mine, like your first tattoo. He smiles, mildly interested, turning each of the charms over with care until he finds it. "Is that . . . ?"

The cross is small, perfect for something like this, and it also seems out of place.

"Rosary beads," I say.

He barks a laugh and pulls up his shirtsleeve to reveal a tattoo on his forearm.

"Is that a slice of cherry pie?" I squeal.

He nods.

"It reminds me of you and reminds me that the right decision might also be the hard one. How much do you remember?"

"After a while it didn't seem to matter what had happened in the past. It was the future that was important. The feelings didn't change, though," I say.

After Auntie O flew to DC to pick me up, my memories of my other lives started to fade. But my memories from this lifetime rose from those ashes. I grieved a long time for my sister and wondered about Fay.

The settlement from the airline, after they determined the explosion was negligence, helped me stay afloat all those years I was searching for a record deal. My therapist thought everything I believed happened had all been a hallucination, and my neurologist thought Fay and I had had a shared delusion, but I needed to mark us with something solid. The bracelet seemed like a good way to commemorate the connection and the break.

"The cherries look, uh . . . juicy?" I say, struggling for words, totally unlike the international star I pay my manager to say I am.

"Your cello looks . . . jingly?" he replies, and laughs. "I used to be smoother than this."

The silence between us stretches out, and it's like we're at the diner again. A choice that needed to be made, but then again, maybe not. He holds out his hand and I lace my fingers into his. His palm is warm, a little calloused, and perfect.

There's no script for this. It's never happened before, and hopefully it won't ever again.

ACKNOWLEDGMENTS

Thank you so much for reading *For All Time*. It was so much fun to write and I hope you loved reading it as much as I loved writing it. I want to thank my editor, Krista Vitola, and copy editor, Karen Sherman, and the entire Simon & Schuster team. I also want to thank my fantastic agent, John Cusick, who believed in the essence of the story from the beginning. Birthing a book isn't something you do on your own; it requires advocates and space to think and dream, so I want to thank my family and my students at South Atlanta High School. In addition to my school family and publishing family, I want to thank my real family, my parents and my husband, who always believe that I can do anything. Finally, a big shout-out is necessary for my critique partners, Megan Cronin and Nicole Lesperance, and the team at #DVPit, without whom this book may never have reached so many of you.

DISCUSSION QUESTIONS

1. Time travel narratives don't commonly feature Black characters. Why do you think that is?

2. Fayard is often depicted as a "hustler." How does this help or harm him in his various lives?

3. Both Tamar and Fayard have characteristics that follow them throughout their lives. Which ones did you notice?

4. Aabidah, Tamar's sister, says that Fay is doing "too much" when he comes to the airport. What is she afraid of and does she have a right to be afraid?

5. Tamar is a music lover and plays an instrument in many of her lives. How does she use this creative outlet to communicate?

6. Fayard mentions the Brotherhood of Sleeping Car Porters, a labor organization that did eventually receive its charter from the American Federation of Labor. Its leader, A. Philip Randolph, advocated for better hours, better wages, and other improvements for the more than 18,000 members of the organization. Social movements are often spearheaded by young people. Why do you think Uncle Max was afraid of change?

7. In what ways were Fay and Tamar afraid of change in their various lives?

8. Fay is a gambler and he's good at it. Once he sees how tips are made on the train, he starts a lottery game to make money. What spurred this change?

9. Tamar is an orphan at the beginning of the book. How do you think that affects her decision-making? Does having her sister as her guardian give her more power over her future or is it harmful?

10. Mansa Musa is said to be the richest man who ever lived. His trek from Mali to Mecca was so disruptive to some cities that their economies collapsed because of all the gold he gave away on his journey. Why would Fay try to downplay his association with the great ruler? Does wealth make you think differently of the people you meet?

11. Tamar avoids calling Fay her boyfriend. Do labels help or harm romantic relationships?

12. Tamar believes her daddy treats her differently than her sister because of her dark skin. Do you believe he does this on purpose? Have you ever witnessed "colorism" in action in your life?

13. James Shepard was a founder of Mechanics and Farmers Bank in the early twentieth century. While he did not have a nephew named Norman, he was a leader in his community. Why would Tamar's daddy want to align himself with the family instead of sending Tamar to Spelman College?

14. Fayard and Tamar are both Geminis, who are said to be curious, adaptable, and affectionate, but they can also be indecisive and nervous. Do either of them live up to the Gemini stereotype? Why or why not?

15. Iyin betrays Tamar by sabotaging her marriage proposal. Think about an alternative ending to that lifetime.

16. On Alpha 9, Tamar is a soldier. Were there any indications in her personality in the previous chapters to indicate that she would be a successful warrior?

17. Tamar and Fayard have met across time in infinite lives. Imagine a setting that wasn't shared in the book where you think they would thrive and share it with your group.

18. Fayard is a polyglot, meaning he can speak many languages. On Alpha 9, he's useful because of his communications skills. Has he been a good communicator in all of his lives?

19. The timing seems to always be a bit off for the couple. Do you believe it is fate that is the problem or their individual choices?

20. At the end of the story, Fayard and Tamar meet many years later and reconnect. Is this a happily ever after?